PENGUIN CLASS

D0240840

# THE PENGUIN BOOK OF
# FIRST WORLD WAR STORIES

BARBARA KORTE is Professor of English Literature at the University of Freiburg, Germany. Recent publications include work on the British short story, English travel writing, Black and Asian British culture and the cultural reception of the First World War in Britain.

ANN-MARIE EINHAUS took her MA degree in English literature and History at the University of Freiburg and is currently working on a PhD project investigating the canonization of First World War short stories in Britain.

# The Penguin Book of First World War Stories

*Edited and Introduced by* BARBARA KORTE
*Assistant editor* ANN-MARIE EINHAUS

PENGUIN BOOKS

PENGUIN CLASSICS

Published by the Penguin Group
Penguin Books Ltd, 80 Strand, London WC2R ORL, England
Penguin Group (USA) Inc., 375 Hudson Street, New York, New York 10014, USA
Penguin Group (Canada), 90 Eglinton Avenue East, Suite 700, Toronto, Ontario, Canada M4P 2Y3
(a division of Pearson Penguin Canada Inc.)
Penguin Ireland, 25 St Stephen's Green, Dublin 2, Ireland
(a division of Penguin Books Ltd)
Penguin Group (Australia), 250 Camberwell Road, Camberwell, Victoria 3124, Australia
(a division of Pearson Australia Group Pty Ltd)
Penguin Books India Pvt Ltd, 11 Community Centre, Panchsheel Park, New Delhi – 110 017, India
Penguin Group (NZ), 67 Apollo Drive, Rosedale, North Shore 0632, New Zealand
(a division of Pearson New Zealand Ltd)
Penguin Books (South Africa) (Pty) Ltd, 24 Sturdee Avenue, Rosebank, Johannesburg 2196, South Africa

Penguin Books Ltd, Registered Offices: 80 Strand, London WC2R ORL, England

www.penguin.com

This collection first published in Penguin Classics 2007
007

Introduction and editorial material copyright © Barbara Korte and Ann-Marie Einhaus, 2007
The Acknowledgements on pp. 399–401 constitute an extension of this page.

Set in 10.25/12.25 pt PostScript Adobe Sabon
Typeset by Rowland Phototypesetting Ltd, Bury St Edmunds, Suffolk
Printed in England by Clays Ltd, St Ives plc

ISBN: 978-0-141-44215-0

www.greenpenguin.co.uk

# Contents

# 4 IN RETROSPECT

# Introduction

## The Literary Memory of the First World War in Britain

As we approach the centenary of the First World War's out-break, its standing in the cultural memory of Britain is high. The war that, it was believed, would end all war[1] set the tone for a catastrophic century and became a pervading historical myth. A 'Great War' of unprecedented scale, with more dead and injured combatants than any earlier conflict in which the British had been involved, it is popularly remembered as a 'great casualty',[2] epitomized by the heavy losses on the first day of the battle of the Somme on 1 July 1916. It also intensely affected the population at home, who faced strict control of civilian life under the Defence of the Realm Act, lived under the threat of air raids and anticipated a German invasion. Women, as well as men, made considerable contributions to the war effort, on the so-called home front as well as in combat zones.

The war's impact on the outlook and transformation of British society in the early twentieth century was significant – for example, with regard to the changing relationships of gender and class. Above all, however, it traumatized a generation, and gave rise to a nationwide process of mourning and remembrance that coloured the collective memory of the war for the entire twentieth century.[3]

The First World War had long-term consequences for all participant nations, but Britain seems exceptional in the extent to which its memory has retained, rather than lost, prominence in public perception, through public commemoration, museums, school curricula, popular history, films, television programmes and, last but not least, literature.

Indeed, the First World War has been characterized as a 'literary war': since education had spread considerably during the preceding decades, there was, according to Paul Fussell, an 'unparalleled literariness of all ranks who fought the Great War'[4] – soldiers who not only consumed but also produced literature, especially poetry. At home, established and amateur writers were equally prolific, providing propaganda and morale-boosting pieces as well as more balanced and openly anti-war views.

In the war's aftermath, fictional and autobiographical narratives played a substantial role in the nation's coping with trauma, bereavement, and the reconstruction of private and public lives. The late 1920s and early 1930s even saw an outright war books 'boom',[5] during which many of the now classic war memoirs and novels were first published: Edmund Blunden's *Undertones of War* (1928), Robert Graves's *Goodbye to All That* (1929), Siegfried Sassoon's Sherston trilogy (1928–36), Vera Brittain's *Testament of Youth* (1933) and Richard Aldington's *Death of a Hero* (1929). These well-known books are marked by 'disenchantment'[6] with the war's just cause and present it as the sacrifice of a whole generation. With the trench poetry, these works have perpetuated a view of the war as a futile endeavour, bungled by incompetent generals, condemning thousands of men to a cruel death. This perception was identified as one-sided even during the war-literature boom,[7] and current research has confirmed that much of the middlebrow and popular fiction of the inter-war years offered a more patriotic, constructive and consolatory interpretation of the war than the handful of works that have become classics.[8]

The widespread neglect of more affirmative views is in part a legacy of the 1960s, when there was a resurgence of interest in the First World War and its literature, which had been overshadowed by the resonance of the Second World War. Faced with the nuclear threat, the decade engendered a strong peace movement, which preferred to see the First World War as pointless slaughter – an image disseminated in republished trench poetry and the war-critical memoirs and novels of the late 1920s.

The sixties' preferred interpretation had a crucial effect on the perception of all those who had no personal recollections of the war and its aftermath. The novelists who turned the war into a major subject during the final decades of the twentieth century, from Susan Hill in the 1970s to Pat Barker and Sebastian Faulks in the 1990s, all tend to retell the 'great casualty' narrative, with its now stereotypical settings and trappings, in particular the muddy, rat-infested trenches of the Western Front, which has become *the* site of the war in Britain's cultural imagination.[9] At the beginning of the twenty-first century even writers of popular crime fiction, like Anne Perry and the Children's Laureate, Michael Morpurgo, have discovered the war as a central theme and keep its literary memory alive.[10]

## The War and the Short Story

While high-street booksellers offer a wide selection of material for the general reader, and academic interest in the war and its literature is also high, the short story is curiously overlooked. A few stories by writers of renown, including Rudyard Kipling, Joseph Conrad, D. H. Lawrence and Katherine Mansfield, are still familiar. Otherwise, British stories about the war have passed into oblivion – although thousands were produced during the war and the two subsequent decades, filling the pages of a broad range of magazines and newspapers. Not all of this vast production was of lasting merit and appeal. Most of the sea stories and sketches by 'Bartimeus' and 'Taffrail',[11] for example, seem removed from contemporary interests and taste, as does the vast number of stories for a juvenile audience, for instance by the prolific Eden Phillpotts (1862–1960).[12] Gilbert Frankau (1884–1952) was a bestselling author of the early twentieth century, but his stories have a xenophobic strain that tends to offend the contemporary reader. Such stories are of interest primarily to today's cultural historian, but others have been undeservedly forgotten.

The majority of stories about the war were written between 1914 and 1918, and then until the early 1930s, when the experience of the war and its consequences were still of

immediate relevance to many readers. These decades were a
heyday for the short story in Britain. A great number of periodi-
cals offered a market for both more traditional storytellers
(such as W. Somerset Maugham and John Galsworthy) and
modernists (including Virginia Woolf and Katherine Mansfield), who explored the short story's potential in terms of a
new aesthetic. Through the latter in particular, the short story
acquired the reputation of a form congenial to the modern
condition. Its emphasis on isolated moments and mere frag-
ments of experience, its art of condensation and ambiguous
expression seemed ideal for capturing modern life with its hasti-
ness, inconclusiveness, uncertainties and distrust of traditional
beliefs.[13] For the same reasons, the short story was deemed to
have an affinity to the first fully technological and industrialized
war, which exploded extant norms of perception, interpretation
and representation. Its aesthetic seemed highly suitable for arti-
culating the experiences of the front with its moments of violence, shock, disorientation and strangeness. In 1930 Edmund
Blunden (1896–1974), poet and memoirist of the war, emphasized, drawing on his own knowledge of the trenches: 'The
mind of the soldier on active service was continually beginning
a new short story, which had almost always to be broken off
without a conclusion.'[14]

During the inter-war years, a time of 'badly shaken values',
the short story became an alternative to the lyric poem for
writers 'hit in the face by a clash of material events it was
impossible to ignore'. H. E. Bates (1905–74), a successful writer
of stories, went on to say that '(n)o poetry of great consequence
came out of that generation . . . , but many short stories did'.[15]

Few stories written during the war and its aftermath were
radically experimental or self-consciously modern, but many
depart from conventional plot-oriented narration, resist closure
and use forms like the impressionistic sketch, the dramatic
monologue or the dialogue scene. In this anthology, such
elements are most clearly discernible in Katherine Mansfield's
'An Indiscreet Journey' and Mary Borden's 'Blind'. At the same
time, a great number of war stories were told in traditional and
sometimes even formulaic ways, aiming to provide accessible

interpretations for a mass audience in modes that encompassed the heroic and tragic as well as the suspenseful and comic.

But if such a vast and various body of war stories *was* produced, why did most of it slip out of literary memory? One possible explanation is that, as soon as it had ended, the First World War became an issue of mourning, intense retrospection and social analysis. In the context of mourning, some of the war's poetry would become, in the words of Andrew Motion, a 'sacred national text'.[16] The memoir and the novel established themselves as major domains for depicting the long processes of trauma and healing, or for analysing the war's impact on an entire society. The short story lacks the scope to investigate individual and social lives in all their dimensions, and although it can address the theme of memory quite effectively (as the final section of this book shows), its strength is the 'momentary' outlook – not only in terms of thematic preferences: stories require a relatively brief time to write and be published and can thus react more immediately to events and attitudes of the day than novels or memoirs. This topicality also means that some stories may date easily and lack interest for the general reader of later decades.

For its survival, a story depends on the more permanent medium of an author's collection or a multi-author anthology. But story compilations, and especially thematic ones, tend to have a restricted market appeal. Of the 'classic' representatives of the war's literature, only Richard Aldington had a volume of stories still in print in the 1990s, and only because the Imperial War Museum decided to republish *Roads to Glory* (1930) in 1992.[17] To date, there has never been a major anthology of British stories of the First World War, although they featured prominently in the multinational anthology that was part of the war-books boom and for which Edmund Blunden wrote an introduction, *Great Short Stories of the War* (1930).[18] Its editor, H. Cotton Minchin, stated in his prefatory note that this was 'the first substantial collection of short stories of the Great War to be published' and expressed his hope that it might be found 'of permanent value'.[19] It was reprinted once in 1933, in a cheap edition, and again in 1994, in time for the eightieth anniversary of the war's outbreak.

## Principles of the Present Selection

This anthology aims to restore the short story to the map of the war's literature. It sets out to illustrate the wide thematic and stylistic range of stories of lasting quality or fascination that writers in Britain have produced from the days of the war until the end of the twentieth century.[20] The volume comprises work by authors famed for the art of their short story (such as Kipling, Conrad, Lawrence, Mansfield and, more recently, Muriel Spark), but also by writers well known during their lifetime but later forgotten, such as Stacy Aumonier and Winifred Holtby. It also includes a number of stories by writers specifically associated with the literature of the First World War, such as Aldington, Graves and Mary Borden. The selection acknowledges the many facets of the war's cultural production and deliberately represents some successful stories in more popular modes: the spy thriller, the 'whodunnit' and the supernatural tale.[21]

The variety of outlooks on the war in the stories assembled here is determined by genre and style, but also other variables: whether a writer is a man or a woman, experienced the war him- or herself or belongs to a later generation, whether and where he or she actively served in the war and, of course, whether a story was written during the war or from a temporal distance. Since there was at no time a unified perception of the war, the stories have been grouped into thematic sections rather than chronologically: 'Front', 'Spies and Intelligence', 'At Home' and 'In Retrospect'. This arrangement brings differences in experience and attitude to the foreground. It juxtaposes, for example, male and female impressions of the front and represents the latter not only with a nurse's story, Mary Borden's 'Blind' (1929), but also with Katherine Mansfield's 'An Indiscreet Journey' (1915), which gives a more unusual and entirely selfish reason for a woman's presence in the 'forbidden' militarized zone of France. The 'Front' section, as with all others, also mixes periods, including Anne Perry's prize-winning mystery story 'Heroes' (2000). It investigates notions of heroism and cowardice from the perspective of the late twentieth

century, but it also illustrates how strongly the memory of
the First World War has now crystallized into an archetypical
Western Front. Other stories in this section remind us of other
theatres of war: Conrad's 'The Tale' (1917) is about the war
at sea, while Arthur Wells's 'Chanson Triste' (1924), an apt
illustration of the 'literary' war, is set in Bulgaria and hence on
a front that has almost completely disappeared from the British
cultural imagination.

Even though various impressions and interpretations of the
war have always existed side by side, we must distinguish the
three major phases of origin for stories about the war: 1914–18;
the inter-war years; and, finally, the resurgence of interest since
the 1960s. The stories collected here date from all these phases,
but with a strong emphasis on the early decades when production of stories was abundant and interpretation of the war
highly contested.

Positive views of the war as a necessary and patriotic event
appear more frequently before rather than after 1918. This is
reflected in this anthology, which starts with one of the first
stories of the war to become famous, Arthur Machen's 'The
Bowmen', published as early as September 1914. A story of the
supernatural, it associates the British soldiers who had bravely
fought heavy German forces before their retreat from Mons on
23 August 1914 with the small victorious army of the battle of
Agincourt in 1415, which has become famous as the patriotic
centrepiece of Shakespeare's *Henry V*. Not only does Machen's
story mask a British defeat, it also suggests that the British
Expeditionary Force (BEF) was guarded by celestial powers.
Conan Doyle's story about the war effort of Sherlock Holmes,
'His Last Bow', was written and published in 1917, after even
more military disasters, and revived a view that had welcomed
the war as a cleansing force: the bitter 'east wind' that Holmes
evokes in his final remark will leave England a cleaner, better
and stronger land. Like Conan Doyle, Rudyard Kipling worked
for the War Office.[22] His story, 'Mary Postgate' (1915), shows
the enemy, a fatally wounded German airman whose plane
has crashed in England, from the perspective of an elderly spinster who seeks revenge for the death of the young man she

helped to bring up. But even stories written during the war sometimes presented a more friendly view of the enemy. In Stacy
Aumonier's 'Them Others' (1917), a woman is concerned about
the fate of the German family she knew before the war. Wartime
stories also vary significantly in their portrayal of the men who
fought. 'Private Meyrick – Company Idiot' (1916), written by
the once-popular 'Sapper', portrays an incompetent who, in
his own tragicomic manner, dies a hero. Conrad's 'The Tale'
describes an officer's dilemma after he has sent the crew of a
ship to certain death.

Stories of the inter-war years are likewise diverse in approach
and sentiment. 'Trench stories' of that period, by such authors
as C. E. Montague ('A Trade Report Only', 1923) and Richard
Aldington ('Victory', 1930), tend to be war-critical and empha-
size the horror and human tragedy of the war. But by that time,
remembrance and healing had also become a major theme.
Katherine Mansfield's 'The Fly' (1922) explores a father's grief
six years after his son was killed. Published in the same year
but in a completely different spirit, Harold Brighouse's 'Once
a Hero' casts a satirical light on a hypocritical cult of public
commemoration that serves the living more than it does the
'glorious' dead.

A decade later, the pain of remembering had abated, as
Winifred Holtby's 'The Casualty List' (1932) suggests: to the
old woman in this story, the daily obituary of natural deaths
has become more real and affecting than the lists of casualties
she recalls from the war. The necessity for 1920s Britain to
recuperate even underlies a story that looks back to the hidden
war of intelligence: in John Buchan's 'The Loathly Opposite'
(1928), two men from a former decoding unit suffer ailments
that may result from their exhausting efforts during the war. That
they find a cure in the former enemy's country reflects late-1920s
pacifism and the desire to achieve reconciliation with Germany.

Other stories of the time raised more controversial issues:
that British soldiers had been shot for desertion, for example,
like the underage volunteer in John Galsworthy's 'Told by
the Schoolmaster' (1927). The difficulties returned soldiers
experienced in readjusting to post-war Britain are the subject

of Hugh Walpole's 'Nobody' (1921); his protagonist only regains a purpose in life when he forms a new affiliation with the working classes and thus stands for the reorientation with which his society as a whole was confronted. The war's impact on conceptions of gender is another prominent theme of the post-war years.[23] While D. H. Lawrence's 'Tickets, Please' (1919) sketches a war caused by women's entry into 'male' working domains, Radclyffe Hall's 'Miss Ogilvy Finds Herself' (written 1926) depicts an ageing lesbian who longs for the active role, freedom and temporary acceptance that work as an ambulance driver had afforded her during the war and which she lost with the Armistice.

Although their number decreased dramatically after the caesura of the Second World War, stories about the First World War continued to be written after 1945. Not unexpectedly, their main concern is how the war is remembered across the gap of time and how this memory is passed on to future generations. Robert Graves's early 1960s story about the 'Christmas Truce' of 1914 explicitly includes a man who wishes his war veteran grandfather to march with the Campaign for Nuclear Disarmament. By the end of the twentieth century, few First World War soldiers were left, and the character in Julian Barnes's 'Evermore' (1995) anticipates that the war's collective memory will fade. But this story itself helps to perpetuate its memory, as do the others in the anthology's final section. Muriel Spark's 'The First Year of My Life' (1975) and Robert Grossmith's 'Company' (1989) indicate in their own original ways how the war continues to haunt later generations, figuratively and, as Grossmith's ghost story suggests, even literally.

Barbara Korte

## NOTES

1.   See for example H. G. Wells, *The War That Will End War* (London: Palmer, 1914).

2.   On the 'great Casualty Myth' see John Terraine, *The Smoke and*

*the Fire: Myths and Anti-myths of War 1861–1945* (London: Leo Cooper, 1992), p. 35.

3. The war's culture of mourning is discussed in Jay Winter's influential study *Sites of Memory, Sites of Mourning: The Great War in European Cultural History* (Cambridge: Cambridge University Press, 1995).

4. See Fussell's seminal *The Great War and Modern Memory* (Oxford: Oxford University Press, 1975), pp. 155f.

5. On this 'great boom of war literature' see, among others, Rosa Maria Bracco, *Merchants of Hope: British Middlebrow Writers and the First World War, 1919–1939* (Providence, Rhode Island: Berg, 1993), p. 14.

6. *Disenchantment* (London: Chatto & Windus, 1922) is the programmatic and frequently quoted title of C. E. Montague's recollections of his war experience.

7. See in particular Douglas Jerrold's *The Lie about the War: A Note on Some Contemporary War Writers* (London: Faber and Faber, 1930). On a 'distorted' popular memory based on canonical literature, see also the recent historical scholarship of Gary D. Sheffield, *Forgotten Victory: The First World War. Myths and Realities* (London: Headline, 2001) and Brian Bond, *The Unquiet Western Front: Britain's Role in Literature and History* (Cambridge: Cambridge University Press, 2002).

8. See Bracco, *Merchants of Hope*; Michael Paris, *Warrior Nation: Images of War in British Popular Culture, 1950–2000* (London: Reaktion Books, 2000).

9. Susan Hill, *Strange Meeting* (1971), Pat Barker, *Regeneration Trilogy* (1991–5) and Sebastian Faulks, *Birdsong* (1993). Other significant novels of the 1990s include Robert Edric's *In Desolate Heaven* (1997), David Hartnett's *Brother to Dragons* (1998) and Helen Dunmore's *Zennor in Darkness* (1993).

10. Perry's series of novels set in the war was begun in 2003, with *No Graves as Yet*; Morpurgo's *Private Peaceful* came out the same year.

11. 'Bartimeus' was the pseudonym of Lewis Anselm da Costa Ricci (1886–1967), 'Taffrail' that of Henry Taprell Dorling (1883–1968).

12. Some of Phillpotts's short stories were collected in *The Human Boy and the War* (London: Methuen, 1916).

13. On the more recent history of the short story in Britain see Clare Hanson, *Short Stories and Short Fictions, 1880–1980* (Basingstoke: Macmillan, 1985) and Dominic Head, *The Modernist*

*Short Story: A Study in Theory and Practice* (Cambridge: Cambridge University Press, 1992). Specifically on the modern short story as an art of the 'significant moment', see Frank O'Connor in *The Lonely Voice: A Study of the Short Story* (London: Macmillan, 1963), p. 23.

14. See Blunden's introduction to the anthology *Great Short Stories of the War: England, France, Germany, America*, ed. 'H.C.M' (London: Eyre and Spottiswoode, 1930), p. ii.

15. H. E. Bates, *The Modern Short Story: A Critical Survey* (1941; Boston: The Writer, 1965), p. 203. Also compare George Walter's observation in the introduction to his *Penguin Book of First World War Poetry* (London: Penguin, 2006) that after the war, 'the market for war poetry dried up almost as quickly as it had appeared' (p. xxiii).

16. See Motion's introduction to his anthology of *First World War Poems* (London: Faber and Faber, 2003), p. xi, also quoted by Walter, *First World War Poetry*, p. 31.

17. Story collections of other well-known writers associated with the war, like C. E. Montague's *Fiery Particles* (1923) and R. H. Mottram's *Armistice* (1929), were last published in the early 1970s, i.e. in the wake of the 1960s' revived interest in the First World War.

18. See note 14.

19. The anthology was also published in the United States (New York: Harper, 1931), with an introduction by H. M. Tomlinson (1873–1958), who had just published his anti-war novel *All Our Yesterdays* (1930). A slightly earlier collection, James G. Dunton's *C'est la Guerre! The Best Stories of the World War* (Boston: Stratford, 1927), had a strong American focus and included only two British examples.

20. Of the writers reprinted here, Katherine Mansfield has a New Zealand and Mary Borden an American background, but the war stories of both were written or published while their authors lived in Britain.

21. Despite the modern technology with which it was fought, the experience of the war sometimes seemed to border on the archaic and the surreal, and for the bereaved, spiritualism became a source of consolation. It is not surprising, therefore, that the supernatural story was perceived to have an affinity to the war. On the war and the supernatural, see also Winter, *Sites of Memory*, pp. 54–77.

22. On the involvement of British writers in the propaganda machine

see also Peter Buitenhuis, *The Great War of Words: Literature as Propaganda 1914–18 and After* (London: Batsford, 1989), pp. 79–116, and Samuel Hynes, *A War Imagined: The First World War and English Culture* (London: The Bodley Head, 1990), pp. 25–56.

23. On the war's importance for a re-conceptualization of masculinity and femininity, see Sandra M. Gilbert's seminal article 'Soldier's Heart: Literary Men, Literary Women, and the Great War', in *Speaking of Gender*, ed. Elaine Showalter (London: Routledge, 1989), pp. 282–309.

# Further Reading

## Anthologies of Short Stories of the First World War

*Great First World War Stories* (London: Chancellor, 1994): this is a reprint of *Great Short Stories of the War*, 1930, and includes, among others: H. M. Tomlinson ('A Raid Night'), F. Britten Austin ('The End of an Epoch'), 'Saki' ('The Square Egg'), R. H. Mottram ('The Devil's Own') and Algernon Blackwood ('Cain's Atonement').

*Women, Men and the Great War*, ed. Trudi Tate (Manchester: Manchester University Press, 1995): has a special interest in the gender experience and perception of the war, and includes, among others: Wyndham Lewis ('The French Poodle'), Ford Madox Ford ('The Scaremonger'), Virginia Woolf ('The Mark on the Wall'), May Sinclair ('Red Tape') and Mary Butts ('Speed the Plough').

## Political and Social History of the First World War

DeGroot, Gerard, *Blighty: British Society in the Era of the Great War* (London: Longman, 1996).

Marwick, Arthur, *The Deluge: British Society and the First World War* (London: Macmillan, 1991 (1965)).

Strachan, Hew (ed.), *The Oxford Illustrated History of the First World War*, (Oxford: Oxford University Press, 1998).

Strachan, Hew, *The First World War: A New Illustrated History* (London: Simon & Schuster, 2003).

## Cultural History and Impact of the First World War

Eksteins, Modris, *Rites of Spring: The Great War and the Birth of the Modern Age* (Boston: Houghton Mifflin; and London: Bantam Press, 1989).

Todman, Dan, *The Great War: Myth and Memory* (London: Hamble-
don and London, 2005).
Tylee, Claire M., *The Great War and Women's Consciousness: Images
of Militarism and Womanhood in Women's Writings, 1914–64*
(Iowa: University of Iowa Press, 1990).

## Studies of the War's Literature

Bergonzi, Bernard, *Heroes' Twilight; A Study of the Literature of the
Great War* (1965; Manchester: Carcanet, 1997 [1965]).
Eby, Cecil, *The Road to Armageddon: The Martial Spirit
in English Popular Literature 1870–1914* (Durham and London:
Duke University Press, 1987).
Higgonet, Margaret R., *Lines of Fire: Women Writers of World War
I* (New York: Plume, 1999).
Onions, John, *English Fiction and Drama of the Great War, 1918–
39* (Basingstoke: Macmillan, 1990).
Parfitt, George, *Fiction of the First World War: A Study* (London:
Faber, 1988).
Raitt, Suzanne, and Tate, Trudi (eds.), *Women's Fiction and the Great
War* (Oxford: Clarendon Press, 1997).
Sherry, Vincent, *The Cambridge Companion to the Literature of the
First World War* (Cambridge: Cambridge University Press, 2000).

# A Note on the Texts

The first published appearance of a short story in a magazine or newspaper is often difficult to trace and obtain. The author may also have revised this version for a later appearance in collected form. Where possible, the text reprinted here is therefore that of its first appearance in an author's collection, assuming that this is the author's definitive version. Where this source was unavailable, other anthologies were considered an acceptable alternative. The respective edition is specified in the note to each story.

The texts are unabridged. Apart from house-styling in minor typographical details, spelling and punctuation have not been altered, but obvious printer's errors have been emended.

I

FRONT

# ARTHUR MACHEN
# THE BOWMEN

It was during the retreat of the eighty thousand,[1] and the authority of the censorship is sufficient excuse for not being more explicit. But it was on the most awful day of that awful time, on the day when ruin and disaster came so near that their shadow fell over London far away; and, without any certain news, the hearts of men failed within them and grew faint; as if the agony of the army in the battlefield had entered into their souls.

On this dreadful day, then, when three hundred thousand men in arms with all their artillery swelled like a flood against the little English company, there was one point above all other points in our battle line that was for a time in awful danger, not merely of defeat, but of utter annihilation. With the permission of the censorship and of the military expert, this corner may, perhaps, be described as a salient, and if this angle were crushed and broken, then the English force as a whole would be shattered, the Allied left would be turned, and Sedan[2] would inevitably follow.

All the morning the German guns had thundered and shrieked against this corner, and against the thousand or so of men who held it. The men joked at the shells, and found funny names for them, and had bets about them, and greeted them with scraps of music-hall songs. But the shells came on and burst, and tore good Englishmen limb from limb, and tore brother from brother, and as the heat of the day increased so did the fury of that terrific cannonade. There was no help, it seemed. The English artillery was good, but there was not nearly enough of it; it was being steadily battered into scrap iron.

There comes a moment in a storm at sea when people say to one another: 'It is at its worst; it can blow no harder,' and then there is a blast ten times more fierce than any before it. So it was in these British trenches.

There were no stouter hearts in the whole world than the hearts of these men; but even they were appalled as this seven-times-heated hell of the German cannonade fell upon them and overwhelmed them and destroyed them. And at this very moment they saw from their trenches that a tremendous host was moving against their lines. Five hundred of the thousand remained, and as far as they could see the German infantry was pressing on against them, column upon column, a grey world of men, ten thousand of them, as it appeared afterwards.

There was no hope at all. They shook hands, some of them. One man improvised a new version of the battle-song, 'Good-bye, Good-bye to Tipperary',[3] ending with 'And we shan't get there.' And they all went on firing steadily. The officers pointed out that such an opportunity for high-class, fancy shooting might never occur again; the Germans dropped line after line; the Tipperary humorist asked: 'What price Sidney Street?'[4] And the few machine-guns did their best. But everybody knew it was of no use. The dead grey bodies lay in companies and battalions, as others came on and on and on, and they swarmed and stirred and advanced from beyond and beyond.

'World without end. Amen,'[5] said one of the British soldiers with some irrelevance as he took aim and fired. And then he remembered – he says he cannot think why or wherefore – a queer vegetarian restaurant in London where he had once or twice eaten eccentric dishes of cutlets made of lentils and nuts that pretended to be steak. On all the plates in this restaurant there was printed a figure of St George in blue, with the motto, *Adsit Anglis Sanctus Georgius* – May St George be a present help to the English. This soldier happened to know Latin and other useless things, and now, as he fired at his man in the grey advancing mass – three hundred yards away – he uttered the pious vegetarian motto. He went on firing to the end, and at last Bill on his right had to clout him cheerfully over the head to make him stop, pointing out as he did so that the King's ammunition cost money and was not lightly to be wasted in drilling funny patterns into dead Germans.

For as the Latin scholar uttered his invocation he felt something between a shudder and an electric shock pass through his body. The roar of the battle died down in his ears to a gentle murmur; instead of it, he says, he heard a great voice and a shout louder than a thunder-peal crying, 'Array, array, array!'

His heart grew hot as a burning coal, it grew cold as ice within him, as it seemed to him that a tumult of voices answered to his summons. He heard, or seemed to hear, thousands shouting: 'St George! St George!'

'Ha! messire; ha! sweet Saint, grant us good deliverance!'

'St George for merry England!'

'Harow! Harow![6] Monseigneur St George, succour us.'

'Ha! St George! Ha! St George! a long bow and a strong bow.'

'Heaven's Knight, aid us!'

And as the soldier heard these voices he saw before him, beyond the trench, a long line of shapes, with a shining about them. They were like men who drew the bow, and with another shout their cloud of arrows flew singing and tingling through the air towards the German hosts.

The other men in the trench were firing all the while. They had no hope; but they aimed just as if they had been shooting at Bisley.

Suddenly one of them lifted up his voice in the plainest English.

'Gawd help us!' he bellowed to the man next to him, 'but we're blooming marvels! Look at those grey ... gentlemen, look at them! D'ye see them? They're not going down in dozens, nor in 'undreds; it's thousands, it is. Look! look! there's a regiment gone while I'm talking to ye.'

'Shut it!' the other soldier bellowed, taking aim, 'what are ye gassing about?'

But he gulped with astonishment even as he spoke, for, indeed, the grey men were falling by the thousands. The English could hear the guttural scream of the German officers, the

crackle of their revolvers as they shot the reluctant; and still
line after line crashed to the earth.

All the while the Latin-bred soldier heard the cry:

'Harow! Harow! Monseigneur, dear Saint, quick to our aid!
St George help us!'

'High Chevalier, defend us!'

The singing arrows fled so swift and thick that they darkened
the air; the heathen horde melted from before them.

'More machine-guns!' Bill yelled to Tom.

'Don't hear them,' Tom yelled back. 'But, thank God, anyway; they've got it in the neck.'

In fact, there were ten thousand dead German soldiers left
before that salient of the English army, and consequently there
was no Sedan. In Germany, a country ruled by scientific prin-
ciples, the great general staff decided that the contemptible
English[7] must have employed shells containing an unknown gas
of a poisonous nature, as no wounds were discernible on the
bodies of the dead German soldiers. But the man who knew
what nuts tasted like when they called themselves steak knew
also that St George had brought his Agincourt bowmen to help
the English.

# 'SAPPER' (HERMAN CYRIL MCNEILE)
# PRIVATE MEYRICK – COMPANY IDIOT

No one who has ever given the matter a moment's thought would deny, I suppose, that a regiment without discipline is like a ship without a rudder. True as that fact has always been, it is doubly so now, when men are exposed to mental and physical shocks such as have never before been thought of.

The condition of a man's brain after he has sat in a trench and suffered an intensive bombardment for two or three hours can only be described by one word, and that is – numbed. The actual physical concussion, apart altogether from the mental terror, caused by the bursting of a succession of large shells in a man's vicinity, temporarily robs him of the use of his thinking faculties. He becomes half-stunned, dazed; his limbs twitch convulsively and involuntarily; he mutters foolishly – he becomes incoherent. Starting with fright he passes through that stage, passes beyond it into a condition bordering on coma; and when a man is in that condition he is not responsible for his actions. His brain has ceased to work . . .

Now it is, I believe, a principle of psychology that the brain or mind of a man can be divided into two parts – the objective and the subjective: the objective being that part of his thought-box which is actuated by outside influences, by his senses, by his powers of deduction; the subjective being that part which is not directly controllable by what he sees and hears, the part which the religious might call his soul, the Buddhist 'the Spark of God', others instinct. And this portion of a man's nature remains acutely active, even while the other part has struck work. In fact, the more numbed and comatose the thinking brain, the more clearly and insistently does subjective instinct hold sway over a man's body. Which all goes to show that discipline, if it is to be of any use to a man at such a time, must be a very different type of thing to what the ordinary, uninitiated, and so-called free civilian believes it to be. It must be an ideal, a thing where the motive counts, almost a religion. It must be an appeal to the soul of man, not merely an order to his body. That the order to his body, the self-control of his daily actions, the general change in his mode of life will infallibly follow on the heels of the appeal to his soul – if that appeal be successful – is obvious. But the appeal must come first: it must be the driving power; it must be the cause and not the effect. Otherwise, when the brain is gone – numbed by causes outside its control; when the reasoning intellect of man is out of action – stunned for the time; when only his soul remains to pull the quivering, helpless body through, – then, unless that soul has the ideal of discipline in it, it will fail. And failure *may* mean death and disaster; it *will* mean shame and disgrace, when sanity returns . . .

To the man seated at his desk in the company office these ideas were not new. He had been one of the original Expeditionary Force;[1] but a sniper had sniped altogether too successfully out by Zillebecke in the early stages of the first battle of Ypres, and when that occurs a rest cure becomes necessary. At that time he was the senior subaltern of one of the finest regiments of 'a contemptible little army';[2] now he was a major commanding a company in the tenth battalion of that same regiment. And in front of him on the desk, a yellow form pinned to a white slip of flimsy paper, announced that No. 8469, Private Meyrick, J., was for office. The charge was 'Late falling in on the 8 a.m. parade', and the evidence against him was being given by CSM Hayton, also an old soldier from that original battalion at Ypres. It was Major Seymour himself who had seen the late appearance of the above-mentioned Private Meyrick, and who had ordered the yellow form to be prepared. And now with it in front of him, he stared musingly at the office fire . . .

There are a certain number of individuals who from earliest infancy have been imbued with the idea that the chief pastime of officers in the army, when they are not making love to another man's wife, is the preparation of harsh and tyrannical rules for the express purpose of annoying their men, and the gloating infliction of drastic punishment on those that break them. The absurdity of this idea has nothing to do with it, it being a well-known fact that the more absurd an idea is, the more utterly fanatical do its adherents become. To them the thought that a man being late on parade should make him any the worse fighter – especially as he had, in all probability, some good and sufficient excuse – cannot be grasped. To them the idea that men may not be a law unto themselves – though possibly agreed to reluctantly in the abstract – cannot possibly be assimilated in the concrete.

'He has committed some trifling offence,' they say; 'now you will give him some ridiculous punishment. That is the curse of militarism – a chosen few rule by Fear.' And if you tell them that any attempt to inculcate discipline by fear alone must of necessity fail, and that far from that being the method in the Army the reverse holds good, they will not believe you. Yet – it is so . . .

'Shall I bring in the prisoner, sir?' The Sergeant-Major was standing by the door.

'Yes, I'll see him now.' The officer threw his cigarette into the fire and put on his hat.

'Take off your 'at. Come along there, my lad – move. You'd go to sleep at your mother's funeral – you would.' Seymour smiled at the conversation outside the door; he had soldiered many years with that Sergeant-Major. 'Now, step up briskly. Quick march. 'Alt. Left turn.' He closed the door and ranged himself alongside the prisoner facing the table.

'No. 8469, Private Meyrick – you are charged with being late on the 8 a.m. parade this morning. Sergeant-Major, what do you know about it?'

'Sir, on the 8 a.m. parade this morning, Private Meyrick came running on 'alf a minute after the bugle sounded. 'Is puttees were not put on tidily. I'd like to say, sir, that it's not the first time this man has been late falling in. 'E seems to me to be always a-dreaming, somehow – not properly awake like. I warned 'im for office.'

The officer's eyes rested on the hatless soldier facing him. 'Well, Meyrick,' he said quietly, 'what have you got to say?'

'Nothing, sir. I'm sorry as 'ow I was late. I was reading, and I never noticed the time.'

'What were you reading?' The question seemed superfluous – almost foolish; but something in the eyes of the man facing him, something in his short, stumpy, uncouth figure interested him.

'I was a-reading Kipling,[3] sir.' The Sergeant-Major snorted as nearly as such an august disciplinarian could snort in the presence of his officer.

' 'E ought, sir, to 'ave been 'elping the cook's mate – until 'e was due on parade.'

'Why do you read Kipling or anyone else when you ought to be doing other things?' queried the officer. His interest in the case surprised himself; the excuse was futile, and two or three days to barracks is an excellent corrective.

'I dunno, sir. 'E sort of gets 'old of me, like. Makes me want to do things – and then I can't. I've always been slow and awkward like, and I gets a bit flustered at times. But I do try 'ard.' Again a doubtful noise from the Sergeant-Major; to him trying 'ard and reading Kipling when you ought to be swabbing up dishes were hardly compatible.

For a moment or two the officer hesitated, while the Sergeant-Major looked frankly puzzled. 'What the blazes 'as come over 'im?' he was thinking; 'surely he ain't going to be guyed by that there wash. Why don't 'e give 'im two days and be done with it – and me with all them returns?'

'I'm going to talk to you, Meyrick.' Major Seymour's voice cut in on these reflections. For the fraction of a moment 'Two days' CB' had been on the tip of his tongue, and then he'd changed his mind. 'I want to try and make you understand why you were brought up to office to-day. In every community – in every body of men – there must be a code of rules which govern what they do. Unless those rules are carried out by all those men, the whole system falls to the ground. Supposing everyone came on to parade half a minute late because they'd been reading Kipling?'

'I know, sir. I see as 'ow I was wrong. But – I dreams some-times as 'ow I'm like them he talks about, when 'e says as 'ow they lifted 'em through the charge as won the day. And then the dream's over, and I know as 'ow I'm not.'

The Sergeant-Major's impatience was barely concealed; those returns were oppressing him horribly.

'You can get on with your work, Sergeant-Major. I know you're busy.' Seymour glanced at the NCO. 'I want to say a little more to Meyrick.'

The scandalized look on his face amused him; to leave a prisoner alone with an officer – impossible, unheard of.

'I am in no hurry, sir, thank you.'

'All right then,' Seymour spoke briefly. 'Now, Meyrick, I want you to realize that the principle at the bottom of all discipline is the motive that makes that discipline. I want you to realize that all these rules are made for the good of the regiment, and that in everything you do and say you have an effect on the regiment. You count in the show, and I count in it, and so does the Sergeant-Major. We're all out for the same thing, my lad, and that is the regiment. We do things not because we're afraid of being punished if we don't, but because we know that they are for the good of the regiment – the finest regiment in the world. You've got to make good, not because you'll be dropped on if you don't, but because you'll pull the regiment down if you fail. And because you count, you, personally, must not be late on parade. It *does* matter what you do yourself. I want you to realize that, and why. The rules you are ordered to comply with are the best rules. Sometimes we alter one – because we find a better; but they're the best we can get, and before you can find yourself in the position of the men you dream about – the men who lift others, the men who lead others – you've got to lift and lead yourself. Nothing is too small to worry about, nothing too insignificant. And because I think that at the back of your head somewhere you've got the right ideas; because I think it's natural to you to be a bit slow and awkward and that your failure isn't due to laziness or slackness, I'm not going to punish you this time for breaking the rules. If you do it again, it will be a different matter. There comes a time when one can't judge motives; when one can only judge results. Case dismissed.'

Thoughtfully the officer lit a cigarette as the door closed, and though for the present there was nothing more for him to do in office, he lingered on, pursuing his train of thoughts. Fully conscious of the aggrieved wrath of his Sergeant-Major at having his time wasted, a slight smile spread over his face. He was not given to making perorations of this sort, and now that it was over he wondered rather why he'd done it. And then he recalled the look in the private's eyes as he had spoken of his dreams.

'He'll make good that man.' Unconsciously he spoke aloud. 'He'll make good.'

The discipline of habit is what we soldiers had before the war, and that takes time. Now it must be the discipline of intelligence, of ideal. And for that fear is the worst conceivable teacher. We have no time to form habits now; the routine of the army is of too short duration before the test comes. And the test is too crushing . . .

The bed-rock now as then is the same, only the methods of getting down to that bed-rock have to be more hurried. Of old habitude and constant association instilled a religion – the religion of obedience, the religion of *esprit de corps*. But it took time. Now we need the same religion, but we haven't the same time.

In the office next door the Sergeant-Major was speaking soft words to the Pay Corporal.[4]

'Blimey, I dunno what's come over the bloke. You know that there Meyrick . . .'

'Who, the Slug?' interpolated the other.

'Yes. Well, 'e come shambling on to parade this morning with 'is puttees flapping round his ankles – late as usual; and 'e told me to run 'im up to office.' A thumb indicated the Major next door. 'When I gets 'im there, instead of giving 'im three days' CB and being done with it, 'e starts a lot of jaw about motives and discipline. 'E hadn't got no ruddy excuse; said 'e was a-reading Kipling, or some such rot – when 'e ought to have been 'elping the cook's mate.'

'What did he give him?' asked the Pay Corporal, interested.

'Nothing. His blessing and dismissed the case. As if I had nothing better to do than listen to 'im talking 'ot air to a perisher like that there Meyrick. 'Ere, pass over them musketry returns.'[5]

Which conversation, had Seymour overheard it, he would have understood and fully sympathized with. For CSM Hayton, though a prince of sergeant-majors, was no student of psychology. To him a spade was a spade only as long as it shovelled earth.

Now, before I go on to the day when the subject of all this trouble and talk was called on to make good, and how he did it, a few words on the man himself might not be amiss. War, the great forcing house of character, admits no lies. Sooner or later it finds out a man, and he stands in the pitiless glare of truth for what he is. And it is not by any means the cheery hail-fellow-well-met type, or the thruster, or the sportsman, who always pools the most votes when the judging starts . . .

John Meyrick, before he began to train for the great adventure, had been something in a warehouse down near Tilbury. And 'something' is about the best description of what he was that you could give. Moreover there wasn't a dog's chance of his ever being 'anything'. He used to help the young man – I should say young gentleman – who checked weigh-bills at one of the dock entrances. More than that I cannot say, and incidentally the subject is not of surpassing importance. His chief interests in life were contemplating the young gentleman, listening open-mouthed to his views on life, and dreaming. Especially the latter. Sometimes he would go after the day's work, and, sitting down on a bollard, his eyes would wander over the lines of some dirty tramp, with her dark-skinned crew. Visions of wonderful seas and tropic islands, of leafy palms with the blue-green surf thundering in towards them, of coral reefs and glorious-coloured flowers, would run riot in his brain. Not that he particularly wanted to go and see these figments of his imagination for himself; it was enough for him to dream of them – to conjure them up for a space in his mind by the help of an actual concrete ship – and then to go back to his work of assisting his loquacious companion. He did not find the work uncongenial; he had no hankerings after other modes of life – in fact the thought of any change never even entered into his calculations. What the future might hold he neither knew nor cared; the expressions of his companion on the rottenness of life in general and their firm in particular awoke no answering chord in his breast. He had enough to live on in his little room at the top of a tenement house – he had enough over for an occasional picture show – and he had his dreams. He was content.

Then came the war. For a long while it passed him by; it was no concern of his, and it didn't enter his head that it was ever likely to be until one night, as he was going in to see *Jumping Jess, or the Champion Girl Cowpuncher* at the local movies, a recruiting sergeant touched him on the arm.

He was not a promising specimen for a would-be soldier, but that recruiting sergeant was not new to the game, and he'd seen worse.

'Why aren't you in khaki, young fellow me lad?' he remarked genially.

The idea, as I say, was quite new to our friend. Even though that very morning his colleague in the weigh-bill pastime had chucked it and joined, even though he'd heard a foreman discussing who they were to put in his place as 'that young Meyrick was habsolutely 'opeless', it still hadn't dawned on him that he might go too. But the recruiting sergeant was a man of some knowledge; in his daily round he encountered many and varied types. In two minutes he had fired the boy's imagination with a glowing and partially true description of the glories of war and the army, and supplied him with another set of dreams to fill his brain. Wasting no time, he struck while the iron was hot, and in a few minutes John Meyrick, sometime checker of weigh-bills, died, and No. 8469, Private John Meyrick came into being.

But though you change a man's vocation with the stroke of a pen, you do not change his character. A dreamer he was in the beginning, and a dreamer he remained to the end. And dreaming, as I have already pointed out, was not a thing which commended itself to Company-Sergeant-Major Hayton, who in due course became one of the chief arbiters of our friend's destinies. True it was no longer coral islands – but such details availed not with cook's mates and other busy movers in the regimental hive. Where he'd got them from, Heaven knows, those tattered volumes of Kipling; but their matchless spirit had caught his brain and fired his soul, with the result – well, the first of them has been given.

There were more results to follow. Not three days after he was again upon the mat for the same offence, only to say much the same as before.

'I do try, sir – I do try; but some'ow —'

And though in the bottom of his heart the officer believed him, though in a very strange way he felt interested in him, there are limits and there are rules. There comes a time, as he had said, when one can't judge by motives, when one can only judge by results.

'You mustn't only try; you must succeed. Three days to barracks.'

That night in mess the officer sat next to the Colonel. 'It's the thrusters, the martinets, the men of action who win the VCs and DCMs, my dear fellow,' said his CO, as he pushed along the wine. 'But it's the dreamers, the idealists who deserve them. They suffer so much more.'

And as Major Seymour poured himself out a glass of port, a face came into his mind – the face of a stumpy, uncouth man with deep-set eyes. 'I wonder,' he murmured – 'I wonder.'

The opportunities for stirring deeds of heroism in France do not occur with great frequency, whatever outsiders may think to the contrary. For months on end a battalion may live a life of peace and utter boredom, getting a few casualties now and then, occasionally bagging an unwary Hun, vegetating continuously in the same unprepossessing hole in the ground – saving only when they go to another, or retire to a town somewhere in rear to have a bath. And the battalion to which No. 8469,

Private Meyrick, belonged was no exception to the general rule.

For five weeks they had lived untroubled by anything except flies – all of them, that is, save various NCOs in A company.[6] To them flies were quite a secondary consideration when compared to their other worry. And that, it is perhaps superfluous to add, was Private Meyrick himself.

Every day the same scene would be enacted; every day some sergeant or corporal would dance with rage as he contemplated the Company Idiot – the title by which he was now known to all and sundry.

'Wake up! Wake up! Lumme, didn't I warn you – didn't I warn yer 'arf an 'our ago over by that there tree, when you was a-staring into the branches looking for nuts or something – didn't I warn yer that the company was parading at ten fifteen for 'ot baths?'

'I didn't 'ear you, Corporal – I didn't really.'

'Didn't 'ear me! Wot yer mean, didn't 'ear me? My voice ain't like the twitter of a grass'opper, is it? It's my belief you're barmy, my boy, B-A-R-M-Y. *Savez*?[7] Get a move on yer, for Gawd's sake! You ought to 'ave a nurse. And when you gets to the bath-'ouse, for 'Eaven's sake pull yerself together! Don't forget to take off yer clothes before yer gets in; and when they lets the water out, don't go stopping in the bath because you forgot to get out. I wouldn't like another regiment to see you lying about when they come. They might say things.'

And so with slight variations the daily strafe went on. Going up to the trenches it was always Meyrick who got lost; Meyrick who fell into shell holes and lost his rifle or the jam for his section; Meyrick who forgot to lie down when a flare went up, but stood vacantly gazing at it until partially stunned by his next-door neighbour. Periodically messages would come through from the next regiment asking if they'd lost the regimental pet, and that he was being returned. It was always Meyrick . . .

'I can't do nothing with 'im, sir.' It was the Company-Sergeant-Major speaking to Seymour. ''E seems soft like in the 'ead. Whenever 'e does do anything and doesn't forget, 'e does it wrong. 'E's always dreaming and 'alf barmy.'

'He's not a flier, I know, Sergeant-Major, but we've got to put up with all sorts nowadays,' returned the officer diplomatically. 'Send him to me, and let me have a talk to him.'

'Very good, sir; but 'e'll let us down badly one of these days.'

And so once again Meyrick stood in front of his company officer, and was encouraged to speak of his difficulties. To an amazing degree he had remembered the discourse he had listened to many months previously; to do something for the regiment was what he desired more than anything – to do something big, really big. He floundered and stopped; he could find no words . . .

'But don't you understand that it's just as important to do the little things? If you can't do them, you'll never do the big ones.'

'Yes, sir – I sees that; I do try, sir, and then I gets thinking, and some'ow – oh! I dunno – but everything goes out of my head like. I wants the regiment to be proud of me – and then they calls me the Company Idiot.' There was something in the man's face that touched Seymour.

'But how can the regiment be proud of you, my lad,' he asked gently, 'if you're always late on parade, and forgetting to do what you're told? If I wasn't certain in my own mind that it wasn't slackness and disobedience on your part, I should ask the Colonel to send you back to England as useless.'

An appealing look came into the man's eyes. 'Oh! don't do that, sir. I will try 'ard – straight I will.'

'Yes, but as I told you once before, there comes a time when one must judge by results. Now, Meyrick, you must understand this finally. Unless you do improve, I shall do what I said. I shall tell the Colonel that you're not fitted to be a soldier, and I shall get him to send you away. I can't go on much longer; you're more trouble than you're worth. We're going up to the trenches again to-night, and I shall watch you. That will do; you may go.'

And so it came about that the Company Idiot entered on what was destined to prove the big scene in his uneventful life under the eyes of a critical audience. To the Sergeant-Major, who was a gross materialist, failure was a foregone conclusion;

to the company officer, who went a little nearer to the heart of things, the issue was doubtful. Possibly his threat would succeed; possibly he'd struck the right note. And the peculiar thing is that both proved right according to their own lights . . .

This particular visit to the trenches was destined to be of a very different nature to former ones. On previous occasions peace had reigned; nothing untoward had occurred to mar the quiet restful existence which trench life so often affords to its devotees. But this time . . .

It started about six o'clock in the morning on the second day of their arrival – a really pleasant little intensive bombardment. A succession of shells came streaming in, shattering every yard of the front line with tearing explosions. Then the Huns turned on the gas and attacked behind it. A few reached the trenches – the majority did not; and the ground outside was covered with grey-green figures, some of which were writhing and twitching and some of which were still. The attack had failed . . .

But that sort of thing leaves its mark on the defenders, and this was their first baptism of real fire. Seymour had passed rapidly down the trench when he realized that for the moment it was over; and though men's faces were covered with the hideous gas masks, he saw by the twitching of their hands and by the ugly high-pitched laughter he heard that it would be well to get into touch with those behind. Moreover, in every piece of trench there lay motionless figures in khaki . . .

It was as he entered his dugout that the bombardment started again. Quickly he went to the telephone, and started to get on to Brigade Headquarters. It took him twenty seconds to realize that the line had been cut, and then he cursed dreadfully. The roar of the bursting shells was deafening; his cursing was inaudible; but in a fit of almost childish rage – he kicked the machine. Men's nerves are jangled at times . . .

It was merely coincidence doubtless, but a motionless figure in a gas helmet crouching outside the dugout saw that kick, and slowly in his bemused brain there started a train of thought. Why should his company officer do such a thing; why should they all be cowering in the trench waiting for death to come to them; why . . . ? For a space his brain refused to act; then it started again.

Why was that man lying full length at the bottom of the trench, with the great hole torn out of his back, and the red stream spreading slowly round him; why didn't it stop instead of filling up the little holes at the bottom of the trench and then overflowing into the next one? He was the corporal who'd called him barmy; but why should he be dead? He was dead – at least the motionless watcher thought he must be. He lay so still, and his body seemed twisted and unnatural. But why should one of the regiment be dead; it was all so unexpected, so sudden? And why did his Major kick the telephone? . . .

For a space he lay still, thinking; trying to figure things out. He suddenly remembered tripping over a wire coming up to the trench, and being cursed by his sergeant for lurching against him. 'You would,' he had been told – 'you would. If it ain't a wire you'd fall over yer own perishing feet.'

'What's the wire for, Sergint?' he had asked.

'What d'you think, softie? Drying the washing on? It's the telephone wire to Headquarters.'

It all came back to him, and it had been over by the stunted pollard that he'd tripped up. Then he looked back at the silent, motionless figure – the red stream had almost reached him – and the Idea came. It came suddenly – like a blow. The wire must be broken, otherwise the officer wouldn't have kicked the telephone, he'd have spoken through it.

'I wants the regiment to be proud of me – and then they calls me the Company Idiot.' He couldn't do the little things – he was always forgetting, but . . . ! What was that about 'lifting 'em through the charge that won the day'?[8] There was no charge, but there was the regiment. And the regiment was wanting him at last. Something wet touched his fingers, and when he looked at them, they were red. 'B-A-R-M-Y. You ought to 'ave a nurse . . .'

Then once again coherent thought failed him – utter physical weakness gripped him – he lay comatose, shuddering, and crying softly over he knew not what. The sweat was pouring down his face from the heat of the gas helmet, but still he held the valve between his teeth, breathing in through the nose and out through the mouth as he had been told. It was automatic, involuntary; he couldn't think, he only remembered certain things by instinct.

Suddenly a high explosive shell burst near him – quite close: and a mass of earth crashed down on his legs and back, half burying him. He whimpered feebly, and after a while dragged himself free. But the action brought him close to that silent figure, with the ripped-up back . . .

'You ought to 'ave a nurse . . .' Why? Gawd above – why? Wasn't he as good a man as that there dead corporal? Wasn't he one of the regiment too? And now the Corporal couldn't do anything; but he – well, he hadn't got no hole torn out of his back. It wasn't his blood that lay stagnant, filling the little holes at the bottom of the trench . . .

Kipling came back to him – feebly, from another world. The dreamer was dreaming once again.

> If your officer's dead and the sergeants look white,
> Remember it's ruin to run from a fight.[9]

Run! Who was talking of running? He was going to save the regiment – once he could think clearly again. Everything was hazy just for the moment.

> And wait for supports like a soldier.

But there weren't no supports, and the telephone wire was broken – the wire he'd tripped over as he came up. Until it was mended there wouldn't be any supports – until it was mended – until –

With a choking cry he lurched to his feet: and staggering, running, falling down, the dreamer crossed the open. A tearing pain through his left arm made him gasp, but he got there – got there and collapsed. He couldn't see very well, so he tore off his gas helmet, and, peering round, at last saw the wire. And the wire was indeed cut. Why the throbbing brain should have imagined it would be cut *there*, I know not; perhaps he associated it particularly with the pollard – and after all he was the Company Idiot. But it was cut there, I am glad to say; let us not begrudge him his little triumph. He found one end, and some few feet off he saw the other. With infinite difficulty he dragged himself towards it. Why did he find it so terribly hard to move? He couldn't see clearly; everything somehow was getting hazy and red. The roar of the shells seemed muffled strangely – faraway, indistinct. He pulled at the wire, and it came towards him; pulled again, and the two ends met. Then he slipped back against the pollard, the two ends grasped in his right hand . . .

The regiment was safe at last. The officer would not have to kick the telephone again. The Idiot had made good. And into his heart there came a wonderful peace.

There was a roaring in his ears; lights danced before his eyes; strange shapes moved in front of him. Then, of a sudden, out of the gathering darkness a great white light seared his senses, a deafening crash overwhelmed him, a sharp stabbing blow struck his head. The roaring ceased, and a limp figure slipped down and lay still, with two ends of wire grasped tight in his hand.

'They are going to relieve us to-night, Sergeant-Major.' The two men with tired eyes faced one another in the Major's dugout. The bombardment was over, and the dying rays of a blood-red sun glinted through the door. 'I think they took it well.'

'They did, sir – very well.'

'What are the casualties? Any idea?'

'Somewhere about seventy or eighty, sir – but I don't know the exact numbers.'

'As soon as it's dark I'm going back to Headquarters. Captain Standish will take command.'

'That there Meyrick is reported missing, sir.'

'Missing! He'll turn up somewhere – if he hasn't been hit.'

'Probably walked into the German trenches by mistake,' grunted the CSM dispassionately, and retired. Outside the dugout men had moved the corporal; but the red pools still remained – stagnant at the bottom of the trench . . .

'Well, you're through all right now, Major,' said a voice in the doorway, and an officer with the white and blue brassard of the signals came in and sat down. 'There are so many wires going back that have been laid at odd times, that it's difficult to trace them in a hurry.' He gave a ring on the telephone, and in a moment the thin, metallic voice of the man at the other end broke the silence.

'All right. Just wanted to make sure we were through. Ring off.'

'I remember kicking that damn thing this morning when I found we were cut off,' remarked Seymour, with a weary smile. 'Funny how childish one is at times.'

'Aye – but natural. This war's damnable.' The two men fell silent. 'I'll have a bit of an easy here,' went on the signal officer after a while, 'and then go down with you.'

A few hours later the two men clambered out of the back of the trench. 'It's easier walking, and I know every stick,' remarked the Major. 'Make for that stunted pollard first.'

Dimly the tree stood outlined against the sky – a conspicuous mark and signpost. It was the signal officer who tripped over it first – that huddled quiet body – and gave a quick ejaculation. 'Somebody caught it here, poor devil. Look out – duck.'

A flare shot up into the night, and by its light the two motionless officers close to the pollard looked at what they had found.

'How the devil did he get here!' muttered Seymour. 'It's one of my men.'

'Was he anywhere near you when you kicked the telephone?' asked the other, and his voice was a little hoarse.

'He may have been – I don't know. Why?'

'Look at his right hand.' From the tightly clenched fingers two broken ends of wire stuck out.

'Poor lad.' The Major bit his lip. 'Poor lad – I wonder. They called him the Company Idiot. Do you think . . . ?'

'I think he came out to find the break in the wire,' said the other quietly. 'And in doing so he found the answer to the big riddle.'

'I knew he'd make good – I knew it all along. He used to dream of big things – something big for the regiment.'

'And he's done a big thing, by Jove,' said the signal officer gruffly, 'for it's the motive that counts. And he couldn't know that he'd got the wrong wire.'

'When 'e doesn't forget, 'e does things wrong.'

As I said, both the Sergeant-Major and his officer proved right according to their own lights.

# C. E. MONTAGUE

# A TRADE REPORT ONLY

No one has said what was wrong with The Garden, nor even why it was called by that name: whether because it had apples in it, and also a devil, like Eden; or after Gethsemane and the agonies there; or, again, from Proserpine's[1] garden, because of the hush filling the foreground. All the air near you seemed like so much held breath, with the long rumble of far-away guns stretching out beyond it like some dreamful line of low hills in the distance of a landscape.

The rest of the Western Front has been well written up – much too well. The Garden alone – the Holy Terror, as some of the men used to call it – has not. It is under some sort of taboo. I think I know why. If you never were in the line there before the smash came and made it like everywhere else, you could not know how it would work on the nerves when it was still its own elfish self. And if you were there and did know, then you knew also that it was no good to try to tell people. They only said, 'Oh, so you all had the wind up?' We had. But who could say why? How is a horse to say what it is that be-devils one empty place more than another? He has to prick up his ears when he gets there. Then he starts sweating. That's all he knows, and it was the same story with us in The Garden. All I can do is to tell you, just roughly, the make of the place, the way that the few honest solids and liquids were fixed that came into it. They were the least part of it, really.

It was only an orchard, to look at; all ancient apple-trees, dead straight in the stem, with fat, wet grass underneath, a little unhealthy in colour for want of more sun. Six feet above ground the lowest apple boughs all struck out level, and kept so; some

beasts, gone in our time, must have eaten every leaf that tried
to grow lower. So the under side of the boughs made a sort of
flat awning or roof. We called the layer of air between it and
the ground The Six-foot Seam, as we were mostly miners. The
light in this seam always appeared to have had something done
to it: sifted through branches, refracted, messed about somehow, it was not at all the stuff you wanted just at that time.
You see the like of it in an eclipse, when the sun gives a queer
wink at the earth round the edge of a black mask. Very nice,
too, in its place; but the war itself was quite enough out of the
common – falling skies all over the place, and half your dead
certainties shaken.

We and the Germans were both in The Garden, and knew it.
But nobody showed. Everywhere else on the front somebody
showed up at last; somebody fired. But here nothing was seen
or heard, ever. You found you were whispering and walking
on tip-toe, expecting you didn't know what. Have you been in
a great crypt at twilight under a church, nothing round you but
endless thin pillars, holding up a low roof? Suppose there's a
wolf at the far end of the crypt and you alone at the other,
staring and staring into the thick of the pillars, and wondering,
wondering – round which of the pillars will that grey nose come
rubbing?

Why not smash up the silly old spell, you may say – let a
good yell, loose a shot, do any sane thing to break out? That's
what I said till we got there. Our unit took over the place from
the French. A French platoon sergeant, my opposite number,
showed me the quarters and posts and the like, and I asked the
usual question, 'How's the old Boche?'

'*Mais assez gentil*,'[2] he pattered. That Gaul was not waiting
to chat. While he showed me the bomb-store, he muttered
something low, hurried, and blurred – '*Le bon Dieu Boche*,'[3] I
think it was, had created the orchard. The Germans themselves
were '*bons bourgeois*' enough, for all he had seen or heard of
them – 'Not a shot in three weeks. *Seulement*' – he grinned,
half-shamefaced and half-confidential, as sergeant to sergeant
– '*ne faut pas les embêter*.'[4]

I knew all about that. French sergeants were always like that:

dervishes in a fight when it came, but dead set, at all other times, on living *paisiblement*,[5] smoking their pipes. *Paisiblement* – they love the very feel of the word in their mouths. Our men were no warrior race, but they all hugged the belief that they really were marksmen, not yet found out by the world. They would be shooting all night at clods, at tops of posts, at anything that might pass for a head. Oh, I knew. Or I thought so.

But no. Not a shot all the night. Nor on any other night either. We were just sucked into the hush of The Garden the way your voice drops in a church – when you go in at the door you become part of the system. I tried to think why. Did nobody fire just because in that place it was so easy for anybody to kill? No trench could be dug; it would have filled in an hour with water filtering through from the full stream flanking The Garden. Sentries stood out among the fruit trees, behind little breastworks of sods, like the things you use to shoot grouse. These screens were merely a form; they would scarcely have slowed down a bullet. They were not defences, only symbols of things that were real elsewhere. Everything else in the place was on queer terms with reality; so were they.

Our first event was the shriek. It was absolutely detached, un-related to anything seen or heard before or soon after, just like the sudden fall of a great tree on a windless day. At three o'clock on a late autumn morning, a calm moonless night, the depths of The Garden in front of our posts yielded a long wailing scream. I was making a round of our posts at the time, and the scream made me think of a kind of dream I had had twice or thrice; not a story dream, but a portrait dream; just a vivid rending vision of the face of some friend with a look on it that made me feel the brute I must have been to have never seen how he or she had suffered, and how little I had known or tried to know. I could not have fancied before that one yell could tell such a lot about anyone. Where it came from there must be some kind of hell going on that went beyond all the hells now in the books, like one of the stars that are still out of sight because the world has not lived long enough to give time for the first ray of light from their blaze to come through to our eyes.

I found the sentries jumpy. 'What is it, Sergeant?' one of them almost demanded of me, as if I were the fellow in charge of the devils. 'There's no one on earth,' he said, 'could live in that misery.' Toomey himself, the red-headed gamekeeper out of the County Fermanagh, betrayed some perturbation. He hinted that 'Them wans' were in it. 'Who?' I asked. 'Ach, the Good People,' he said, with a trace of reluctance. Then I remembered, from old days at school, that the Greeks, too, had been careful; they called their Furies 'The Well-disposed Ladies'.

All the rest of the night there was not a sound but the owls. The sunless day that followed was quiet till 2.30 p.m., when the Hellhound appeared. He came trotting briskly out of the orchard, rounding stem after stem of the fruit trees, leaped our little pretence of barbed wire, and made straight for Toomey, then on guard, as any dog would. It was a young male black-and-tan. It adored Toomey till three, when he was relieved. Then it came capering around him in ecstasy, back to the big living cellar, a hundred yards in the rear. At the door it heard voices within and let down its tail, ready to plead lowliness and contrition before any tribunal less divine than Toomey.

The men, or most of them, were not obtrusively divine just then. They were out to take anything ill that might come. All the hushed days had first drawn their nerves tight, and then the scream had cut some of them. All bawled or squeaked in the cellar, to try to feel natural after the furtive business outside.

'Gawd a'mighty!' Looker shrilled at the entry of Toomey, 'if Fritz ain't sold 'im a pup!'

Jeers flew from all parts of the smoky half-darkness. 'Where's licence, Toomey?'

'Sure 'e's clean in th' 'ouse?'

' 'Tain't no Dogs' 'Ome 'ere. Over the way!'

Corporal Mullen, the ever-friendly, said to Toomey, more mildly, 'Wot? Goin' soft?'

'A daycent dog, Corp,' said Toomey. 'He's bruk wi' the Kaiser. An' I'll engage he's through the distemper. Like as not he'll be an Alsatian.' Toomey retailed these commendations slowly, with pauses between, to let them sink in.

'What'll you feed him?' asked Mullen, inspecting the points of the beast with charity.

'Feed 'im!' Looker squealed. 'Feed 'im into th' incinerator!'

Toomey turned on him. 'Aye, an' be et be the rats!'

'Fat lot o' talk about rats,' growled Brunt, the White Hope, the company's only prize-fighter. 'Tha'd think rats were struttin' down fairway, shovin' folk off duck-board.'

'Ah!' Looker agreed. 'An' roostin' up yer armpit.'

'Thot's reet,' said Brunt.

'I'll bet 'arf a dollar,' said Looker, eyeing the Hellhound malignantly, 'the 'Uns 'ave loaded 'im up with plague fleas. Sent 'im acrorse. Wiv instructions.'

Toomey protested. 'Can't ye see the dog has been hit, ye blind man?' In fact, the immigrant kept his tail licking expressively under his belly except when it lifted under the sunshine of Toomey's regard.

Brunt rumbled out slow gloomy prophecies from the gloom of his corner. ''E'll be tearin' 'imself t'bits wi' t'mange in a fortneet. Rat for breakfas', rat for dinner, rat for tea; bit o' rat las' thing at neet, 'fore 'e'll stretch down to 't.'

'An' that's the first sinse ye've talked,' Toomey conceded. 'A rotten diet-sheet is ut. An' dirt! An' no kennel the time the roof'll start drippin'. A dog's life for a man, an' God knows what for a dog.'

We felt the force of that. We all had dogs at home. The Hellhound perhaps felt our ruth in the air like a rise of temperature, for at this point he made a couple of revolutions on his wheel base, to get the pampas-grass of his imagination comfortable about him, and then collapsed in a curve and lay at rest with his nose to the ground and two soft enigmatic gleams from his eyes raking the twilight recesses of our dwelling. For the moment he was relieved of the post of nucleus-in-chief for the vapours of fractiousness to condense upon.

He had a distinguished successor. The company sergeant-major, no less, came round about five minutes after with 'word from the colonel'. Some mischief, all our hearts told us at once. They were right too. The Corps had sent word – just what it would, we inwardly groaned. The Corps had sent word that

GHQ – Old GHQ! At it again! we savagely thought. We knew what was coming. Yes, GHQ wanted to know what German unit was opposite to us. That meant a raid, of course. The colonel couldn't help it. Like all sane men below brigade staffs, he hated raids. But orders were orders. He did all he could. He sent word that if anyone brought in a German, dead or alive, on his own, by this time to-morrow, he, the colonel, would give him a fiver. Of course nobody could, but it was an offer, meant decently.

Darkness and gnashing of teeth, grunts and snarls of disgust, filled the cellar the moment the CSM had departed. 'Gawd 'elp us!' 'A ride! In The Gawden!' ''Oo says Gawd made gawdens?' 'Ow! Everythink in The Gawden is lovely!' 'Come into The Gawden, Maud!' You see, the wit of most of us was not a weapon of precision. Looker came nearest, perhaps, to the point. 'As if we 'ad a chawnce,' he said, 'to gow aht rattin' Germans, wiv a sack!'

'We gotten dog for't ahl reet,' said Brunt. This was the only audible trace of good humour. Toomey looked at Brunt quickly.

Toomey was destined to trouble that afternoon: one thing came after another. At 3.25 I sent him and Brunt, with a clean sack apiece, to the sergeant-major's dug-out for the rations. They came back in ten minutes. As Toomey gave me his sack, I feared that I saw a thin train of mixed black and white dust trending across the powdered mortar floor to the door. Then I saw Looker, rage in his face, take a candle and follow this trail, stooping down, and once tasting the stuff on a wet finger-tip.

And then the third storm burst. 'Christ!' Looker yelled. 'If 'e ain't put the tea in the sack wiv a 'ole in it!'

We all knew that leak in a bottom corner of that special sack as we knew every very small thing in our life of small things – the cracked dixie-lid,[6] the brazier's short leg, the way that Mynns had of clearing his throat, and Brunt of working his jaws before spitting. Of course, the sack was all right for loaves and the tinned stuff. But tea! – loose tea mixed with powdered sugar! It was like loading a patent seed-sowing machine with your fortune in gold-dust. There was a general groan of 'God help us!' with extras. In this report I leave out, all along, a great many extras. Print and paper are dear.

Looker was past swearing. 'Plyin' a piper-chise!' he ejaculated with venom. 'All owver Frawnce! Wiv our grub!'

Toomey was sorely distressed. He, deep in whose heart was lodged the darling vision of Toomey the managing head, the contriver, the 'ould lad that was in ut', had bungled a job fit for babes. 'Ah, then, who could be givin' his mind to the tea,' he almost moaned, 'an' he with a grand thought in ut?'

At any other time and place the platoon would have settled down, purring, under those words. 'A grand thought', 'a great idaya' – when Toomey in happier days had owned to being in labour with one of these heirs of his invention, some uncovenanted mercy had nearly always accrued before long to his friends – a stew of young rabbits, two brace of fat pheasants, once a mighty wild goose. The tactician, we understood in a general way, had 'put the comether upon' them. Now even those delicious memories were turned to gall. 'Always the sime!' Looker snarled at the fallen worker of wonders. 'Always the sime! Ye cawn't 'ave a bit o' wire sived up for pipe-cleanin' without 'e'll loan it off yer to go snarin' 'ares.' Looker paused for a moment, gathering all the resources of wrath, and then he swiftly scaled the high top-gallant of ungraciousness: ' 'E wiv the 'ole platoon workin' awye for 'im, pluckin' pawtridge an' snipes, the 'ole wye up from the sea! Top end o' Frawnce is all a muck o' feathers wiv 'im!'

All were good men; Looker, like Toomey, a very good man. It was only their nerves that had gone, and the jolly power of gay and easy relentment after a jar. However they tried, they could not cease yapping. I went out for a drink of clean air. If you are to go on loving mankind, you must take a rest from it sometimes. As I went up the steps from the cellar the rasping jangle from below did not cease; it only sank on my ears as I went. 'Ow, give us 'Owm Rule for England, Gord's sike!' 'Sye there ain't no towds in Irelan', do they?' 'Looker, I've tould you I'm sorry, an' –' 'Garn, both on yer! Ol' gas-projectors!' 'Begob, if ye want an eye knocked from ye then –!' I was going back, but then I heard Corporal Mullen, paternal and firm, like

Neptune rebuking the winds. 'Now, then, we don't none of us want to go losing our heads about nothing.' No need to trouble. Mullen would see to the children.

I went east, into The Garden. Ungathered apples were going to loss on its trees. I stood looking at one of them for a time, and then it suddenly detached itself and fell to the ground with a little thud and a splash of squashed brown rottenness, as if my eye had plucked it. After that sound the stillness set in again: stillness of autumn, stillness of vigilant fear, and now the stillness of oncoming evening, the nun, to make it more cloistral. No silence so deep but that it can be deepened! As minutes passed, infinitesimal whispers – I think from mere wisps of eddies, twisting round snags in the stream – began to lift into hearing. Deepening silence is only the rise in clearness, of this or that more confidential utterance.

I must have been sucking that confidence in for a good twenty minutes before I turned with a start. I had to, I did not know why. It seemed as if some sense, which I did not know I had got, told me that someone was stealing up behind me. No one there; nothing but Arras, the vacuous city, indistinct among her motionless trees. She always seemed to be listening and frightened. It was as if the haggard creature had stirred.

I looked to my front again, rather ashamed. Was I losing hold too, I wondered, as I gazed level out into the Seam and watched the mist deepening? Each evening that autumn, a quilt of very white mist would come out of the soaked soil of The Garden, lay itself out, flat and dense, but shallow at first, over the grass, and then deepen upward as twilight advanced, first submerging the tips of the grass and the purple snake-headed flowers; and then thickening steadily up till the whole Six-foot Seam was packed with milky opaqueness.

Sixty yards out from our front a heron was standing, immobilized, in the stream, staring down – for a last bit of fishing no doubt. As I watched him, his long head came suddenly round and half up. He listened. He stood like that, warily, for a minute, then seemed to decide it was no place for him, hoisted himself off the ground, and winged slowly away with great flaps. I felt cold, and thought, 'What a time I've been loafing round here!' But I found it was four o'clock only. I thought I would go on and visit my sentries, the three-o'clock men who would come off duty at five. It would warm me; and one or two of the young ones were apt to be creepy about sundown.

Schofield, the lad in one of our most advanced posts, was waist-deep in the mist when I reached him.

'Owt, boy?' I whispered. He was a North-country man.

'Nowt, Sergeant,' he answered, 'barrin' –' He checked. He was one of the stout ones you couldn't trust to yell out for help if the Devil were at them.

'What's wrong?' I asked pretty sharply.

'Nobbut t'way,' he said slowly, 'they deucks doan't seem t'be gettin' down to it to-neet.' My eye followed his through the boughs to the pallid sky. A flight of wild-duck were whirling and counter-whirling aloft in some odd *pas d'inquiétude*.[7] Yes; no doubt our own ducks that had come during the war, with the herons and snipe, to live in The Garden, the untrodden marsh where, between the two lines of rifles never unloaded, no shot was ever heard and snipe were safe from all snipers. A good lad, Schofield; he took a lot of notice of things. But what possessed the creatures? What terror infested their quarters to-night?

I looked Schofield over. He was as near to dead white as a tanned man can come – that is, a bad yellow. But he could be left. A man that keeps on taking notice of things he can see, instead of imagining ones that he can't, is a match for the terror that walketh by twilight. I stole on to our most advanced post of all. There I was not so sure of my man. He was Mynns. We called him Billy Wisdom, because he was a schoolmaster in civil life – some council school at Hoggerston. 'What cheer, Billy?' I whispered. 'Anything to report?'

The mist was armpit deep on him now, but the air quite clear above that; so that from three feet off I saw his head and shoulders well, and his bayonet; nothing else at all. He did not turn when I spoke, nor unfix his eyes from the point he had got them set on, in front of his post and a little below their own level. 'All – quiet – and – correct – Sergeant,' he said, as if each

word were a full load and had to be hauled by itself. I had once
seen a man drop his rifle and bolt back overland from his post,
to trial and execution and anything rather than that ever-lasting
wait for a bayonet's point to come lunging up out of thick mist
in front and a little below him, into the gullet, under the chin.
Billy was near bolting-point, I could tell by more senses than
one. He was losing hold on one bodily function after another,
but still hanging on hard to something, some grip of the spirit
that held from second to second, after muscle had mutinied and
nerve was gone.

He had hardly spoken before a new torment wrung him.
The whole landscape suddenly gave a quick shiver. The single
poplar, down the stream, just perceptibly shuddered and
rustled, and then was dead still again. A bed of rushes, nearer
us, swayed for an instant, and stood taut again. Absurd, you
will say. And, of course, it was only a faint breath of wind, the
only stir in the air all that day. But you were not there. So you
cannot feel how the cursed place had tried to shake itself free
of its curse, and had failed and fallen rigid again, dreeing its
weird, and poor Billy with it. His hold on his tongue was what
he lost now. He began to wail under his breath, 'Christ, pity
me! Oh, suffering Christ, pity me!' He was still staring hard to
his front, but I had got a hand ready to grab at his belt when,
from somewhere out in the mist before us, there came, short
and crisp, the crack of a dead branch heavily trodden upon.

Billy was better that instant. Better an audible enemy, one
with a body, one that could trample on twigs, than that vague
infestation of life with impalpable sinisterness. Billy turned with
a grin – ghastly enough, but a grin.

'Hold your fire,' I said in his ear, 'till I order.' I made certain
dispositions of bombs on a little shelf. Then we waited, listening, second by second. I think both our ears must have flicked
like a mule's. But the marvel came in at the eye. We both saw
the vision at just the same instant. It was some fifty yards from
us, straight to our front. It sat on the top of the mist as though
mist were ice and would bear. It was a dog, of the very same
breed as the Hellhound, sitting upright like one of the beasts
that support coats-of-arms; all proper, too, as the heralds would

say, with the black and tan hues as in life. The image gazed at us fixedly. How long? Say, twenty seconds. Then it about-turned without any visible use of its limbs, and receded some ten or twelve yards, still sitting up and now rhythmically rising and falling as though the mist it rode upon were undulating. Then it clean vanished. I thought it sank, as if the mist had ceased to bear. Billy thought the beast just melted into the air radially, all round, as rings made of smoke do.

You know the crazy coolness, a sort of false presence of mind, that will come in and fool you a little bit further at these moments of staggering dislocation of cause and effect. One of these waves of mad rationalism broke on me now. I turned quickly round to detect the cinema lantern behind us which must have projected the dog's moving figure upon the white sheet of mist. None there, of course. Only the terrified city, still there, aghast, with held breath.

Then all my anchors gave together. I was adrift; there was nothing left certain. I thought, 'What if all we are sure of be just a mistake, and our sureness about it conceit, and we no better than puppies ourselves to wonder that dogs should be taking their ease in mid-air and an empty orchard be shrieking?' While I was drifting, I happened to notice the sleepy old grumble of guns from the rest of the front, and I envied those places. Sane, normal places; happy all who were there; only their earth-works were crumbling, not the last few certainties that we men think we have got hold of.

All this, of course, had to go on in my own mind behind a shut face. For Billy was one of the nerve specialists; he might get a VC, or be shot in a walled yard at dawn, according to how he was handled. So I was pulling my wits together a little, to dish out some patter fit for his case – you know: the 'bright, breezy, brotherly' bilge – when the next marvel came. A sound this time – a voice, too; no shriek, not even loud, but tranquil, articulate, slow, and so distant that only the deathly stillness which gave high relief to every bubble that burst with a plop, out in the marsh, could bring the words to us at all. 'Has annywan here lost a dog? Annywan lost a good dog? *Hoond? Goot Hoond?* Annywan lost a *goot Hoond?*'

You never can tell how things will take you. I swear I was right out of that hellish place for a minute or more, alive and free and back at home among the lost delights of Epsom Downs, between the races; the dear old smelly crowd all over the course, and the merchant who carries a tray crying, 'Oo'll 'ave a good cigar, gents? Twopence! 'Oo wants a good cigar? Twopence! 'Oo says a good smoke?' And the sun shining good on all the bookies and crooks by the rails, the just and the unjust, all jolly and natural. Better than Lear's blasted heath and your mind running down!

You could see the relief settle on Mynns like oil going on to a burn on your hand. Have you seen an easy death in bed? – the yielding sigh of peace and the sinking inwards, the weary job over? It was like that. He breathed, 'That Irish swine!' in a voice that made it a blessing. I felt the same, but more uneasily. One of my best was out there in the wide world, having God knew what truck with the enemy. Any Brass Hat that came loafing round might think, in his blinded soul, that Toomey was fraternizing; whereas Toomey was dead or prisoner by now, or as good, unless delivered by some miracle of gumption surpassing all his previous practices against the brute creation. We could do nothing, could not even guess where he was in the fog. It had risen right up to the boughs; the whole Seam was packed with it, tight. No one but he who had put his head into the mouth of the tiger could pull it out now.

We listened on, with pricked ears. Voices we certainly heard; yes, more than one; but not a word clear. And voices were not what I harked for – it was for the shot that would be the finish of Toomey. I remembered during the next twenty minutes quite a lot of good points about Toomey. I found that I had never had a sulky word from him, for one. At the end of the twenty minutes the voices finally stopped. But no shot came. A prisoner, then?

The next ten minutes were bad. Towards the end of the two hours for which they lasted I could have fancied the spook symptoms were starting again. For out of the mist before us there came something that was not seen, or heard, or felt; no one sense could fasten upon it; only a mystic consciousness came of some approaching displacement of the fog. The blind, I believe, feel the same when they come near a lamp-post. Slowly this undefined source of impressions drew near, from out the uncharted spaces beyond, to the frontiers of hearing and sight, slipped across them and took form, at first as the queerest tangle of two sets of limbs, and then as Toomey, bearing on one shoulder a large corpse, already stiff, clothed in field-grey.

'May I come in, Sergeant?' said Toomey, 'an' bring me sheaves wid me?' The pride of 'cuteness shone from his eyes like a lamp through the fog; his voice had the urbanely affected humility of the consciously great.

'You may,' said I, 'if you've given nothing away.'

'I have not,' said he. 'I'm an importer entirely. Me exports are nil.' He rounded the flank of the breastwork and laid the body tenderly down, as a collector would handle a Strad. 'There wasn't the means of an identification about me. Me shoulder titles, me badge, me pay-book, me small-book, me disc, an' me howl correspondence – I left all beyant in the cellar. They'd not have got value that tuk me.' Toomey's face was all one wink. To value himself on his courage would never enter his head. It was the sense of the giant intellect within that filled him with triumph.

I inspected the bulging eyes of the dead. 'Did you strangle him sitting?' I asked.

'Not at all. Amn't I just after tradin' the dog for him?' Then, in the proper whisper, Toomey made his report:

'Ye'll remember the whillabalooin' there was at meself in the cellar. Leppin' they were, at the loss of the tea. The end of it was that "I'm goin' out now," said I, "to speak to a man," said I, "about a dog," an' I quitted the place, an' the dog with me, knockin' his nose against every lift of me heel. I'd a grand thought in me head, to make them whisht thinkin' bad of me. Very near where the lad Schofiel' is, I set out for Germ'ny, stoopin' low to get all the use of the fog. Did you notus me, Sergeant?'

'Breaking the firewood?' I said.

'Aye, I med sure that ye would. So I signalled.'

Now I perceived. Toomey went on. 'I knew, when I held up

the dog on the palm of me hand, ye'd see where I was, an' where goin'. Then I wint on, deep into th' East. Their wire is nothin' at all; it's the very spit of our own. I halted among ut, and gev out a notus, in English an' German, keepin' well down in the fog to rejuce me losses. They didn't fire – ye'll have heard that. They sint for the man with the English. An', be the will o' God, he was the same man that belonged to the dog.'

'"Hans," says I, courcheous but firm, "the dog is well off where he is. Will you come to him quietly?"'

'I can't jus' give ye his words, but the sinse of them only. "What are ye doin' at all," he says, "askin' a man to desert?"'

'There was serious trouble in that fellow's voice. It med me ashamed. But I wint on, an' only put double strength in me temptin's. "Me colonel," I told him, "is offerin' five pounds for a prisoner. Come back with me now and ye'll have fifty francs for yourself when I get the reward. Think over ut well. Fifty francs down. There's a grand lot of spendin' in that. An' ye'll be wi' the dog." As I offered him each injucement, I lifted th' an'mal clear of the fog for two seconds or three, to keep the man famished wid longin'. You have to be crool in a war. Each time that I lowered the dog I lep' two paces north, under the fog, to be-divvil their aim if they fired.

'"Ach, to hell wi' your francs an' your pounds," says he in his ag'ny. "Give me the dog or I'll shoot. I see where you are."'

'"I'm not there at all," says I, "an' the dog's in front of me bosom."'

'Ye'll understan', Sergeant,' Toomey said to me gravely, 'that last was a ruse. I'd not do the like o' that to a dog, anny more than yourself.

'The poor divvil schewed in his juice for a while, very quiet. Then he out with an offer. "Will ye take sivinty francs for the dog? It's the whole of me property. An' it only comes short be five francs of th' entire net profuts ye'd make on the fiver, an' I comin' with you."'

'"I will not," says I, faint and low. It was tormint refusin' the cash.

'"Won't *annythin*' do ye," says he in despair, "but a live wan?"'

' "Depinds," says I pensively, playin' me fish. I held up the
dog for a second again, to keep his sowl workin'.

'He plunged, at the sight of the creature. "Couldn't ye do
with a body?" he says very low.

' "Depinds," says I, marvellin' was ut a human sacrifice he
was for makin', the like of the Druids, to get back the dog.

' "Not fourteen hours back," says he, "he died on us."

' "Was he wan of yourselves?" says I. "A nice fool I'd look if
I came shankin' back from the fair wid a bit of the wrong unit."

' "He was," says he, "an' the best of us all." An' then he went
on, wid me puttin' in just a word now and then, or a glimpse
of the dog, to keep him desirous and gabbin'. There's no use in
cheapenin' your wares. He let on how this fellow he spoke of
had never joyed since they came to that place, an' gone mad at
the finish wi' not gettin' his sleep without he'd be seein' Them
Wans in a dream and hearin' the Banshies; the way he bruk out
at three in the morning that day, apt to cut anny in two that
would offer to hold him. "Here's out of it all," he appeared to
have said; "I've lived through iv'ry room in hell, how long, O
Lord, how long, but it's glory an' victory now," an' off an'
away wid him West, through The Garden. "Ye'll not have seen
him at all?" says me friend. We hadn't notussed, I told him.
"We were right then," says he; "he'll have died on the way. For
he let a scream in the night that a man couldn't give an' live
after. If he'd fetched up at your end," says he, "you'd have
known, for he was as brave as a lion."

' "A livin' dog's better," says I, "than anny dead lion. It's a
Jew's bargain you're makin'. Where's the deceased?"

' "Pass me the dog," says he, "an' I'll give you his route
out from here to where he'll have dropped. It's his point of
deparchure I stand at."

' "I'll come to ye there," says I, "an' ye'll give me his bearin's,
an' when I've set eyes on me man I'll come back an' hand ye
the dog, an' not sooner."

'He was spaichless a moment. "Come now," says I, from me
lair in the fog, "wan of the two of us has to be trustful. I'll not
let ye down."

' "Ye'll swear to come back?" says he in great anguish.

'I said, "Tubbe sure."

'"Come on with ye, then," he answered.

'I went stoopin' along to within six feet of his voice, the way ye'd swim under water, an' then I came to the surface. The clayey-white face that he had, an' the top of his body showed over a breastwork the moral of ours. An', be cripes, it was all right. The red figures were plain on his shoulder-strap – wan-eighty-six. Another breastwork the fellow to his was not thirty yards south. There was jus' the light left me to see that the sentry there was wan-eighty-six too. I'd inspicted the goods in bulk now, an' only had to see to me sample an' off home with it.'

Toomey looked benedictively down on the long stiff frame with its Iron Cross ribbon and red worsted '186'. 'An ould storm-throoper!' Toomey commendingly said. 'His friend gev me the line to him. Then he got anxious. "Ye'll bury him fair?" he said. "Is he a Prod'stant?" says I, "or a Cath'lic?" "A good Cath'lic," says he; "we're Bavarians here." "Good," says I, "I'll speak to Father Moloney meself." "An' ye'll come back," says he, "wi' the dog?" "I will not," says I, "I shall hand him ye now. Ye're a straight man not to ha' shot me before. Besides, ye're a Cath'lic." So I passed him the an'mal and off on me journey. Not the least trouble at all, findin' the body. The birds were all pointin' to ut. They hated ut. Faith, but that fellow had seen the quare things!' Toomey looked down again at the monstrously staring eyes of his capture, bursting with agonies more fantastic, I thought, than any that stare from the bay-oneted dead in a trench.

'The man wi' the dog,' Toomey said, 'may go the same road. His teeth are all knockin' together. A match for your own, Billy.' In trenches you did not pretend not to know all about one another, the best and the worst. In that screenless life friendship frankly condoled with weak nerves or an ugly face or black temper.

'Sergeant,' said Toomey, 'ye'll help me indent for the fiver? A smart drop of drink it'll be for the whole of the boys.'

I nodded. 'Bring him along,' I said, 'now.'

'Well, God ha' mercy on his sowl,' said Toomey, hoisting the load on to his back.

'And of all Christian souls, I pray God.' I did not say it. Only Ophelia's echo, crossing my mind. How long would Mynns last? Till I could wangle his transfer to the divisional laundry or gaff?

I brought Toomey along to claim the fruit of his guile. We had to pass Schofield. He looked more at ease in his mind than before. I asked the routine question. 'All correct, Sergeant,' he answered. 'Deucks is coom dahn. Birds is all stretchin' dahn to it, proper.'

Its own mephitic mock-peace was re-filling The Garden. But no one can paint a miasma. Anyhow, I am not trying to. This is a trade report only.

# RICHARD ALDINGTON
# VICTORY

A motor despatch-rider, with a broad blue and white band on his khaki arm, chugged and bumped along the *pavé* road. He slowed down as he came to two infantry officers, arguing over maps, and straddled his legs out like a hobby-horse rider as he handed over a slip of folded paper.

'From Division, sir. Urgent.'

Captain Baron, commanding C Company,[1] shoved his transparent map case under his arm and irritatedly thrust back his tin hat, which was new and chafed his head. He was a plump, stuggy little man in gold-rimmed glasses, in peace time the head of the clerical department of a large London commercial firm, and enormously devoted to 'bumph,' *i.e.* all the vast paper apparatus of war. His conscientiousness in answering paper questions drew down on him and his cursing subalterns unending streams of chits and reports. He spent hours a day in useless writing. This made him so tired that he was always dropping off to sleep, like the Dormouse in *Alice*.[2] Under the stress of perpetual insomnia and conscientiousness this mildest of men had become frightfully irritable. He liked a well-planned unalterable routine, and his conscientiousness was always flabbergasted by any scrimshanking in his subordinates. He petulantly disapproved of the open warfare which had suddenly come after years of trench routine: unexpected things kept happening and decisions had to be made at once without any guiding precedent – which was most incorrect. Consequently, much of the practical work of the company was performed by his second-in-command, a tall young man, who submitted to his superior's fantasies with bored resignation – an attitude he adopted to the whole war.

'Tch, tch, tch! Now what are we to make of this, Ellerton? Another of these *wretched* counter-orders!'

Ellerton glanced at the despatch. It was marked 'Urgent', and contained a peremptory order to all units not to cross the Mons–Maubeuge road. Baron mechanically pushed up his ill-fitting helmet again, and continued irritatedly:

'What *do* they want us to do? First we get urgent orders to push on at all costs and establish contact with the Boche – the Colonel strafed me not fifteen minutes ago because I hadn't made good that bally[3] road. I sent Hogbin with a chit to Warburton, telling him to take his platoon and establish posts three hundred yards beyond the road. And now comes this order from Division! What the devil do they mean?'

Ellerton looked slowly round him and took a deep breath. The dull misty twilight of a greyish November afternoon was deepening about them. The worn *pavé* road, still littered with débris from the retreating German armies, ran with dreary straightness through bare blank fields. A few hundred yards in front were the meagre leafless trees of the main road from Maubeuge to Mons. To their left was a dirty little hamlet, intact except for the smoke-blackened ruins of the church, burned in 1914.

'I should say the war is ending.'

Baron was amazed and annoyed by this remark.

'Don't talk such nonsense! Why, we're scarcely in Belgium yet, and we've got to get to Berlin. The old Boche will make a stand at every river, especially the Rhine. We're miles ahead of our transport and most of the artillery. You know we're tired out – ought to have been relieved days ago. The colonel says we're going so fast the relieving division can't overtake us. A regular staff yarn . . .'

The motor despatch-rider had turned his machine and chugged off into the gloom. Ellerton sighed at Baron's eloquent complaints. He more than half shared his pessimism about the duration of the war, though the Boches certainly were retreating in undisguised panic, and had made no attempt at a real stand

for days. Still, you never knew with the old Boche. He had
blown bridges, culverts, crossroads, with exemplary military
destructiveness. Every railway they passed had each alternative
rail most neatly blown about six inches – the maximum of
destructiveness with the minimum of effort. The whole railway
would have to be re-laid. They must be forty to sixty miles from
rail-head. It certainly was impossible to fight even one more big
battle at present . . . Ellerton sighed again.

'I suppose you're right. Probably they don't want us to over-
run our objective and get involved in a premature action. I'll
go myself and tell Warburton to bring his platoon back.'

'All right. I'd better go and see the colonel again. He told me
we were to continue the pursuit at dawn – I expect he's changed
his mind, too!'

And the agitated little man, still occasionally pushing up his
helmet, plodded off irritatedly.

Ellerton found Warburton, a round-faced, yellow-haired
young man, with a perpetual frown of perplexity giving verbose
orders to a couple of sections.

'Hullo, Ellerton. I say, there must be a Boche machine-gun
post somewhere to our front. I sent out a couple of patrols, and
Corporal Eliot was killed – damn nuisance, one of our best
NCOs. I'm going out with a couple of sections to try and snaffle
the post after dark.'

'No, you're not! There's an order from Division just arrived
– we're to retire behind the Mons–Maubeuge road.'

'What on earth for?'

'God knows. But that's the order.'

Warburton swore copiously.

'And my best corporal's killed!'


C Company officers bivouacked that night in a cold empty
cottage, which however had the luxury of a roof and of an
undamaged board floor to sleep on. Iron rations. Baron
denounced the lack of organization in the ASC, with several
pointed hints to Warburton, the Company Mess President. The
night was very cold, and they shivered as they lay on the floor
in their trench coats. Gusts of raw, damp air flowed into the

room each time one of the sleeping officers was roused to relieve his predecessor on duty.

Ellerton took the two-to-four watch, after nearly four hours' sleep. Seated on the only available chair, in front of a biscuit-box table with a guttering candle stuck in a bottle, the conscientious Baron was drearily bowed asleep over masses of Situation Reports, Ration Indents, Casualty Reports, and letters from and to relatives of men killed. Baron's kindliness and paper fever involved him in long carefully docketed correspondence with the relatives of the dead; once, five minutes before zero hour,[4] Ellerton had found him in a dugout agitatedly explaining by letter to an indignant parent why the pocket-knife was missing from the effects of a man killed two months before.

'Why don't you lie down, Baron? You're worn out, old man, and you're only nodding asleep there. Chuck that silly bumph, and go to sleep.'

Baron sat up with a jerk.

'Wha's time?'

'Two o'clock.'

'Tch, tch! And I *must* get all this done before dawn!'

Ellerton knew it was useless to argue further, and slowly got into his equipment. As he shut the door, he saw Baron was already beginning to nod again.

And Baron was not the only one who was tired. The whole battalion was tired, tired to a mortal indifference. The last newspapers they had seen, dating from the end of October, informed them they had won splendid victories. It was, of course, interesting to get news about this big war which was going on, but they were too much absorbed in their own job, and far too tired to give much attention to it.

The cold wind smote Ellerton's cheek as he stumbled wearily along, with a weary, silent runner behind him. Overhead a wasted-looking moon sagged westwards, encumbered by heavy clouds. Ellerton was leg-weary, body-weary, mind-weary, heart-weary, so sick of the war that he had ceased to think about it, and simply plodded on, resigned to an eternity of trench duty, hopeless about the infernal thing ever ending. Even the sudden return to open warfare, even the large map outside

Divisional Headquarters, almost daily marked with new bulging advances in blue pencil, failed to alter him. Shut inside the
blinkers of duty as an infantry officer, his intelligence was dead
or somnolent – he almost believed Baron's imbecility about
having to get to Berlin, which was only Baron's conscientious
feeling that the routine even of war must be carried out to the
end predetermined by 'the authorities'. Who the devil are 'the
authorities', though, Ellerton reflected as he stumbled along?
God knows. Anyhow it doesn't matter. Nothing matters. Not
a button. And talking of buttons, I must tell that idiot, Fen-
church, that he forgot again to sew that fly-button on my
slacks . . .

He came to the first of the three sentry positions, established
about fifty yards from the main road. Damn funny, not having
any trenches; so awkward and unprotected. The sentries, too,
felt awkward without the customary fire-step and parapet . . .
You never knew what might happen with the old Boche. Yet it
was very quiet, unbelievably quiet. But for an occasional Very
light and a little artillery fire to the left they might have been
on night ops. in England.

'Anything to report, Corporal?'

'No, sir, all quiet, sir.'

'Let the men rest as much as you can.'

'Very good, sir.'

'You know we're being relieved to-morrow?'

' 'Eard that tale before, sir.'

'Well, there's another division bivouacked just behind us.
Captain Baron saw one of their officers at Battalion HQ. I think
we've earned a few days' rest.'

'Men are worn out, sir, and them iron rations . . .'

'I know, I know, but they'll get hot food to-morrow, or the
QM shall perish . . .'

'Very good, sir.'

'Good-night, Corporal.'

'Good-night, sir.'

Undoubtedly it was amazingly quiet. Ellerton peered through
the dim air – not a light, not a bullet, not a shell, not a sound
from the German army. A surprise attack pending? Or had they

retreated faster than ever, and fallen back on another prepared line? True, their Siegfried line[5] had proved a wash-out, a mere rough trench with scarcely any wire. But still, you never knew. He went back to Number I post, and warned the corporal to keep a good watch, and instantly report anything unusual. He repeated this order to the other posts.

How still it was! How slowly the time went! Only twenty minutes gone. The runner stumbled heavily and nearly fell. Poor devil, tired out.

'Tired, Hogbin?'

'Yessir, a bit, sir.'

'All right, go and sleep. It's so quiet I shan't need you.'

'Very good, sir, thank y' very much, sir.'

He listened to the sound of the man's heavy hobnailed boots on the cobbled side road. How awkward-animal a man is when he's tired out. Good to be alone, though. Ellerton established a sort of beat for himself, more to keep awake than for any other reason. Quiet and cold. Nothing to report. The moon suddenly jumped into clear sky from behind a heavy cloud. He gazed eagerly in the direction of the enemy. Nothing but dim fields and the vague forms of trees. To the right was a sort of round valley, half-filled with very white mist, so level that it looked like cream in a large brown bowl . . .

He continued his beat.

An hour after dawn next morning, Ellerton was marching with Warburton at the head of Number I platoon on their way back to rest billets. Baron came jolting along on the Company Rosinante,[6] which his prudent sedentary spirit preferred to the more sprightly animals offered by the transport officer. Ellerton fell out of the ranks to speak to him.

'Just going along to Batt. HQ,' explained Baron. 'I'm taking those reports – whoa! you brute!' – (the horse had tossed its head) – 'the runners are so careless.'

He patted his buttoned pocket, which was bulging with documents.

'And, by the bye, Ellerton, I ought to strafe you. In the casualty report for the last action, you didn't mark how the men were hit. Don't you remember there's an order that casualties are to be marked "G" for gas, "S" for shell, "B" for bullet, and so on?'

Ellerton laughed.

'Rot! How the hell are we to know? We can't stay behind to discover how each casualty happens. If Whitehall are so keen on statistics, why the hell don't they come and collect 'em themselves?'

'All very well, old man, but an order's an order.'

'So long, old man, get us a good billet.'

'So long.'

Baron bobbed off uneasily ahead, and Ellerton rejoined the first platoon. The men were singing one of the worst of their drawling songs:

> 'It's a long, loong traiiil a-wiiinding,
>     Into the laaand of my dreeeeams,
>  Where the niiightingaaales are siiinging . . .'

Suddenly, round a bend in the road, appeared a staff officer on a chestnut, as handsome and fiery as Baron's Rosinante was ugly and tame. Ellerton hastily called the men to attention, but before they could unsling their rifles for the salute the staff officer waved his hand and shouted:

'Armistice was signed at six this morning, and comes into force at eleven. The war's over.'

A languid cheer came from the platoon.

''Oo-ray.'

And then, as the staff man rode on, they at once continued:

> 'It's a long, looong traiiil a-wiiinding . . .'

Ellerton was amazed at their phlegm. He turned his head aside so that Warburton should not see his emotion. So it was over, really over, incredibly over! In a flash a dozen scenes of the war leaped into his mind, a dozen occasions when death had seemed inevitable, memories of the interminable months when it had seemed impossible that the war could ever end . . .

It was like the gift of another life! It *was* another life. Instead of living from minute to minute with the menace perpetually staring at you, instead of getting up and lying down with death . . . Incredible.

He would not be killed. Warburton and Baron and Hogbin would not be killed. No one else in the battalion would be killed. Incredible. A thrill of almost painful exultation went through him, as if the first rush of returning hope and vitality were a hurt like blood flowing back into a crushed limb. Then with a worse, almost unendurable pang, he thought of the millions of men of many nations who would never feel that ecstasy, who were gone for ever, rotting in desolate battlefields and graveyards all over the world. He turned his head further from Warburton to hide the tears which, to his amazement, came into his eyes. Would they dare to 'maffick'[7] in London and Paris? Probably. Well, let them. A lot of cheering idiots in an unlimited cemetery would make a good emblem for the first quarter of the twentieth century. Perhaps the men's quietness and lack of demonstration meant that they too felt this – they were extraordinarily quick now in refusing to be taken in by humbug. Ellerton (like them) was indeed quietly and deeply grateful that the long torture was over, but neither he nor they could join with the Captains and the Kings in shouting for the Victory. The only victory that had resulted was in fact the victory of death over life, of stupidity over intelligence, of hatred over humanity. It must never happen again, never, never. It was the duty of the survivors to the dead so to warn the world that this abomination never occurred again. Even the dullest of them would see that and help. He turned to Warburton:

'Well, what are you thinking about it all?'

From the more than ever perplexed frown on Warburton's babyish face, Ellerton expected some revelation of deep emotion, perhaps a solemn pledge to labour for the abolition of war. What Warburton said, however, was:

'I'm wondering if Baron'd lend me the horse. If I could ride over to the Divisional Canteen I might be able to get some better grub for us.'

# ANNE PERRY
# HEROES

Nights were always the worst, and in winter they lasted from dusk at about four o'clock until dawn again towards eight the following morning. Sometimes star shells lit the sky, showing the black zigzags of the trenches stretching as far as the eye could see to left and right. Apparently now they went right across France and Belgium all the way from the Alps to the Channel. But Joseph was only concerned with this short stretch of the Ypres Salient.

In the gloom near him someone coughed, a deep, hacking sound coming from down in the chest. They were in the support line, farthest from the front, the most complex of the three rows of trenches. Here were the kitchens, the latrines and the stores and mortar positions. Fifteen-foot shafts led to caves about five paces wide and high enough for most men to stand upright. Joseph made his way in the half-dark now, the slippery wood under his boots and his hands feeling the mud walls, held up by timber and wire. There was an awful lot of water. One of the sumps must be blocked.

There was a glow of light ahead and a moment later he was in the comparative warmth of the dugout. There were two candles burning and the brazier gave off heat and a sharp smell of soot. The air was blue with tobacco smoke, and a pile of boots and greatcoats steamed a little. Two officers sat on canvas chairs talking together. One of them recited a joke – gallows humour, and they both laughed. A gramophone sat silent on a camp table, and a small pile of records of the latest music-hall songs was carefully protected in a tin box.

'Hello, Chaplain,' one of them said cheerfully. 'How's God these days?'

'Gone home on sick leave,' the other answered quickly, before Joseph could reply. There was disgust in his voice, but no intended irreverence. Death was too close here for men to mock faith.

'Have a seat,' the first offered, waving towards a third chair. 'Morris got it today. Killed outright. That bloody sniper again.'

'He's somewhere out there, just about opposite us,' the second said grimly. 'One of those blighters the other day claimed he'd got forty-three for sure.'

'I can believe it,' Joseph answered, accepting the seat. He knew better than most what the casualties were. It was his job to comfort the terrified, the dying, to carry stretchers, often to write letters to the bereaved. Sometimes he thought it was harder than actually fighting, but he refused to stay back in the comparative safety of the field hospitals and depots. This was where he was most needed.

'Thought about setting up a trench raid,' the major said slowly, weighing his words and looking at Joseph. 'Good for morale. Make it seem as if we were actually doing something. But our chances of getting the blighter are pretty small. Only lose a lot of men for nothing. Feel even worse afterwards.'

The captain did not add anything. They all knew morale was sinking. Losses were high, the news bad. Word of terrible slaughter seeped through from the Somme and Verdun and all along the line right to the sea. Physical hardship took its toll, the dirt, the cold, and the alternation between boredom and terror. The winter of 1916 lay ahead.

'Cigarette?' The major held out his pack to Joseph.

'No thanks,' Joseph declined with a smile. 'Got any tea going?'

They poured him a mugful, strong and bitter, but hot. He drank it, and half an hour later made his way forward to the open air again and the travel trench. A star shell exploded high and bright. Automatically he ducked, keeping his head below the rim. They were about four feet deep, and in order not to provide a target, a man had to move in a half-crouch. There was a rattle of machine-gun fire out ahead and, closer to, a thud as a rat was dislodged and fell into the mud beside the duckboards.

Other men were moving about close to him. The normal order of things was reversed here. Nothing much happened during the day. Trench repair work was done, munitions shifted, weapons cleaned, a little rest taken. Most of the activity was at night, most of the death.

' 'Lo, Chaplain,' a voice whispered in the dark. 'Say a prayer we get that bloody sniper, will you?'

'Maybe God's a Jerry?' someone suggested in the dark.

'Don't be stupid!' a third retorted derisively. 'Everyone knows God's an Englishman![1] Didn't they teach you nothing at school?'

There was a burst of laughter. Joseph joined in. He promised to offer up the appropriate prayers and moved on forward. He had known many of the men all his life. They came from the same Northumbrian town as he did, or the surrounding villages. They had gone to school together, nicked apples from the same trees, fished in the same rivers, and walked the same lanes.

It was a little after six when he reached the firing trench beyond whose sandbag parapet lay no man's land with its four or five hundred yards of mud, barbed wire, and shell holes. Half a dozen burned tree stumps looked in the sudden flares like men. Those grey wraiths could be fog, or gas.

Funny that in summer this blood- and horror-soaked soil could still bloom with honeysuckle, forget-me-nots, and wild larkspur, and most of all with poppies. You would think nothing would ever grow there again.

More star shells went up, lighting the ground, the jagged scars of the trenches black, the men on the fire steps with rifles on their shoulders illuminated for a few, blinding moments. Sniper shots rang out.

Joseph stood still. He knew the terror of the night watch out beyond the parapet, crawling around in the mud. Some of them would be at the head of saps out from the trench, most would be in shell holes, surrounded by heavy barricades of wire. Their purpose was to check enemy patrols for unusual movement, any signs of increased activity, as if there might be an attack planned.

More star shells lit the sky. It was beginning to rain. A crackle of machine-gun fire, and heavier artillery somewhere over to the left. Then the sharp whine of sniper fire, again and again.

Joseph shuddered. He thought of the men out there, beyond his vision, and prayed for strength to endure with them in their pain, not to try to deaden himself to it.

There were shouts somewhere ahead, heavy shells now, shrapnel bursting. There was a flurry of movement, flares, and a man came sliding over the parapet, shouting for help.

Joseph plunged forward, slithering in the mud, grabbing for the wooden props to hold himself up. Another flare of light. He saw quite clearly Captain Holt lurching towards him, another man over his shoulder, deadweight.

'He's hurt!' Holt gasped. 'Pretty badly. One of the night patrol. Panicked. Just about got us all killed.' He eased the man down into Joseph's arms and let his rifle slide forward, bayonet covered in an old sock to hide its gleam. His face was grotesque in the lantern light, smeared with mud and a wide streak of blood over the burned cork that blackened it, as all night patrol had.

Others were coming to help. There was still a terrible noise of fire going on and the occasional flare.

The man in Joseph's arms did not stir. His body was limp and it was difficult to support him. Joseph felt the wetness and the smell of blood. Wordlessly others materialized out of the gloom and took the weight.

'Is he alive?' Holt said urgently. 'There was a hell of a lot of shot up there.' His voice was shaking, almost on the edge of control.

'Don't know,' Joseph answered. 'We'll get him back to the bunker and see. You've done all you can.' He knew how desperate men felt when they risked their lives to save another man and did not succeed. A kind of despair set in, a sense of very personal failure, almost a guilt for having survived themselves. 'Are you hurt?'

'Not much,' Holt answered. 'Couple of grazes.'

'Better have them dressed, before they get poisoned,' Joseph advised, his feet slipping on the wet boards and banging his shoulder against a jutting post. The whole trench wall was crooked, giving way under the weight of mud. The founds had eroded.

The man helping him swore.

Awkwardly carrying the wounded man, they staggered back through the travel line to the support trench and into the light and shelter of a bunker.

Holt looked dreadful. Beneath the cork and blood his face was ashen. He was soaked with rain and mud and there were dark patches of blood across his back and shoulders.

Someone gave him a cigarette. Back here it was safe to strike a match. He drew in smoke deeply. 'Thanks,' he murmured, still staring at the wounded man.

Joseph looked down at him now, and it was only too plain where the blood had come from. It was young Ashton. He knew him quite well. He had been at school with his older brother.

The soldier who had helped carry him in let out a cry of dismay, strangled in his throat. It was Mordaff, Ashton's closest friend, and he could see what Joseph now could also. Ashton was dead, his chest torn open, the blood no longer pumping, and a bullet-hole through his head.

'I'm sorry,' Holt said quietly. 'I did what I could. I can't have got to him in time. He panicked.'

Mordaff jerked his head up. 'He never would!' The cry was desperate, a shout of denial against a shame too great to be borne. 'Not Will!'

Holt stiffened. 'I'm sorry,' he said hoarsely. 'It happens.'

'Not with Will Ashton, it don't!' Mordaff retorted, his eyes blazing, pupils circled with white in the candlelight, his face grey. He had been in the front line two weeks now, a long stretch without a break from the ceaseless tension, filth, cold, and intermittent silence and noise. He was nineteen.

'You'd better go and get that arm dressed, and your side,' Joseph said to Holt. He made his voice firm, as to a child.

Holt glanced again at the body of Ashton, then up at Joseph.

'Don't stand there bleeding,' Joseph ordered. 'You did all you could. There's nothing else. I'll look after Mordaff.'

'I tried!' Holt repeated. 'There's nothing but mud and darkness and wire, and bullets coming in all directions.' There was a sharp thread of terror under his shell-thin veneer of control. He had seen too many men die. 'It's enough to make anyone lose his nerve. You want to be a hero – you mean to be – and then it overwhelms you –'

'Not Will!' Mordaff said again, his voice choking off in a sob.

Holt looked at Joseph again, then staggered out.

Joseph turned to Mordaff. He had done this before, too many times, tried to comfort men who had just seen childhood friends blown to pieces, or killed by a sniper's bullet, looking as if they should still be alive, perfect except for the small, blue hole through the brain. There was little to say. Most men found talk of God meaningless at that moment. They were shocked, fighting against belief and yet seeing all the terrible waste and loss in front of them. Usually it was best just to stay with them, let them speak about the past, what the friend had been like, times they had shared, just as if he were only wounded and would be back, at the end of the war, in some world one could only imagine, in England, perhaps on a summer day with sunlight on the grass, birds singing, a quiet riverbank somewhere, the sound of laughter, and women's voices.

Mordaff refused to be comforted. He accepted Ashton's death; the physical reality of that was too clear to deny, and he had seen too many other men he knew killed in the year and a half he had been in Belgium. But he could not, would not accept that Ashton had panicked. He knew what panic out there cost, how many other lives it jeopardized. It was the ultimate failure.

'How am I going to tell his mam?' he begged Joseph. 'It'll be all I can do to tell her he's dead! His pa'll never get over it. That proud of him, they were. He's the only boy. Three sisters he had, Mary, Lizzie, and Alice. Thought he was the greatest lad in the world. I can't tell 'em he panicked! He couldn't have, Chaplain! He just wouldn't!'

Joseph did not know what to say. How could people at home in England even begin to imagine what it was like in the mud and noise out here? But he knew how deep shame burned. A lifetime could be consumed by it.

'Maybe he just lost sense of direction,' he said gently. 'He wouldn't be the first.' War changed men. People did panic. Mordaff knew that, and half his horror was because it could be true. But Joseph did not say so. 'I'll write to his family,' he went on. 'There's a lot of good to say about him. I could send pages. I'll not need to tell them much about tonight.'

'Will you?' Mordaff was eager. 'Thanks . . . thanks, Chaplain. Can I stay with him . . . until they come for him?'

'Yes, of course,' Joseph agreed. 'I'm going forward anyway. Get yourself a hot cup of tea. See you in an hour or so.'

He left Mordaff squatting on the earth floor beside Ashton's body and fumbled his way back over the slimy duckboards towards the travel line, then forward again to the front and the crack of gunfire and the occasional high flare of a star shell.

He did not see Mordaff again, but he thought nothing of it. He could have passed twenty men he knew and not recognized them, muffled in greatcoats, heads bent as they moved, rattling along the duckboards, or standing on the fire steps, rifles to shoulder, trying to see in the gloom for something to aim at.

Now and again he heard a cough, or the scamper of rats' feet and the splash of rain and mud. He spent a little time with two men swapping jokes, joining in their laughter. It was black humour, self-mocking, but he did not miss the courage in it, or the fellowship, the need to release emotion in some sane and human way.

About midnight the rain stopped.

A little after five the night patrol came scrambling through the wire, whispered passwords to the sentries, then came tumbling over the parapet of sandbags down into the trench, shivering with cold and relief. One of them had caught a shot in the arm.

Joseph went back with them to the support line. In one of the dugouts a gramophone was playing a music-hall song. A couple of men sang along with it; one of them had a beautiful voice, a soft, lyric tenor. It was a silly song, trivial, but it sounded almost like a hymn out here, a praise of life.

A couple of hours and the day would begin: endless, methodical duties of housekeeping, mindless routine, but it was better than doing nothing.

There was still a sporadic crackle of machine-gun fire and the whine of sniper bullets.

An hour till dawn.

Joseph was sitting on an upturned ration case when Sergeant Renshaw came into the bunker, pulling the gas curtain aside to peer in.

'Chaplain?'

Joseph looked up. He could see bad news in the man's face.

'I'm afraid Mordaff got it tonight,' he said, coming in and letting the curtain fall again. 'Sorry. Don't really know what happened. Ashton's death seems to have . . . well, he lost his nerve. More or less went over the top all by himself. Suppose he was determined to go and give Fritz a bloody nose, on Ashton's account. Stupid bastard! Sorry, Chaplain.'

He did not need to explain himself, or to apologize. Joseph knew exactly the fury and the grief he felt at such a futile waste. To this was added a sense of guilt that he had not stopped it. He should have realized Mordaff was so close to breaking. He should have seen it. That was his job.

He stood up slowly. 'Thanks for telling me, Sergeant. Where is he?'

'He's gone, Chaplain.' Renshaw remained near the doorway. 'You can't help 'im now.'

'I know that. I just want to . . . I don't know . . . apologize to him. I let him down. I didn't understand he was . . . so . . .'

'You can't be everybody's keeper,' Renshaw said gently. 'Too many of us. It's not been a bad night otherwise. Got a trench raid coming off soon. Just wish we could get that damn sniper across the way there.' He scraped a match and lit his cigarette. 'But morale's good. That was a brave thing Captain Holt did out there. He wanted the chance to do something to hearten the men. He saw it and took it. Pity about Ashton, but that doesn't alter Holt's courage. Could see him, you know, by the star shells. Right out there beyond the last wire, bent double, carrying Ashton on his back. Poor devil went crazy. Running around like a fool. Have got the whole patrol killed if Holt hadn't gone after him. Hell of a job getting him back. Fell a couple of times. Reckon that's worth a mention in despatches, at least. Heartens the men, knowing our officers have got that kind of spirit.'

'Yes . . . I'm sure,' Joseph agreed. He could only think of Ashton's white face, and Mordaff's desperate denial, and how Ashton's mother would feel, and the rest of his family. 'I think I'll go and see Mordaff just the same.'

'Right you are,' Renshaw conceded reluctantly, standing aside for Joseph to pass.

Mordaff lay in the support trench just outside the bunker two hundred yards to the west. He looked even younger than he had in life, as if he were asleep. His face was oddly calm, even though it was smeared with mud. Someone had tried to clean most of it off in a kind of dignity, so that at least he was recognizable. There was a large wound in the left side of his forehead. It was bigger than most sniper wounds. He must have been a lot closer.

Joseph stood in the first paling of the darkness and looked at him by candlelight from the open bunker curtain. He had been so alive only a few hours ago, so full of anger and loyalty and dismay. What had made him throw his life away in a useless gesture? Joseph racked his mind for some sign that should have warned him Mordaff was so close to breaking, but he could not see it even now.

There was a cough a few feet away, and the tramp of boots on duckboards. The men were stood down, just one sentry per platoon left. They had returned for breakfast. If he thought about it he could smell cooking.

Now would be the time to ask around and find out what had happened to Mordaff.

He made his way to the field kitchen. It was packed with men, some standing to be close to the stoves and catch a bit of their warmth, others choosing to sit, albeit farther away. They had survived the night. They were laughing and telling stories, most of them unfit for delicate ears, but Joseph was too used to it to take any offence. Now and then someone new would apologize for such language in front of a chaplain, but most knew he understood too well.

'Yeah,' one answered his question through a mouthful of bread and jam. 'He came and asked me if I saw what happened to Ashton. Very cut up, he was.'

'And what did you tell him?' Joseph asked.

The man swallowed. 'Told him Ashton seemed fine to me when he went over. Just like anyone else, nervous . . . but, then, only a fool isn't scared to go over the top!'

Joseph thanked him and moved on. He needed to know who else was on the patrol.

'Captain Holt,' the next man told him, a ring of pride in his voice. Word had got around about Holt's courage. Everyone stood a little taller because of it, felt a little braver, more confident. 'We'll pay Fritz back for that,' he added. 'Next raid – you'll see.'

There was a chorus of agreement.

'Who else?' Joseph pressed.

'Seagrove, Noakes, Willis,' a thin man replied, standing up. 'Want some breakfast, Chaplain? Anything you like, on the house – as long as it's bread and jam and half a cup of tea. But you're not particular, are you? Not one of those fussy eaters who'll only take kippers and toast?'

'What I wouldn't give for a fresh Craster kipper,' another sighed, a faraway look in his eyes. 'I can smell them in my dreams.'

Someone told him good-naturedly to shut up.

'Went over the top beside me,' Willis said when Joseph found him quarter of an hour later. 'All blacked up like the rest of us. Seemed okay to me then. Lost him in no man's land. Had a hell of a job with the wire. As bloody usual, it wasn't where we'd been told. Got through all right, then Fritz opened up on us. Star shells all over the sky.' He sniffed and then coughed violently. When he had control of himself again, he continued. 'Then I saw someone outlined against the flares, arms high, like a wild man, running around. He was going towards the German lines, shouting something. Couldn't hear what in the noise.'

Joseph did not interrupt. It was now broad daylight and beginning to drizzle again. Around them men were starting the duties of the day: digging, filling sandbags, carrying ammu-

nition, strengthening the wire, resetting duckboards. Men took
an hour's work, an hour's sentry duty, and an hour's rest.

Near them somebody was expending his entire vocabulary
of curses against lice. Two more were planning elaborate
schemes to hold the water at bay.

'Of course that lit us up like a target, didn't it!' Willis went
on. 'Sniper fire and machine-guns all over the place. Even a
couple of shells. How none of us got hit I'll never know. Perhaps
the row woke God up, and He came back on duty!' He laughed
hollowly. 'Sorry, Chaplain. Didn't mean it. I'm just so damn
sorry poor Ashton got it. Holt just came out of nowhere and
ran after him. Obsessed with being a hero, or he'd not even
have tried. I can see him in my mind's eye floundering through
the mud. If Ashton hadn't got caught in the wire he'd never
have got him.'

'Caught in the wire?' Joseph asked, memory pricking at him.

'Yeah. Ashton must have run right into the wire, because he
stopped sudden – teetering, like – and fell over. A hell of a
barrage came over just after that. We all threw ourselves down.'

'What happened then?' Joseph said urgently, a slow, sick
thought taking shape in his mind.

'When it died down I looked up again, and there was Holt
staggering back with poor Ashton across his shoulders. Hell of
a job he had carrying him, even though he's bigger than Ashton
– well, taller, anyway. Up to his knees in mud, he was, shot and
shell all over, sky lit up like a Christmas tree. Of course we
gave him what covering fire we could. Maybe it helped.' He
coughed again. 'Reckon he'll be mentioned in despatches,
Chaplain? He deserves it.' There was admiration in his voice, a
lift of hope.

Joseph forced himself to answer. 'I should think so.' The
words were stiff.

'Well, if he isn't, the men'll want to know why!' Willis said
fiercely. 'Bloody hero, he is.'

Joseph thanked him and went to find Seagrove and Noakes.
They told him pretty much the same story.

'You going to have him recommended?' Noakes asked. 'He
earned it this time. Mordaff came and we said just the same to

him. Reckon he wanted the Captain given a medal. He made us say it over and over again, exactly what happened.'

'That's right.' Seagrove nodded, leaning on a sandbag.

'You told him the same?' Joseph asked. 'About the wire, and Ashton getting caught in it?'

'Yes, of course. If he hadn't got caught by the legs he'd have gone straight on and landed up in Fritz's lap, poor devil.'

'Thank you.'

'Welcome, Chaplain. You going to write up Captain Holt?'

Joseph did not answer, but turned away, sick at heart.

He did not need to look again, but he trudged all the way back to the field hospital anyway. It would be his job to say the services for both Ashton and Mordaff. The graves would be already dug.

He looked at Ashton's body again, looked carefully at his trousers. They were stained with mud, but there were no tears in them, no marks of wire. The fabric was perfect.

He straightened up.

'I'm sorry,' he said quietly to the dead man. 'Rest in peace.' And he turned and walked away.

He went back to where he had left Mordaff's body, but it had been removed. Half an hour more took him to where it also was laid out. He touched the cold hand and looked at the brow. He would ask. He would be sure. But in his mind he already was. He needed time to know what he must do about it. The men would be going over the top on another trench raid soon. Today morale was high. They had a hero in their number, a man who would risk his own life to bring back a soldier who had lost his nerve and panicked. Led by someone like that, they were equal to Fritz any day. Was one pistol bullet, one family's shame, worth all that?

What were they fighting for anyway? The issues were so very big, and at the same time so very small and immediate.

He found Captain Holt alone just after dusk, standing on the duckboards below the parapet, near one of the firing steps.

'Oh, it's you, Chaplain. Ready for another night?'

'It'll come, whether I am or not,' Joseph replied.

Holt gave a short bark of laughter. 'That doesn't sound like you. Tired of the firing line, are you? You've been up here a couple of weeks; you should be in turn for a step back any day. Me too, thank God.'

Joseph faced forward, peering through the gloom towards no man's land and the German lines beyond. He was shaking. He must control himself. This must be done in the silence, before the shooting started up again. Then he might not get away with it.

'Pity about that sniper over there,' he remarked. 'He's taken out a lot of our men.'

'Damnable,' Holt agreed. 'Can't get a line on him, though. Keeps his own head well down.'

'Oh, yes.' Joseph nodded. 'We'd never get him from here. It needs a man to go over in the dark and find him.'

'Not a good idea, Chaplain. He'd not come back. Not advocating suicide, are you?'

Joseph chose his words very carefully and kept his voice as unemotional as he could.

'I wouldn't have put it like that,' he answered. 'But he has cost us a lot of men. Mordaff today, you know?'

'Yes . . . I heard. Pity.'

'Except that wasn't the sniper, of course. But the men think it was, so it comes to the same thing, as far as morale is concerned.'

'Don't know what you mean, Chaplain.' There was a slight hesitation in Holt's voice in the darkness.

'Wasn't a rifle wound, it was a pistol,' Joseph replied. 'You can tell the difference, if you're actually looking for it.'

'Then he was a fool to be that close to German lines,' Holt said, facing forward over the parapet and the mud. 'Lost his nerve, I'm afraid.'

'Like Ashton,' Joseph said. 'Can understand that, up there in no man's land, mud everywhere, wire catching hold of you, tearing at you, stopping you from moving. Terrible thing to be caught in the wire with the star shells lighting up the night. Makes you a sitting target. Takes an exceptional man not to panic, in those circumstances . . . a hero.'

Hold did not answer.

There was silence ahead of them, only the dull thump of feet and a squelch of duckboards in mud behind, and the trickle of water along the bottom of the trench.

'I expect you know what it feels like,' Joseph went on. 'I notice you have some pretty bad tears in your trousers, even one in your blouse. Haven't had time to mend them yet.'

'I daresay I got caught in a bit of wire out there last night,' Holt said stiffly. He shifted his weight from one foot to the other.

'I'm sure you did,' Joseph agreed with him. 'Ashton didn't. His clothes were muddy, but no wire tears.'

There were several minutes of silence. A group of men passed by behind them, muttering words of greeting. When they were gone the darkness closed in again. Someone threw up a star shell and there was a crackle of machine-gun fire.

'I wouldn't repeat that, if I were you, Chaplain,' Holt said at last. 'You might make people think unpleasant things, doubts. And right at the moment morale is high. We need that. We've had a hard time recently. We're going over the top in a trench raid soon. Morale is important . . . trust. I'm sure you know that, maybe even better than I do. That's your job, isn't it? Morale, spiritual welfare of the men?'

'Yes . . . spiritual welfare is a good way of putting it. Remember what it is we are fighting for, and that it is worth all that it costs . . . even this.' Joseph gestured in the dark to all that surrounded them.

More star shells went up, illuminating the night for a few garish moments, then a greater darkness closed in.

'We need our heroes,' Holt said very clearly. 'You should know that. Any man who would tear them down would be very unpopular, even if he said he was doing it in the name of truth, or justice, or whatever it was he believed in. He would do a lot of harm, Chaplain. I expect you can see that . . .'

'Oh, yes,' Joseph agreed. 'To have their hero shown to be a coward who laid the blame for his panic on another man, and let him be buried in shame, and then committed murder to hide that, would devastate men who are already wretched and exhausted by war.'

'You are perfectly right.' Holt sounded as if he were smiling. 'A very wise man, Chaplain. Good of the regiment first. The right sort of loyalty.'

'I could prove it,' Joseph said very carefully.

'But you won't. Think what it would do to the men.'

Joseph turned a little to face the parapet. He stood up on to the fire step and looked forward over the dark expanse of mud and wire.

'We should take that sniper out. That would be a very heroic thing to do. Good thing to try, even if you didn't succeed. You'd deserve a mention in despatches for that, possibly a medal.'

'It would be posthumous!' Holt said bitterly.

'Possibly. But you might succeed and come back. It would be so daring, Fritz would never expect it,' Joseph pointed out.

'Then you do it, Chaplain!' Holt said sarcastically.

'It wouldn't help you, Captain. Even if I die, I have written a full account of what I have learned today, to be opened should anything happen to me. On the other hand, if you were to mount such a raid, whether you returned or not, I should destroy it.'

There was silence again, except for the distant crack of sniper fire a thousand yards away and the drip of mud.

'Do you understand me, Captain Holt?'

Holt turned slowly. A star shell lit his face for an instant. His voice was hoarse.

'You're sending me to my death!'

'I'm letting you be the hero you're pretending to be and Ashton really was,' Joseph answered. 'The hero the men need. Thousands of us have died out here, no one knows how many more there will be. Others will be maimed or blinded. It isn't whether you die or not, it's how well.'

A shell exploded a dozen yards from them. Both men ducked, crouching automatically.

Silence again.

Slowly Joseph unbent.

Holt lifted his head. 'You're a hard man, Chaplain. I misjudged you.'

'Spiritual care, Captain,' Joseph said quietly. 'You wanted

the men to think you a hero, to admire you. Now you're going to justify that and become one.'

Holt stood still, looking towards him in the gloom, then slowly he turned and began to walk away, his feet sliding on the wet duckboards. Then he climbed up the next fire step and up over the parapet.

Joseph stood still and prayed.

# MARY BORDEN

# BLIND

The door at the end of the baraque kept opening and shutting
to let in the stretcher-bearers. As soon as it opened a crack the
wind scurried in and came hopping towards me across the bodies
of the men that covered the floor, nosing under the blankets, lifting the flaps of heavy coats, and burrowing among the loose
heaps of clothing and soiled bandages. Then the grizzled head
of a stretcher-bearer would appear, butting its way in, and he
would emerge out of the black storm into the bright fog that
seemed to fill the place, dragging the stretcher after him, and
then the old one at the other end of the load would follow, and
they would come slowly down the centre of the hut looking for
a clear place on the floor.

The men were laid out in three rows on either side of the
central alleyway. It was a big hut, and there were about sixty
stretchers in each row. There was space between the heads of
one row and the feet of another row, but no space to pass
between the stretchers in the same row; they touched. The old
territorials who worked with me passed up and down between
the heads and feet. I had a squad of thirty of these old orderlies
and two sergeants and two priests, who were expert dressers.
Wooden screens screened off the end of the hut opposite the
entrance. Behind these were the two dressing-tables where the
priests dressed the wounds of the new arrivals and got them
ready for the surgeons, after the old men had undressed them
and washed their feet. In one corner was my kitchen where
I kept all my syringes and hypodermic needles and stimulants.

It was just before midnight when the stretcher-bearers
brought in the blind man, and there was no space on the floor

anywhere; so they stood waiting, not knowing what to do with him.

I said from the floor in the second row: 'Just a minute, old ones. You can put him here in a minute.' So they waited with the blind man suspended in the bright, hot, misty air between them, like a pair of old horses in shafts with their heads down, while the little boy who had been crying for his mother died with his head on my breast. Perhaps he thought the arms holding him when he jerked back and died belonged to some woman I had never seen, some woman waiting somewhere for news of him in some village, somewhere in France. How many women, I wondered, were waiting out there in the distance for news of these men who were lying on the floor? But I stopped thinking about this the minute the boy was dead. It didn't do to think. I didn't as a rule, but the boy's very young voice had startled me. It had come through to me as a real voice will sound sometimes through a dream, almost waking you, but now it had stopped, and the dream was thick round me again, and I laid him down, covered his face with the brown blanket, and called two other old ones.

'Put this one in the corridor to make more room here,' I said; and I saw them lift him up. When they had taken him away, the stretcher-bearers who had been waiting brought the blind one and put him down in the cleared space. They had to come round to the end of the front row and down between the row of feet and row of heads; they had to be very careful where they stepped; they had to lower the stretcher cautiously so as not to jostle the men on either side (there was just room), but these paid no attention. None of the men lying packed together on the floor noticed each other in this curious dream-place.

I had watched this out of the corner of my eye, busy with something that was not very like a man. The limbs seemed to be held together only by the strong stuff of the uniform. The head was unrecognizable. It was a monstrous thing, and a dreadful rattling sound came from it. I looked up and saw the chief surgeon standing over me. I don't know how he got there. His small shrunken face was wet and white; his eyes were brilliant and feverish; his incredible hands that saved so many men so exquisitely, so quickly, were in the pockets of his white coat.

'Give him morphine,' he said, 'a double dose. As much as you like.' He pulled a cigarette out of his pocket. 'In cases like this, if I am not about, give morphine; enough, you understand.' Then he vanished like a ghost. He went back to his operating room, a small white figure with round shoulders, a magician, who performed miracles with knives. He went away through the dream.

I gave the morphine, then crawled over and looked at the blind man's ticket. I did not know, of course, that he was blind until I read his ticket. A large round white helmet covered the top half of his head and face; only his nostrils and mouth and chin were uncovered. The surgeon in the dressing station behind the trenches had written on his ticket, 'Shot through the eyes. Blind.'

Did he know? I asked myself. No, he couldn't know yet. He would still be wondering, waiting, hoping, down there in that deep, dark silence of his, in his own dark personal world. He didn't know he was blind; no one would have told him. I felt his pulse. It was strong and steady. He was a long, thin man, but his body was not very cold and the pale lower half of his clear-cut face was not very pale. There was something beautiful about him In his case there was no hurry, no necessity to rush him through the operating room. There was plenty of time. He would always be blind.

One of the orderlies was going up and down with hot tea in a bucket. I beckoned to him.

I said to the blind one: 'Here is a drink.' He didn't hear me, so I said it more loudly against the bandage, and helped him lift his head, and held the tin cup to his mouth below the thick edge of the bandage. I did not think then of what was hidden under the bandage. I think of it now. Another head case across the hut had thrown off his blanket and risen from his stretcher. He was standing stark naked except for his head bandage, in the middle of the hut, and was haranguing the crowd in a loud voice with the gestures of a political orator. But the crowd, lying on the floor, paid no attention to him. They did not notice him. I called to Gustave and Pierre to go to him.

The blind man said to me: 'Thank you, Sister, you are very kind. That is good. I thank you.' He had a beautiful voice. I noticed the great courtesy of his speech. But they were all courteous. Their courtesy when they died, their reluctance to cause me any trouble by dying or suffering, was one of the things it didn't do to think about.

Then I left him, and presently forgot that he was there waiting in the second row of stretchers on the left side of the long crowded floor.

Gustave and Pierre had got the naked orator back on to his stretcher and were wrapping him up again in his blankets. I let them deal with him and went back to my kitchen at the other end of the hut, where my syringes and hypodermic needles were boiling in saucepans. I had received by post that same morning a dozen beautiful new platinum needles. I was very pleased with them. I said to one of the dressers as I fixed a needle on my syringe and held it up, squirting the liquid through it: 'Look. I've some lovely new needles.' He said: 'Come and help me a moment. Just cut this bandage, please.' I went over to his dressing-table. He darted off to a voice that was shrieking somewhere. There was a man stretched on the table. His brain came off in my hands when I lifted the bandage from his head.

When the dresser came back I said: 'His brain came off on the bandage.'

'Where have you put it?'

'I put it in the pail under the table.'

'It's only one half of his brain,' he said, looking into the man's skull. 'The rest is here.'

I left him to finish the dressing and went about my own business. I had much to do.

It was my business to sort out the wounded as they were brought in from the ambulances and to keep them from dying before they got to the operating rooms: it was my business to sort out the nearly dying from the dying. I was there to sort them out and tell how fast life was ebbing in them. Life was leaking away from all of them; but with some there was no hurry, with others it was a case of minutes. It was my business to create a counter-wave of life, to create the flow against the

ebb. It was like a tug of war with the tide. The ebb of life was
cold. When life was ebbing the man was cold; when it began to
flow back, he grew warm. It was all, you see, like a dream. The
dying men on the floor were drowned men cast up on the beach,
and there was the ebb of life pouring away over them, sucking
them away, an invisible tide; and my old orderlies, like old
sea-salts out of a lifeboat, were working to save them. I had to
watch, to see if they were slipping, being dragged away. If a
man were slipping quickly, being sucked down rapidly, I sent
runners to the operating rooms. There were six operating rooms
on either side of my hut. Medical students in white coats hurried
back and forth along the covered corridors between us. It was
my business to know which of the wounded could wait and
which could not. I had to decide for myself. There was no one
to tell me. If I made any mistakes, some would die on their
stretchers on the floor under my eyes who need not have died.
I didn't worry. I didn't think. I was too busy, too absorbed in
what I was doing. I had to judge from what was written on
their tickets and from the way they looked and the way they
felt to my hand. My hand could tell of itself one kind of cold
from another. They were all half frozen when they arrived, but
the chill of their icy flesh wasn't the same as the cold inside them
when life was almost ebbed away. My hands could instantly tell
the difference between the cold of the harsh bitter night and
the stealthy cold of death. Then there was another thing, a
small fluttering thing. I didn't think about it or count it. My
fingers felt it. I was in a dream, led this way and that by my
cute eyes and hands that did many things, and seemed to know
what to do.

Sometimes there was no time to read the ticket or touch
the pulse. The door kept opening and shutting to let in the
stretcher-bearers whatever I was doing. I could not watch when
I was giving piqures; but, standing by my table filling a syringe,
I could look down over the rough forms that covered the floor
and pick out at a distance this one and that one. I had been
doing this for two years, and had learned to read the signs. I
could tell from the way they twitched, from the peculiar shade
of a pallid face, from the look of tight pinched-in nostrils, and

in other ways which I could not have explained, that this or
that one was slipping over the edge of the beach of life. Then I
would go quickly with my long saline needles, or short thick
camphor-oil needles, and send one of the old ones hurrying
along the corridor to the operating rooms. But sometimes there
was no need to hurry; sometimes I was too late; with some
there was no longer any question of the ebb and flow of life
and death; there was nothing to do.

The hospital throbbed and hummed that night like a dynamo.
The operating rooms were ablaze; twelve surgical *équipes* were
at work; boilers steamed and whistled; nurses hurried in and
out of the sterilizing rooms carrying big shining metal boxes
and enamelled trays; feet were running, slower feet shuffling.
The hospital was going full steam ahead. I had a sense of great
power, exhilaration and excitement. A loud wind was howling.
It was throwing itself like a pack of wolves against the flimsy
wooden walls, and the guns were growling. Their voices were
dying away. I thought of them as a pack of beaten dogs, slinking
away across the dark waste where the dead were lying and the
wounded who had not yet been picked up, their only cover the
windy blanket of the bitter November night.

And I was happy. It seemed to me that the crazy crowded
bright hot shelter was a beautiful place. I thought, 'This is the
second battlefield. The battle now is going on over the helpless
bodies of these men. It is we who are doing the fighting now,
with their real enemies.' And I thought of the chief surgeon, the
wizard working like lightning through the night, and all the
others wielding their flashing knives against the invisible enemy.
The wounded had begun to arrive at noon. It was now past
midnight, and the door kept opening and shutting to let in the
stretcher-bearers, and the ambulances kept lurching in at the
gate. Lanterns were moving through the windy dark from shed
to shed. The nurses were out there in the scattered huts, putting
the men to bed when they came over the dark ground, asleep,
from the operating rooms. They would wake up in clean warm
beds – those who did wake up.

'We will send you the dying, the desperate, the moribund,'
the Inspector-General had said. 'You must expect a thirty per

cent mortality.' So we had got ready for it; we had organized to dispute that figure.

We had built brick ovens, four of them, down the centre of the hut, and on top of these, galvanized iron cauldrons of boiling water were steaming. We had driven nails all the way down the wooden posts that held up the roof and festooned the posts with red rubber hot-water bottles. In the corner near to my kitchen we had partitioned off a cubicle, where we built a light bed, a rough wooden frame lined with electric light bulbs, where a man could be cooked back to life again. My own kitchen was an arrangement of shelves for saucepans and syringes and needles of different sizes, and cardboard boxes full of ampoules of camphor oil and strychnine and caffeine and morphine, and large ampoules of sterilized salt and water, and dozens of beautiful sharp shining needles were always on the boil.

It wasn't much to look at, this reception hut. It was about as attractive as a goods yard in a railway station, but we were very proud of it, my old ones and I. We had got it ready, and it was good enough for us. We could revive the cold dead there; snatch back the men who were slipping over the edge; hoist them out of the dark abyss into life again. And because our mortality at the end of three months was only nineteen per cent, not thirty, well, it was the most beautiful place in the world to me and my old grizzled Pépères, Gaston and Pierre and Leroux and the others were to me like shining archangels. But I didn't think about this. I think of it now. I only knew it then, and was happy. Yes, I was happy there.

Looking back, I do not understand that woman – myself – standing in that confused goods yard filled with bundles of broken human flesh. The place by one o'clock in the morning was a shambles. The air was thick with steaming sweat, with the effluvia of mud, dirt, blood. The men lay in their stiff uniforms that were caked with mud and dried blood, their great boots on their feet; stained bandages showing where a trouser leg or a sleeve had been cut away. Their faces gleamed faintly, with a faint phosphorescence. Some who could not breathe lying down were propped up on their stretchers against the

wall, but most were prone on their backs, staring at the steep
iron roof.

The old orderlies moved from one stretcher to another, carefully, among the piles of clothing, boots and blood-soaked
bandages – careful not to step on a hand or a sprawling twisted
foot. They carried zinc pails of hot water and slabs of yellow
soap and scrubbing brushes. They gathered up the heaps of
clothing, and made little bundles of the small things out of
pockets, or knelt humbly, washing the big yellow stinking feet
that protruded from under the brown blankets. It was the
business of these old ones to undress the wounded, wash them,
wrap them in blankets, and put hot-water bottles at their feet
and sides. It was a difficult business peeling the stiff uniform
from a man whose hip or shoulder was fractured, but the old
ones were careful. Their big peasant hands were gentle – very,
very gentle and careful. They handled the wounded men as if
they were children. Now, looking back, I see their rough powerful visages, their shaggy eye-brows, their big clumsy, gentle
hands. I see them go down on their stiff knees; I hear their
shuffling feet and their soft gruff voices answering the voices of
the wounded, who are calling to them for drinks, or to God for
mercy.

The old ones had orders from the commandant not to cut
the good cloth of the uniforms if they could help it, but they
had orders from me not to hurt the men, and they obeyed me.
They slit up the heavy trousers and slashed across the stiff
tunics with long scissors, and pulled very slowly, very carefully
at the heavy boots, and the wounded men did not groan or cry
out very much. They were mostly very quiet. When they did
cry out they usually apologized for the annoyance of their
agony. Only now and then a wind of pain would sweep over
the floor, tossing the legs and arms, then subside again.

I think that woman, myself, must have been in a trance, or
under some horrid spell. Her feet are lumps of fire, her face
is clammy, her apron is splashed with blood; but she moves
ceaselessly about with bright burning eyes and handles the
dreadful wreckage of men as if in a dream. She does not seem
to notice the wounds or the blood. Her eyes seem to be watching

something that comes and goes and darts in and out among the prone bodies. Her eyes and her hands and her ears are alert, intent on the unseen thing that scurries and hides and jumps out of the corner on to the face of a man when she's not looking. But quick, something makes her turn. Quick, she is over there, on her knees fighting the thing off, driving it away, and now it's got another victim. It's like a dreadful game of hide and seek among the wounded. All her faculties are intent on it. The other things that are going on, she deals with automatically.

There is a constant coming and going. Medical students run in and out.

'What have you got ready?'

'I've got three knees, two spines, five abdomens, twelve heads. Here's a lung case – hæmorrhage. He can't wait.' She is binding the man's chest; she doesn't look up.

'Send him along.'

'Pierre! Gaston! Call the stretcher-bearers to take the lung to Monsieur D—.' She fastens the tight bandage, tucks the blanket quickly round the thin shoulders. The old men lift him. She hurries back to her saucepans to get a new needle.

A surgeon appears.

'Where's that knee of mine? I left it in the saucepan on the window ledge. I had boiled it up for an experiment.'

'One of the orderlies must have taken it,' she says, putting her old needle on to boil.

'Good God! Did he mistake it?'

'Jean, did you take a saucepan you found on the windowsill?'

'Yes, sister, I took it. I thought it was for the *casse croûte*;[1] it looked like a ragoût of *mouton*. I have it here.'

'Well, it was lucky he didn't eat it. It was a knee I had cut out, you know.'

It is time for the old ones' '*casse croûte*'. It is after one o'clock. At one o'clock the orderlies have cups of coffee and chunks of bread and meat. They eat their supper gathered round the stoves where the iron cauldrons are boiling. The surgeons and the sisters attached to the operating rooms are drinking coffee too in the sterilizing rooms. I do not want any supper. I am not hungry. I am not tired. I am busy. My eyes are busy and my fingers. I am conscious of nothing about myself but my eyes, hands and feet. My feet are a nuisance, they are swollen, hurting lumps, but my fingers are perfectly satisfactory. They are expert in the handling of frail glass ampoules and syringes and needles. I go from one man to another jabbing the sharp needles into their sides, rubbing their skins with iodine, and each time I pick my way back across their bodies to fetch a fresh needle I scan the surface of the floor where the men are spread like a carpet, for signs, for my special secret signals of death.

'Aha! I'll catch you out again.' Quick, to that one. That jerking! That sudden livid hue spreading over his form. 'Quick, Emile! Pierre!' I have lifted the blanket. The blood is pouring out on the floor under the stretcher. 'Get the tourniquet. Hold his leg up. Now then, tight – tighter. Now call the stretcher-bearers.'

Someone near is having a fit. Is it epilepsy? I don't know. His mouth is frothy. His eyes are rolling. He tries to fling himself on the floor. He falls with a thud across his neighbour, who does not notice. The man just beyond propped up against the wall, watches as if from a great distance. He has a gentle patient face; this spectacle does not concern him.

The door keeps opening and shutting to let in the stretcher-bearers. The wounded are carried in at the end door and are carried out to the operating rooms at either side. The sergeant is counting the treasures out of a dead man's pockets. He is tying his little things, his letters and *briquet*,[2] etc., up in a handkerchief. Some of the old ones are munching their bread and meat in the centre of the hut under the electric light. The others are busy with their pails and scissors. They shuffle about, kneeling, scrubbing, filling hot-water bottles. I see it all through a mist. It is misty but eternal. It is a scene in eternity, in some strange dream-hell where I am glad to be employed, where I belong, where I am happy. How crowded together we are here. How close we are in this nightmare. The wounded are packed into this place like sardines, and we are so close to them, my old ones and I. I've never been so close before to human beings. We are locked together, the old ones and I, and the wounded men; we are bound together. We all feel it. We all know it. The same thing is throbbing in us, the single thing, the one life. We are one body, suffering and bleeding. It is a kind of bliss to me to feel this. I am a little delirious, but my head is cool enough, it seems to me.

'No, not that one. He can wait. Take the next one to Monsieur D—, and this one to Monsieur Guy, and this one to Monsieur Robert. We will put this one on the electric light bed; he has no pulse. More hot-water bottles here, Gaston.

'Do you feel cold, *mon vieux?*'

'Yes, I think so, but pray do not trouble.'

I go with him into the little cubicle, turn on the light bulbs, leave him to cook there; and as I come out again to face the strange heaving dream, I suddenly hear a voice calling me, a new far-away hollow voice.

'Sister! My sister! Where are you?'

I am startled. It sounds so far away, so hollow and so sweet. It sounds like a bell high up in the mountains. I do not know where it comes from. I look down over the rows of men lying on their backs, one close to the other, packed together on the floor, and I cannot tell where the voice comes from. Then I hear it again.

'Sister! Oh, my sister, where are you?'

A lost voice. The voice of a lost man, wandering in the mountains, in the night. It is the blind man calling. I had forgotten him. I had forgotten that he was there. He could wait. The others could not wait. So I had left him and forgotten him.

Something in his voice made me run, made my heart miss a beat. I ran down the centre alleyway, round and up again, between the two rows, quickly, carefully stepping across to him over the stretchers that separated us. He was in the second row. I could just squeeze through to him.

'I am coming,' I called to him. 'I am coming.'

I knelt beside him. 'I am here,' I said; but he lay quite still on his back; he didn't move at all; he hadn't heard me. So I took his hand and put my mouth close to his bandaged head and called to him with desperate entreaty.

'I am here. What is it? What is the matter?'

He didn't move even then, but he gave a long shuddering sigh of relief.

'I thought I had been abandoned here, all alone,' he said softly in his far-away voice.

I seemed to awake then. I looked round me and began to tremble, as one would tremble if one awoke with one's head over the edge of a precipice. I saw the wounded packed round us, hemming us in. I saw his comrades, thick round him, and the old ones shuffling about, working and munching their hunks of bread, and the door opening to let in the stretcher-bearers. The light poured down on the rows of faces. They gleamed faintly. Four hundred faces were staring up at the roof, side by side. The blind man didn't know. He thought he was alone, out in the dark. That was the precipice, that reality.

'You are not alone,' I lied. 'There are many of your comrades here, and I am here, and there are doctors and nurses. You are with friends here, not alone.'

'I thought,' he murmured in that far-away voice, 'that you had gone away and forgotten me, and that I was abandoned here alone.'

My body rattled and jerked like a machine out of order. I was awake now, and I seemed to be breaking to pieces.

'No,' I managed to lie again. 'I had not forgotten you, nor left you alone.' And I looked down again at the visible half of his face and saw that his lips were smiling.

At that I fled from him. I ran down the long, dreadful hut and hid behind my screen and cowered, sobbing, in a corner, hiding my face.

The old ones were very troubled. They didn't know what to do. Presently I heard them whispering:

'She is tired,' one said.

'Yes, she is tired.'

'She should go off to bed,' another said.

'We will manage somehow without her,' they said.

Then one of them timidly stuck a grizzled head round the corner of the screen. He held his tin cup in his hands. It was full of hot coffee. He held it out, offering it to me. He didn't know of anything else that he could do for me.

# KATHERINE MANSFIELD
# AN INDISCREET JOURNEY

She is like St Anne. Yes, the concierge is the image of St Anne, with that black cloth over her head, the wisps of grey hair hanging, and the tiny smoking lamp in her hand. Really very beautiful, I thought, smiling at St Anne, who said severely: 'Six o'clock. You have only just got time. There is a bowl of milk on the writing-table.' I jumped out of my pyjamas and into a basin of cold water like any English lady in any French novel. The concierge, persuaded that I was on my way to prison cells and death by bayonets, opened the shutters and the cold clear light came through. A little steamer hooted on the river; a cart with two horses at a gallop flung past. The rapid swirling water; the tall black trees on the far side, grouped together like Negroes conversing. Sinister, very, I thought, as I buttoned on my age-old Burberry. (That Burberry was very significant. It did not belong to me. I had borrowed it from a friend. My eye lighted upon it hanging in her little dark hall. The very thing! The perfect and adequate disguise – an old Burberry. Lions have been faced in a Burberry. Ladies have been rescued from open boats in mountainous seas wrapped in nothing else. An old Burberry seems to me the sign and the token of the undisputed venerable traveller, I decided, leaving my purple peg-top with the real seal collar and cuffs in exchange.)

'You will never get there,' said the concierge, watching me turn up the collar. 'Never! Never!' I ran down the echoing stairs – strange they sounded, like a piano flicked by a sleepy housemaid – and on to the Quai. 'Why so fast, *ma mignonne*?'[1] said a lovely little boy in coloured socks, dancing in front of the electric lotus buds that curve over the entrance to the Métro.

Alas! there was not even time to blow him a kiss. When I arrived at the big station I had only four minutes to spare, and the platform entrance was crowded and packed with soldiers, their yellow papers in one hand and big untidy bundles. The Commissaire of Police stood on one side, a Nameless Official on the other. Will he let me pass? Will he? He was an old man with a fat swollen face covered with big warts. Horn-rimmed spectacles squatted on his nose. Trembling, I made an effort. I conjured up my sweetest early-morning smile and handed it with the papers. But the delicate thing fluttered against the horn spectacles and fell. Nevertheless, he let me pass, and I ran, ran in and out among the soldiers and up the high steps into the yellow-painted carriage.

'Does one go direct to X?' I asked the collector who dug at my ticket with a pair of forceps and handed it back again. 'No, Mademoiselle, you must change at X.Y.Z.'

'At – ?'

'X.Y.Z.'

Again I had not heard. 'At what time do we arrive there, if you please?'

'One o'clock.' But that was no good to me. I hadn't a watch. Oh, well – later.

Ah! the train had begun to move. The train was on my side. It swung out of the station, and soon we were passing the vegetable gardens, passing the tall, blind houses to let, passing the servants beating carpets. Up already and walking in the fields, rosy from the rivers and the red-fringed pools, the sun lighted upon the swinging train and stroked my muff and told me to take off that Burberry. I was not alone in the carriage. An old woman sat opposite, her skirt turned back over her knees, a bonnet of black lace on her head. In her fat hands, adorned with a wedding and two mourning rings, she held a letter. Slowly, slowly she sipped a sentence, and then looked up and out of the window, her lips trembling a little, and then another sentence, and again the old face turned to the light, tasting it ... Two soldiers leaned out of the window, their heads nearly touching – one of them was whistling, the other had his coat fastened with some rusty safety-pins. And now there were soldiers everywhere working on the railway line, leaning against trucks or standing hands on hips, eyes fixed on the train as though they expected at least one camera at every window. And now we were passing big wooden sheds like rigged-up dancing halls or seaside pavilions, each flying a flag. In and out of them walked the Red Cross men; the wounded sat against the walls sunning themselves. At all the bridges, the crossings, the stations, a *petit soldat*, all boots and bayonet. Forlorn and desolate he looked, like a little comic picture waiting for the joke to be written underneath. Is there really such a thing as war? Are all these laughing voices really going to the war? These dark woods lighted so mysteriously by the white stems of the birch and the ash – these watery fields with the big birds flying over – these rivers green and blue in the light – have battles been fought in places like these?

What beautiful cemeteries we are passing! They flash gay in the sun. They seem to be full of cornflowers and poppies and daisies. How can there be so many flowers at this time of the year? But they are not flowers at all. They are bunches of ribbons tied on to the soldiers' graves.

I glanced up and caught the old woman's eye. She smiled and folded the letter. 'It is from my son – the first we have had since October. I am taking it to my daughter-in-law.'

'. . . ?'

'Yes, very good,' said the old woman, shaking down her skirt and putting her arm through the handle of her basket. 'He wants me to send him some handkerchiefs and a piece of stout string.'

What is the name of the station where I have to change? Perhaps I shall never know. I got up and leaned my arms across the window rail, my feet crossed. One cheek burned as in infancy on the way to the seaside. When the war is over I shall have a barge and drift along these rivers with a white cat and a pot of mignonette[2] to bear me company.

Down the side of the hill filed the troops, winking red and blue in the light. Far away, but plainly to be seen, some more flew by on bicycles. But really, *ma France adorée*,[3] this uniform is ridiculous. Your soldiers are stamped upon your bosom like bright irreverent transfers.

The train slowed down, stopped . . . Everybody was getting out except me. A big boy, his *sabots* tied to his back with a piece of string, the inside of his tin wine cup stained a lovely impossible pink, looked very friendly. Does one change here perhaps for X? Another whose kepi[4] had come out of a wet paper cracker swung my suit-case to earth. What darlings soldiers are! '*Merci bien, Monsieur, vous êtes tout à fait aimable* . . .'[5] 'Not this way,' said a bayonet. 'Nor this,' said another. So I followed the crowd. 'Your passport, Mademoiselle . . .' '*We, Sir Edward Grey* . . .' I ran through the muddy square and into the buffet.

A green room with a stove jutting out and tables on each side. On the counter, beautiful with coloured bottles, a woman leans, her breasts in her folded arms. Through an open door I can see a kitchen, and the cook in a white coat breaking eggs into a bowl and tossing the shells into a corner. The blue and red coats of the men who are eating hang upon the walls. Their short swords and belts are piled upon chairs. Heavens! what a noise. The sunny air seemed all broken up and trembling with it. A little boy, very pale, swung from table to table, taking the orders, and poured me out a glass of purple coffee. *Ssssh*, came from the eggs. They were in a pan. The woman rushed from behind the counter and began to help the boy. *Toute de suite, tout' suite!*[6] she chirruped to the loud impatient voices. There came a clatter of plates and the pop-pop of corks being drawn.

Suddenly in the doorway I saw someone with a pail of fish – brown speckled fish, like the fish one sees in a glass case, swimming through forests of beautiful pressed sea-weed. He was an old man in a tattered jacket, standing humbly, waiting for someone to attend to him. A thin beard fell over his chest, his eyes under the tufted eyebrows were bent on the pail he carried. He looked as though he had escaped from some holy picture, and was entreating the soldiers' pardon for being there at all . . .

But what could I have done? I could not arrive at X with two fishes hanging on a straw; and I am sure it is a penal offence in France to throw fish out of railway-carriage windows, I thought, miserably climbing into a smaller, shabbier train.

Perhaps I might have taken them to – *ah, mon Dieu* – I had forgotten the name of my uncle and aunt again! Buffard, Buffon – what was it? Again I read the unfamiliar letter in the familiar handwriting.

My Dear Niece,
Now that the weather is more settled, your uncle and I would be charmed if you would pay us a little visit. Telegraph me when you are coming. I shall meet you outside the station if I am free. Otherwise our good friend, Madame Grinçon, who lives in the little toll-house by the bridge, *juste en face de le gare*,[7] will conduct you to our home. *Je vous embrasse bien tendrement*.
                                                                Julie Boiffard.

A visiting card was enclosed: *M. Paul Boiffard*.

Boiffard – of course that was the name. *Ma tante Julie et mon oncle Paul* – suddenly they were there with me, more real, more solid than any relations I had ever known. I saw Tante Julie bridling, with the soup-tureen in her hands, and Oncle Paul sitting at the table with a red and white napkin tied round his neck. Boiffard – Boiffard – I must remember the name. Supposing the Commissaire Militaire should ask me who the relations were I was going to and I muddled the name – Oh, how fatal! Buffard – no, Boiffard. And then for the first time, folding Aunt Julie's letter, I saw scrawled in a corner of the empty back page: *Venez vite, vite*.[8] Strange impulsive woman! My heart began to beat . . .

'Ah, we are not far off now,' said the lady opposite. 'You are going to X, Mademoiselle?'

'*Oui, Madame*.'

'I also . . . You have been there before?'

'No, Madame. This is the first time.'

'Really, it is a strange time for a visit.'

I smiled faintly, and tried to keep my eyes off her hat. She was quite an ordinary little woman, but she wore a black velvet toque, with an incredibly surprised-looking sea-gull camped on the very top of it. Its round eyes, fixed on me so inquiringly, were almost too much to bear. I had a dreadful

impulse to shoo it away, or to lean forward and inform her of
its presence . . .

'*Excusez-moi, Madame*, but perhaps you have not remarked
there is an *espèce de* sea-gull *coucheé sur votre chapeau*.'[9]

Could the bird be there on purpose? I must not laugh . . . I
must not laugh. Had she ever looked at herself in a glass with
that bird on her head?

'It is very difficult to get into X at present, to pass the station,'
she said, and she shook her head with the sea-gull at me.
'Ah, such an affair. One must sign one's name and state one's
business.'

'Really, is it as bad as all that?'

'But naturally. You see, the whole place is in the hands of the
military, and' – she shrugged – 'they have to be strict. Many
people do not get beyond the station at all. They arrive. They
are put in the waiting-room, and there they remain.'

Did I or did I not detect in her voice a strange, insulting
relish?

'I suppose such strictness is absolutely necessary,' I said
coldly, stroking my muff.

'Necessary,' she cried. 'I should think so. Why, Mademoiselle, you cannot imagine what it would be like otherwise! You
know what women are like about soldiers' – she raised a final
hand – 'mad, completely mad. But –' and she gave a little laugh
of triumph – 'they could not get into X. *Mon Dieu*, no! There
is no question about that.'

'I don't suppose they even try,' said I.

'Don't you?' said the sea-gull.

Madame said nothing for a moment. 'Of course the authorities are very hard on the men. It means instant imprisonment,
and then – off to the firing-line without a word.'

'What are *you* going to X for?' said the sea-gull. 'What on
earth are *you* doing here?'

'Are you making a long stay in X, Mademoiselle?'

She had won, she had won. I was terrified. A lamp-post swam
past the train with the fatal name upon it. I could hardly breathe
– the train had stopped. I smiled gaily at Madame and danced
down the steps to the platform . . .

It was a hot little room, completely furnished, with two colonels seated at two tables. They were large, grey-whiskered men with a touch of burned red on their cheeks. Sumptuous and omnipotent they looked. One smoked what ladies love to call a heavy Egyptian cigarette, with a long creamy ash, the other toyed with a gilded pen. Their heads rolled on their tight collars, like big over-ripe fruits. I had a terrible feeling, as I handed my passport and ticket, that a soldier would step forward and tell me to kneel. I would have knelt without question.

'What's this?' said God I, querulously. He did not like my passport at all. The very sight of it seemed to annoy him. He waved a dissenting hand at it, with a 'Non, je ne peux pas manger ça'[10] air.

'But it won't do. It won't do at all, you know. Look – read for yourself,' and he glanced with extreme distaste at my photograph, and then with even greater distaste his pebble eyes looked at me.

'Of course the photograph is deplorable,' I said, scarcely breathing with terror, 'but it has been vised and vised.'

He raised his big bulk and went over to God II.

'Courage!' I said to my muff and held it firmly, 'Courage!'

God II held up a finger to me, and I produced Aunt Julie's letter and her card. But he did not seem to feel the slightest interest in her. He stamped my passport idly, scribbled a word on my ticket and I was on the platform again.

'That way – you pass out that way.'

Terribly pale, with a faint smile on his lips, his hand at salute, stood the little corporal. I gave no sign, I am sure I gave no sign. He stepped behind me.

'And then follow me as though you do not see me,' I heard him half whisper, half sing.

How fast he went, through the slippery mud towards a bridge. He had a postman's bag on his back, a paper parcel and the Matin[11] in his hand. We seemed to dodge through a maze of policemen, and I could not keep up at all with the little corporal who began to whistle. From the toll-house 'our good friend, Madame Grinçon', her hands wrapped in a shawl, watched our coming, and against the toll-house there leaned a tiny faded cab. *Montez vite, vite!*[12] said the little corporal, hurling my suit-case, the postman's bag, the paper parcel and the *Matin* on to the floor.

'A-ie! A-ie! Do not be so mad. Do not ride yourself. You will be seen,' wailed 'our good friend, Madame Grinçon'.

'*Ah, je m'en f . . .*'[13] said the little corporal.

The driver jerked into activity. He lashed the bony horse and away we flew, both doors, which were the complete sides of the cab, flapping and banging.

'*Bon jour, mon amie.*'

'*Bon jour, mon ami.*'

And then we swooped down and clutched at the banging doors. They would not keep shut. They were fools of doors.

'Lean back, let me do it!' I cried. 'Policemen are as thick as violets everywhere.'

At the barracks the horse reared up and stopped. A crowd of laughing faces blotted the window.

'*Prends ça, mon vieux,*'[14] said the little corporal, handing the paper parcel.

'It's all right,' called someone.

We waved, we were off again. By a river, down a strange white street, with little houses on either side, gay in the late sunlight.

'Jump out as soon as he stops again. The door will be open. Run straight inside. I will follow. The man is already paid. I know you will like the house. It is quite white. And the room is white too, and the people are –'

'White as snow.'

We looked at each other. We began to laugh. 'Now,' said the little corporal.

Out I flew and in at the door. There stood, presumably, my aunt Julie. There in the background hovered, I supposed, my uncle Paul.

'*Bon jour, Madame!*'

'*Bon jour, Monsieur!*'

'It is all right, you are safe,' said my aunt Julie. Heavens, how I loved her! And she opened the door of the white room and shut it upon us. Down went the suit-case, the postman's bag, the *Matin*. I threw my passport up into the air, and the little corporal caught it.

What an extraordinary thing. We had been there to lunch and to dinner each day; but now in the dusk and alone I could not find it. I clop-clopped in my borrowed *sabots* through the greasy mud, right to the end of the village, and there was not a sign of it. I could not even remember what it looked like, or if there was a name painted on the outside, or any bottles or tables showing at the window. Already the village houses were sealed for the night behind big wooden shutters. Strange and mysterious they looked in the ragged drifting light and thin rain, like a company of beggars perched on the hill-side, their bosoms full of rich unlawful gold. There was nobody about but the soldiers. A group of wounded stood under a lamp-post, petting a mangy, shivering dog. Up the street came four big boys singing:

> '*Dodo, mon homme, fais vit' dodo . . .*'[15]

and swung off down the hill to their sheds behind the railway station. They seemed to take the last breath of the day with them. I began to walk slowly back.

'It must have been one of these houses. I remember it stood far back from the road – and there were no steps, not even a porch – one seemed to walk right through the window.' And then quite suddenly the waiting-boy came out of just such a place. He saw me and grinned cheerfully, and began to whistle through his teeth.

'*Bon soir, mon petit.*'

'*Bon soir, Madame.*' And he followed me up the café to our special table, right at the far end by the window, and marked by a bunch of violets that I had left in a glass there yesterday.

'You are two?' asked the waiting-boy, flicking the table with a red and white cloth. His long swinging steps echoed over the bare floor. He disappeared into the kitchen and came back to light the lamp that hung from the ceiling under a spreading shade, like a haymaker's hat. Warm light shone on the empty place that was really a barn, set out with dilapidated tables and chairs. Into the middle of the room a black stove jutted. At one side of it there was a table with a row of bottles on it, behind which Madame sat and took the money and made entries in a red book. Opposite her desk a door led into the kitchen. The walls were covered with a creamy paper patterned all over with green and swollen trees – hundreds and hundreds of trees reared their mushroom heads to the ceiling. I began to wonder who had chosen the paper and why. Did Madame think it was beautiful, or that it was a gay and lovely thing to eat one's dinner at all seasons in the middle of a forest . . . On either side of the clock there hung a picture: one, a young gentleman in black tights wooing a pear-shaped lady in yellow over the back of a garden seat, *Premier Rencontre*;[16] two, the black and yellow in amorous confusion, *Triomphe d'Amour*.[17]

The clock ticked to a soothing lilt, *C'est ça c'est ça*. In the kitchen the waiting-boy was washing up. I heard the ghostly chatter of the dishes.

And years passed. Perhaps the war is long since over – there is no village outside at all – the streets are quiet under the grass. I have an idea this is the sort of thing one will do on the very last day of all – sit in an empty café and listen to a clock ticking until –

Madame came through the kitchen door, nodded to me and took her seat behind the table, her plump hands folded on the red book. *Ping* went the door. A handful of soldiers came in, took off their coats and began to play cards, chaffing and poking fun at the pretty waiting-boy, who threw up his little round head, rubbed his thick fringe out of his eyes and cheeked them back in his broken voice. Sometimes his voice boomed up from his throat, deep and harsh, and then in the middle of a sentence it broke and scattered in a funny squeaking. He seemed to enjoy it himself. You would not have been surprised if he had walked into the kitchen on his hands and brought back your dinner turning a catherine-wheel.

*Ping* went the door again. Two more men came in. They sat at the table nearest Madame, and she leaned to them with a birdlike movement, her head on one side. Oh, they had a grievance! The Lieutenant was a fool – nosing about – springing out at them – and they'd only been sewing on buttons. Yes, that was all – sewing on buttons, and up comes this young spark. 'Now then, what you up to?' They mimicked the idiotic voice. Madame drew down her mouth, nodding sympathy. The waiting-boy served them with glasses. He took a bottle of some orange-coloured stuff and put it on the table edge. A shout from the card-players made him turn sharply, and crash! over went the bottle, spilling on the table, the floor – smash! to tinkling atoms. An amazed silence. Through it the drip-drip of the wine from the table on to the floor. It looked very strange dropping so slowly, as though the table were crying. Then there came a roar from the card-players. 'You'll catch it, my lad! That's the style! Now you've done it! . . . *Sept, huit, neuf.*' They started playing again. The waiting-boy never said a word. He stood, his head bent, his hands spread out, and then he knelt and gathered up the glass, piece by piece and soaked the wine up with a cloth. Only when Madame cried cheerfully, 'You wait till *he* finds out,' did he raise his head.

'He can't say anything, if I pay for it,' he muttered, his face jerking, and he marched off into the kitchen with the soaking cloth.

'*Il pleure de colère,*'[18] said Madame delightedly, patting her hair with her plump hands.

The café slowly filled. It grew very warm. Blue smoke mounted from the tables and hung about the haymaker's hat in misty wreaths. There was a suffocating smell of onion soup and boots and damp cloth. In the din the door sounded again. It opened to let in a weed of a fellow, who stood with his back against it, one hand shading his eyes.

'Hullo! you've got the bandage off?'

'How does it feel, *mon vieux*?'

'Let's have a look at them.'

But he made no reply. He shrugged and walked unsteadily to a table, sat down and leaned against the wall. Slowly his hand fell. In his white face his eyes showed, pink as a rabbit's. They brimmed and spilled, brimmed and spilled. He dragged a white cloth out of his pocket and wiped them.

'It's the smoke,' said someone. 'It's the smoke tickles them up for you.'

His comrades watched him a bit, watched his eyes fill again, again brim over. The water ran down his face, off his chin on to the table. He rubbed the place with his coat-sleeve, and then, as though forgetful, went on rubbing, rubbing with his hand across the table, staring in front of him. And then he started shaking his head to the movement of his hand. He gave a loud strange groan and dragged out the cloth again.

'*Huit, neuf, dix*,' said the card-players.

'*P'tit*, some more bread.'

'Two coffees.'

'*Un Picon!*'[19]

The waiting-boy, quite recovered, but with scarlet cheeks, ran to and fro. A tremendous quarrel flared up among the card-players, raged for two minutes, and died in flickering laughter. 'Ooof!' groaned the man with the eyes, rocking and mopping. But nobody paid any attention to him except Madame. She made a little grimace at her two soldiers.

'*Mais vous savez c'est un peu dégoûtant, ça*,'[20] she said severely.

'*Ah, oui, Madame*,' answered the soldiers, watching her bent head and pretty hands, as she arranged for the hundredth time a frill of lace on her lifted bosom.

'*V'là, Monsieur!*' cawed the waiting-boy over his shoulder to me. For some silly reason I pretended not to hear, and I leaned over the table smelling the violets, until the little corporal's hand closed over mine.

'Shall we have *un peu de charcuterie* to begin with?' he asked tenderly.

'In England,' said the blue-eyed soldier, 'you drink whisky with your meals. *N'est-ce pas, Mademoiselle?*[21] A little glass of whisky neat before eating. Whisky and soda with your *bifteks*,[22] and after, more whisky with hot water and lemon.'

'Is it true that?' asked his great friend who sat opposite, a big red-faced chap with a black beard and large moist eyes and hair that looked as though it had been cut with a sewing-machine.

'Well, not quite true,' said I.

'*Si, si,*' cried the blue-eyed soldier. 'I ought to know. I'm in business. English travellers come to my place, and it's always the same thing.'

'Bah, I can't stand whisky,' said the little corporal. 'It's too disgusting the morning after. Do you remember, *ma fille*, the whisky in that little bar at Montmartre?'

'*Souvenir tendre,*'[23] sighed Blackbeard, putting two fingers in the breast of his coat and letting his head fall. He was very drunk.

'But I know something that you've never tasted,' said the blue-eyed soldier, pointing a finger at me; 'something really good.' *Cluck* he went with his tongue. '*É-patant!*[24] And the curious thing is that you'd hardly know it from whisky except that it's' – he felt with his hand for the word – 'finer, sweeter perhaps, not so sharp, and it leaves you feeling gay as a rabbit next morning.'

'What is it called?'

'*Mirabelle!*' He rolled the word round his mouth, under his tongue. 'Ah-ah, that's the stuff.'

'I could eat another mushroom,' said Blackbeard. 'I would like another mushroom very much. I am sure I could eat another mushroom if Mademoiselle gave it to me out of her hand.'

'You ought to try it,' said the blue-eyed soldier, leaning both hands on the table and speaking so seriously that I began to wonder how much more sober he was than Blackbeard. 'You ought to try it, and tonight. I would like you to tell me if you don't think it's like whisky.'

'Perhaps they've got it here,' said the little corporal, and he called the waiting-boy. '*P'tit!*'

'*Non, Monsieur,*' said the boy, who never stopped smiling. He served us with dessert plates painted with blue parrots and horned beetles.

'What is the name for this in English?' said Blackbeard, pointing. I told him 'Parrot'.

'Ah, *mon Dieu!* . . . Pair-rot . . .' He put his arms round his plate. 'I love you, *ma petite* pair-rot. You are sweet, you are blonde, you are English. You do not know the difference between whisky and *mirabelle*.'

The little corporal and I looked at each other, laughing. He squeezed up his eyes when he laughed, so that you saw nothing but the long curly lashes.

'Well, I know a place where they do keep it,' said the blue-eyed soldier. 'Café des Amis. We'll go there – I'll pay – I'll – I'll pay for the whole lot of us.' His gesture embraced thousands of pounds.

But with a loud whirring noise the clock on the wall struck half past eight; and no soldier is allowed in a café after eight o'clock at night.

'It is fast,' said the blue-eyed soldier. The little corporal's watch said the same. So did the immense turnip that Blackbeard produced and carefully deposited on the head of one of the horned beetles.

'Ah, well, we'll take the risk,' said the blue-eyed soldier, and he thrust his arms into his immense cardboard coat. 'It's worth it,' he said. 'It's worth it. You just wait.'

Outside, stars shone between wispy clouds and the moon fluttered like a candle flame over a pointed spire. The shadows of the dark plume-like trees waved on the white houses. Not a soul to be seen. No sound to be heard but the *Hsh! Hsh!* of a far-away train, like a big beast shuffling in its sleep.

'You are cold,' whispered the little corporal. 'You are cold, *ma fille.*'

'No, really not.'

'But you are trembling.'

'Yes, but I'm not cold.'

'What are the women like in England?' asked Blackbeard. 'After the war is over I shall go to England. I shall find a little English woman and marry her – and her pair-rot.' He gave a loud choking laugh.

'Fool!' said the blue-eyed soldier, shaking him; and he leaned over to me. 'It is only after the second glass that you really taste it,' he whispered. 'The second little glass and then – ah! – then you know.'

Café des Amis gleamed in the moonlight. We glanced quickly up and down the road. We ran up the four wooden steps, and opened the ringing glass door into a low room lighted with a hanging lamp, where about ten people were dining. They were seated on two benches at a narrow table.

'Soldiers!' screamed a woman, leaping up from behind a white soup-tureen – a scrag of a woman in a black shawl. 'Soldiers! At this hour! Look at that clock, look at it.' And she pointed to the clock with the dripping ladle.

'It's fast,' said the blue-eyed soldier. 'It's fast, Madame. And don't make so much noise, I beg of you. We will drink and we will go.'

'Will you?' she cried, running round the table and planting herself in front of us. 'That's just what you won't do. Coming into an honest woman's house this hour of the night – making a scene – getting the police after you. Ah, no! Ah, no! It's a disgrace, that's what it is.'

'Sh!' said the little corporal, holding up his hand. Dead silence. In the silence we heard steps passing.

'The police,' whispered Blackbeard, winking at a pretty girl with rings in her ears, who smiled back at him, saucy. 'Sh!'

The faces lifted, listening. 'How beautiful they are!' I thought. 'They are like a family party having supper in the New Testament . . .' The steps died away.

'Serve you very well right if you had been caught,' scolded the angry woman. 'I'm sorry on your account that the police didn't come. You deserve it – you deserve it.'

'A little glass of *mirabelle* and we will go,' persisted the blue-eyed soldier.

Still scolding and muttering she took four glasses from the cupboard and a big bottle. 'But you're not going to drink in here. Don't you believe it.' The little corporal ran into the kitchen. 'Not there! Not there! Idiot!' she cried. 'Can't you see there's a window there, and a wall opposite where the police come every evening to –'

'Sh!' Another scare.

'You are mad and you will end in prison – all four of you,' said the woman. She flounced out of the room. We tiptoed after her into a dark smelling scullery, full of pans of greasy water, of salad leaves and meat-bones.

'There now,' she said, putting down the glasses. 'Drink and go!'

'Ah, at last!' The blue-eyed soldier's happy voice trickled
through the dark. 'What do you think? Isn't it just as I said?
Hasn't it got a taste of excellent – *ex-cellent* whisky?'

# JOSEPH CONRAD
# THE TALE

Outside the large single window the crepuscular light was dying out slowly in a great square gleam without colour, framed rigidly in the gathering shades of the room.

It was a long room. The irresistible tide of the night ran into the most distant part of it, where the whispering of a man's voice, passionately interrupted and passionately renewed, seemed to plead against the answering murmurs of infinite sadness.

At last no answering murmur came. His movement when he rose slowly from his knees by the side of the deep, shadowy couch holding the shadowy suggestion of a reclining woman revealed him tall under the low ceiling, and sombre all over except for the crude discord of the white collar under the shape of his head and the faint, minute spark of a brass button here and there on his uniform.

He stood over her a moment, masculine and mysterious in his immobility, before he sat down on a chair near by. He could see only the faint oval of her upturned face and, extended on her black dress, her pale hands, a moment before abandoned to his kisses and now as if too weary to move.

He dared not make a sound, shrinking as a man would do from the prosaic necessities of existence. As usual, it was the woman who had the courage. Her voice was heard first – almost conventional while her being vibrated yet with conflicting emotions.

'Tell me something,' she said.

The darkness hid his surprise and then his smile. Had he not just said to her everything worth saying in the world – and that not for the first time!

'What am I to tell you?' he asked, in a voice creditably steady. He was beginning to feel grateful to her for that something final in her tone which had eased the strain.

'Why not tell me a tale?'

'A tale!' He was really amazed.

'Yes. Why not?'

These words came with a slight petulance, the hint of a loved woman's capricious will, which is capricious only because it feels itself to be a law, embarrassing sometimes and always difficult to elude.

'Why not?' he repeated, with a slightly mocking accent, as though he had been asked to give her the moon. But now he was feeling a little angry with her for that feminine mobility that slips out of an emotion as easily as out of a splendid gown.

He heard her say, a little unsteadily with a sort of fluttering intonation which made him think suddenly of a butterfly's flight:

'You used to tell – your – your simple and – and professional – tales very well at one time. Or well enough to interest me. You had a – a sort of art – in the days – the days before the war.'

'Really?' he said, with involuntary gloom. 'But now, you see, the war is going on,' he continued in such a dead, equable tone that she felt a slight chill fall over her shoulders. And yet she persisted. For there's nothing more unswerving in the world than a woman's caprice.

'It could be a tale not of this world,' she explained.

'You want a tale of the other, the better world?' he asked, with a matter-of-fact surprise. 'You must evoke for that task those who have already gone there.'

'No. I don't mean that. I mean another – some other – world. In the universe – not in heaven.'

'I am relieved. But you forget that I have only five days' leave.'

'Yes. And I've also taken a five days' leave from – from my duties.'

'I like that word.'

'What word?'

'Duty.'

'It is horrible – sometimes.'

'Oh, that's because you think it's narrow. But it isn't. It contains infinities, and – and so –'

'What is this jargon?'

He disregarded the interjected scorn. 'An infinity of absolution, for instance,' he continued. 'But as to this "another world" – who's going to look for it and for the tale that is in it?'

'You,' she said, with a strange, almost rough, sweetness of assertion.

He made a shadowy movement of assent in his chair, the irony of which not even the gathered darkness could render mysterious.

'As you will. In that world, then, there was once upon a time a Commanding Officer and a Northman. Put in the capitals, please, because they had no other names. It was a world of seas and continents and islands –'

'Like the earth,' she murmured, bitterly.

'Yes. What else could you expect from sending a man made of our common, tormented clay on a voyage of discovery? What else could he find? What else could you understand or care for, or feel the existence of even? There was comedy in it, and slaughter.'

'Always like the earth,' she murmured.

'Always. And since I could find in the universe only what was deeply rooted in the fibres of my being there was love in it, too. But we won't talk of that.'

'No. We won't,' she said, in a neutral tone which concealed perfectly her relief – or her disappointment. Then after a pause she added: 'It's going to be a comic story.'

'Well –' He paused, too. 'Yes. In a way. In a very grim way. It will be human, and, as you know, comedy is but a matter of the visual angle. And it won't be a noisy story. All the long guns in it will be dumb – as dumb as so many telescopes.'

'Ah, there are guns in it, then! And may I ask – where?'

'Afloat. You remember that the world of which we speak had its seas. A war was going on in it. It was a funny world and terribly in earnest. Its war was being carried on over the land, over the water, under the water, up in the air, and even under the ground. And many young men in it, mostly in wardrooms and messrooms, used to say to each other – pardon the unparliamentary word – they used to say, "It's a damned bad war, but it's better than no war at all." Sounds flippant, doesn't it?'

He heard a nervous, impatient sigh in the depths of the couch while he went on without a pause.

'And yet there is more in it than meets the eye. I mean more wisdom. Flippancy, like comedy, is but a matter of visual first-impression. That world was not very wise. But there was in it a certain amount of common working sagacity. That, however, was mostly worked by the neutrals in diverse ways, public and private, which had to be watched; watched by acute minds and also by actual sharp eyes. They had to be very sharp indeed, too, I assure you.'

'I can imagine,' she murmured, appreciatively.

'What is there that you can't imagine?' he pronounced, soberly. 'You have the world in you. But let us go back to our Commanding Officer, who, of course, commanded a ship of a sort. My tales if often professional (as you remarked just now) have never been technical. So I'll just tell you that the ship was of a very ornamental sort once, with lots of grace and elegance and luxury about her. Yes, once! She was like a pretty woman who had suddenly put on a suit of sackcloth and stuck revolvers in her belt. But she floated lightly, she moved nimbly, she was quite good enough.'

'That was the opinion of the Commanding Officer?' said the voice from the couch.

'It was. He used to be sent out with her along certain coasts to see – what he could see. Just that. And sometimes he had some preliminary information to help him, and sometimes he had not. And it was all one, really. It was about as useful as information trying to convey the locality and intentions of a cloud, of a phantom taking shape here and there and impossible to seize, would have been.

'It was in the early days of the war. What at first used to amaze the Commanding Officer was the unchanged face of the waters, with its familiar expression, neither more friendly nor more hostile. On fine days the sun strikes sparks upon the blue; here and there a peaceful smudge of smoke hangs in the distance, and it is impossible to believe that the familiar clear horizon traces the limit of one great circular ambush.

'Yes, it is impossible to believe, till some day you see a ship not your own ship (that isn't so impressive), but some ship in company, blow up all of a sudden and plop under almost before you know what has happened to her. Then you begin to believe. Henceforth you go out for the work to see – what you can see, and you keep on at it with the conviction that some day you will die from something you have not seen. One envies the soldiers at the end of the day, wiping the sweat and blood from their faces, counting the dead fallen to their hands, looking at the devastated fields, the torn earth that seems to suffer and bleed with them. One does, really. The final brutality of it – the taste of primitive passion – the ferocious frankness of the blow struck with one's hand – the direct call and the straight response. Well, the sea gave you nothing of that, and seemed to pretend that there was nothing the matter with the world.'

She interrupted, stirring a little.

'Oh, yes. Sincerity – frankness – passion – three words of your gospel. Don't I know them!'

'Think! Isn't it ours – believed in common?' he asked, anxiously, yet without expecting an answer, and went on at once: 'Such were the feelings of the Commanding Officer. When the night came trailing over the sea, hiding what looked like the hypocrisy of an old friend, it was a relief. The night blinds you frankly – and there are circumstances when the sunlight may grow as odious to one as falsehood itself. Night is all right.

'At night the Commanding Officer could let his thoughts get away – I won't tell you where. Somewhere where there was no choice but between truth and death. But thick weather, though it blinded one, brought no such relief. Mist is deceitful, the dead luminosity of the fog is irritating. It seems that you *ought* to see.

'One gloomy, nasty day the ship was steaming along her beat in sight of a rocky, dangerous coast that stood out intensely black like an India-ink drawing on grey paper. Presently the

second in command spoke to his chief. He thought he saw
something on the water, to seaward. Small wreckage, perhaps.

'"But there shouldn't be any wreckage here, sir," he
remarked.

'"No," said the Commanding Officer. "The last reported
submarined ships were sunk a long way to the westward. But
one never knows. There may have been others since then not
reported nor seen. Gone with all hands."

'That was how it began. The ship's course was altered to pass
the object close; for it was necessary to have a good look at
what one could see. Close, but without touching; for it was not
advisable to come in contact with objects of any form whatever
floating casually about. Close, but without stopping or even
diminishing speed; for in those times it was not prudent to
linger on any particular spot, even for a moment. I may tell you
at once that the object was not dangerous in itself. No use in
describing it. It may have been nothing more remarkable than,
say, a barrel of a certain shape and colour. But it was significant.

'The smooth bow-wave hove it up as if for a closer inspection,
and then the ship, brought again to her course, turned her back
on it with indifference, while twenty pairs of eyes on her deck
stared in all directions trying to see – what they could see.

'The Commanding Officer and his second-in-command discussed the object with understanding. It appeared to them to
be not so much a proof of the sagacity as of the activity of
certain neutrals. This activity had in many cases taken the form
of replenishing the stores of certain submarines at sea. This was
generally believed, if not absolutely known. But the very nature
of things in those early days pointed that way. The object,
looked at closely and turned away from with apparent indifference, put it beyond doubt that something of the sort had been
done somewhere in the neighbourhood.

'The object in itself was more than suspect. But the fact of its
being left in evidence roused other suspicions. Was it the result
of some deep and devilish purpose? As to that all speculation
soon appeared to be a vain thing. Finally the two officers came
to the conclusion that it was left there most likely by accident,
complicated possibly by some unforeseen necessity; such, per-

haps, as the sudden need to get away quickly from the spot, or
something of that kind.

'Their discussion had been carried on in curt, weighty
phrases, separated by long, thoughtful silences. And all the time
their eyes roamed about the horizon in an everlasting, almost
mechanical effort of vigilance. The younger man summed up
grimly:

' "Well, it's evidence. That's what this is. Evidence of what
we were pretty certain of before. And plain, too."

' "And much good it will do to us," retorted the Commanding
Officer. "The parties are miles away; the submarine, devil only
knows where, ready to kill; and the noble neutral slipping away
to the eastward, ready to lie!"

'The second-in-command laughed a little at the tone. But he
guessed that the neutral wouldn't even have to lie very much.
Fellows like that, unless caught in the very act, felt themselves
pretty safe. They could afford to chuckle. That fellow was
probably chuckling to himself. It's very possible he had been
before at the game and didn't care a rap for the bit of evidence
left behind. It was a game in which practice made one bold and
successful, too.

'And again he laughed faintly. But his Commanding Officer
was in revolt against the murderous stealthiness of methods
and the atrocious callousness of complicities that seemed to
taint the very source of men's deep emotions and noblest activities; to corrupt their imagination which builds up the final
conceptions of life and death. He suffered –'

The voice from the sofa interrupted the narrator.

'How well I can understand that in him!'

He bent forward slightly.

'Yes. I, too. Everything should be open in love and war. Open
as the day, since both are the call of an ideal which it is so easy,
so terribly easy, to degrade in the name of Victory.'

He paused; then went on:

'I don't know that the Commanding Officer delved so deep
as that into his feelings. But he did suffer from them – a sort of
disenchanted sadness. It is possible, even, that he suspected
himself of folly. Man is various. But he had no time for much

introspection, because from the south-west a wall of fog had advanced upon his ship. Great convolutions of vapours flew over, swirling about masts and funnel, which looked as if they were beginning to melt. Then they vanished.

'The ship was stopped, all sounds ceased, and the very fog became motionless, growing denser and as if solid in its amazing dumb immobility. The men at their stations lost sight of each other. Footsteps sounded stealthy; rare voices, impersonal and remote, died out without resonance. A blind white stillness took possession of the world.

'It looked, too, as if it would last for days. I don't mean to say that the fog did not vary a little in its density. Now and then it would thin out mysteriously, revealing to the men a more or less ghostly presentment of their ship. Several times the shadow of the coast itself swam darkly before their eyes through the fluctuating opaque brightness of the great white cloud clinging to the water.

'Taking advantage of these moments, the ship had been moved cautiously nearer the shore. It was useless to remain out in such thick weather. Her officers knew every nook and cranny of the coast along their beat. They thought that she would be much better in a certain cove. It wasn't a large place, just ample room for a ship to swing at her anchor. She would have an easier time of it till the fog lifted up.

'Slowly, with infinite caution and patience, they crept closer and closer, seeing no more of the cliffs than an evanescent dark loom with a narrow border of angry foam at its foot. At the moment of anchoring the fog was so thick that for all they could see they might have been a thousand miles out in the open sea. Yet the shelter of the land could be felt. There was a peculiar quality in the stillness of the air. Very faint, very elusive, the wash of the ripple against the encircling land reached their ears, with mysterious sudden pauses.

'The anchor dropped, the leads were laid in. The Commanding Officer went below into his cabin. But he had not been there very long when a voice outside his door requested his presence on deck. He thought to himself: 'What is it now?' He felt some impatience at being called out again to face the wearisome fog.

'He found that it had thinned again a little and had taken on a gloomy hue from the dark cliffs, which had no form, no outline, but asserted themselves as a curtain of shadows all round the ship, except in one bright spot, which was the entrance from the open sea. Several officers were looking that way from the bridge. The second-in-command met him with the breathlessly whispered information that there was another ship in the cove.

'She had been made out by several pairs of eyes only a couple of minutes before. She was lying at anchor very near the entrance – a mere vague blot on the fog's brightness. And the Commanding Officer by staring in the direction pointed out to him by eager hands ended by distinguishing it at last himself. Indubitably a vessel of some sort.

' "It's a wonder we didn't run slap into her when coming in," observed the second-in-command.

' "Send a boat on board before she vanishes," said the Commanding Officer. He surmised that this was a coaster. It could hardly be anything else. But another thought came into his head suddenly. "It is a wonder," he said to his second in command, who had rejoined him after sending the boat away.

'By that time both of them had been struck by the fact that the ship so suddenly discovered had not manifested her presence by ringing her bell.

' "We came in very quietly, that's true," concluded the younger officer. "But they must have heard our leadsmen at least. We couldn't have passed her more than fifty yards off. The closest shave! They may even have made us out, since they were aware of something coming in. And the strange thing is that we never heard a sound from her. The fellows on board must have been holding their breath."

' "Aye," said the Commanding Officer, thoughtfully.

'In due course the boarding-boat returned, appearing suddenly alongside, as though she had burrowed her way under the fog. The officer in charge came up to make his report, but the Commanding Officer didn't give him time to begin. He cried from a distance:

' "Coaster, isn't she?"

'"No, sir. A stranger – a neutral," was the answer.

'"No. Really! Well, tell us all about it. What is she doing here?"

'The young man stated then that he had been told a long and complicated story of engine troubles. But it was plausible enough from a strictly professional point of view and it had the usual features: disablement, dangerous drifting along the shore, weather more or less thick for days, fear of a gale, ultimately a resolve to go in and anchor anywhere on the coast, and so on. Fairly plausible.

'"Engines still disabled?" inquired the Commanding Officer.

'"No, sir. She has steam on them."

'The Commanding Officer took his second aside. "By Jove!" he said, "you were right! They were holding their breaths as we passed them. They were."

'But the second-in-command had his doubts now.

'"A fog like this does muffle small sounds, sir," he remarked. "And what could his object be, after all?"

'"To sneak out unnoticed," answered the Commanding Officer.

'"Then why didn't he? He might have done it, you know. Not exactly unnoticed, perhaps. I don't suppose he could have slipped his cable without making some noise. Still, in a minute or so he would have been lost to view – clean gone before we had made him out fairly. Yet he didn't."

'They looked at each other. The Commanding Officer shook his head. Such suspicions as the one which had entered his head are not defended easily. He did not even state it openly. The boarding officer finished his report. The cargo of the ship was of a harmless and useful character. She was bound to an English port. Papers and everything in perfect order. Nothing suspicious to be detected anywhere.

'Then passing to the men, he reported the crew on deck as the usual lot. Engineers of the well-known type, and very full of their achievement in repairing the engines. The mate surly. The master rather a fine specimen of a Northman, civil enough, but appeared to have been drinking. Seemed to be recovering from a regular bout of it.

'"I told him I couldn't give him permission to proceed. He said he wouldn't dare to move his ship her own length out in such weather as this, permission or no permission. I left a man on board, though."

'"Quite right."

'The Commanding Officer, after communing with his suspicions for a time, called his second aside.

'"What if she were the very ship which had been feeding some infernal submarine or other?" he said in an undertone.

'The other started. Then, with conviction:

'"She would get off scot-free. You couldn't prove it, sir."

'"I want to look into it myself."

'"From the report we've heard I am afraid you couldn't even make a case for reasonable suspicion, sir."

'"I'll go on board all the same."

'He had made up his mind. Curiosity is the great motive power of hatred and love. What did he expect to find? He could not have told anybody – not even himself.

'What he really expected to find there was the atmosphere, the atmosphere of gratuitous treachery, which in his view nothing could excuse; for he thought that even a passion of unrighteousness for its own sake could not excuse that. But could he detect it? Sniff it? Taste it? Receive some mysterious communication which would turn his invincible suspicions into a certitude strong enough to provoke action with all its risks?

'The master met him on the after-deck, looming up in the fog amongst the blurred shapes of the usual ship's fittings. He was a robust Northman, bearded, and in the force of his age. A round leather cap fitted his head closely. His hands were rammed deep into the pockets of his short leather jacket. He kept them there while he explained that at sea he lived in the chart-room, and led the way there, striding carelessly. Just before reaching the door under the bridge he staggered a little, recovered himself, flung it open, and stood aside, leaning his shoulder as if involuntarily against the side of the house, and staring vaguely into the fog-filled space. But he followed the Commanding Officer at once, flung the door to, snapped on the electric light, and hastened to thrust his hands back into his pockets, as though afraid of being seized by them either in friendship or in hostility.

'The place was stuffy and hot. The usual chart-rack overhead was full, and the chart on the table was kept unrolled by an empty cup standing on a saucer half-full of some spilt dark liquid. A slightly nibbled biscuit reposed on the chronometer-case. There were two settees, and one of them had been made up into a bed with a pillow and some blankets, which were now very much tumbled. The Northman let himself fall on it, his hands still in his pockets.

'"Well, here I am," he said, with a curious air of being surprised at the sound of his own voice.

'The Commanding Officer from the other settee observed the handsome, flushed face. Drops of fog hung on the yellow beard and moustaches of the Northman. The much darker eyebrows ran together in a puzzled frown, and suddenly he jumped up.

'"What I mean is that I don't know where I am. I really don't," he burst out, with extreme earnestness. 'Hang it all! I got turned around somehow. The fog has been after me for a week. More than a week. And then my engines broke down. I will tell you how it was.'

'He burst out into loquacity. It was not hurried, but it was insistent. It was not continuous for all that. It was broken by the most queer, thoughtful pauses. Each of these pauses lasted no more than a couple of seconds, and each had the profundity of an endless meditation. When he began again nothing betrayed in him the slightest consciousness of these intervals. There was the same fixed glance, the same unchanged earnestness of tone. He didn't know. Indeed, more than one of these pauses occurred in the middle of a sentence.

'The Commanding Officer listened to the tale. It struck him as more plausible than simple truth is in the habit of being. But that, perhaps, was prejudice. All the time the Northman was speaking the Commanding Officer had been aware of an inward voice, a grave murmur in the depth of his very own self, telling another tale, as if on purpose to keep alive in him his indignation and his anger with that baseness of greed or of mere outlook which lies often at the root of simple ideas.

'It was the story that had been already told to the boarding officer an hour or so before. The Commanding Officer nodded slightly at the Northman from time to time. The latter came to an end and turned his eyes away. He added, as an afterthought:

'"Wasn't it enough to drive a man out of his mind with worry? And it's my first voyage to this part, too. And the ship's my own. Your officer has seen the papers. She isn't much, as you can see for yourself. Just an old cargo-boat. Bare living for my family."

'He raised a big arm to point at a row of photographs plastering the bulkhead. The movement was ponderous, as if the arm had been made of lead. The commanding officer said, carelessly:

'"You will be making a fortune yet for your family with this old ship."

'"Yes, if I don't lose her," said the Northman, gloomily.

'"I mean – out of this war," added the Commanding Officer.

'The Northman stared at him in a curiously unseeing and at the same time interested manner, as only eyes of a particular blue shade can stare.

'"And you wouldn't be angry at it," he said, "would you? You are too much of a gentleman. We didn't bring this on you. And suppose we sat down and cried. What good would that be? Let those cry who made the trouble," he concluded, with energy. "Time's money, you say. Well – *this* time *is* money. Oh! isn't it!"

'The Commanding Officer tried to keep under the feeling of immense disgust. He said to himself that it was unreasonable. Men were like that – moral cannibals feeding on each other's misfortunes. He said aloud:

'"You have made it perfectly plain how it is that you are here. Your log-book confirms you very minutely. Of course, a log-book may be cooked. Nothing easier."

'The Northman never moved a muscle. He was gazing at the floor; he seemed not to have heard. He raised his head after a while.

'"But you can't suspect me of anything," he muttered, negligently.

'The Commanding Officer thought: "Why should he say this?"'

'Immediately afterwards the man before him added: "My cargo is for an English port."'

'His voice had turned husky for the moment. The Commanding Officer reflected: "That's true. There can be nothing. I can't suspect him. Yet why was he lying with steam up in this fog – and then, hearing us come in, why didn't he give some sign of life? Why? Could it be anything else but a guilty conscience? He could tell by the leadsmen that this was a man-of-war."'

'Yes – why? The Commanding Officer went on thinking: "Suppose I ask him and then watch his face. He will betray himself in some way. It's perfectly plain that the fellow *has* been drinking. Yes, he has been drinking; but he will have a lie ready all the same." The Commanding Officer was one of those men who are made morally and almost physically uncomfortable by the mere thought of having to beat down a lie. He shrank from the act in scorn and disgust, which were invincible because more temperamental than moral.

'So he went out on deck instead and had the crew mustered formally for his inspection. He found them very much what the report of the boarding officer had led him to expect. And from their answers to his questions he could discover no flaw in the log-book story.

'He dismissed them. His impression of them was – a picked lot; have been promised a fistful of money each if this came off; all slightly anxious, but not frightened. Not a single one of them likely to give the show away. They don't feel in danger of their life. They know England and English ways too well!

'He felt alarmed at catching himself thinking as if his vaguest suspicions were turning into a certitude. For, indeed, there was no shadow of reason for his inferences. There was nothing to give away.

'He returned to the chart-room. The Northman had lingered behind there; and something subtly different in his bearing, more bold in his blue, glassy stare, induced the Commanding Officer to conclude that the fellow had snatched at the opportunity to take another swig at the bottle he must have had concealed somewhere.

'He noticed, too, that the Northman on meeting his eyes put on an elaborately surprised expression. At least, it seemed elaborated. Nothing could be trusted. And the Englishman felt himself with astonishing conviction faced by an enormous lie, solid like a wall, with no way round to get at the truth, whose ugly murderous face he seemed to see peeping over at him with a cynical grin.

'"I dare say," he began, suddenly, "you are wondering at my proceedings, though I am not detaining you, am I? You wouldn't dare to move in this fog?"

'"I don't know where I am," the Northman ejaculated, earnestly. "I really don't."

'He looked around as if the very chart-room fittings were strange to him. The Commanding Officer asked him whether he had not seen any unusual objects floating about while he was at sea.

'"Objects! What objects? We were groping blind in the fog for days."

'"We had a few clear intervals," said the Commanding Officer. "And I'll tell you what we have seen and the conclusion I've come to about it."

'He told him in a few words. He heard the sound of a sharp breath indrawn through closed teeth. The Northman with his hand on the table stood absolutely motionless and dumb. He stood as if thunderstruck. Then he produced a fatuous smile.

'Or at least so it appeared to the Commanding Officer. Was this significant, or of no meaning whatever? He didn't know, he couldn't tell. All the truth had departed out of the world as if drawn in, absorbed in this monstrous villainy this man was – or was not – guilty of.

'"Shooting's too good for people that conceive neutrality in this pretty way," remarked the Commanding Officer, after a silence.

'"Yes, yes, yes," the Northman assented, hurriedly – then added an unexpected and dreamy-voiced "Perhaps."

'Was he pretending to be drunk, or only trying to appear sober? His glance was straight, but it was somewhat glazed. His lips outlined themselves firmly under his yellow moustache.

But they twitched. Did they twitch? And why was he drooping like this in his attitude?

'"There's no perhaps about it," pronounced the Commanding Officer sternly.

'The Northman had straightened himself. And unexpectedly he looked stern, too.

'"No. But what about the tempters? Better kill that lot off. There's about four, five, six million of them," he said, grimly; but in a moment changed into a whining key. "But I had better hold my tongue. You have some suspicions."

'"No, I've no suspicions," declared the Commanding Officer.

'He never faltered. At that moment he had the certitude. The air of the chart-room was thick with guilt and falsehood braving the discovery, defying simple right, common decency, all humanity of feeling, every scruple of conduct.

'The Northman drew a long breath. "Well, we know that you English are gentlemen. But let us speak the truth. Why should we love you so very much? You haven't done anything to be loved. We don't love the other people, of course. They haven't done anything for that either. A fellow comes along with a bag of gold . . . I haven't been in Rotterdam my last voyage for nothing."

'"You may be able to tell something interesting, then, to our people when you come into port," interjected the officer.

'"I might. But you keep some people in your pay at Rotterdam. Let them report. I am a neutral – am I not? . . . Have you ever seen a poor man on one side and a bag of gold on the other? Of course, I couldn't be tempted. I haven't the nerve for it. Really I haven't. It's nothing to me. I am just talking openly for once.'

'"Yes. And I am listening to you," said the Commanding Officer, quietly.

'The Northman leaned forward over the table. "Now that I know you have no suspicions, I talk. You don't know what a poor man is. I do. I am poor myself. This old ship, she isn't much, and she is mortgaged, too. Bare living, no more. Of course, I wouldn't have the nerve. But a man who has nerve! See. The stuff he takes aboard looks like any other cargo –

packages, barrels, tins, copper tubes – what not. He doesn't see it work. It isn't real to him. But he sees the gold. That's real. Of course, nothing could induce me. I suffer from an internal disease. I would either go crazy from anxiety – or – or – take to drink or something. The risk is too great. Why – ruin!"

' "It should be death." The Commanding Officer got up, after this curt declaration, which the other received with a hard stare oddly combined with an uncertain smile. The officer's gorge rose at the atmosphere of murderous complicity which surrounded him, denser, more impenetrable, more acrid than the fog outside.

' "It's nothing to me," murmured the Northman, swaying visibly.

' "Of course not," assented the Commanding Officer, with a great effort to keep his voice calm and low. The certitude was strong within him. "But I am going to clear all you fellows off this coast at once. And I will begin with you. You must leave in half an hour."

'By that time the officer was walking along the deck with the Northman at his elbow.

' "What! In this fog?" the latter cried out, huskily.

' "Yes, you will have to go in this fog."

' "But I don't know where I am. I really don't."

'The Commanding Officer turned round. A sort of fury possessed him. The eyes of the two men met. Those of the Northman expressed a profound amazement.

' "Oh, you don't know how to get out." The Commanding Officer spoke with composure, but his heart was beating with anger and dread. "I will give you your course. Steer south-by-east-half-east for about four miles and then you will be clear to haul to the eastward for your port. The weather will clear up before very long."

' "Must I? What could induce me? I haven't the nerve."

' "And yet you must go. Unless you want to –"

' "I don't want to," panted the Northman. "I've enough of it."

'The Commanding Officer got over the side. The Northman remained still as if rooted to the deck. Before his boat reached his ship the Commanding Officer heard the steamer beginning to pick up her anchor. Then, shadowy in the fog, she steamed out on the given course.

'"Yes," he said to his officers, "I let him go."'

The narrator bent forward towards the couch, where no movement betrayed the presence of a living person.

'Listen,' he said, forcibly. 'That course would lead the Northman straight on a deadly ledge of rock. And the Commanding Officer gave it to him. He steamed out – ran on it – and went down. So he had spoken the truth. He did not know where he was. But it proves nothing. Nothing either way. It may have been the only truth in all his story. And yet . . . He seems to have been driven out by a menacing stare – nothing more.'

He abandoned all pretence.

'Yes, I gave that course to him. It seemed to me a supreme test. I believe – no, I don't believe. I don't know. At the time I was certain. They all went down; and I don't know whether I have done stern retribution – or murder; whether I have added to the corpses that litter the bed of the unreadable sea the bodies of men completely innocent or basely guilty. I don't know. I shall never know.'

He rose. The woman on the couch got up and threw her arms round his neck. Her eyes put two gleams in the deep shadow of the room. She knew his passion for truth, his horror of deceit, his humanity.

'Oh, my poor, poor –'

'I shall never know,' he repeated, sternly, disengaged himself, pressed her hands to his lips, and went out.

# A. W. WELLS

# 'CHANSON TRISTE'

I have sometimes thought that if I put it all down on paper, precisely and exactly as it occurred, my mind might become easier. Certainly nothing has given me relief up to now. One, two, three, seven years ago it must be since it happened, and at a spot four or five thousand miles away, to which I am never likely to return; and yet there still come days, nights, sometimes even weeks, when the whole thing will break out in my brain again as though everything took place only yesterday. Curious – the odd, queerly inconsequent sort of causes to which I trace these outbreaks. Always, for instance, I seem to find myself worst when the grapes are in season (especially the small 'black' variety), or when the plovers are crying on bright moonlight nights; while there is one place which I have learned to shun as I might shun a plague. If I can possibly avoid it, nothing will ever induce me to climb the hill that stretches along the Surrey suburb in which I live, and look across the twenty-miles-wide valley to where the next range of hills loom, across the horizon.

But perhaps the most weird result of all is that I can never stay in a room for long where Tschaikovsky is being played – particularly his 'Chanson Triste'.[1] I like Tschaikovsky; yet when the orchestra played 'Chanson Triste' to-night I simply had to come out. I couldn't stand it any longer. Joan, I could see, was as nearly furious with me as she has ever been since our marriage. She's forgiven me now, for I have told her all about it, shown her the photograph and kept not a single detail back from her ... but I could see quite plainly that she did not understand. And I want somebody to understand. Most of all, of course, I want Dimitri to understand. I'd give ten, twenty years of my life, I believe, if I could only make Dimitri understand.

No, Dimitri was not a woman: a soldier, just a common Bulgar soldier,[2] but with this one supreme and startling difference – that of the men who died in the Great War Dimitri died the worst death of all. And although it was no weapon of mine – either held, directed, or commanded by me – that killed him, I am afraid I was responsible for that death. Of one thing, at least, I am certain: Dimitri thinks I was responsible. The whole tragedy lies in that.

It would be the most foolish, in some ways the most tragic, mistake in the world to suppose that this is just an ordinary war story that I have to relate. I wish it were. If I could only trace one experience similar to mine (as, indeed, I have spent hours and hours browsing over bookstalls trying to find it) I should feel comforted; but nowhere have I been able to discover the vaguest hint of a resemblance. It all happened not far from a town called Dorrain,[3] which is situated at the far end of the valley where the river Struma runs between Bulgaria and Macedonia; but I would rather you immediately forgot those names, and pictured to yourself only the town and the valley – the town a poor, war-battered heap of buildings, and the valley a twenty-miles stretch of country, lying between ranges of hills so high and formidable that the military experts had long since given them up as impregnable. And I would have you imagine that while in the town war is being carried on in the best modern manner – two opposing swarms of rats gradually nibbling into one another's territory – all the warfare that exists in the valley is conducted by small groups of men who creep down from their respective hills in the night-time, wander vaguely about the valley until dawn comes, and then creep weariedly back again. All night long the shriek of the shrapnel and the glare of the Very lights may be hovering over the town; but in the twenty-miles-wide valley the darkness may pass without the sound or the flash of a single rifle shot. And the valley is so strewn with ravines and little clumps of trees, and men are so very scarce there, that a group of men from one range of hills may pass a group of men from the other, barely a hundred yards away, and never be aware of it.

So I think you may very fairly visualize the scene in which the experience I have to relate to you occurred; and yet I find myself altogether at a loss to convey the feeling of a man suddenly withdrawn from his little rat-hole in the town, and sent roaming about the valley wherever the fancy moved him – the groping, childlike fright of it all, those first few nights, and then, as time wore on, the sweet, civilian scent of liberty that suddenly seemed to breathe over everything. I wish I could convey to you, for instance, only a fraction of the divine joy there was to be had in those secret little pilgrimages to the pomegranate orchard, near the five tall poplar trees; the breathless, perspiring excitement that was to be felt in stealing into those ruined, deserted little villages – deserted, that is, except perhaps by the fellows from the opposite hills. But most of all, I wish I could convey to you something of the sudden sense of awe that fell on me one night, when, entirely alone, and trying to locate a certain fig-tree, I came across a small straw-thatched hut, tucked away in a little ravine I never remembered having seen before.

Softly I crept up to the doorway, waited for a moment to make sure that no sound came from within, and then entered. Marking first that there were no cracks through which the moonlight was piercing, I struck a match and looked anxiously round the room. A small, rickety-looking table, and an equally rickety-looking chair drawn up to it – that was all. Then I noticed that on the table was a small piece of candle, and lying only a foot away from this, a thin, black-bound book – a copy of Rupert Brooke[4] with the leaves turned down at the page:

> . . . And I shall find some girl, perhaps,
> A better girl than you,
> With eyes as wise, but kindlier,
> And lips as soft, but true.
> And I dare say she will do.[5]

Oh God, this was rich! Who, in the name of all that was wonderful, was the lovesick buffoon in the battalion who stole away into this lonely little straw-thatched hut at nights so that he might the more reflectively read Rupert Brooke? Then I turned to the fly-leaf and read the name:

NICOLAS DIMITRI.

Several moments, I think, must have elapsed before I realized the tremendous significance of my discovery – that the book in my hand belonged to a man from the opposite hills, who, even as I stood there, might enter to claim it. Quivering with excitement I thrust the book hurriedly into my pocket, blew out the light, and went outside.

Do not ask me to explain why it was that the next time I visited the straw-thatched hut in the ravine I should leave on the rickety little table the only book of poetry I ever carried during the war – a small, leather-bound edition of Omar Khayyám.[6] All that I know is that it seemed to me the only and natural thing to do; and I can still recall very vividly the excitement I felt when, a night or two later, I crept away from my patrol to see if the exchange had been accepted. Yes, the table was quite empty – quite empty except for the same innocent stump of candle. And then I suddenly noticed a certain peculiarity about that candle. Instead of standing erect, as I first saw it, it was now lying on its side, and trailing away from the wick was a long line of grease spots, stretching not only across the table, but half-way across the floor to where lay a large, flat boulder. In a flash the thought came to me that I was intended to lift that boulder; and two minutes later, hands quivering with excitement and heart throbbing against my ribs, I was eagerly deciphering, as a raw youth might read his first love-letter, the curiously stilted, Latin-looking hand of a man who told me that, although born a Bulgar, and now fighting as a Bulgar, he had spent the greater part of his life in America, where he had learned to understand and appreciate English art and literature beyond all other.

That letter still lies before me – one of the dozen, tattered, carefully hoarded pages I have just revealed to Joan; but little purpose could be served, I am afraid, by quoting it in full. He makes great fun, I see, because, above all poets, I should choose as my grand consoler in the war an old Persian who died eight hundred years ago. 'I think you must be very, very English,' he writes. 'I do not wonder that the *Rubáiyát* so appeals to you. You English like to think yourselves stolid, unshakeable and imperturbable; but how much of this, I sometimes wonder, is due to some curious kink of Oriental fatalism about you?' And then there is the letter in which he reflects on the mutually futile, bloody butchery that went on all round us in those sublime spring evenings of that mournful year of 1917. Bitter, searing things he writes, as only a man can write who has recently returned from ghastly, naked realities. But I will not trouble you with these. Poor Dimitri! To quote them now would be to mock him.

I leave it entirely to the psychologists to explain the strange compelling attraction, the almost romantic glamour, that somehow pervaded this friendship of ours, right from the very beginning. Times there must have been, of course, when both of us must have reflected that what we were doing was utterly wrong and deceitful: that we were committing a crime for which, had they discovered it, the countries whose uniforms we wore would immediately have had us shot, and buried like so much loathsome carrion; and yet, speaking for myself, I can only say that always uppermost in my mind was a feeling of stupendous glamour about our association – heightened a hundredfold, I suppose, because only two people in the world knew of it. And the very fact that it was illicit, I think, only grew in time to be a still further attraction. I began to understand, I am afraid, something of the irresistible lure that men have felt in illicit dealing and illicit love, ever since the world began. I am persuaded to think, indeed, that there were many ways in which this association between Dimitri and myself resembled very much an illicit love affair. All that I seemed to live for, at that time, was the weekly letters, hidden under the large, flat boulder in the little straw-thatched hut; and at all sorts of odd moments during the day I would find myself staring across that twenty-miles-wide valley picturing, somewhere on those opposite hills, the writer of them – wondering what he was doing and whether he ever similarly wondered about me.

And then, as time went on, it seemed that letters would no longer suffice; we began to make gifts to one another. I started by directing attention to a small box of cigarettes and a packet of chocolate that might be found hidden in the hollow of a certain fig-tree a dozen yards farther down the ravine; he responded by leaving me a bunch of grapes, of a small black variety I have never known surpassed for sweetness. Then the gifts no longer sufficed: Dimitri began to talk of photographs – 'civilian preferred', as he expressed it. For a long time I hesitated about that. Either of us, I pointed out, might at any time be killed, and to be found with enemy photographs in our possession might lead to an infamy which certainly neither of us deserved. But in the end I yielded; and even now, as I write, there stares mutely, half-defiantly up at me from the midst of the tattered letters the picture of a tall, rather lanky sort of youth, with that peculiarly elusive kind of face we are inclined to call 'temperamental', and with a mass of jet black hair brushed abruptly back from his forehead.

Only one thing remained for us now, of course, and that was to meet; but both of us, I think, shrank from mentioning this. For here, it seemed, we reached the one great forbidden sin: the pitch, once touched, that must inevitably defile. The wonder was, I often thought, that we did not meet by accident, and one night, I remember, we nearly did meet by accident. For some reason or other Dimitri seems to have been unusually indiscreet. When within twenty yards of the hut I could see the tiniest glimmer of light piercing through the door, which had evidently been closed with insufficient care. Then the light suddenly went out, and a minute later I heard footsteps moving towards the opposite end of the ravine, and a soft musical whistle mournfully mingling with the melancholy croaking of the frogs. The tune was Tschaikovsky's 'Chanson Triste'. For fully a quarter of an hour I must have remained there and listened, a cold sweat breaking over me lest on his return journey he should run into my patrol, whose duty (as, indeed, it was mine) would be either to take him prisoner or to kill him. But nothing happened.

Quietly I stole into the hut and sought for my usual letter under the large flat boulder. It amounted to nothing more than a note: 'Shall be going from here end of this week,' he had scribbled; 'hope we shall meet sometime.' What those words may convey to you – set out, as you will see them, in cold, matter-of-fact print – I do not know. I only know that as I stood there in that dull, flickering candle-light, and with the guns of the town ringing greedily, unappeasingly in my ears, there only seemed one course open to me.

'We must meet now, Dimitri,' I wrote. 'Wednesday, midnight. Come, I shall be here. I shall not fail.'

Sometimes I find myself believing that hidden away some-where in this stricken, blighted world lies some grim, smirking God of War whose awful charge it is to keep inviolate the relentless, age-long tenets of his creed. The fact remains that I never did meet Dimitri – not, at least, in the manner I had suggested. A thousand times my mind must have rehearsed, and endured again, the crowded incident of that tragic Wednesday – the wild, poignant fluctuation of it all: the glorious elation at our imagined meeting, the unspeakably abysmal depths of its realization. And a thousand times still, I am afraid, my mind must rehearse and endure it again.

Almost with the fastidiousness of a woman preparing to meet her lover you see me that Wednesday afternoon pottering about my little dugout, and paying what little attention I could to my personal appearance, my heart throbbing the while its mad, unrestrainable song of secret exultation. Emperors, Prime Min-isters, Commanders, not even the 'Bloody Beast of War' itself, I sing to myself, can keep Dimitri and me – apostles of the new world that is to arise from all this crimson chaos – from meeting. Then, almost more quickly than I can write it down, the blow fell. Ryan suddenly came blundering into my dugout.

'Heard?' he said.

'Heard what?' I demanded.

'Stunt on,' he answered. 'Patrol's going out to-night with a definite job on. Going out to see if we can get hold of a "Johnny",[7] or nobble him. Don't know whether you've ever seen it, old man, but in one of the ravines down there, there's a little straw-thatched hut. Somehow had my suspicions about that hut for a long time; thought I saw a light there once, but wasn't quite sure. But other night not only saw light but saw a "Johnny" too – passed within ten yards of me, other side of some trees, whistling away as cool as a cucumber. So surprised, didn't know what the 'ell to do. Frightened to say anything about it at first; and then I thought I'd miss out that bit about being only ten yards away and tell the OC that I'd observed a whole outpost of 'em concentrating on this hut. "What time was this?" says the Old Man, as keen as mustard. "Somewhere about midnight, sir," I said. "Right-o," says the Old Man, "we'll give 'em outpost to-night." '

The glass by which I had been shaving threw back at me the ashen, livid impotence of my face. What happened in the next minute or two I cannot exactly say, but as soon as ever I decently could, I think, I forced my way out of the dugout, and stumbled half-blindly to where I could gaze, as I had gazed a hundred times before, across that twenty-miles-wide valley, over which Nicolas Dimitri, unless I could stop him, must shortly march to his death – and die thinking that I, the man whom he had hailed as an affinity of a nobler, cleaner world, had lured him to that death. Unless I could stop him! But how could I stop him? Even if it were possible for me to get to him I had not the slightest idea where to go. For that had always been an unwritten law of honour between us: we knew of no destination other than the little straw-thatched hut. All that I knew was that he was somewhere over there, somewhere spread over twenty miles, and unless I could stop him to-night he would be killed – thinking himself as surely killed by me as though mine were the hand that pierced a dagger through his heart.

I will not harass you with all the frenzied detail of that night. Only one agony seemed to be spared to me – and that was that, instead of being sent with the party actually attacking the hut, I was detailed to assist in cutting off any escape at the far end of the ravine. Of my reflections as we trailed down the hill into the valley that night I am afraid I can tell you very little. I do not think I had any. Why, I don't know; but somehow I seem to have decided quite definitely that Dimitri would be killed, so that my mind became blank and numbed, as a man's mind becomes numbed on the funeral journey of a very dear relative. I do not seem to have been aware of anything until, after we had been waiting at the end of the ravine for about half an hour, a dozen rifle shots rang out. Then immediately the stupor left me and I raced up the ravine.

'Too late, old man.' Ryan met me and laughed into my face. 'Only one of 'em, but would persist in fighting. Fought like 'ell. Got it clean in the stomach – two places, poor beggar! Peg out any minute. Got a fag on you?'

Less than a dozen yards away, lying in the centre of the ravine, along which, less than five minutes ago, he had raced like a hunted beast, I could see him dying – not dying as the war artists so sinfully and successfully paint men dying, but in all the vulgar agony of a badly butchered animal.

He had just been feebly gulping at a bottle of water held to his lips by a stretcher-bearer when the moonlight fell on my face, and I could see that he knew me. A minute later and he was dead – but in that minute there came over his face such a look as I do not remember having seen on any human face before. The stretcher-bearer, I could see, accepted it as simply the dying spasm of a particularly painful death. But I knew differently. Physical pain was the least thing I saw there. I knew that Nicolas Dimitri died the most hopeless, the most despairing death that it is possible for any man to die – died thinking himself not only sacrificed to a world in madness, but taunted, in his last dying glimpse, by the irrefutable betrayal and degradation of all those finer, nobler impulses he had worshipped as a world's redemption. Not pain, not hatred, not longing was written on that face, but just a look of infinite, unutterable despair . . .

And to-night, rising hazily above the violins, as they throbbed out 'Chanson Triste', gradually taking form and consolidating, until I could see every line and twinge of it, I saw that face again.

# 2

# SPIES AND INTELLIGENCE

# ARTHUR CONAN DOYLE
# HIS LAST BOW

It was nine o'clock at night upon the second of August – the most terrible August in the history of the world. One might have thought already that God's curse hung heavy over a degenerate earth, for there was an awesome hush and a feeling of vague expectancy in the sultry and stagnant air. The sun had long set, but one blood-red gash, like an open wound, lay low in the distant west. Above the stars were shining brightly, and below the lights of the shipping glimmered in the bay. The two famous Germans stood beside the stone parapet of the garden walk, with the long, low, heavily-gabled house behind them, and they looked down upon the broad sweep of the beach at the foot of the great chalk cliff on which Von Bork, like some wandering eagle, had perched himself four years before. They stood with their heads close together talking in low, confidential tones. From below the two glowing ends of their cigars might have been the smouldering eyes of some malignant fiend looking down in the darkness.

A remarkable man this Von Bork – a man who could hardly be matched among all the devoted agents of the Kaiser.[1] It was his talents which had first recommended him for the English mission, the most important mission of all, but since he had taken it over those talents had become more and more manifest to the half-dozen people in the world who were really in touch with the truth. One of these was his present companion, Baron Von Herling, the Chief Secretary of the Legation, whose huge hundred-horse-power Benz car was blocking the country lane as it waited to carry its owner back to London.

'Things are moving very fast now and quite in accordance with the time-table. So far as I can judge the trend of events, you will probably be back in Berlin within the week,' the secretary was saying. 'When you get there, my dear Von Bork, I think you will be surprised at the warm welcome you will receive. I happen to know what is thought in the All-Highest quarters of your work in this country.' He was a huge man, the secretary, deep, broad, and tall, with a slow, heavy fashion of speech which had been his main asset in his political career.

Von Bork laughed in a deprecating way.

'They are not very hard to deceive, these Englanders,' he remarked. 'A more docile, simple folk could not be imagined.'

'I don't know about that,' said the other, thoughtfully. 'They have strange, unexpected limits, and one must learn to allow for them. It is that surface simplicity of theirs which makes a trap for the stranger. One's first impression is that they are entirely soft. Then you come suddenly upon something very hard, and you know that you have reached the limit and must adapt yourself to the fact. They have, for example, their insular conventions, which simply *must* be observed.'

'Meaning "good form" and "playing the game" and that sort of thing?' Von Bork sighed as one who had suffered much.

'Meaning British prejudice and convention, in all its queer manifestations. As an example I may quote one of my own worst blunders – I can afford to talk of my blunders, for you know my work well enough to be aware of my successes. It was on my first arrival. I was invited to a week-end gathering at the country-house of a Cabinet Minister. The conversation was amazingly indiscreet.'

Von Bork nodded. 'I've been there,' said he, drily.

'Exactly. Well, I naturally sent a *résumé* of the information to Berlin. Unfortunately, our good Chancellor[2] is a little heavy-handed in these matters, and he transmitted a remark which showed that he was aware of what had been said. This, of course, took the trail straight up to me. You've no idea the harm that it did me. There was nothing soft about our British hosts on that occasion, I can assure you. I was two years living it down. Now you, with this sporting pose of yours –'

'No, no; don't call it a pose. A pose is an artificial thing. This is quite natural. I am a born sportsman. I enjoy it.'

'Well, that makes it the more effective. You yacht against them, you hunt with them, you play polo, you match them in every game. Your four-in-hand[3] takes the prize at Olympia – I have even heard that you go the length of boxing with the young officers. What is the result? Nobody takes you seriously. You are "a good old sport", "quite a decent fellow for a German", a hard-drinking, night-club, knock-about-town, devil-may-care young fellow. And all the time this quiet country-house of yours is the centre of half the mischief in England, and the sporting squire – the most astute secret-service man in Europe. Genius, my dear Von Bork – genius!'

'You flatter me, Baron. But certainly I may claim that my four years in this country have not been unproductive. I've never shown you my little store. Would you mind stepping in for a moment?'

The door of the study opened straight on to the terrace. Von Bork pushed it back, and, leading the way, he clicked the switch of the electric light. He then closed the door behind the bulky form which followed him, and carefully adjusted the heavy curtain over the latticed window. Only when all these precautions had been taken and tested did he turn his sunburned, aquiline face to his guest.

'Some of my papers have gone,' said he. 'When my wife and the household left yesterday for Flushing they took the less important with them. I must, of course, claim the protection of the Embassy for the others.'

'Everything has been most carefully arranged. Your name has already been filed as one of the personal suite. There will be no difficulties for you or your baggage. Of course, it is just possible that we may not have to go. England may leave France to her fate. We are sure that there is no binding treaty between them.'

'And Belgium?' He stood listening intently for the answer.

'Yes, and Belgium too.'

Von Bork shook his head. 'I don't see how that could be. There is a definite treaty there. It would be the end of her – and what an end! She could never recover from such a humiliation.'

'She would at least have peace for the moment.'

'But her honour?'

'Tut, my dear sir, we live in a utilitarian age. Honour is a mediaeval conception. Besides, England is not ready. It is an inconceivable thing, but even our special war-tax of fifty millions, which one would think made our purpose as clear as if we had advertised it on the front page of *The Times*, has not roused these people from their slumbers. Here and there one hears a question. It is my business to find an answer. Here and there also there is irritation. It is my business to soothe it. But I can assure you that so far as the essentials go – the storage of munitions, the preparation for submarine attack, the arrangements for making high explosives – nothing is prepared. How then can England come in, especially when we have stirred her up such a devil's brew of Irish civil war, window-breaking furies,[4] and God knows what to keep her thoughts at home?'

'She must think of her future.'

'Ah, that is another matter. I fancy that in the future we have our own very definite plans about England, and that your information will be very vital to us. It is to-day or to-morrow with Mr John Bull. If he prefers to-day we are perfectly ready, and the readier, my dear Von Bork, for your labours. If it is to-morrow, I need not tell you that we shall be more ready still. I should think they would be wiser to fight with allies than without them, but that is their own affair. This week is their week of destiny. But let us get away from speculation and back to *real-politik*. You were speaking of your papers.'

He sat in the armchair with the light shining upon his broad, bald head, while he puffed sedately at his cigar and watched the movements of his companion.

The large oak-panelled, book-lined room had a curtain hung in the farther corner. When this was drawn it disclosed a large brass-bound safe. Von Bork detached a small key from his watch-chain, and after some considerable manipulation of the lock he swung open the heavy door.

'Look!' said he, standing clear, with a wave of his hand.

The light shone vividly into the opened safe, and the secretary of the Embassy gazed with an absorbed interest at the rows of stuffed pigeon-holes with which it was furnished. Each pigeon-hole had its label, and his eyes, as he glanced along them, read a long series of such titles as 'Fords', 'Harbour-Defences', 'Aeroplanes', 'Ireland', 'Egypt', 'Portsmouth Forts', 'The Channel', 'Rosyth',[5] and a score of others. Each compartment was bristling with papers and plans.

'Colossal!' said the secretary. Putting down his cigar he softly clapped his fat hands.

'And all in four years, Baron. Not such a bad show for the hard-drinking, hard-riding country squire. But the gem of my collection is coming, and there is the setting all ready for it.' He pointed to a space over which 'Naval Signals' was printed.

'But you have a good dossier there already?'

'Out of date and waste paper. The Admiralty in some way got the alarm and every code has been changed. It was a blow, Baron – the worst set-back in my whole campaign. But, thanks to my cheque-book and the good Altamont, all will be well to-night.'

The Baron looked at his watch, and gave a guttural exclamation of disappointment.

'Well, I really can wait no longer. You can imagine that things are moving at present in Carlton House Terrace[6] and that we have all to be at our posts. I had hoped to be able to bring news of your great *coup*. Did Altamont name no hour?'

Von Bork pushed over a telegram.

'Will come without fail to-night and bring new sparking-plugs. – ALTAMONT.'

'Sparking-plugs, eh?'

'You see, he poses as a motor expert, and I keep a full garage. In our code everything likely to come up is named after some spare part. If he talks of a radiator it is a battleship, of an oil-pump a cruiser, and so on. Sparking-plugs are naval signals.'

'From Portsmouth at midday,' said the secretary, examining the superscription. 'By the way, what do you give him?'

'Five hundred pounds for this particular job. Of course, he has a salary as well.'

'The greedy rogue. They are useful, these traitors, but I grudge them their blood-money.'

'I grudge Altamont nothing. He is a wonderful worker. If I pay him well, at least he delivers the goods, to use his own phrase. Besides, he is not a traitor. I assure you that our most Pan-Germanic Junker is a peaceful sucking-dove in his feelings towards England as compared with a real bitter Irish-American.'

'Oh, an Irish-American?'

'If you heard him talk you would not doubt it. Sometimes I assure you I can hardly understand him. He seems to have declared war on the King's English as well as on the English King. Must you really go? He may be here any moment.'

'No; I'm sorry, but I have already overstayed my time. We shall expect you early to-morrow, and when you get that signal-book through the little door on the Duke of York's steps[7] you can put a triumphant *Finis* to your record in England. What! Tokay!' He indicated a heavily-sealed, dust-covered bottle which stood with two high glasses upon a salver.

'May I offer you a glass before your journey?'

'No, thanks. But it looks like revelry.'

'Altamont has a nice taste in wines, and he took a fancy to my Tokay. He is a touchy fellow and needs humouring in small things. He is absolutely vital to my plans, and I have to study him, I assure you.' They had strolled out on to the terrace again, and along it to the farther end, where, at a touch from the Baron's chauffeur, the great car shivered and chuckled. 'Those are the lights of Harwich, I suppose,' said the secretary, pulling on his dust-coat. 'How still and peaceful it all seems! There may be other lights within the week, and the English coast a less tranquil place! The heavens, too, may not be quite so peaceful, if all that the good Zeppelin promises us comes true. By the way, who is that?'

Only one window showed a light behind them. In it there stood a lamp, and beside it, seated at a table, was a dear old ruddy-faced woman in a country cap. She was bending over her knitting and stopping occasionally to stroke a large black cat upon a stool beside her.

'That is Martha, the only servant I have left.'

The secretary chuckled.

'She might almost personify Britannia,' said he, 'with her

complete self-absorption and general air of comfortable som-
nolence. Well, *au revoir*, Von Bork!' With a final wave of his
hand he sprang into the car, and a moment later the two golden
cones from the headlights shot forward through the darkness.
The secretary lay back in the cushions of the luxurious limou-
sine with his thoughts full of the impending European tragedy,
and hardly observing that as his car swung round the village
street it nearly passed over a little Ford coming in the opposite
direction.

Von Bork walked slowly back to the study when the last
gleams of the motor lamps had faded into the distance. As he
passed he observed that his old housekeeper had put out her
lamp and retired. It was a new experience to him, the silence
and darkness of his widespread house, for his family and household had been a large one. It was a relief to him, however, to
think that they were all in safety, and that, but for that one old
woman who lingered in the kitchen, he had the whole place to
himself. There was a good deal of tidying up to do inside his
study, and he set himself to do it until his keen, handsome face
was flushed with the heat of the burning papers. A leather valise
stood beside his table, and into this he began to pack very
neatly and systematically the precious contents of his safe. He
had hardly got started with the work, however, when his quick
ears caught the sound of a distant car. Instantly he gave an
exclamation of satisfaction, strapped up the valise, shut the
safe, locked it, and hurried out on to the terrace. He was just
in time to see the lights of a small car come to a halt at the gate.
A passenger sprang out of it and advanced swiftly towards
him, while the chauffeur, a heavily-built, elderly man with a
grey moustache, settled down like one who resigns himself to
a long vigil.

'Well?' asked Von Bork, eagerly, running forward to meet
his visitor.

For answer the man waved a small brown-paper parcel triumphantly above his head.

'You can give me the glad hand to-night, mister,' he cried.
'I'm bringin' home the bacon at last.'

'The signals?'

'Same as I said in my cable. Every last one of them – sema-phore,[8] lamp-code,[9] Marconi[10] – a copy, mind you, not the original. The sucker that sold it would have handed over the book itself. That was too dangerous. But it's the real goods, and you can lay to that.' He slapped the German upon the shoulder with a rough familiarity from which the other winced.

'Come in,' he said. 'I'm all alone in the house. I was only waiting for this. Of course, a copy is better than the original. If an original were missing they would change the whole thing. You think it's all safe about this copy?'

The Irish-American had entered the study and stretched his long limbs from the arm-chair. He was a tall, gaunt man of sixty, with clear-cut features and a small goatee beard, which gave him a general resemblance to the caricatures of Uncle Sam. A half-smoked sodden cigar hung from the corner of his mouth, and as he sat down he struck a match and relit it. 'Makin' ready for a move?' he remarked, as he looked round him. 'Say, Mister,' he added, as his eyes fell upon the safe from which the curtain was now removed, 'you don't tell me you keep your papers in that?'

'Why not?'

'Gosh, in a wide-open contraption like that! And they reckon you to be some spy. Why, a Yankee crook would be into that with a can-opener. If I'd known that any letter of mine was goin' to lie loose in a thing like that I'd have been a mutt to write to you at all.'

'It would puzzle any of your crooks to force that safe,' Von Bork answered. 'You won't cut that metal with any tool.'

'But the lock?'

'No; it's a double combination lock. You know what that is?'

'Search me,' said the American, with a shrug.

'Well, you need a word as well as a set of figures before you can get the lock to work.' He rose and showed a double radiat-ing disc round the keyhole. 'This outer one is for the letters, the inner one for the figures.'

'Well, well, that's fine.'

'So it's not quite so simple as you thought. It was four years ago that I had it made, and what do you think I chose for the word and figures?'

'It's beyond me.'

'Well, I chose "August" for the word, and "1914" for the figures, and here we are.'

The American's face showed his surprise and admiration.

'My, but that was smart! You had it down to a fine thing.'

'Yes; a few of us even then could have guessed the date. Here it is, and I'm shutting down to-morrow morning.'

'Well, I guess you'll have to fix me up too. I'm not stayin' in this goldarned country all on my lonesome. In a week or less, from what I see, John Bull will be on his hind legs and fair rampin'. I'd rather watch him from over the water.'

'But you're an American citizen?'

'Well, so was Jack James an American citizen, but he's doin' time in Portland[11] all the same. It cuts no ice with a British copper to tell him you're an American citizen. "It's British law and order over here," says he. By the way, Mister, talking of Jack James, it seems to me you don't do much to cover your men.'

'What do you mean?' Von Bork asked, sharply.

'Well, you are their employer, ain't you? It's up to you to see that they don't fall down. But they do fall down, and when did you ever pick them up? There's James –'

'It was James's own fault. You know that yourself. He was too self-willed for the job.'

'James was a bonehead – I give you that. Then there was Hollis.'

'The man was mad.'

'Well, he went a bit woozy towards the end. It's enough to make a man bughouse when he has to play a part from mornin' to night, with a hundred guys all ready to set the coppers wise to him. But now there is Steiner –'

Von Bork started violently, and his ruddy face turned a shade paler.

'What about Steiner?'

'Well, they've pulled him, that's all. They raided his store last night, and he and his papers are all in Portsmouth Jail. You'll go off and he, poor devil, will have to stand the racket, and lucky if he gets clear with his life. That's why I want to get over the salt water as soon as you do.'

Von Bork was a strong, self-contained man, but it was easy to see that the news had shaken him.

'How could they have got on to Steiner?' he muttered. 'That's the worst blow yet.'

'Well, you nearly had a darned sight worse one, for I believe they are not far off me.'

'You don't mean that!'

'Sure thing. My landlady down Fratton way had some inquiries, and when I heard of it I guessed it was time for me to hustle. But what I want to know, Mister, is how the coppers know these things? Steiner is the fifth man you've lost since I signed on for you, and I know the name of the sixth if I don't get a move on. How do you explain it, and ain't you ashamed to see your men go down like this?'

Von Bork flushed crimson.

'How dare you speak in such a way?'

'If I didn't dare things, Mister, I wouldn't be in your service. But I'll tell you straight what is in my mind. I've heard that with you German politicians when an agent has done his work you are not very sorry to see him put away where he can't talk too much.'

Von Bork sprang to his feet.

'Do you dare to suggest that I have given away my own agents?'

'I don't stand for that, Mister, but there's a stool pigeon or a cross somewhere, and it's up to you to find out where it is. Anyhow, I am taking no more chances. It's me for little Holland, and the sooner the better.'

Von Bork had mastered his anger.

'We have been allies too long to quarrel now at the very hour of victory,' said he. 'You've done splendid work and taken big risks, and I can't forget it. By all means go to Holland, and you can come with us to Berlin or get a boat from Rotterdam to New York. No other line will be safe a week from now, when Von Tirpitz gets to work. But let us settle up, Altamont. I'll take that book and pack it with the rest.'

The American held the small parcel in his hand, but made no motion to give it up.

'What about the dough?' he asked.

'The what?'

'The boodle. The reward. The five hundred pounds. The gunner turned durned nasty at the last, and I had to square him with an extra hundred dollars or it would have been nitsky for you and me. "Nothin' doin'!" says he, and he meant it too, but the last hundred did it. It's cost me two hundred pounds from first to last, so it isn't likely I'd give it up without gettin' my wad.'

Von Bork smiled with some bitterness. 'You don't seem to have a very high opinion of my honour,' said he; 'you want the money before you give up the book.'

'Well, Mister, it is a business proposition.'

'All right. Have your way.' He sat down at the table and scribbled a cheque, which he tore from the book, but he refrained from handing it to his companion. 'After all, since we are to be on such terms, Mr Altamont,' said he, 'I don't see why I should trust you any more than you trust me. Do you understand?' he added, looking back over his shoulder at the American. 'There's the cheque upon the table. I claim the right to examine that parcel before you pick the money up.'

The American passed it over without a word. Von Bork undid a winding of string and two wrappers of paper. Then he sat gazing for a moment in silent amazement at a small blue book which lay before him. Across the cover was printed in golden letters, *Practical Handbook of Bee Culture*. Only for one instant did the master-spy glare at this strangely-irrelevant inscription. The next he was gripped at the back of his neck by a grasp of iron, and a chloroformed sponge was held in front of his writhing face.

'Another glass, Watson?' said Mr Sherlock Holmes, as he extended the dusty bottle of Imperial Tokay. 'We must drink to this joyous reunion.'

The thick-set chauffeur, who had seated himself by the table, pushed forward his glass with some eagerness.

'It is a good wine, Holmes,' he said, when he had drunk heartily to the sentiment.

'A remarkable wine, Watson. Our noisy friend upon the sofa has assured me that it is from Franz Joseph's[12] special cellar at the Schoenbrunn Palace.[13] Might I trouble you to open the window, for chloroform vapour does not help the palate.'

The safe was ajar, and Holmes, who was now standing in front of it, was removing dossier after dossier, swiftly examining each, and then packing it neatly in Von Bork's valise. The German lay upon the sofa sleeping stertorously, with a strap round his upper arms and another round his legs.

'We need not hurry ourselves, Watson. We are safe from interruption. Would you mind touching the bell? There is no one in the house except old Martha, who has played her part to admiration. I got her the situation here when first I took the matter up. Ah, Martha, you will be glad to hear that all is well.'

The pleasant old lady had appeared in the doorway. She curtsied with a smile to Mr Holmes, but glanced with some apprehension at the figure upon the sofa.

'It is all right, Martha. He has not been hurt at all.'

'I am glad of that, Mr Holmes. According to his lights he has been a kind master. He wanted me to go with his wife to Germany yesterday, but that would hardly have suited your plans, would it, sir?'

'No, indeed, Martha. So long as you were here I was easy in my mind. We waited some time for your signal to-night.'

'It was the secretary, sir; the stout gentleman from London.'

'I know. His car passed ours. But for your excellent driving, Watson, we should have been the very type of Europe under the Prussian juggernaut. What more, Martha?'

'I thought he would never go. I knew that it would not suit your plans, sir, to find him here.'

'No, indeed. Well, it only meant that we waited half an hour or so on the hill until I saw your lamp go out and knew that the coast was clear. You can report to me to-morrow in London, Martha, at Claridge's Hotel.'

'Very good, sir.'

'I suppose you have everything ready to leave?'

'Yes, sir. He posted seven letters to-day. I have the addresses, as usual. He received nine; I have these also.'

'Very good, Martha. I will look into them to-morrow. Good-night. These papers,' he continued, as the old lady vanished, 'are not of very great importance, for, of course, the information which they represent has been sent off long ago to the German Government. These are the originals, which could not safely be got out of the country.'

'Then they are of no use?'

'I should not go so far as to say that, Watson. They will at least show our people what is known and what is not. I may say that a good many of these documents have come to him through me, and I need not add are thoroughly untrustworthy. It would brighten my declining years to see a German cruiser navigating the Solent according to the mine-field plans which I have furnished. But you, Watson' – he stopped his work and took his old friend by the shoulders – 'I've hardly seen you in the light yet. How have the years used you? You look the same blithe boy as ever.'

'I feel twenty years younger, Holmes. I have seldom felt so happy as when I got your wire asking me to meet you at Harwich with the car. But you, Holmes – you have changed very little – save for that horrible goatee.'

'Those are the sacrifices one makes for one's country, Watson,' said Holmes, pulling at his little tuft. 'To-morrow it will be but a dreadful memory. With my hair cut and a few other superficial changes I shall no doubt reappear at Claridge's to-morrow as I was before this American stunt – I beg your pardon, Watson; my well of English seems to be permanently defiled – before this American job came my way.'

'But you had retired, Holmes. We heard of you as living the life of a hermit among your bees and your books in a small farm upon the South Downs.'

'Exactly, Watson. Here is the fruit of my leisured ease, the *magnum opus* of my latter years!' He picked up the volume from the table and read out the whole title, *Practical Handbook of Bee Culture, with some Observations upon the Segregation of the Queen.* Alone I did it. Behold the fruit of pensive nights and laborious days,[14] when I watched the little working gangs as once I watched the criminal world of London.'

'But how did you get to work again?'

'Ah! I have often marvelled at it myself. The Foreign Minister alone I could have withstood, but when the Premier also deigned to visit my humble roof –! The fact is, Watson, that this gentleman upon the sofa was a bit too good for our people. He was in a class by himself. Things were going wrong, and no one could understand why they were going wrong. Agents were suspected or even caught, but there was evidence of some strong and secret central force. It was absolutely necessary to expose it. Strong pressure was brought upon me to look into the matter. It has cost me two years, Watson, but they have not been devoid of excitement. When I say that I started my pilgrimage at Chicago, graduated in an Irish secret society at Buffalo, gave serious trouble to the constabulary at Skibbereen,[15] and so eventually caught the eye of a subordinate agent of Von Bork, who recommended me as a likely man, you will realize that the matter was complex. Since then I have been honoured by his confidence, which has not prevented most of his plans going subtly wrong and five of his best agents being in prison. I watched them, Watson, and I picked them as they ripened. Well, sir, I hope that you are none the worse?'

The last remark was addressed to Von Bork himself, who, after much gasping and blinking, had lain quietly listening to Holmes's statement. He broke out now into a furious stream of German invective, his face convulsed with passion. Holmes continued his swift investigation of documents, his long, nervous fingers opening and folding the papers while his prisoner cursed and swore.

'Though unmusical, German is the most expressive of all languages,' he observed, when Von Bork had stopped from pure exhaustion. 'Halloa! Halloa!' he added, as he looked hard at the corner of a tracing before putting it in the box. 'This should put another bird in the cage. I had no idea that the paymaster was such a rascal, though I have long had an eye upon him. Dear me, Mister Von Bork, you have a great deal to answer for!'

The prisoner had raised himself with some difficulty upon the sofa and was staring with a strange mixture of amazement and hatred at his captor.

'I shall get level with you, Altamont,' he said, speaking with slow deliberation. 'If it takes me all my life I shall get level with you.'

'The old sweet song,' said Holmes. 'How often have I heard it in days gone by! It was a favourite ditty of the late lamented Professor Moriarty. Colonel Sebastian Moran has also been known to warble it. And yet I live and keep bees upon the South Downs.'

'Curse you, you double traitor!' cried the German, straining against his bonds and glaring murder from his furious eyes.

'No, no, it is not so bad as that,' said Holmes, smiling. 'As my speech surely shows you, Mr Altamont of Chicago had no existence in fact. He was a concoction, a myth, an isolated strand from my bundle of personalities. I used him and he is gone.'

'Then who are you?'

'It is really immaterial who I am, but since the matter seems to interest you, Mr Von Bork, I may say that this is not my first acquaintance with the members of your family. I have done a good deal of business in Germany in the past, and my name is probably familiar to you.'

'I would wish to know it,' said the Prussian, grimly.

'It was I who brought about the separation between Irene Adler and the late King of Bohemia when your cousin Heinrich was the Imperial Envoy. It was I also who saved from murder by the Nihilist Klopman, Count Von und Zu Grafenstein, who was your mother's elder brother. It was I –'

Von Bork sat up in amazement.

'There is only one man –' he cried.

'Exactly,' said Holmes.

Von Bork groaned and sank back on the sofa. 'And most of that information came through you!' he cried. 'What is it worth? What have I done? It is my ruin for ever!'

'It is certainly a little untrustworthy,' said Holmes. 'It will require some checking, and you have little time to check it.

Your admiral may find the new guns rather larger than he expects and the cruisers perhaps a trifle faster.'

Von Bork clutched at his own throat in despair.

'There are a good many other points of detail which will no doubt come to light in good time. But you have one quality which is very rare in a German, Mr Von Bork: you are a sportsman, and you will bear me no ill will when you realize that you, who have outwitted so many other people, have at last been outwitted yourself. After all, you have done your best for your country and I have done my best for mine, and what could be more natural? Besides,' he added, not unkindly, as he laid his hand upon the shoulder of the prostrate man, 'it is better than to fall before some more ignoble foe. These papers are now ready, Watson. If you will help me with our prisoner I think that we may get started for London at once.'

It was no easy task to move Von Bork, for he was a strong and a desperate man. Finally, holding either arm, the two friends walked him very slowly down the garden path, which he had trod with such proud confidence when he received the congratulations of the famous diplomatist only a few hours before. After a short final struggle he was hoisted, still bound hand and foot, into the spare seat of the little car. His precious valise was wedged in beside him.

'I trust that you are as comfortable as circumstances permit,' said Holmes, when the final arrangements were made. 'Should I be guilty of a liberty if I lit a cigar and placed it between your lips?'

But all amenities were wasted upon the angry German.

'I suppose you realize, Mr Sherlock Holmes,' said he, 'that if your Government bears you out in this treatment it becomes an act of war?'

'What about your Government and all this treatment?' said Holmes, tapping the valise.

'You are a private individual. You have no warrant for my arrest. The whole proceeding is absolutely illegal and out-rageous.'

'Absolutely,' said Holmes.

'Kidnapping a German subject.'

'And stealing his private papers.'

'Well, you realize your position, you and your accomplice here. If I were to shout for help as we pass through the village –'

'My dear sir, if you did anything so foolish you would probably enlarge the too-limited titles of our village inns by giving us The Dangling Prussian as a sign-post. The Englishman is a patient creature, but at present his temper is a little inflamed, and it would be as well not to try him too far. No, Mr Von Bork, you will go with us in a quiet, sensible fashion to Scotland Yard, whence you can send for your friend Baron Von Herling and see if even now you may not fill that place which he has reserved for you in the Ambassadorial suite. As to you, Watson, you are joining up with your old service, as I understand, so London won't be out of your way. Stand with me here upon the terrace, for it may be the last quiet talk that we shall ever have.'

The two friends chatted in intimate converse for a few minutes, recalling once again the days of the past, whilst their prisoner vainly wriggled to undo the bonds that held him. As they turned to the car Holmes pointed back to the moonlit sea and shook a thoughtful head.

'There's an east wind coming, Watson.'

'I think not, Holmes. It is very warm.'

'Good old Watson! You are the one fixed point in a changing age. There's an east wind coming all the same, such a wind as never blew on England yet. It will be cold and bitter, Watson, and a good many of us may wither before its blast. But it's God's own wind none the less, and a cleaner, better, stronger land will lie in the sunshine when the storm has cleared. Start her up, Watson, for it's time that we were on our way. I have a cheque for five hundred pounds which should be cashed early, for the drawer is quite capable of stopping it, if he can.'

# W. SOMERSET MAUGHAM
# GIULIA LAZZARI

The train started at eight. When he had disposed of his bag Ashenden walked along the platform. He found the carriage in which Giulia Lazzari was, but she sat in a corner, looking away from the light, so that he could not see her face. She was in charge of two detectives who had taken her over from English police at Boulogne. One of them worked with Ashenden on the French side of the Lake Geneva, and as Ashenden came up he nodded to him.

'I've asked the lady if she will dine in the restaurant-car, but she prefers to have dinner in the carriage, so I've ordered a basket. Is that quite correct?'

'Quite,' said Ashenden.

'My companion and I will go into the diner in turn so that she will not remain alone.'

'That is very considerate of you. I will come along when we've started and have a chat with her.'

'She's not disposed to be very talkative,' said the detective.

'One could hardly expect it,' replied Ashenden.

He walked on to get his ticket for the second service and then returned to his own carriage. Giulia Lazzari was just finishing her meal when he went back to her. From a glance at the basket he judged that she had not eaten with too poor an appetite. The detective who was guarding her opened the door when Ashenden appeared and at Ashenden's suggestion left them alone.

Giulia Lazzari gave him a sullen look.

'I hope you've had what you wanted for dinner,' he said as he sat down in front of her.

She bowed slightly, but did not speak. He took out his case. 'Will you have a cigarette?'

She gave him a glance, seemed to hesitate, and then, still without a word, took one. He struck a match, and lighting it, looked at her. He was surprised. For some reason he had expected her to be fair, perhaps from some notion that an Oriental would be more likely to fall for a blonde; but she was almost swarthy. Her hair was hidden by a close-fitting hat, but her eyes were coal-black. She was far from young, she might have been thirty-five, and her skin was lined and sallow. She had at the moment no make-up on and she looked haggard. There was nothing beautiful about her but her magnificent eyes. She was big, and Ashenden thought she must be too big to dance gracefully; it might be that in Spanish costume she was a bold and flaunting figure, but there in the train, shabbily dressed, there was nothing to explain the Indian's infatuation. She gave Ashenden a long, appraising stare. She wondered evidently what sort of man he was. She blew a cloud of smoke through her nostrils and gave it a glance, then looked back at Ashenden. He could see that her sullenness was only a mask, she was nervous and frightened. She spoke in French with an Italian accent.

'Who are you?'

'My name would mean nothing to you, Madame. I am going to Thonon. I have taken a room for you at the Hôtel de la Place. It is the only one open now. I think you will find it quite comfortable.'

'Ah, it is you the Colonel spoke to me of. You are my jailer.'

'Only as a matter of form. I shall not intrude upon you.'

'All the same you are my jailer.'

'I hope not for very long. I have in my pocket your passport with all the formalities completed to permit you to go to Spain.'

She threw herself back into the corner of the carriage. White, with those great black eyes, in the poor light, her face was suddenly a mask of despair.

'It's infamous. Oh, I think I could die happy if I could only kill that old Colonel. He has no heart. I'm so unhappy.'

'I am afraid you have got yourself into a very unfortunate

situation. Did you not know that espionage was a dangerous game?'

'I never sold any of the secrets. I did no harm.'

'Surely only because you had no opportunity. I understand that you signed a full confession.'

Ashenden spoke to her as amiably as he could, a little as though he were talking to a sick person, and there was no harshness in his voice.

'Oh, yes, I made a fool of myself. I wrote the letter the Colonel said I was to write. Why isn't that enough? What is to happen to me if he does not answer? I cannot force him to come if he does not want to.'

'He has answered,' said Ashenden. 'I have the answer with me.'

She gave a gasp and her voice broke.

'Oh, show it to me, I beseech you to let me see it.'

'I have no objection to doing that. But you must return it to me.'

He took Chandra's letter from his pocket and gave it to her. She snatched it from his hand. She devoured it with her eyes, there were eight pages of it, and as she read the tears streamed down her cheeks. Between her sobs she gave little exclamations of love, calling the writer by pet names French and Italian. This was the letter that Chandra had written in reply to hers telling him, on R.'s instructions, that she would meet him in Switzerland. He was mad with joy at the prospect. He told her in passionate phrases how long the time had seemed to him since they were parted, and how he had yearned for her, and now that he was to see her again so soon he did not know how he was going to bear his impatience. She finished it and let it drop to the floor.

'You can see he loves me, can't you? There's no doubt about that. I know something about it, believe me.'

'Do you really love him?' asked Ashenden.

'He's the only man who's ever been kind to me. It's not very gay the life one leads in these music-halls, all over Europe, never resting, and men – they are not much, the men who haunt those places. At first I thought he was just like the rest of them.'

Ashenden picked up the letter and replaced it in his pocket-book.

'A telegram was sent in your name to the address in Holland to say that you would be at the Hôtel Gibbons at Lausanne on the fourteenth.'

'That is to-morrow.'

'Yes.'

She threw up her head and her eyes flashed.

'Oh, it is an infamous thing that you are forcing me to do. It is shameful.'

'You are not obliged to do it,' said Ashenden.

'And if I don't?'

'I'm afraid you must take the consequences.'

'I can't go to prison,' she cried out suddenly, 'I can't, I can't; I have such a short time before me; he said ten years. Is it possible I could be sentenced to ten years?'

'If the Colonel told you so it is very possible.'

'Oh, I know him. That cruel face. He would have no mercy. And what should I be in ten years? Oh, no, no.'

At that moment the train stopped at a station and the detective waiting in the corridor tapped on the window. Ashenden opened the door and the man gave him a picture-postcard. It was a dull little view of Pontarlier, the frontier station between France and Switzerland, and showed a dusty *place* with a statue in the middle and a few plane trees. Ashenden handed her a pencil.

'Will you write this postcard to your lover? It will be posted at Pontarlier. Address it to the hotel at Lausanne.'

She gave him a glance, but without answering took it and wrote as he directed.

'Now on the other side write: "Delayed at frontier but everything all right. Wait at Lausanne." Then add whatever you like, *tendresses*, if you like.'

He took the postcard from her, read it to see that she had done as he directed and then reached for his hat.

'Well, I shall leave you now, I hope you will have a sleep. I will fetch you in the morning when we arrive at Thonon.'

The second detective had now returned from his dinner

and as Ashenden came out of the carriage the two men went in. Giulia Lazzari huddled back into her corner. Ashenden gave the postcard to an agent who was waiting to take it to Pontarlier and then made his way along the crowded train to his sleeping-car.

It was bright and sunny, though cold, next morning when they reached their destination. Ashenden, having given his bags to a porter, walked along the platform to where Giulia Lazzari and the two detectives were standing. Ashenden nodded to them.

'Well, good morning. You need not trouble to wait.'

They touched their hats, gave a word of farewell to the woman, and walked away.

'Where are they going?' she asked.

'Off. You will not be bothered with them any more.'

'Am I in your custody then?'

'You're in nobody's custody. I'm going to permit myself to take you to your hotel and then I shall leave you. You must try to get a good rest.'

Ashenden's porter took her hand-luggage and she gave him the ticket for her trunk. They walked out of the station. A cab was waiting for them and Ashenden begged her to get in. It was a longish drive to the hotel and now and then Ashenden felt that she gave him a sidelong glance. She was perplexed. He sat without a word. When they reached the hotel the proprietor – it was a small hotel, prettily situated at the corner of a little promenade and it had a charming view – showed them the room that had been prepared for Madame Lazzari. Ashenden turned to him.

'That'll do very nicely, I think. I shall come down in a minute.'

The proprietor bowed and withdrew.

'I shall do my best to see that you are comfortable, Madame,' said Ashenden. 'You are here absolutely your own mistress and you may order pretty well anything you like. To the proprietor you are just a guest of the hotel like any other. You are absolutely free.'

'Free to go out?' she asked quickly.

'Of course.'

'With a policeman on either side of me, I suppose.'

'Not at all. You are as free in the hotel as though you were in your own house and you are free to go out and come in when you choose. I should like an assurance from you that you will not write any letters without my knowledge or attempt to leave Thonon without my permission.'

She gave Ashenden a long stare. She could not make it out at all. She looked as though she thought it a dream.

'I am in a position that forces me to give you any assurance you ask. I give you my word of honour that I will not write a letter without showing it to you or attempt to leave this place.'

'Thank you. Now I will leave you. I will do myself the pleasure of coming to see you to-morrow morning.'

Ashenden nodded and went out. He stopped for five minutes at the police-station to see that everything was in order and then took the cab up the hill to a little secluded house on the outskirts of the town at which on his periodical visits to this place he stayed. It was pleasant to have a bath and a shave and get into slippers. He felt lazy and spent the rest of the morning reading a novel.

Soon after dark – for even at Thonon, though it was in France, it was thought desirable to attract attention to Ashenden as little as possible – an agent from the police-station came to see him. His name was Félix. He was a little dark Frenchman with sharp eyes and an unshaven chin, dressed in a shabby grey suit and rather down at heel, so that he looked like a lawyer's clerk out of work. Ashenden offered him a glass of wine and they sat down by the fire.

'Well, your lady lost no time,' he said. 'Within a quarter of an hour of her arrival she was out of the hotel with a bundle of clothes and trinkets that she sold in a shop near the market. When the afternoon boat came in she went down to the quay and bought a ticket to Evian.'

Evian, it should be explained, was the next place along the lake in France and from there, crossing over, the boat went to Switzerland.

'Of course she hadn't a passport, so permission to embark was denied her.'

'How did she explain that she had no passport?'

'She said she'd forgotten it. She said she had an appointment to see friends in Evian and tried to persuade the official in charge to let her go. She attempted to slip a hundred francs into his hand.'

'She must be a stupider woman than I thought,' said Ashenden.

But when next day he went about eleven in the morning to see her he made no reference to her attempt to escape. She had had time to arrange herself, and now, her hair elaborately done, her lips and cheeks painted, she looked less haggard than when he had first seen her.

'I've brought you some books,' said Ashenden. 'I'm afraid the time hangs heavy on your hands.'

'What does that matter to you?'

'I have no wish that you should suffer anything that can be avoided. Anyhow, I will leave them and you can read them or not as you choose.'

'If you only knew how I hated you.'

'It would doubtless make me very uncomfortable. But I really don't know why you should. I am only doing what I have been ordered to do.'

'What do you want of me now? I do not suppose you have come only to ask after my health.'

Ashenden smiled.

'I want you to write a letter to your lover telling him that owing to some irregularity in your passport the Swiss authorities would not let you cross the frontier, so you have come here, where it is very nice and quiet, so quiet that one can hardly realize there is a war, and you propose that Chandra should join you.'

'Do you think he is a fool? He will refuse.'

'Then you must do your best to persuade him.'

She looked at Ashenden a long time before she answered. He suspected that she was debating within herself whether by writing the letter and so seeming docile she could not gain time.

'Well, dictate and I will write what you say.'

'I should prefer you to put it in your own words.'

'Give me half an hour and the letter shall be ready.'

'I will wait here,' said Ashenden.

'Why?'

'Because I prefer to.'

Her eyes flashed angrily, but controlling herself she said nothing. On the chest of drawers were writing materials. She sat down at the dressing-table and began to write. When she handed Ashenden the letter he saw even through her rouge that she was very pale. It was the letter of a person not much used to expressing herself by means of pen and ink, but it was well enough, and when towards the end, starting to say how much she loved the man, she had been carried away and wrote with all her heart, it had really a certain passion.

'Now add: "The man who is bringing this is Swiss, you can trust him absolutely. I didn't want the censor to see it."'

She hesitated an instant, but then wrote as he directed.

'How do you spell "absolutely"?'

'As you like. Now address an envelope and I will relieve you of my unwelcome presence.'

He gave the letter to the agent who was waiting to take it across the lake. Ashenden brought her the reply the same evening. She snatched it from his hands and for a moment pressed it to her heart. When she read it she uttered a little cry of relief.

'He won't come.'

The letter, in the Indian's flowery, stilted English, expressed his bitter disappointment. He told her how intensely he had looked forward to seeing her and implored her to do everything in the world to smooth the difficulties that prevented her from crossing the frontier. He said that it was impossible for him to come, impossible; there was a price on his head, and it would be madness for him to think of risking it. He attempted to be jocular, she did not want her little fat lover to be shot, did she?

'He won't come,' she repeated, 'he won't come.'

'You must write and tell him that there is no risk. You must say that if there were you would not dream of asking him. You must say that if he loves you he will not hesitate.'

'I won't. I won't.'

'Don't be a fool. You can't help yourself.'

She burst into a sudden flood of tears. She flung herself on the floor and seizing Ashenden's knees implored him to have mercy on her.

'I will do anything in the world for you if you will let me go.'

'Don't be absurd,' said Ashenden. 'Do you think I want to become your lover? Come, come, you must be serious. You know the alternative.'

She raised herself to her feet and changing on a sudden to fury flung at Ashenden one foul name after another.

'I like you much better like that,' he said. 'Now will you write or shall I send for the police?'

'He will not come. It is useless.'

'It is very much to your interest to make him come.'

'What do you mean by that? Do you mean that if I do everything in my power and fail, that . . .'

She looked at Ashenden with wild eyes.

'Yes, it means either you or him.'

She staggered. She put her hand to her heart. Then without a word she reached for pen and paper. But the letter was not to Ashenden's liking and he made her write it again. When she had finished she flung herself on the bed and burst once more into passionate weeping. Her grief was real, but there was something theatrical in the expression of it that prevented it from being peculiarly moving to Ashenden. He felt his relation to her as impersonal as a doctor's in the presence of a pain that he cannot alleviate. He saw now why R. had given him this peculiar task; it needed a cool head and an emotion well under control.

He did not see her next day. The answer to the letter was not delivered to him till after dinner, when it was brought to Ashenden's little house by Félix.

'Well, what news have you?'

'Our friend is getting desperate,' smiled the Frenchman. 'This afternoon she walked up to the station just as a train was about to start for Lyons. She was looking up and down uncertainly, so I went to her and asked if there was anything I could do. I introduced myself as an agent of the Sûreté. If looks could kill I should not be standing here now.'

'Sit down, *mon ami*,' said Ashenden.

'*Merci*. She walked away, she evidently thought it was no use to try to get on the train, but I have something more interesting to tell you. She has offered a boatman on the lake a thousand francs to take her across to Lausanne.'

'What did he say to her?'

'He said he couldn't risk it.'

'Yes?'

The little agent gave his shoulders a slight shrug and smiled.

'She's asked him to meet her on the road that leads to Evian at ten o'clock to-night so that they can talk of it again, and she's given him to understand that she will not repulse too fiercely the advances of a lover. I have told him to do what he likes so long as he comes and tells me everything that is of importance.'

'Are you sure you can trust him?' asked Ashenden.

'Oh, quite. He knows nothing, of course, but that she is under surveillance. You need have no fear about him. He is a good boy. I have known him all his life.'

Ashenden read Chandra's letter. It was eager and passionate. It throbbed strangely with the painful yearning of his heart. Love? Yes, if Ashenden knew anything of it there was the real thing. He told her how he spent the long, long hours walking by the lakeside and looking towards the coast of France. How near they were and yet so desperately parted! He repeated again and again that he could not come, and begged her not to ask him; he would do everything in the world for her, but that he dared not do, and yet if she insisted how could he resist her? He besought her to have mercy on him. And then he broke into a long wail at the thought that he must go away without seeing her, he asked her if there were not some means by which she could slip over, he swore that if he could ever hold her in his arms again he would never let her go. Even the forced and elaborate language in which it was written could not dim the hot fire that burned the pages; it was the letter of a madman.

'When will you hear the result of her interview with the boatman?' asked Ashenden.

'I have arranged to meet him at the landing-stage between eleven and twelve.'

Ashenden looked at his watch.

'I will come with you.'

They walked down the hill and reaching the quay for shelter from the cold wind stood in the lea of the custom-house. At last they saw a man approaching and Félix stepped out of the shadow that hid them.

'Antoine.'

'Monsieur Félix? I have a letter for you; I promised to take it to Lausanne by the first boat to-morrow.'

Ashenden gave the man a brief glance, but did not ask what had passed between him and Giulia Lazzari. He took the letter and by the light of Félix's electric torch read it. It was in faulty German.

'*On no account come. Pay no attention to my letters. Danger. I love you. Sweetheart. Don't come.*'

He put it in his pocket, gave the boatman fifty francs, and went home to bed. But the next day when he went to see Giulia Lazzari he found her door locked. He knocked for some time, there was no answer. He called her.

'Madame Lazzari, you must open the door. I want to speak to you.'

'I am in bed. I am ill and can see no one.'

'I am sorry, but you must open the door. If you are ill I will send for a doctor.'

'No, go away. I will see no one.'

'If you do not open the door I shall send for a locksmith and have it broken open.'

There was a silence and then he heard the key turned in the lock. He went in. She was in a dressing-gown and her hair was dishevelled. She had evidently just got out of bed.

'I am at the end of my strength. I can do nothing more. You have only to look at me to see that I am ill. I have been sick all night.'

'I shall not keep you long. Would you like to see a doctor?'

'What good can a doctor do me?'

He took out of his pocket the letter she had given the boatman and handed it to her.

'What is the meaning of this?' he asked.

She gave a gasp at the sight of it and her sallow face went green.

'You gave me your word that you would neither attempt to escape nor write a letter without my knowledge.'

'Did you think I would keep my word?' she cried, her voice ringing with scorn.

'No. To tell you the truth it was not entirely for your convenience that you were placed in a comfortable hotel rather than in the local jail, but I think I should tell you that though you have your freedom to go in and out as you like you have no more chance of getting away from Thonon than if you were chained by the leg in a prison cell. It is silly to waste your time writing letters that will never be delivered.'

'*Cochon.*'[1]

She flung the opprobrious word at him with all the violence that was in her.

'But you must sit down and write a letter that *will* be delivered.'

'Never. I will do nothing more. I will not write another word.'

'You came here on the understanding that you would do certain things.'

'I will not do them. It is finished.'

'You had better reflect a little.'

'Reflect! I have reflected. You can do what you like; I don't care.'

'Very well, I will give you five minutes to change your mind.'

Ashenden took out his watch and looked at it. He sat down on the edge of the unmade bed.

'Oh, it has got on my nerves, this hotel. Why did you not put me in the prison? Why, why? Everywhere I went I felt that spies were on my heels. It is infamous what you are making me do. Infamous! What is my crime? I ask you, what have I done? Am I not a woman? It is infamous what you are asking me to do. Infamous.'

She spoke in a high shrill voice. She went on and on. At last the five minutes were up. Ashenden had not said a word. He rose.

'Yes, go, go,' she shrieked at him.

She flung foul names at him.

'I shall come back,' said Ashenden.

He took the key out of the door as he went out of the room and locked it behind him. Going downstairs he hurriedly scribbled a note, called the boots and dispatched him with it to the police-station. Then he went up again. Giulia Lazzari had thrown herself on her bed and turned her face to the wall. Her body was shaken with hysterical sobs. She gave no sign that she heard him come in. Ashenden sat down on the chair in front of the dressing-table and looked idly at the odds and ends that littered it. The toilet things were cheap and tawdry and none too clean. There were little shabby pots of rouge and cold-cream and little bottles of black for the eyebrows and eyelashes. The hairpins were horrid and greasy. The room was untidy and the air was heavy with the smell of cheap scent. Ashenden thought of the hundreds of rooms she must have occupied in third-rate hotels in the course of her wandering life from provincial town to provincial town in one country after another. He wondered what had been her origins. She was a coarse and vulgar woman, but what had she been when young? She was not the type he would have expected to adopt that career, for she seemed to have no advantages that could help her, and he asked himself whether she came of a family of entertainers (there are all over the world families in which for generations the members have become dancers or acrobats or comic singers) or whether she had fallen into the life accident- ally through some lover in the business who had for a time made her his partner. And what men must she have known in all these years, the comrades of the shows she was in, the agents and managers who looked upon it as a perquisite of their position that they should enjoy her favours, the merchants or well-to-do tradesmen, the young sparks of the various towns she played in, who were attracted for the moment by the glamour of the dancer or the blatant sensuality of the woman! To her they were the paying customers and she accepted them indifferently as the recognized and admitted supplement to her miserable salary, but to them perhaps she was romance. In her bought arms they caught sight for a moment of the brilliant world of the capitals, and ever so distantly and however shoddily of the adventure and the glamour of a more spacious life.

There was a sudden knock at the door and Ashenden immediately cried out:

'*Entrez*.'

Giulia Lazzari sprang up in bed to a sitting posture.

'Who is it?' she called.

She gave a gasp as she saw the two detectives who had brought her from Boulogne and handed her over to Ashenden at Thonon.

'You! What do you want?' she shrieked.

'*Allons, levez-vous*,'[2] said one of them, and his voice had a sharp abruptness that suggested that he would put up with no nonsense.

'I'm afraid you must get up, Madame Lazzari,' said Ashenden. 'I am delivering you once more to the care of these gentlemen.'

'How can I get up? I'm ill, I tell you. I cannot stand. Do you want to kill me?'

'If you won't dress yourself, we shall have to dress you, and I'm afraid we shouldn't do it very cleverly. Come, come, it's no good making a scene.'

'Where are you going to take me?'

'They're going to take you back to England.'

One of the detectives took hold of her arm.

'Don't touch me, don't come near me,' she screamed furiously.

'Let her be,' said Ashenden. 'I'm sure she'll see the necessity of making as little trouble as possible.'

'I'll dress myself.'

Ashenden watched her as she took off her dressing-gown and slipped a dress over her head. She forced her feet into shoes obviously too small for her. She arranged her hair. Every now and then she gave the detectives a hurried, sullen glance. Ashenden wondered if she would have the nerve to go through with it. R. would call him a damned fool, but he almost wished she would. She went up to the dressing-table and Ashenden stood up in order to let her sit down. She greased her face quickly and then rubbed off the grease with a dirty towel, she powdered herself and made up her eyes. But her hand shook. The three men watched her in silence. She rubbed the rouge on her cheeks and painted her mouth. Then she crammed a hat down on her head. Ashenden made a gesture to the first detective and he took a pair of handcuffs out of his pocket and advanced towards her.

At the sight of them she started back violently and flung her arms wide.

'*Non, non, non. Je ne veux pas.* No, not them. No. No.'

'Come, *ma fille*, don't be silly,' said the detective roughly.

As though for protection (very much to his surprise) she flung her arms round Ashenden.

'Don't let them take me, have mercy on me, I can't, I can't.'

Ashenden extricated himself as best he could.

'I can do nothing more for you.'

The detective seized her wrists and was about to affix the handcuffs when with a great cry she threw herself down on the floor.

'I will do what you wish. I will do everything.'

On a sign from Ashenden the detectives left the room. He waited for a little till she had regained a certain calm. She was lying on the floor, sobbing passionately. He raised her to her feet and made her sit down.

'What do you want me to do?' she gasped.

'I want you to write another letter to Chandra.'

'My head is in a whirl. I could not put two phrases together. You must give me time.'

But Ashenden felt that it was better to get her to write a letter while she was under the effect of her terror. He did not want to give her time to collect herself.

'I will dictate the letter to you. All you have to do is to write exactly what I tell you.'

She gave a deep sigh, but took the pen and the paper and sat down before them at the dressing-table.

'If I do this and . . . and you succeed, how do I know that I shall be allowed to go free?'

'The Colonel promised that you should. You must take my word for it that I shall carry out his instructions.'

'I *should* look a fool if I betrayed my friend and then went to prison for ten years.'

'I'll tell you your best guarantee of our good faith. Except by reason of Chandra you are not of the smallest importance to us. Why should we put ourselves to the bother and expense of keeping you in prison when you can do us no harm?'

She reflected for an instant. She was composed now. It was as though, having exhausted her emotion, she had become on a sudden a sensible and practical woman.

'Tell me what you want me to write.'

Ashenden hesitated. He thought he could put the letter more or less in the way she would naturally have put it, but he had to give it consideration. It must be neither fluent nor literary. He knew that in moments of emotion people are inclined to be melodramatic and stilted. In a book or on the stage this always rings false and the author has to make his people speak more simply and with less emphasis than in fact they do. It was a serious moment, but Ashenden felt that there were in it elements of the comic.

'I didn't know I loved a coward,' he started. 'If you loved me you couldn't hesitate when I ask you to come ... Underline *couldn't* twice.' He went on. 'When I promise you there is no danger. If you don't love me, you are right not to come. Don't come. Go back to Berlin where you are in safety. I am sick of it. I am alone here. I have made myself ill by waiting for you and every day I have said he is coming. If you loved me you would not hesitate so much. It is quite clear to me that you do not love me. I am sick and tired of you. I have no money. This hotel is impossible. There is nothing for me to stay for. I can get an engagement in Paris. I have a friend there who has made me serious propositions. I have wasted long enough over you and look what I have got from it. It is finished. Good-bye. You will never find a woman who will love you as I have loved you. I cannot afford to refuse the proposition of my friend, so I have telegraphed to him and as soon as I shall receive his answer I go to Paris. I do not blame you because you do not love me, that is not your fault, but you must see that I should be a stupid to go on wasting my life. One is not young for ever. Good-bye. Giulia.'

When Ashenden read over the letter he was not altogether satisfied. But it was the best he could do. It had an air of verisimilitude which the words lacked because, knowing little English, she had written phonetically, the spelling was atrocious and the handwriting like a child's; she had crossed out words and written them over again. Some of the phrases he had put in French. Once or twice tears had fallen on the pages and blurred the ink.

'I leave you now,' said Ashenden. 'It may be that when next you see me I shall be able to tell you that you are free to go where you choose. Where do you want to go?'

'Spain.'

'Very well, I will have everything prepared.'

She shrugged her shoulders. He left her.

There was nothing now for Ashenden to do but wait. He sent a messenger to Lausanne in the afternoon, and next morning went down to the quay to meet the boat. There was a waiting-room next to the ticket-office and here he told the detectives to hold themselves in readiness. When a boat arrived the passengers advanced along the pier in line and their passports were examined before they were allowed to go ashore. If Chandra came and showed his passport, and it was very likely that he was travelling with a false one, issued probably by a neutral nation, he was to be asked to wait and Ashenden was to identify him. Then he would be arrested. It was with some excitement that Ashenden watched the boat come in and the little group of people gathered at the gangway. He scanned them closely but saw no one who looked in the least like an Indian. Chandra had not come. Ashenden did not know what to do. He had played his last card. There were not more than half a dozen passengers for Thonon, and when they had been examined and gone their way he strolled slowly along the pier.

'Well, it's no go,' he said to Félix, who had been examining the passports. 'The gentleman I expected hasn't turned up.'

'I have a letter for you.'

He handed Ashenden an envelope addressed to Madame Lazzari on which he immediately recognized the spidery hand-writing of Chandra Lal. At that moment the steamer from

Geneva which was going to Lausanne and the end of the lake
hove in sight. It arrived at Thonon every morning twenty
minutes after the steamer going in the opposite direction had
left. Ashenden had an inspiration.

'Where is the man who brought it?'

'He's in the ticket-office.'

'Give him the letter and tell him to return to the person who
gave it to him. He is to say that he took it to the lady and she
sent it back. If the person asks him to take another letter he is
to say that it is not much good as she is packing her trunk and
leaving Thonon.'

He saw the letter handed over and the instructions given and
then walked back to his little house in the country.

The next boat on which Chandra could possibly come arrived
about five, and having at that hour an important engagement
with an agent working in Germany, he warned Félix that he
might be a few minutes late. But if Chandra came he could
easily be detained; there was no great hurry since the train in
which he was to be taken to Paris did not start till shortly after
eight. When Ashenden had finished his business he strolled
leisurely down to the lake. It was light still and from the top of
the hill he saw the steamer pulling out. It was an anxious
moment and instinctively he quickened his steps. Suddenly he
saw someone running towards him and recognized the man
who had taken the letter.

'Quick, quick,' he cried. 'He's there.'

Ashenden's heart gave a great thud against his chest.

'At last.'

He began to run too and as they ran the man, panting, told
him how he had taken back the unopened letter. When he put
it in the Indian's hand he turned frightfully pale ('I should never
have thought an Indian could turn that colour,' he said), and
turned it over and over in his hand as though he could not
understand what his own letter was doing there. Tears sprang
to his eyes and rolled down his cheeks. ('It was grotesque,
he's fat, you know.') He said something in a language the man
did not understand and then in French asked him when the
boat went to Thonon. When he got on board he looked about,

but did not see him, then he caught sight of him, huddled up in an ulster with his hat drawn down over his eyes, standing alone in the bows. During the crossing he kept his eyes fixed on Thonon.

'Where is he now?' asked Ashenden.

'I got off first and Monsieur Félix told me to come for you.'

'I suppose they're holding him in the waiting-room.'

Ashenden was out of breath when they reached the pier. He burst into the waiting-room. A group of men, talking at the top of their voices and gesticulating wildly, were clustered round a man lying on the ground.

'What's happened?' he cried.

'Look,' said Monsieur Félix.

Chandra Lal lay there, his eyes wide open and a thin line of foam on his lips, dead. His body was horribly contorted.

'He's killed himself. We've sent for the doctor. He was too quick for us.'

A sudden thrill of horror passed through Ashenden.

When the Indian landed Félix recognized from the description that he was the man they wanted. There were only four passengers. He was the last. Félix took an exaggerated time to examine the passports of the first three, and then took the Indian's. It was a Spanish one and it was all in order. Félix asked the regulation questions and noted them on the official sheet. Then he looked at him pleasantly and said:

'Just come into the waiting-room for a moment. There are one or two formalities to fulfil.'

'Is my passport not in order?' the Indian asked.

'Perfectly.'

Chandra hesitated, but then followed the official to the door of the waiting-room. Félix opened it and stood aside.

'*Entrez.*'

Chandra went in and the two detectives stood up. He must have suspected at once that they were police-officers and realized that he had fallen into a trap.

'Sit down,' said Félix. 'I have one or two questions to put to you.'

'It is hot in here,' he said, and in point of fact they had a little stove there that kept the place like an oven. 'I will take off my coat if you permit.'

'Certainly,' said Félix graciously.

He took off his coat, apparently with some effort, and he turned to put it on a chair, and then before they realized what had happened they were startled to see him stagger and fall heavily to the ground. While taking off his coat Chandra had managed to swallow the contents of a bottle that was still clasped in his hand. Ashenden put his nose to it. There was a very distinct odour of almonds.

For a little while they looked at the man who lay on the floor. Félix was apologetic.

'Will they be very angry?' he asked nervously.

'I don't see that it was your fault,' said Ashenden. 'Anyhow, he can do no more harm. For my part I am just as glad he killed himself. The notion of his being executed did not make me very comfortable.'

In a few minutes the doctor arrived and pronounced life extinct.

'Prussic acid,' he said to Ashenden.

Ashenden nodded.

'I will go and see Madame Lazzari,' he said. 'If she wants to stay a day or two longer I shall let her. But if she wants to go to-night of course she can. Will you give the agents at the station instructions to let her pass?'

'I shall be at the station myself,' said Félix.

Ashenden once more climbed the hill. It was night now, a cold, bright night with an unclouded sky and the sight of the new moon, a white shining thread, made him turn three times the money in his pocket. When he entered the hotel he was seized on a sudden with distaste for its cold banality. It smelled of cabbage and boiled mutton. On the walls of the hall were coloured posters of railway companies advertising Grenoble, Carcassonne and the bathing places of Normandy. He went upstairs and after a brief knock opened the door of Giulia Lazzari's room. She was sitting in front of her dressing-table, looking at herself in the glass, just idly or despairingly, apparently doing nothing, and it was in this that she saw Ashenden as he came in. Her face changed suddenly as she caught sight of his and she sprang up so vehemently that the chair fell over.

'What is it? Why are you so white?' she cried.

She turned round and stared at him and her features were gradually twisted to a look of horror.

'*Il est pris*,' she gasped.

'*Il est mort*,' said Ashenden.

'Dead! He took the poison. He had the time for that. He's escaped you after all.'

'What do you mean? How did you know about the poison?'

'He always carried it with him. He said that the English should never take him alive.'

Ashenden reflected for an instant. She had kept that secret well. He supposed the possibility of such a thing should have occurred to him. How was he to anticipate these melodramatic devices?

'Well, now you are free. You can go wherever you like and no obstacle shall be put in your way. Here are your ticket and your passport and here is the money that was in your possession when you were arrested. Do you wish to see Chandra?'

She started.

'No, no.'

'There is no need. I thought you might care to.'

She did not weep. Ashenden supposed that she had exhausted all her emotion. She seemed apathetic.

'A telegram will be sent to-night to the Spanish frontier to instruct the authorities to put no difficulties in your way. If you will take my advice you will get out of France as soon as you can.'

She said nothing, and since Ashenden had no more to say he made ready to go.

'I am sorry that I have had to show myself so hard to you. I am glad to think that now the worst of your troubles are over and I hope that time will assuage the grief that I know you must feel for the death of your friend.'

Ashenden gave her a little bow and turned to the door. But she stopped him.

'One little moment,' she said. 'There is one thing I should like to ask. I think you have some heart.'

'Whatever I can do for you, you may be sure I will.'

'What are they going to do with his things?'

'I don't know. Why?'

Then she said something that confounded Ashenden. It was the last thing he expected.

'He had a wrist-watch that I gave him last Christmas. It cost twelve pounds. Can I have it back?'

# JOHN BUCHAN
# THE LOATHLY OPPOSITE

Burminster had been to a Guildhall dinner the night before, which had been attended by many – to him – unfamiliar celebrities. He had seen for the first time in the flesh people whom he had long known by reputation, and he declared that in every case the picture he had formed of them had been cruelly shattered. An eminent poet, he said, had looked like a starting-price bookmaker, and a financier of world-wide fame had been exactly like the music-master at his preparatory school. Wherefore Burminster made the profound deduction that things were never what they seemed.

'That's only because you have a feeble imagination,' said Sandy Arbuthnot. 'If you had really understood Timson's poetry you would have realized that it went with close-cropped red hair and a fat body, and you should have known that Macintyre [this was the financier] had the music-and-metaphysics type of mind. That's why he puzzles the City so. If you understand a man's work well enough you can guess pretty accurately what he'll look like. I don't mean the colour of his eyes and his hair, but the general atmosphere of him.'

It was Sandy's agreeable habit to fling an occasional paradox at the table with the view of starting an argument. This time he stirred up Pugh, who had come to the War Office from the Indian Staff Corps. Pugh had been a great figure in Secret Service work in the East, but he did not look the part, for he had the air of a polo-playing cavalry subaltern. The skin was stretched as tight over his cheekbones as over the knuckles of a clenched fist, and was so dark that it had the appearance of beaten bronze. He had black hair, rather beady black eyes, and the hooky nose which in the Celt often goes with that colouring. He was himself a very good refutation of Sandy's theory.

'I don't agree,' Pugh said. 'At least not as a general principle. One piece of humanity whose work I studied with the micro-scope for two aching years upset all my notions when I came to meet it.'

Then he told us this story.

'When I was brought to England in November '17 and given a "hush" department on three floors of an eighteenth-century house in a back street, I had a good deal to learn about my business. That I learned it in reasonable time was due to the extraordinarily fine staff that I found provided for me. Not one of them was a regular soldier. They were all educated men – they had to be in that job – but they came out of every sort of environment. One of the best was a Shetland laird, another was an Admiralty Court KC, and I had, besides, a metallurgical chemist, a golf champion, a leader-writer, a popular dramatist, several actuaries, and an East End curate. None of them thought of anything but his job, and at the end of the War, when some ass proposed to make them OBEs, there was a very fair imitation of a riot. A more loyal crowd never existed, and they accepted me as their chief as unquestioningly as if I had been with them since 1914.

'To the War in the ordinary sense they scarcely gave a thought. You found the same thing in a lot of other behind-the-lines departments, and I daresay it was a good thing – it kept their nerves quiet and their minds concentrated. After all, our business was only to decode and decipher German messages; we had nothing to do with the use which was made of them. It was a curious little nest, and when the Armistice came my people were flabbergasted – they hadn't realized that their job was bound up with the War.

'The one who most interested me was my second-in-command, Philip Channell. He was a man of forty-three, about five foot four in height, weighing, I fancy, under nine stone, and almost as blind as an owl. He was good enough at papers with his double glasses, but he could hardly recognize you three yards off. He had been a professor at some Midland college –

mathematics or physics, I think – and as soon as the War began
he had tried to enlist. Of course they wouldn't have him – he
was about E5 in any physical classification, besides being well
over age – but he would take no refusal, and presently he
worried his way into the Government service. Fortunately he
found a job which he could do superlatively well, for I do not
believe there was a man alive with more natural genius for
cryptography.

'I don't know if any of you have ever given your mind to that
heart-breaking subject. Anyhow, you know that secret writing
falls under two heads – codes and ciphers, and that codes are
combinations of words and ciphers of numerals. I remember
how one used to be told that no code or cipher which was
practically useful was really undiscoverable, and in a sense that
is true, especially of codes. A system of communication which
is in constant use must obviously not be too intricate, and a
working code, if you get long enough for the job, can generally
be read. That is why a code is periodically changed by the
users. There are rules in worrying out the permutations and
combinations of letters in most codes, for human ingenuity
seems to run in certain channels, and a man who has been a
long time at the business gets surprisingly clever at it. You begin
by finding out a little bit, and then empirically building up the
rules of decoding, till in a week or two you get the whole
thing. Then, when you are happily engaged in reading enemy
messages, the code is changed suddenly, and you have to start
again from the beginning . . . You can make a code, of course,
that it is simply impossible to read except by accident – the key
to which is a page of some book, for example – but fortunately
that kind is not of much general use.

'Well, we got on pretty well with the codes, and read the
intercepted enemy messages, cables and wireless, with considerable ease and precision. It was mostly diplomatic stuff, and not
very important. The more valuable stuff was in cipher, and that
was another pair of shoes. With a code you can build up the
interpretation by degrees, but with a cipher you either know it
or you don't – there are no half-way houses. A cipher, since it
deals with numbers, is a horrible field for mathematical ingen-

uity. Once you have written out the letters of a message in numerals there are many means by which you can lock it and double-lock it. The two main devices, as you know, are transposition and substitution, and there is no limit to the ways one or other or both can be used. There is nothing to prevent a cipher having a double meaning, produced by two different methods, and, as a practical question, you have to decide which meaning is intended. By way of an extra complication, too, the message, when deciphered, may turn out to be itself in a difficult code. I can tell you our job wasn't exactly a rest cure.'

Burminster, looking puzzled, inquired as to the locking of ciphers.

'It would take too long to explain. Roughly, you write out a message horizontally in numerals; then you pour it into vertical columns, the number and order of which are determined by a key-word; then you write out the contents of the columns horizontally, following the lines across. To unlock it you have to have the key-word, so as to put it back into the vertical columns, and then into the original horizontal form.'

Burminster cried out like one in pain. 'It can't be done. Don't tell me that any human brain could solve such an acrostic.'

'It was frequently done,' said Pugh.

'By you?'

'Lord bless you, not by me. I can't do a simple cross-word puzzle. By my people.'

'Give me the trenches,' said Burminster in a hollow voice. 'Give me the trenches any day. Do you seriously mean to tell me that you could sit down before a muddle of numbers and travel back the way they had been muddled to an original that made sense?'

'I couldn't, but Channell could – in most cases. You see, we didn't begin entirely in the dark. We already knew the kind of intricacies that the enemy favoured, and the way we worked was by trying a variety of clues till we lit on the right one.'

'Well, I'm blessed! Go on about your man Channell.'

'This isn't Channell's story,' said Pugh. 'He only comes into it accidentally . . . There was one cipher which always defeated us, a cipher used between the German General Staff and their forces in the East. It was a locked cipher, and Channell had given more time to it than to any dozen of the others, for it put him on his mettle. But he confessed himself absolutely beaten. He wouldn't admit that it was insoluble, but he declared that he would need a bit of real luck to solve it. I asked him what kind of luck, and he said a mistake and a repetition. That, he said, might give him a chance of establishing equations.

'We called this particular cipher "PY", and we hated it poisonously. We felt like pygmies battering at the base of a high stone tower. Dislike of the thing soon became dislike of the man who had conceived it. Channell and I used to – I won't say amuse, for it was too dashed serious – but torment ourselves by trying to picture the fellow who owned the brain that was responsible for PY. We had a pretty complete dossier of the German Intelligence Staff, but of course we couldn't know who was responsible for this particular cipher. We knew no more than his code name, Reinmar, with which he signed the simpler messages to the East, and Channell, who was a romantic little chap for all his science, had got it into his head that it was a woman. He used to describe her to me as if he had seen her – a she-devil, young, beautiful, with a much-painted white face, and eyes like a cobra's. I fancy he read a rather low class of novel in his off-time.

'My picture was different. At first I thought of the histrionic type of scientist, the "ruthless brain" type, with a high forehead and a jaw puckered like a chimpanzee's. But that didn't seem to work, and I settled on a picture of a first-class *Generalstabsoffizier*,[1] as handsome as Falkenhayn,[2] trained to the last decimal, absolutely passionless, with a mind that worked with the relentless precision of a fine machine. We all of us at the time suffered from the bogy of this kind of German, and, when things were going badly, as in March '18, I couldn't sleep for hating him. The infernal fellow was so water-tight and armourplated, a Goliath who scorned the pebbles from our feeble slings.

'Well, to make a long story short, there came a moment in September '18 when PY was about the most important thing in the world. It mattered enormously what Germany was doing

in Syria, and we knew that it was all in PY. Every morning a pile
of the intercepted German wireless messages lay on Channell's
table, which were as meaningless to him as a child's scrawl. I
was prodded by my chiefs and in turn I prodded Channell. We
had a week to find the key to the cipher, after which things
must go on without us, and if we had failed to make anything
of it in eighteen months of quiet work, it didn't seem likely that
we would succeed in seven feverish days. Channell nearly went
off his head with overwork and anxiety. I used to visit his dingy
little room and find him fairly grizzled and shrunken with
fatigue.

'This isn't a story about him, though there is a good story
which I may tell you another time. As a matter of fact, we won
on the post. PY made a mistake. One morning we got a long
message dated *en clair*, then a very short message, and then a
third message almost the same as the first. The second must
mean "Your message of to-day's date unintelligible, please
repeat", the regular formula. This gave us a translation of a
bit of the cipher. Even that would not have brought it out, and
for twelve hours Channell was on the verge of lunacy, till it
occurred to him that Reinmar might have signed the long message with his name, as we used to do sometimes in cases of
extreme urgency. He was right, and, within three hours of the
last moment Operations could give us, we had the whole thing
pat. As I have said, that is a story worth telling, but it is not
this one.

'We both finished the War too tired to think of much except
that the darned thing was over. But Reinmar had been so long
our unseen but constantly pictured opponent that we kept up
a certain interest in him. We would like to have seen how he
took the licking, for he must have known that we had licked
him. Mostly when you lick a man at a game you rather like
him, but I didn't like Reinmar. In fact, I made him a sort of
compost of everything I had ever disliked in a German. Channell
stuck to his she-devil theory, but I was pretty certain that he
was a youngish man with an intellectual arrogance which his
country's débâcle would in no way lessen. He would never
acknowledge defeat. It was highly improbable that I should

ever find out who he was, but I felt that if I did, and met him face to face, my dislike would be abundantly justified.

'As you know, for a year or two after the Armistice I was a pretty sick man. Most of us were. We hadn't the fillip of getting back to civilized comforts, like the men in the trenches. We had always been comfortable enough in body, but our minds were fagged out, and there is no easy cure for that. My digestion went nobly to pieces, and I endured a miserable space of lying in bed and living on milk and olive-oil. After that I went back to work, but the darned thing always returned, and every leech had a different régime to advise. I tried them all – dry meals, a snack every two hours, lemon juice, sour milk, starvation, knocking off tobacco – but nothing got me more than half-way out of the trough. I was a burden to myself and a nuisance to others, dragging my wing through life, with a constant pain in my tummy.

'More than one doctor advised an operation, but I was chary about that, for I had seen several of my friends operated on for the same mischief and left as sick as before. Then a man told me about a German fellow called Christoph, who was said to be very good at handling my trouble. The best hand at diagnosis in the world, my informant said – no fads – treated every case on its merits – a really original mind. Dr Christoph had a modest *Kurhaus* at a place called Rosensee in the Sächischen Sweitz.[3] By this time I was getting pretty desperate, so I packed a bag and set off for Rosensee.

'It was a quiet little town at the mouth of a narrow valley, tucked in under wooded hills, a clean fresh place with open channels of running water in the streets. There was a big church with an onion spire, a Catholic seminary, and a small tanning industry. The *Kurhaus* was half-way up a hill, and I felt better as soon as I saw my bedroom, with its bare scrubbed floors and its wide veranda looking into a forest glade. I felt still better when I saw Dr Christoph. He was a small man with a grizzled beard, a high forehead, and a limp, rather like what I imagine the Apostle Paul must have been. He looked wise, as wise as an old owl. His English was atrocious, but even when he found that I talked German fairly well hc didn't expand in speech. He would deliver no opinion of any kind until he had had me at least a week under observation; but somehow I felt comforted, for I concluded that a first-class mind had got to work on me.

'The other patients were mostly Germans, with a sprinkling of Spaniards, but to my delight I found Channell. He also had been having a thin time since we parted. Nerves were his trouble – general nervous debility and perpetual insomnia, and his college had given him six months' leave of absence to try to get well. The poor chap was as lean as a sparrow, and he had the large dull eyes and the dry lips of the sleepless. He had arrived a week before me, and like me was under observation. But his vetting was different from mine, for he was a mental case, and Dr Christoph used to devote hours to trying to unriddle his nervous tangles. "He is a good man for a German," said Channell, "but he is on the wrong tack. There's nothing wrong with my mind. I wish he'd stick to violet rays[4] and massage, instead of asking me silly questions about my great-grandmother."

'Channell and I used to go for invalidish walks in the woods, and we naturally talked about the years we had worked together. He was living mainly in the past, for the War had been the great thing in his life, and his professorial duties seemed trivial by comparison. As we tramped among the withered bracken and heather, his mind was always harking back to the dingy little room where he had smoked cheap cigarettes and worked fourteen hours out of the twenty-four. In particular, he was as eagerly curious about our old antagonist, Reinmar, as he had been in 1918. He was more positive than ever that she was a woman, and I believe that one of the reasons that had induced him to try a cure in Germany was a vague hope that he might get on her track. I had almost forgotten about the thing, and I was amused by Channell in the part of the untiring sleuth-hound.

'"You won't find her in the *Kurhaus*," I said. "Perhaps she is in some old *Schloss* in the neighbourhood, waiting for you like the Sleeping Beauty."

'"I'm serious," he said plaintively. "It is purely a matter of intellectual curiosity, but I confess I would give a great deal to see her face to face. After I leave here, I thought of going to

Berlin to make some inquiries. But I'm handicapped, for I know nobody and I have no credentials. Why don't you, who have a large acquaintance and far more authority, take the thing up?"

'I told him that my interest in the matter had flagged and that I wasn't keen on digging into the past, but I promised to give him a line to our Military Attaché if he thought of going to Berlin. I rather discouraged him from letting his mind dwell too much on events in the War. I said that he ought to try to bolt the door on all that had contributed to his present breakdown.

' "That is not Dr Christoph's opinion," he said emphatically. "He encourages me to talk about it. You see, with me it is a purely intellectual interest. I have no emotion in the matter. I feel quite friendly towards Reinmar, whoever she may be. It is, if you like, a piece of romance. I haven't had so many romantic events in my life that I want to forget this."

' "Have you told Dr Christoph about Reinmar?" I asked.

' "Yes," he said, "and he was mildly interested. You know the way he looks at you with his solemn grey eyes. I doubt if he quite understood what I meant; for a little provincial doctor, even though he is a genius in his own line, is not likely to know much about the ways of the Great General Staff . . . I had to tell him, for I have to tell him all my dreams, and lately I have taken to dreaming about Reinmar."

' "What's she like?" I asked.

' "Oh, a most remarkable figure. Very beautiful, but uncanny. She has long fair hair down to her knees."

'Of course I laughed. "You're mixing her up with the Valkyries," I said. "Lord, it would be an awkward business if you met that she-dragon in the flesh."

'But he was quite solemn about it, and declared that his waking picture of her was not in the least like his dreams. He rather agreed with my nonsense about the old *Schloss*. He thought that she was probably some penniless grandee, living solitary in a moated grange, with nothing now to exercise her marvellous brain on, and eating her heart out with regret and shame. He drew so attractive a character of her that I began to think that Channell was in love with a being of his own creation, till he ended with, "But all the same she's utterly damnable. She must be, you know."

'After a fortnight I began to feel a different man. Dr Christoph thought that he had got on the track of the mischief, and certainly, with his deep massage and a few simple drugs, I had more internal comfort than I had known for three years. He was so pleased with my progress that he refused to treat me as an invalid. He encouraged me to take long walks into the hills, and presently he arranged for me to go out roebuck-shooting with some of the local Junkers.[5]

'I used to start before daybreak on the chilly November mornings and drive to the top of one of the ridges, where I would meet a collection of sportsmen and beaters, shepherded by a fellow in a green uniform. We lined out along the ridge, and the beaters, assisted by a marvellous collection of dogs, including the sporting dachshund, drove the roe towards us. It wasn't very cleverly managed, for the deer generally broke back, and it was chilly waiting in the first hours with a powdering of snow on the ground and the fir boughs heavy with frost crystals. But later, when the sun grew stronger, it was a very pleasant mode of spending a day. There was not much of a bag, but whenever a roe or a capercailzie[6] fell, all the guns would assemble and drink little glasses of *Kirschwasser*. I had been lent a rifle, one of those appalling contraptions which are double-barrelled shot-guns and rifles in one, and to transpose from one form to the other requires a mathematical calculation. The rifle had a hair-trigger too, and when I first used it I was nearly the death of a respectable Saxon peasant.

'We all ate our midday meal together, and in the evening, before going home, we had coffee and cakes in one or other of the farms. The party was an odd mixture, big farmers and small squires, an hotel-keeper or two, a local doctor, and a couple of lawyers from the town. At first they were a little shy of me, but presently they thawed, and after the first day we were good friends. They spoke quite frankly about the War, in which every one of them had had a share, and with a great deal of dignity and good sense.

'I learned to walk in Sikkim, and the little Saxon hills seemed to me inconsiderable. But they were too much for most of the guns, and instead of going straight up or down a slope they always chose a circuit, which gave them an easy gradient. One evening, when we were separating as usual, the beaters taking a short-cut and the guns a circuit, I felt that I wanted exercise, so I raced the beaters downhill, beat them soundly, and had the better part of an hour to wait for my companions, before we adjourned to the farm for refreshment. The beaters must have talked about my pace, for as we walked away one of the guns, a lawyer called Meissen, asked me why I was visiting Rosensee at a time of year when few foreigners came. I said I was staying with Dr Christoph.

' "Is he then a private friend of yours?" he asked.

'I told him no, that I had come to his *Kurhaus* for treatment, being sick. His eyes expressed polite scepticism. He was not prepared to regard as an invalid a man who went down a hill like an avalanche.

'But, as we walked in the frosty dusk, he was led to speak of Dr Christoph, of whom he had no personal knowledge, and I learned how little honour a prophet may have in his own country. Rosensee scarcely knew him, except as a doctor who had an inexplicable attraction for foreign patients. Meissen was curious about his methods and the exact diseases in which he specialized. "Perhaps he may yet save me a journey to Homburg!"[7] He laughed. "It is well to have a skilled physician at one's door-step. The doctor is something of a hermit, and, except for his patients, does not appear to welcome his kind. Yet he is a good man, beyond doubt, and there are those who say that in the War he was a hero."

'This surprised me, for I could not imagine Dr Christoph in any fighting capacity, apart from the fact that he must have been too old. I thought that Meissen might refer to work in the base hospitals. But he was positive; Dr Christoph had been in the trenches; the limping leg was a war wound.

'I had had very little talk with the doctor, owing to my case being free from nervous complications. He would say a word to me morning and evening about my diet, and pass the time of day when we met, but it was not till the very eve of my departure that we had anything like a real conversation. He sent a message that he wanted to see me for not less than one hour, and he arrived with a batch of notes from which he delivered a kind of lecture on my case. Then I realized what an immense amount of care and solid thought he had expended on me. He had decided that his diagnosis was right – my rapid improvement suggested that – but it was necessary for some time to observe a simple régime, and to keep an eye on certain symptoms. So he took a sheet of notepaper from the table, and in his small precise hand wrote down for me a few plain commandments.

'There was something about him, the honest eyes, the mouth which looked as if it had been often compressed in suffering, the air of grave goodwill, which I found curiously attractive. I wished that I had been a mental case like Channell, and had had more of his society. I detained him in talk, and he seemed not unwilling. By and by we drifted to the War, and it turned out that Meissen was right.

'Dr Christoph had gone as medical officer in November '14 to the Ypres Salient with a Saxon regiment, and had spent the winter there. In '15 he had been in Champagne,[8] and in the early months of '16 at Verdun, till he was invalided with rheumatic fever. That is to say, he had had about seventeen months of consecutive fighting in the worst areas with scarcely a holiday. A pretty good record for a frail little middle-aged man!

'His family was then at Stuttgart, his wife and one little boy. He took a long time to recover from the fever, and after that was put on home duty. "Till the War was almost over," he said, "almost over, but not quite. There was just time for me to go back to the front and get my foolish leg hurt." I must tell you that whenever he mentioned his war experience it was with a comical deprecating smile, as if he agreed with anyone who might think that gravity like his should have remained in bed.

'I assumed that this home duty was medical, until he said something about getting rusty in his professional work. Then it appeared that it had been some job connected with Intelligence. "I am reputed to have a little talent for mathematics,"

he said. "No. I am no mathematical scholar, but, if you understand me, I have a certain mathematical aptitude. My mind has
always moved happily among numbers. Therefore I was set to
construct and to interpret ciphers, a strange interlude in the
noise of war. I sat in a little room and excluded the world, and
for a little I was happy.'

'He went on to speak of the enclave of peace in which he had
found himself, and as I listened to his gentle monotonous voice,
I had a sudden inspiration.

'I took a sheet of note-paper from the stand, scribbled the
word *Reinmar* on it, and shoved it towards him. I had a notion,
you see, that I might surprise him into helping Channell's
researches.

'But it was I who got the big surprise. He stopped thunderstruck as soon as his eye caught the word, blushed scarlet over
every inch of face and bald forehead, seemed to have difficulty
in swallowing, and then gasped, "How did you know?"

'I hadn't known, and now that I did, the knowledge left me
speechless. This was the loathly opposite for which Channell
and I had nursed our hatred. When I came out of my stupefac-
tion I found that he had recovered his balance and was speaking
slowly and distinctly, as if he were making a formal confession.

' "You were among my opponents . . . that interests me deeply
. . . I often wondered . . . You beat me in the end. You are aware
of that?"

'I nodded. "Only because you made a slip," I said.

' "Yes, I made a slip. I was to blame – very gravely to blame,
for I let my private grief cloud my mind."

'He seemed to hesitate, as if he were loath to stir something
very tragic in his memory.

' "I think I will tell you," he said at last. "I have often wished
– it is a childish wish – to justify my failure to those who profited
by it. My chiefs understood, of course, but my opponents could
not. In that month when I failed I was in deep sorrow. I had a
little son – his name was Reinmar – you remember that I took
that name for my code signature?"

'His eyes were looking beyond me into some vision of the
past.

'"He was, as you say, my mascot. He was all my family, and I adored him. But in those days food was not plentiful. We were no worse off than many million Germans, but the child was frail. In the last summer of the War he developed phthisis due to malnutrition, and in September he died. Then I failed my country, for with him some virtue seemed to depart from my mind. You see, my work was, so to speak, his also, as my name was his, and when he left me he took my power with him . . . So I stumbled. The rest is known to you."

'He sat staring beyond me, so small and lonely, that I could have howled. I put my hand on his shoulder and stammered some platitude about being sorry. We sat quite still for a minute or two, and then I remembered Channell. Channell must have poured his views of Reinmar into Dr Christoph's ear. I asked him if Channell knew.

'A flicker of a smile crossed his face.

'"Indeed no. And I will exact from you a promise never to breathe to him what I have told you. He is my patient, and I must first consider his case. At present he thinks that Reinmar is a wicked and beautiful lady whom he may some day meet. That is romance, and it is good for him to think so . . . If he were told the truth, he would be pitiful, and in Herr Channell's condition it is important that he should not be vexed with such emotions as pity."'

# 3

# AT HOME

# RUDYARD KIPLING
# MARY POSTGATE

Of Miss Mary Postgate, Lady McCausland wrote that she was 'thoroughly conscientious, tidy, companionable, and ladylike. I am very sorry to part with her, and shall always be interested in her welfare.'

Miss Fowler engaged her on this recommendation, and to her surprise, for she had had experience of companions, found that it was true. Miss Fowler was nearer sixty than fifty at the time, but though she needed care she did not exhaust her attendant's vitality. On the contrary, she gave out, stimulatingly and with reminiscences. Her father had been a minor Court official in the days when the Great Exhibition of 1851 had just set its seal on Civilization made perfect. Some of Miss Fowler's tales, none the less, were not always for the young. Mary was not young, and though her speech was as colourless as her eyes or her hair, she was never shocked. She listened unflinchingly to every one; said at the end, 'How interesting!' or 'How shocking!' as the case might be, and never again referred to it, for she prided herself on a trained mind, which 'did not dwell on these things'. She was, too, a treasure at domestic accounts, for which the village tradesmen, with their weekly books, loved her not. Otherwise she had no enemies; provoked no jealousy even among the plainest; neither gossip nor slander had ever been traced to her; she supplied the odd place at the Rector's or the Doctor's table at half an hour's notice; she was a sort of public aunt to very many small children of the village street, whose parents, while accepting everything, would have been swift to resent what they called 'patronage'; she served on the Village Nursing Committee as Miss Fowler's nominee when

Miss Fowler was crippled by rheumatoid arthritis, and came out of six months' fortnightly meetings equally respected by all the cliques.

And when Fate threw Miss Fowler's nephew, an unlovely orphan of eleven, on Miss Fowler's hands, Mary Postgate stood to her share of the business of education as practised in private and public schools. She checked printed clothes-lists, and un-itemized bills of extras; wrote to Head and House masters, matrons, nurses and doctors, and grieved or rejoiced over half-term reports. Young Wyndham Fowler repaid her in his holidays by calling her 'Gatepost', 'Postey', or 'Packthread', by thumping her between her narrow shoulders, or by chasing her bleating, round the garden, her large mouth open, her large nose high in the air, at a stiff-necked shamble very like a camel's. Later on he filled the house with clamour, argument, and harangues as to his personal needs, likes and dislikes, and the limitations of 'you women', reducing Mary to tears of physical fatigue, or, when he chose to be humorous, of helpless laughter. At crises, which multiplied as he grew older, she was his ambassadress and his interpretress to Miss Fowler, who had no large sympathy with the young; a vote in his interest at the councils on his future; his sewing-woman, strictly accountable for mislaid boots and garments; always his butt and his slave.

And when he decided to become a solicitor, and had entered an office in London; when his greeting had changed from 'Hullo Postey, you old beast,' to 'Mornin', Packthread', there came a war which, unlike all wars that Mary could remember, did not stay decently outside England and in the newspapers, but intruded on the lives of people whom she knew. As she said to Miss Fowler, it was 'most vexatious'. It took the Rector's son who was going into business with his elder brother; it took the Colonel's nephew on the eve of fruit-farming in Canada; it took Mrs Grant's son who, his mother said, was devoted to the ministry; and, very early indeed, it took Wynn Fowler, who announced on a postcard that he had joined the Flying Corps and wanted a cardigan waistcoat.

'He must go, and he must have the waistcoat,' said Miss Fowler. So Mary got the proper-sized needles and wool, while

Miss Fowler told the men of her establishment – two gardeners and an odd man, aged sixty – that those who could join the Army had better do so. The gardeners left. Cheape, the odd man, stayed on, and was promoted to the gardener's cottage. The cook, scorning to be limited in luxuries, also left, after a spirited scene with Miss Fowler, and took the housemaid with her. Miss Fowler gazetted Nellie, Cheape's seventeen-year-old daughter, to the vacant post; Mrs Cheape to the rank of cook, with occasional cleaning bouts; and the reduced establishment moved forward smoothly.

Wynn demanded an increase in his allowance. Miss Fowler, who always looked facts in the face, said, 'He must have it. The chances are he won't live long to draw it, and if three hundred makes him happy –'

Wynn was grateful, and came over, in his tight-buttoned uniform, to say so. His training centre was not thirty miles away, and his talk was so technical that it had to be explained by charts of the various types of machines. He gave Mary such a chart.

'And you'd better study it, Postey,' he said. 'You'll be seeing a lot of 'em soon.' So Mary studied the chart, but when Wynn next arrived to swell and exalt himself before his womenfolk, she failed badly in cross-examination, and he rated her as in the old days.

'You *look* more or less like a human being,' he said in his new Service voice. 'You *must* have had a brain at some time in your past. What have you done with it? Where d'you keep it? A sheep would know more than you do, Postey. You're lamentable. You are less use than an empty tin can, you dowey old cassowary.'[1]

'I suppose that's how your superior officer talks to *you*?' said Miss Fowler from her chair.

'But Postey doesn't mind,' Wynn replied. 'Do you, Pack-thread?'

'Why? Was Wynn saying anything? I shall get this right next time you come,' she muttered, and knitted her pale brows again over the diagrams of Taubes, Farmans, and Zeppelins.

In a few weeks the mere land and sea battles which she

read to Miss Fowler after breakfast passed her like idle breath. Her heart and her interest were high in the air with Wynn, who had finished 'rolling' (whatever that might be) and had gone on from a 'taxi' to a machine more or less his own. One morning it circled over their very chimneys, alighted on Vegg's Heath, almost outside the garden gate, and Wynn came in, blue with cold, shouting for food. He and she drew Miss Fowler's bath-chair, as they had often done, along the Heath foot-path to look at the biplane. Mary observed that 'it smelled very badly'.

'Postey, I believe you think with your nose,' said Wynn. 'I know you don't with your mind. Now, what type's that?'

'I'll go and get the chart,' said Mary.

'You're hopeless! You haven't the mental capacity of a white mouse,' he cried, and explained the dials and the sockets for bomb-dropping till it was time to mount and ride the wet clouds once more.

'Ah!' said Mary, as the stinking thing flared upward. 'Wait till our Flying Corps gets to work! Wynn says it's much safer than in the trenches.'

'I wonder,' said Miss Fowler. 'Tell Cheape to come and tow me home again.'

'It's all downhill. I can do it,' said Mary, 'if you put the brake on.' She laid her lean self against the pushing-bar and home they trundled.

'Now, be careful you aren't heated and catch a chill,' said overdressed Miss Fowler.

'Nothing makes me perspire,' said Mary. As she bumped the chair under the porch she straightened her long back. The exertion had given her a colour, and the wind had loosened a wisp of hair across her forehead. Miss Fowler glanced at her.

'What do you ever think of, Mary?' she demanded suddenly.

'Oh, Wynn says he wants another three pairs of stockings – as thick as we can make them.'

'Yes. But I mean the things that women think about. Here you are, more than forty –'

'Forty-four,' said truthful Mary.

'Well?'

'Well?' Mary offered Miss Fowler her shoulder as usual.

'And you've been with me ten years now.'

'Let's see,' said Mary. 'Wynn was eleven when he came. He's twenty now, and I came two years before that. It must be eleven.'

'Eleven! And you've never told me anything that matters in all that while. Looking back, it seems to me that I've done all the talking.'

'I'm afraid I'm not much of a conversationalist. As Wynn says, I haven't the mind. Let me take your hat.'

Miss Fowler, moving stiffly from the hip, stamped her rubber-tipped stick on the tiled hall floor. 'Mary, aren't you *anything* except a companion? Would you *ever* have been anything except a companion?'

Mary hung up the garden hat on its proper peg. 'No,' she said after consideration. 'I don't imagine I ever should. But I've no imagination, I'm afraid.'

She fetched Miss Fowler her eleven o'clock glass of Contrexeville.[2]

That was the wet December when it rained six inches to the month, and the women went abroad as little as might be. Wynn's flying chariot visited them several times, and for two mornings (he had warned her by postcard) Mary heard the thresh of his propellers at dawn. The second time she ran to the window, and stared at the whitening sky. A little blur passed overhead. She lifted her lean arms towards it.

That evening at six o'clock there came an announcement in an official envelope that Second Lieutenant W. Fowler had been killed during a trial flight. Death was instantaneous. She read it and carried it to Miss Fowler.

'I never expected anything else,' said Miss Fowler; 'but I'm sorry it happened before he had done anything.'

The room was whirling round Mary Postgate, but she found herself quite steady in the midst of it.

'Yes,' she said. 'It's a great pity he didn't die in action after he had killed somebody.'

'He was killed instantly. That's one comfort,' Miss Fowler went on.

'But Wynn says the shock of a fall kills a man at once –
whatever happens to the tanks,' quoted Mary.

The room was coming to rest now. She heard Miss Fowler
say impatiently, 'But why can't we cry, Mary?' and herself
replying, 'There's nothing to cry for. He has done his duty as
much as Mrs Grant's son did.'

'And when he died, *she* came and cried all the morning,' said
Miss Fowler. 'This only makes me feel tired – terribly tired.
Will you help me to bed, please, Mary? – And I think I'd like
the hot-water bottle.'

So Mary helped her and sat beside her, talking of Wynn in
his riotous youth.

'I believe,' said Miss Fowler suddenly, 'that old people and
young people slip from under a stroke like this. The middle-aged
feel it most.'

'I expect that's true,' said Mary, rising. 'I'm going to put
away the things in his room now. Shall we wear mourning?'

'Certainly not,' said Miss Fowler. 'Except, of course, at the
funeral. I can't go. You will. I want you to arrange about
his being buried here. What a blessing it didn't happen at
Salisbury!'

Everyone, from the Authorities of the Flying Corps to the
Rector, was most kind and sympathetic. Mary found herself
for the moment in a world where bodies were in the habit of
being despatched by all sorts of conveyances to all sorts of
places. And at the funeral two young men in buttoned-up uniforms stood beside the grave and spoke to her afterwards.

'You're Miss Postgate, aren't you?' said one. 'Fowler told me
about you. He was a good chap – a first-class fellow – a great
loss.'

'Great loss!' growled his companion. 'We're all awfully
sorry.'

'How high did he fall from?' Mary whispered.

'Pretty nearly four thousand feet, I should think, didn't he?
You were up that day, Monkey?'

'All of that,' the other child replied. 'My bar made three
thousand, and I wasn't as high as him by a lot.'

'Then *that*'s all right,' said Mary. 'Thank you very much.'

They moved away as Mrs Grant flung herself weeping on Mary's flat chest, under the lych-gate, and cried, '*I* know how it feels! *I* know how it feels!'

'But both his parents are dead,' Mary returned, as she fended her off. 'Perhaps they've all met by now,' she added vaguely as she escaped towards the coach.

'I've thought of that too,' wailed Mrs Grant; 'but then he'll be practically a stranger to them. Quite embarrassing!'

Mary faithfully reported every detail of the ceremony to Miss Fowler, who, when she described Mrs Grant's outburst, laughed aloud.

'Oh, how Wynn would have enjoyed it! He was always utterly unreliable at funerals. D'you remember –' And they talked of him again, each piecing out the other's gaps. 'And now,' said Miss Fowler, 'we'll pull up the blinds and we'll have a general tidy. That always does us good. Have you seen to Wynn's things?'

'Everything – since he first came,' said Mary. 'He was never destructive – even with his toys.'

They faced that neat room.

'It can't be natural not to cry,' Mary said at last. 'I'm *so* afraid you'll have a reaction.'

'As I told you, we old people slip from under the stroke. It's you I'm afraid for. Have you cried yet?'

'I can't. It only makes me angry with the Germans.'

'That's sheer waste of vitality,' said Miss Fowler. 'We must live till the war's finished.' She opened a full wardrobe. 'Now, I've been thinking things over. This is my plan. All his civilian clothes can be given away – Belgian refugees, and so on.'

Mary nodded. 'Boots, collars, and gloves?'

'Yes. We don't need to keep anything except his cap and belt.'

'They came back yesterday with his Flying Corps clothes' – Mary pointed to a roll on the little iron bed.

'Ah, but keep his Service things. Someone may be glad of them later. Do you remember his sizes?'

'Five feet eight and a half; thirty-six inches round the chest. But he told me he's just put on an inch and a half. I'll mark it on a label and tie it on his sleeping-bag.'

'So that disposes of *that*,' said Miss Fowler, tapping the palm of one hand with the ringed third finger of the other. 'What waste it all is! We'll get his old school trunk to-morrow and pack his civilian clothes.'

'And the rest?' said Mary. 'His books and pictures and the games and the toys – and – and the rest?'

'My plan is to burn every single thing,' said Miss Fowler. 'Then we shall know where they are and no one can handle them afterwards. What do you think?'

'I think that would be much the best,' said Mary. 'But there's such a lot of them.'

'We'll burn them in the destructor,' said Miss Fowler.

This was an open-air furnace for the consumption of refuse; a little circular four-foot tower of pierced brick over an iron grating. Miss Fowler had noticed the design in a gardening journal years ago, and had had it built at the bottom of the garden. It suited her tidy soul, for it saved unsightly rubbish-heaps, and the ashes lightened the stiff clay soil.

Mary considered for a moment, saw her way clear, and nodded again. They spent the evening putting away well-remembered civilian suits, underclothes that Mary had marked, and the regiments of very gaudy socks and ties. A second trunk was needed, and, after that, a little packing-case, and it was late next day when Cheape and the local carrier lifted them to the cart. The Rector luckily knew of a friend's son, about five feet eight and a half inches high, to whom a complete Flying Corps outfit would be most acceptable, and sent his gardener's son down with a barrow to take delivery of it. The cap was hung up in Miss Fowler's bedroom, the belt in Miss Postgate's; for, as Miss Fowler said, they had no desire to make tea-party talk of them.

'That disposes of *that*,' said Miss Fowler. 'I'll leave the rest to you, Mary. I can't run up and down the garden. You'd better take the big clothes-basket and get Nellie to help you.'

'I shall take the wheelbarrow and do it myself,' said Mary, and for once in her life closed her mouth.

Miss Fowler, in moments of irritation, had called Mary deadly methodical. She put on her oldest waterproof and

gardening-hat and her ever-slipping goloshes, for the weather
was on the edge of more rain. She gathered fire-lighters from
the kitchen, a half-scuttle of coals, and a faggot of brushwood.
These she wheeled in the barrow down the mossed paths to the
dank little laurel shrubbery where the destructor stood under
the drip of three oaks. She climbed the wire fence into the
Rector's glebe just behind, and from his tenant's rick pulled
two large armfuls of good hay, which she spread neatly on
the fire-bars. Next, journey by journey, passing Miss Fowler's
white face at the morning-room window each time, she brought
down in the towel-covered clothes-basket, on the wheelbarrow,
thumbed and used Hentys, Marryats, Levers, Stevensons,
Baroness Orczys, Garvices,[3] schoolbooks, and atlases, unre-
lated piles of the *Motor Cyclist*, the *Light Car*, and catalogues
of Olympia Exhibitions; the remnants of a fleet of sailing-ships
from ninepenny cutters to a three-guinea yacht; a prep-school
dressing-gown; bats from three-and-sixpence to twenty-four
shillings; cricket and tennis balls; disintegrated steam and clock-
work locomotives with their twisted rails; a grey and red tin
model of a submarine; a dumb gramophone and cracked
records; golf-clubs that had to be broken across the knee, like
his walking-sticks, and an assegai;[4] photographs of private and
public-school cricket and football elevens, and his OTC on the
line of march; Kodaks, and film-rolls; some pewters, and one
real silver cup, for boxing competitions and Junior Hurdles;
sheaves of school photographs; Miss Fowler's photograph; her
own which he had borne off in fun and (good care she took not
to ask!) had never returned; a playbox with a secret drawer; a
load of flannels, belts, and jerseys, and a pair of spiked shoes
unearthed in the attic; a packet of all the letters that Miss
Fowler and she had ever written to him, kept for some absurd
reason through all these years; a five-day attempt at a diary;
framed pictures of racing motors in full Brooklands[5] career, and
load upon load of undistinguishable wreckage of tool-boxes,
rabbit-hutches, electric batteries, tin soldiers, fret-saw outfits,
and jig-saw puzzles.

Miss Fowler at the window watched her come and go, and
said to herself, 'Mary's an old woman. I never realized it before.'

After lunch she recommended her to rest.

'I'm not in the least tired,' said Mary. 'I've got it all arranged. I'm going to the village at two o'clock for some paraffin. Nellie hasn't enough, and the walk will do me good.'

She made one last quest round the house before she started, and found that she had overlooked nothing. It began to mist as soon as she had skirted Vegg's Heath, where Wynn used to descend – it seemed to her that she could almost hear the beat of his propellers overhead, but there was nothing to see. She hoisted her umbrella and lunged into the blind wet till she had reached the shelter of the empty village. As she came out of Mr Kidd's shop with a bottle full of paraffin in her string shopping-bag, she met Nurse Eden, the village nurse, and fell into talk with her, as usual, about the village children. They were just parting opposite the Royal Oak, when a gun, they fancied, was fired immediately behind the house. It was followed by a child's shriek dying into a wail.

'Accident!' said Nurse Eden promptly, and dashed through the empty bar, followed by Mary. They found Mrs Gerritt, the publican's wife, who could only gasp and point to the yard, where a little cart-lodge was sliding sideways amid a clatter of tiles. Nurse Eden snatched up a sheet drying before the fire, ran out, lifted something from the ground, and flung the sheet round it. The sheet turned scarlet and half her uniform too, as she bore the load into the kitchen. It was little Edna Gerritt, aged nine, whom Mary had known since her perambulator days.

'Am I hurted bad?' Edna asked, and died between Nurse Eden's dripping hands. The sheet fell aside and for an instant, before she could shut her eyes, Mary saw the ripped and shredded body.

'It's a wonder she spoke at all,' said Nurse Eden. 'What in God's name was it?'

'A bomb,' said Mary.

'One o' the Zeppelins?'

'No. An aeroplane. I thought I heard it on the Heath, but I fancied it was one of ours. It must have shut off its engines as it came down. That's why we didn't notice it.'

'The filthy pigs!' said Nurse Eden, all white and shaken. 'See the pickle I'm in! Go and tell Dr Hennis, Miss Postgate.' Nurse looked at the mother, who had dropped face down on the floor. 'She's only in a fit. Turn her over.'

Mary heaved Mrs Gerritt right side up, and hurried off for the doctor. When she told her tale, he asked her to sit down in the surgery till he got her something.

'But I don't need it, I assure you,' said she. 'I don't think it would be wise to tell Miss Fowler about it, do you? Her heart is so irritable in this weather.'

Dr Hennis looked at her admiringly as he packed up his bag.

'No. Don't tell anybody till we're sure,' he said, and hastened to the Royal Oak, while Mary went on with the paraffin. The village behind her was as quiet as usual, for the news had not yet spread. She frowned a little to herself, her large nostrils expanded uglily, and from time to time she muttered a phrase which Wynn, who never restrained himself before his women-folk, had applied to the enemy. 'Bloody pagans! They *are* bloody pagans. But,' she continued, falling back on the teaching that had made her what she was, 'one mustn't let one's mind dwell on these things.'

Before she reached the house Dr Hennis, who was also a special constable, overtook her in his car.

'Oh, Miss Postgate,' he said, 'I wanted to tell you that that accident at the Royal Oak was due to Gerritt's stable tumbling down. It's been dangerous for a long time. It ought to have been condemned.'

'I thought I heard an explosion too,' said Mary.

'You might have been misled by the beams snapping. I've been looking at 'em. They were dry-rotted through and through. Of course, as they broke, they would make a noise just like a gun.'

'Yes?' said Mary politely.

'Poor little Edna was playing underneath it,' he went on, still holding her with his eyes, 'and that and the tiles cut her to pieces, you see?'

'I saw it,' said Mary, shaking her head. 'I heard it too.'

'Well, we cannot be sure.' Dr Hennis changed his tone completely. 'I know both you and Nurse Eden (I've been speaking to her) are perfectly trustworthy, and I can rely on you not to say anything – yet at least. It is no good to stir up people unless –'

'Oh, I never do – anyhow,' said Mary, and Dr Hennis went on to the county town.

After all, she told herself, it might, just possibly, have been the collapse of the old stable that had done all those things to poor little Edna. She was sorry she had even hinted at other things, but Nurse Eden was discretion itself. By the time she reached home the affair seemed increasingly remote by its very monstrosity. As she came in, Miss Fowler told her that a couple of aeroplanes had passed half an hour ago.

'I thought I heard them,' she replied. 'I'm going down to the garden now. I've got the paraffin.'

'Yes, but – what *have* you got on your boots? They're soaking wet. Change them at once.'

Not only did Mary obey but she wrapped the boots in a newspaper, and put them into the string bag with the bottle. So, armed with the longest kitchen poker, she left.

'It's raining again,' was Miss Fowler's last word, 'but – I know you won't be happy till that's disposed of.'

'It won't take long. I've got everything down there, and I've put the lid on the destructor to keep the wet out.'

The shrubbery was filling with twilight by the time she had completed her arrangements and sprinkled the sacrificial oil. As she lit the match that would burn her heart to ashes, she heard a groan or a grunt behind the dense Portugal laurels.

'Cheape?' she called impatiently, but Cheape, with his ancient lumbago, in his comfortable cottage would be the last man to profane the sanctuary. 'Sheep,' she concluded, and threw in the fusee. The pyre went up in a roar, and the immediate flame hastened night around her.

'How Wynn would have loved this!' she thought, stepping back from the blaze.

By its light she saw, half hidden behind a laurel not five paces away, a bareheaded man sitting very stiffly at the foot of one of the oaks. A broken branch lay across his lap – one booted leg protruding from beneath it. His head moved ceaselessly from side to side, but his body was as still as the tree's trunk. He was dressed – she moved sideways to look more closely – in a uniform something like Wynn's, with a flap buttoned across the chest. For an instant, she had some idea that it might be one of the young flying men she had met at the funeral. But their heads were dark and glossy. This man's was as pale as a baby's, and so closely cropped that she could see the disgusting pinky skin beneath. His lips moved.

'What do you say?' Mary moved towards him and stooped.

'Laty! Laty! Laty!'[6] he muttered, while his hands picked at the dead wet leaves. There was no doubt as to his nationality. It made her so angry that she strode back to the destructor, though it was still too hot to use the poker there. Wynn's books seemed to be catching well. She looked up at the oak behind the man; several of the light upper and two or three rotten lower branches had broken and scattered their rubbish on the shrubbery path. On the lowest fork a helmet with dependent strings, showed like a bird's-nest in the light of a long-tongued flame. Evidently this person had fallen through the tree. Wynn had told her that it was quite possible for people to fall out of aeroplanes. Wynn told her, too, that trees were useful things to break an aviator's fall, but in this case the aviator must have been broken or he would have moved from his queer position. He seemed helpless except for his horrible rolling head. On the other hand, she could see a pistol case at his belt – and Mary loathed pistols. Months ago, after reading certain Belgian reports together, she and Miss Fowler had had dealings with one – a huge revolver with flat-nosed bullets, which latter, Wynn said, were forbidden by the rules of war to be used against civilized enemies. 'They're good enough for us,' Miss Fowler had replied. 'Show Mary how it works.' And Wynn, laughing at the mere possibility of any such need, had led the craven winking Mary into the Rector's disused quarry, and had shown her how to fire the terrible machine. It lay now in the top-left-hand drawer of her toilet-table – a memento not included in the burning. Wynn would be pleased to see how she was not afraid.

She slipped up to the house to get it. When she came through

the rain, the eyes in the head were alive with expectation. The
mouth even tried to smile. But at sight of the revolver its corners
went down just like Edna Gerritt's. A tear trickled from one
eye, and the head rolled from shoulder to shoulder as though
trying to point out something.

'*Cassée. Toute cassée,*'[7] it whimpered.

'What do you say?' said Mary disgustedly, keeping well to
one side, though only the head moved.

'*Cassée,*' it repeated. '*Che me rends.* Le médicin! Toctor!'[8]

'*Nein!*' said she, bringing all her small German to bear with
the big pistol. '*Ich haben der todt Kinder gesehn.*'[9]

The head was still. Mary's hand dropped. She had been
careful to keep her finger off the trigger for fear of accidents.
After a few moments' waiting, she returned to the destructor,
where the flames were falling, and churned up Wynn's charring
books with the poker. Again the head groaned for the doctor.

'Stop that!' said Mary, and stamped her foot. 'Stop that, you
bloody pagan!'

The words came quite smoothly and naturally. They were
Wynn's own words, and Wynn was a gentleman who for no
consideration on earth would have torn little Edna into those
vividly coloured strips and strings. But this thing hunched under
the oak-tree had done that thing. It was no question of reading
horrors out of newspapers to Miss Fowler. Mary had seen it
with her own eyes on the Royal Oak kitchen table. She must
not allow her mind to dwell upon it. Now Wynn was dead, and
everything connected with him was lumping and rustling and
tinkling under her busy poker into red black dust and grey
leaves of ash. The thing beneath the oak would die too. Mary
had seen death more than once. She came of a family that
had a knack of dying under, as she told Miss Fowler, 'most
distressing circumstances'. She would stay where she was till
she was entirely satisfied that It was dead – dead as dear Papa
in the late 'eighties; aunt Mary in 'eighty-nine; Mamma in
'ninety-one; cousin Dick in 'ninety-five; Lady McCausland's
housemaid in 'ninety-nine; Lady McCausland's sister in nineteen hundred and one; Wynn buried five days ago; and Edna
Gerritt still waiting for decent earth to hide her. As she thought

– her underlip caught up by one faded canine, brows knit and nostrils wide – she wielded the poker with lunges that jarred the grating at the bottom, and careful scrapes round the brickwork above. She looked at her wrist-watch. It was getting on to half past four, and the rain was coming down in earnest. Tea would be at five. If It did not die before that time, she would be soaked and would have to change. Meantime, and this occupied her, Wynn's things were burning well in spite of the hissing wet, though now and again a book-back with a quite distinguishable title would be heaved up out of the mass. The exercise of stoking had given her a glow which seemed to reach to the marrow of her bones. She hummed – Mary never had a voice – to herself. She had never believed in all those advanced views – though Miss Fowler herself leaned a little that way – of woman's work in the world; but now she saw there was much to be said for them. This, for instance, was *her* work – work which no man, least of all Dr Hennis, would ever have done. A man, at such a crisis, would be what Wynn called a 'sportsman'; would leave everything to fetch help, and would certainly bring It into the house. Now a woman's business was to make a happy home for – for a husband and children. Failing these – it was not a thing one should allow one's mind to dwell upon – but –

'Stop it!' Mary cried once more across the shadows. '*Nein*, I tell you! *Ich haben der todt Kinder gesehn.*'

*But* it was a fact. A woman who had missed these things could still be useful – more useful than a man in certain respects. She thumped like a paviour through the settling ashes at the secret thrill of it. The rain was damping the fire, but she could feel – it was too dark to see – that her work was done. There was a dull red glow at the bottom of the destructor, not enough to char the wooden lid if she slipped it half over against the driving wet. This arranged, she leaned on the poker and waited, while an increasing rapture laid hold on her. She ceased to think. She gave herself up to feel. Her long pleasure was broken by a sound that she had waited for in agony several times in her life. She leaned forward and listened, smiling. There could be no mistake. She closed her eyes and drank it in. Once it ceased abruptly.

'Go on,' she murmured, half aloud. 'That isn't the end.'

Then the end came very distinctly in a lull between two rain-gusts. Mary Postgate drew her breath short between her teeth and shivered from head to foot. '*That*'s all right,' said she contentedly, and went up to the house, where she scandalized the whole routine by taking a luxurious hot bath before tea, and came down looking, as Miss Fowler said when she saw her lying all relaxed on the other sofa, 'quite handsome'!

# STACY AUMONIER
# THEM OTHERS

It is always disturbing to me when things fall into pattern form, when, in fact, incidents of real life dovetail with each other in such a manner as to suggest the shape of a story. A story is a nice neat little thing with what is called a 'working-up' and a climax, and life is a clumsy, ungraspable thing, very incomplete in its periods, and with a poor sense of climax. In fact, death – which is a very uncertain quantity – is the only definite note it strikes, and even death has an uncomfortable way of setting other things in motion. If, therefore, in telling you about my friend Mrs Ward, I am driven to the usual shifts of the story-teller, you must believe me that it is because this narrative concerns visions: Mrs Ward's visions, my visions, and your visions. Consequently I am dependent upon my own poor powers of transcription to mould these visions into some sort of shape, and am driven into the position of a story-teller against my will.

The first vision, then, concerns the back view of the Sheldrake Road, which, as you know, butts on to the railway embankment near Dalston Junction station. If you are of an adventurous turn of mind you shall accompany me, and we will creep up on to the embankment together and look down into these back yards. (We shall be liable to a fine of £2, according to a bye-law of the Railway Company, for doing so, but the experience will justify us.)

There are twenty-two of these small buff-brick houses huddled together in this road, and there is surely no more certain way of judging not only the character of the individual inhabitants but of their mode of life than by a survey of these

somewhat pathetic yards. Is it not, for instance, easy to determine the timid, well-ordered mind of little Miss Porson, the
dressmaker at number nine, by its garden of neat mud paths,
with its thin patch of meagre grass, and the small bed of skimpy
geraniums? Cannot one read the tragedy of those dreadful
Alleson people at number four? The garden is a wilderness of
filth and broken bottles, where even the weeds seem chary of
establishing themselves. In fact, if we listen carefully – and the
trains are not making too much noise – we can hear the shrill
crescendo of Mrs Alleson's voice cursing at her husband in the
kitchen, the half-empty gin bottle between them.

The methodical pushfulness and practicability of young Mr
and Mrs Andrew MacFarlane is evident at number fourteen.
They have actually grown a patch of potatoes, and some scarlet-
runners, and there is a chicken-run near the house.

Those irresponsible people, the O'Neals, have grown a bed
of hollyhocks, but for the rest the garden is untidy and unkempt.
One could almost swear they were connected in some obscure
way with the theatrical profession.

Mrs Abbot's garden is a sort of playground. It has asphalt
paths, always swarming with small and not too clean children,
and there are five lines of washing suspended above the mud.
Every day seems to be Mrs Abbot's washing day. Perhaps she
'does' for others. Sam Abbot is certainly a lazy, insolent old
rascal, and such always seem destined to be richly fertile. Mrs
Abbot is a pleasant 'body', though.

The Greens are the swells of the road. George Green is in the
grocery line, and both his sons are earning good money, and
one daughter has piano lessons. The narrow strip of yard is
actually divided into two sections, a flower-garden and a
kitchen-garden. And they are the only people who have flower-
boxes in the front.

Number eight is a curious place. Old Mr Bilge lives there. He
spends most of his time in the garden, but nothing ever seems
to come up. He stands about in his shirt-sleeves, and with a
circular paper hat on his head, like a printer. They say he was
formerly a corn merchant, but has lost all his money. He keeps
the garden very neat and tidy, but nothing seems to grow.

He stands there staring at the beds, as though he found their barrenness quite unaccountable.

Number eleven is unoccupied, and number twelve is Mrs Ward's.

We come now to an important vision, and I want you to come down with me from the embankment and to view Mrs Ward's garden from inside, and also Mrs Ward as I saw her on that evening when I had occasion to pay my first visit.

It had been raining, but the sun had come out. We wandered round the paths together, and I can see her old face now, lined and seamed with years of anxious toil and struggle; her long bony arms, slightly withered, but moving restlessly in the direction of snails and slugs.

'Oh dear! Oh dear!' she was saying. 'What with the dogs, and the cats, and the snails, and the trains, it's wonderful anything comes up at all!'

Mrs Ward's garden has a character of its own, and I cannot account for it. There is nothing very special growing – a few pansies and a narrow border of London Pride, several clumps of unrecognizable things that haven't flowered, the grass patch in only fair order, and at the bottom of the garden an unfinished rabbit-hutch. But there is about Mrs Ward's garden an atmosphere. There is something about it that reflects in her placid eye the calm, somewhat contemplative way she has of looking right through things, as though they didn't concern her too closely. As though, in fact, she were too occupied with her own inner visions.

'No,' she says in answer to my query. 'We don't mind the trains at all. In fact, me and my Tom we often come out here and sit after supper. And Tom smokes his pipe. We like to hear the trains go by.'

She gazes abstractedly at the embankment.

'I like to hear things ... going on and that. It's Dalston Junction a little further on. The trains go from there to all parts, right out into the country they do ... ever so far ... My Ernie went from Dalston.'

She adds the last in a changed tone of voice. And now perhaps we come to the most important vision of all – Mrs Ward's vision of 'my Ernie'.

I ought perhaps to mention that I had never met 'my Ernie'.
I can only see him through Mrs Ward's eyes. At the time when I
met her, he had been away at the War for nearly a year. I need
hardly say that 'my Ernie' was a paragon of sons. He was
brilliant, handsome, and incredibly clever. Everything that
'my Ernie' said was treasured. Every opinion that he expressed
stood. If 'my Ernie' liked anyone, that person was always a
welcome guest. If 'my Ernie' disliked anyone they were not to
be tolerated, however plausible they might appear.

I had seen Ernie's photograph, and I must confess that he
appeared a rather weak, extremely ordinary-looking young
man, but then I would rather trust to Mrs Ward's visions than
the art of any photographer.

Tom Ward was a mild, ineffectual-looking old man, with
something of Mrs Ward's placidity but with nothing of her
strong individual poise. He had some job in a gasworks. There
was also a daughter named Lily, a brilliant person who served
in a tea-shop, and sometimes went to theatres with young
men. To both husband and daughter Mrs Ward adopted an
affectionate, mothering, almost pitying attitude. But with 'my
Ernie', it was quite a different thing. I can see her stooping
figure, and her silver-white hair gleaming in the sun as we come
to the unfinished rabbit-hutch, and the curious wistful tones of
her voice as she touches it and says:

'When my Ernie comes home . . .'

The War to her was some unimaginable but disconcerting
affair centred round Ernie. People seemed to have got into some
desperate trouble, and Ernie was the only one capable of getting
them out of it. I could not at that time gauge how much Mrs
Ward realized the dangers the boy was experiencing. She always
spoke with conviction that he would return safely. Nearly every
other sentence contained some reference to things that were
to happen 'when my Ernie comes home'. What doubts and
fears she had were only recognizable by the subtlest shades in
her voice.

When we looked over the wall into the deserted garden next
door, she said:

'Oh dear! I'm afraid they'll never let that place. It's been

empty since the Stellings went away. Oh, years ago, before this
old war.'

It was on the occasion of my second visit that Mrs Ward told
me more about the Stellings. It appeared that they were a
German family, of all things! There was a Mr Stelling, and
a Mrs Frow Stelling, and two boys.

Mr Stelling was a watchmaker, and he came from a place
called Bremen. It was a very sad story, Mrs Ward told me. They
had only been over here for ten months when Mr Stelling died,
and Mrs Frow Stelling and the boys went back to Germany.

During the time of the Stellings' sojourn in the Sheldrake
Road it appeared that the Wards had seen quite a good deal of
them, and though it would be an exaggeration to say that they
ever became great friends, they certainly got through that period
without any unpleasantness, and even developed a certain
degree of intimacy.

'Allowing for their being foreigners,' Mrs Ward explained,
'they were quite pleasant people.'

On one or two occasions they invited each other to supper,
and I wish my visions were sufficiently clear to envisage those
two families indulging this social habit.

According to Mrs Ward, Mr Stelling was a kind little man
with a round fat face. He spoke English fluently, but Mrs Ward
objected to his table manners.

'When my Tom eats,' she said, 'you don't hear a sound –
I look after that! But that Mr Stelling . . . Oh dear!'

The trouble with Mrs Stelling was that she could only speak
a few words of English, but Mrs Ward said 'she was a pleasant
enough little body', and she established herself quite definitely
in Mrs Ward's affections for the reason that she was so obviously and so passionately devoted to her two sons.

'Oh, my word, though, they do have funny ways – these
foreigners,' she continued. 'The things they used to eat! Most
peculiar! I've known them eat stewed prunes with hot meat!'

Mrs Ward repeated, 'Stewed prunes with hot meat!' several
times, and shook her head, as though this exotic mixture was
a thing to be sternly discouraged. But she acknowledged that

Mrs Frow Stelling was in some ways a very good cook; in fact, her cakes were really wonderful, 'the sort of thing you can't ever buy in a shop'.

About the boys there seemed to be a little divergence of opinion. They were both also fat-faced, and their heads were 'almost shaved like convicts'. The elder one wore spectacles and was rather noisy, but 'My Ernie liked the younger one. Oh yes, my Ernie said that young Hans was quite a nice boy. It was funny the way they spoke, funny and difficult to understand.'

It was very patent that between the elder boy and Ernie, who were of about the same age, there was an element of rivalry which was perhaps more accentuated in the attitude of the mothers than in the boys themselves. Mrs Ward could find little virtue in this elder boy. Most of her criticism of the family was levelled against him. The rest she found only a little peculiar. She said she had never heard such a funny Christian name as Frow. Florrie she had heard of, and even Flora, but not *Frow*. I suggested that perhaps Frow might be some sort of title, but she shook her head and said that that was what she was always known as in the Sheldrake Road, 'Mrs Frow Stelling'.

In spite of Mrs Ward's lack of opportunity for greater intimacy on account of the language problem, her own fine imaginative qualities helped her a great deal. And in one particular she seemed curiously vivid. She gathered an account from one of them – I'm not sure whether it was Mr or Mrs Frow Stelling or one of the boys – of a place they described near their home in Bremen. There was a narrow street of high buildings by a canal, and a little bridge that led over into a gentleman's park. At a point where the canal turned sharply eastwards there was a clump of linden-trees, where one could go in the summer-time, and under their shade one might sit and drink light beer, and listen to a band that played in the early part of the evening.

Mrs Ward was curiously clear about that. She said she often thought about Mr Stelling sitting there after his day's work. It must have been very pleasant for him, and he seemed to miss this luxury in Dalston more than anything. Once Ernie, in a friendly mood, had taken him into the four-ale bar of the Unicorn at the corner of the Sheldrake Road, but Mr Stelling did not seem happy. Ernie acknowledged afterwards that it had been an unfortunate evening. The bar had been rather crowded, and there was a man and two women who had all been drinking too much. In any case, Mr Stelling had been obviously restless there, and he had said afterwards:

'It is not that one wishes to drink only . . .'

And he had shaken his fat little head, and had never been known to visit the Unicorn again.

Mr Stelling died quite suddenly of some heart trouble, and Mrs Ward could not get it out of her head that his last illness was brought about by his disappointment and grief in not being able to go and sit quietly under the linden-trees after his day's work and listen to a band.

'You know, my dear,' she said, 'when you get accustomed to a thing it's *bad* for you to leave it off.'

When poor Mr Stelling died, Mrs Frow Stelling was heart-broken, and I have reason to believe that Mrs Ward went in and wept with her, and in their dumb way they forged the chains of some desperate understanding. When Mrs Frow Stelling went back to Germany they promised to write to each other. But they never did, and for a very good reason. As Mrs Ward said, she was 'no scholard', and as for Mrs Frow Stelling, her English was such a doubtful quantity, she probably never got beyond addressing the envelope.

'That was three years ago,' said Mrs Ward. 'Them boys must be eighteen and nineteen now.'

If I had intruded too greatly into the intimacy of Mrs Ward's life, one of my excuses must be, not that I am 'a scholard', but that I am in any case able to read a simple English letter. I was, in fact, on several occasions 'requisitioned'. When Lily was not at home, someone had to read Ernie's letters out loud. The arrival of Ernie's letters was always an inspiring experience. I should perhaps be in the garden with Mrs Ward when Tom would come hurrying out to the back, and call out:

'Mother! a letter from Ernie!'

And then there would be such excitement and commotion. The first thing was always to hunt for Mrs Ward's spectacles.

They were never where she had put them. Tom would keep on turning the letter over in his hands, and examining the postmark, and he would reiterate:

'Well, what did you do with them, Mother?'

At length they would be found in some unlikely place, and she would take the letter tremblingly to the light. I never knew quite how much Mrs Ward could read. She could certainly read a certain amount. I saw her old eyes sparkling and her tongue moving jerkily between her parted lips, as though she were formulating the words she read, and she would keep on repeating:

'T'ch! T'ch! Oh dear, oh dear, the *things* he says!'

And Tom impatiently by the door would say:

'Well, what *does* he say?'

She never attempted to read the letter out loud, but at last she would wipe her spectacles and say:

'Oh, you read it, sir. The *things* he says!'

They were indeed very good letters of Ernie's, written apparently in the highest spirits. There was never a grumble, not a word. One might gather that he was away with a lot of young bloods on some sporting expedition, in which football, rags, sing-songs, and strange feeds played a conspicuous part. I read a good many of Ernie's letters, and I do not remember that he ever made a single reference to the horrors of war, or said anything about his own personal discomforts. The boy must have had something of his mother in him in spite of the photograph.

And between the kitchen and the yard Mrs Ward would spend her day placidly content, for Ernie never failed to write. There was sometimes a lapse of a few days, but the letter seldom failed to come every fortnight.

It would be difficult to know what Mrs Ward's actual conception of the War was. She never read the newspapers, for the reason, as she explained, that 'There was nothing in them these days except about this old war.' She occasionally dived into *Reynolds' Newspaper* on Sundays to see if there were any interesting law cases or any news of a romantic character. There was nothing romantic in the war news. It was all preposterous. She did indeed read the papers for the first few weeks, but this was for the reason that she had some vague idea that they might contain some account of Ernie's doings. But as they did not, she dismissed them with contempt.

But I found her one night in a peculiarly preoccupied mood. She was out in the garden, and she kept staring abstractedly over the fence into the unoccupied ground next door. It appeared that it had dawned upon her that the War was to do with 'these Germans', that in fact we were fighting the Germans, and then she thought of the Stellings. Those boys would now be about eighteen and nineteen. They would be fighting too. They would be fighting against Ernie. This seemed very peculiar.

'Of course,' she said, 'I never took to that elder boy – a greedy, rough sort of a boy he was. But I'm sure my Ernie wouldn't hurt young Hans.'

She meditated for a moment as though she were contemplating what particular action Ernie would take in the matter. She knew he didn't like the elder boy, but she doubted whether he would want to do anything very violent to him.

'They went out to a music-hall one night together,' she explained, as though a friendship cemented in this luxurious fashion could hardly be broken by an unreasonable display of passion.

It was a few weeks later that the terror suddenly crept into Mrs Ward's life. Ernie's letters ceased abruptly. The fortnight passed, then three weeks, four weeks, five weeks, and not a word. I don't think that Mrs Ward's character at any time stood out so vividly as during those weeks of stress. It is true she appeared a little feebler, and she trembled in her movements, whilst her eyes seemed abstracted as though all the power in them were concentrated in her ears, alert for the bell or the knock. She started visibly at odd moments, and her imagination was always carrying her tempestuously to the front door, only to answer – a milkman or a casual hawker. But she never expressed her fear in words. When Tom came home – he seemed to have aged rapidly – he would come bustling into the garden, and cry out tremblingly:

'There ain't been no letter to-day, Mother?'

And she would say quite placidly:

'No, not to-day, Tom. It'll come to-morrow, I expect.'

And she would rally him and talk of little things, and get busy with his supper. And in the garden I would try and talk to her about her clumps of pansies, and the latest yarn about the neighbours, and I tried to get between her and the rabbit-hutch with its dumb appeal of incompletion. And I would notice her staring curiously over into the empty garden next door, as though she were being assailed by some disturbing apprehensions. Ernie would not hurt that eldest boy . . . but suppose . . . if things were reversed . . . There was something inexplicable and terrible lurking in this passive silence.

During this period the old man was suddenly taken very ill. He came home one night with a high temperature and developed pneumonia. He was laid up for many weeks, and she kept back the telegram that came while he was almost unconscious, and she tended him night and day, nursing her own anguish with a calm face.

For the telegram told her that her Ernie was 'missing and believed wounded'.

I do not know at what period she told the father this news, but it was certainly not till he was convalescent. And the old man seemed to sink into a kind of apathy. He sat feebly in front of the kitchen fire, coughing and making no effort to control his grief.

Outside the great trains went rushing by, night and day. Things were 'going on', but they were all meaningless, cruel.

We made inquiries at the War Office, but they could not amplify the laconic telegram.

And then the winter came on, and the gardens were bleak in the Sheldrake Road. And Lily ran away and married a young tobacconist, who was earning twenty-five shillings a week. And old Tom was dismissed from the gasworks. His work was not proving satisfactory. And he sat about at home and moped. And in the meantime the price of foodstuffs was going up, and coals were a luxury. And so in the early morning Mrs Ward would go off and work for Mrs Abbot at the wash-tub, and she would earn eight or twelve shillings a week.

It is difficult to know how they managed during those days,

but one could see that Mrs Ward was buoyed up by some
poignant hope. She would not give way. Eventually old Tom
did get some work to do at a stationer's. The work was comparatively light, and the pay equally so, so Mrs Ward still
continued to work for Mrs Abbot.

My next vision of Mrs Ward concerns a certain winter
evening. I could not see inside the kitchen, but the old man
could be heard complaining. His querulous voice was rambling
on, and Mrs Ward was standing by the door leading into the
garden. She had returned from her day's work and was scraping
a pan out into a bin near the door. A train shrieked by, and the
wind was blowing a fine rain against the house. Suddenly she
stood up and looked at the sky; then she pushed back her hair
from her brow and frowned at the dark house next door. Then
she turned and said:

'Oh, I don't know, Tom; if we've got to do it, we *must* do it.
If them others can stand it, we can stand it. Whatever them
others do, we can do.'

And then my visions jump rather wildly. And the War becomes to me epitomized in two women. One in this dim doorway in our obscure suburb of Dalston, scraping out a pan,
and the other perhaps in some dark high house near a canal
on the outskirts of Bremen. Them others! These two women
silently enduring. And the trains rushing by, and all the dark,
mysterious forces of the night operating on them equivocally.

Poor Mrs Frow Stelling! Perhaps those boys of hers are 'missing, believed killed'. Perhaps they are killed for certain. She is
as much outside 'the things going on' as Mrs Ward. Perhaps
she is equally as patient, as brave.

And Mrs Ward enters the kitchen, and her eyes are blazing
with a strange light as she says:

'We'll hear to-morrow, Tom. And if we don't hear to-
morrow, we'll hear the next day. And if we don't hear the next
day, we'll hear the day after. And if we don't . . . if we don't
never hear . . . again . . . if them others can stand it, we can
stand it, I say.'

And then her voice breaks, and she cries a little, for endurance
has its limitations, and – the work is hard at Mrs Abbot's.

And the months go by, and she stoops a little more as she walks, and – someone has thrown a cloth over the rabbit-hutch with its unfinished roof. And Mrs Ward is curiously introspective. It is useless to tell her of the things of the active world. She listens politely but she does not hear. She is full of reminiscences of Ernie's and Lily's childhood. She recounts again and again the story of how Ernie when he was a little boy ordered five tons of coal from a coal merchant to be sent to a girls' school in Dalston High Road. She describes the coal carts arriving in the morning, and the consternation of the head-mistress.

'Oh dear, oh dear,' she says; 'the things he did!'

She does not talk much of the Stellings, but one day she says meditatively:

'Mrs Frow Stelling thought a lot of that boy Hans. So she did of the other, as far as that goes. It's only natural like, I suppose.'

As time went on Tom Ward lost all hope. He said he was convinced that the boy was killed. Having arrived at this conclusion he seemed to become more composed. He gradually began to accustom himself to the new point of view. But with Mrs Ward the exact opposite was the case.

She was convinced that the boy was alive, but she suffered terribly.

There came a time – it was in early April – when one felt that the strain could not last. She seemed to lose all interest in the passing world and lived entirely within herself. Even the arrival of Lily's baby did not rouse her. She looked at the child queerly, as though she doubted whether any useful or happy purpose was served by its appearance.

It was a boy.

In spite of her averred optimism she lost her tremulous sense of apprehension when the bell went or the front door was tapped. She let the milkman – and even the postman – wait.

When she spoke it was invariably of things that happened years ago.

Sometimes she talked about the Stellings, and one Sunday she made a strange pilgrimage out to Finchley and visited Mr

Stelling's grave. I don't know what she did there, but she returned looking very exhausted and unwell. As a matter of fact she was unwell for some days after this visit, and she suffered violent twinges of rheumatism in her legs.

I now come to my most unforgettable vision of Mrs Ward.

It was a day at the end of April, and warm for the time of the year. I was standing in the garden with her and it was nearly dark. A goods train had been shunting, and making a great deal of noise in front of the house, and at last had disappeared. I had not been able to help noticing that Mrs Ward's garden was curiously neglected for her for the time of year. The grass was growing on the paths, and the snails had left their silver trail over all the fences.

I was telling her a rumour I had heard about the railway porter and his wife at number twenty-three, and she seemed fairly interested, for she had known John Hemsley, the porter, fifteen years ago, when Ernie was a baby. There were two old broken Windsor chairs in the garden, and on one was a zinc basin in which were some potatoes. She was peeling them, as Lily and her husband were coming to supper. By the kitchen door was a small sink. When she had finished the potatoes, she stood up and began to pour the water down the sink, taking care not to let the skins go too. I was noticing her old bent back, and her long bony hands gripping the sides of the basin, when suddenly a figure came limping round the bend of the house from the side passage, and two arms were thrown around her waist, and a voice said:

'Mind them skins don't go down the sink, Mother. They'll stop it up!'

As I explained to Ernie afterwards, it was an extremely foolish thing to do. If his mother had had anything wrong with her heart, it might have been very serious. There have been many cases of people dying from the shock of such an experience.

As it was, she merely dropped the basin and stood there trembling like a leaf, and Ernie laughed loud and uproariously. It must have been three or four minutes before she could regain her speech, and then all she could manage to say was:

'Ernie! . . . My Ernie!'

And the boy laughed and ragged his mother, and pulled her into the house, and Tom appeared and stared at his son, and said feebly:

'Well, I never!'

I don't know how it was that I found myself intruding upon the sanctity of the inner life of the Ward family that evening. I had never had a meal there before, but I felt I was holding a sort of watching brief over the soul and body of Mrs Ward. I had had a little medical training in my early youth, and this may have been one of the reasons which prompted me to stay.

When Lily and her husband appeared we sat down to a meal of mashed potatoes and onions stewed in milk, with bread and cheese, and very excellent it was.

Lily and her husband took the whole thing in a boisterous, high comedy manner that fitted in with the mood of Ernie. Old Tom sat there staring at his son, and repeating at intervals:

'Well, I never!'

And Mrs Ward hovered round the boy's plate. Her eyes divided their time between his plate and his face, and she hardly spoke all the evening.

Ernie's story was remarkable enough. He told it disconnectedly and rather incoherently. There were moments when he rambled in a rather peculiar way, and sometimes he stammered, and seemed unable to frame a sentence. Lily's husband went out to fetch some beer to celebrate the joyful occasion, and Ernie drank his in little sips, and spluttered. The boy must have suffered considerably, and he had a wound in the abdomen, and another in the right forearm which for a time had paralysed him.

As far as I could gather, his story was this:

He and a platoon of men had been ambushed and had had to surrender. When being sent back to a base, three of them tried to escape from the train, which had been held up at night. He did not know what had happened to the other two men, but it was on this occasion that he received his abdominal wound at the hands of a guard.

He had then been sent to some infirmary, where he was fairly well treated; but as soon as his wound had healed a little, he had been suddenly sent to some fortress prison, presumably as a punishment. He hadn't the faintest idea how long he had been confined there. He said it seemed like fifteen years. It was probably nine months. He had solitary confinement in a cell, which was like a small lavatory. He had fifteen minutes' exercise every day in a yard with some other prisoners, who were Russians, he thought. He spoke to no one. He used to sing and recite in his cell, and there were times when he was quite convinced that he was 'off his chump'. He said he had lost 'all sense of everything' when he was suddenly transferred to another prison. Here the conditions were somewhat better and he was made to work. He said he wrote six or seven letters home from there, but received no reply. The letters certainly never reached Dalston. The food was execrable, but a big improvement on the dungeon. He was only there a few weeks when he and some thirty prisoners were sent suddenly to work on the land at a kind of settlement. He said that the life there would have been tolerable if it hadn't been for the fact that the Commandant was an absolute brute. The food was worse than in the prison, and they were punished severely for the most trivial offences.

It was here, however, that he met a sailor named Martin, a Royal Naval Reservist, an elderly, thick-set man with a black beard and only one eye. Ernie said that this Martin 'was an artist. He wangled everything. He had a genius for getting what he wanted. He would get a beef-steak out of a stone.' In fact, it was obvious that the whole of Ernie's narrative was coloured by his vision of Martin. He said he'd never met such a chap in his life. He admired him enormously, and he was also a little afraid of him.

By some miraculous means peculiar to sailors, Martin acquired a compass. Ernie hardly knew what a compass was, but the sailor explained to him that it was all that was necessary to take you straight to England. Ernie said he 'had had enough of escaping. It didn't agree with his health,' but so strong was his faith and belief in Martin that he ultimately agreed to try with him.

He said Martin's method of escape was the coolest thing he'd ever seen. He planned it all beforehand. It was the fag-end of the day, and the whistle had gone, and the prisoners were trooping back across a potato field. Martin and Ernie were very slow. They lingered apparently to discuss some matter connected with the soil. There were two sentries in sight, one near them and the other perhaps a hundred yards away. The potato field was on a slope; at the bottom of the field were two lines of barbed-wire entanglements. The other prisoners passed out of sight, and the sentry near them called out something, probably telling them to hurry up. They started to go up the field when suddenly Martin staggered and clutched his throat. Then he fell over backwards and commenced to have an epileptic fit. Ernie said it was the realest thing he'd ever seen. The sentry ran up, at the same time whistling to his comrade. Ernie released Martin's collar-band and tried to help him. Both the sentries approached, and Ernie stood back. He saw them bending over the prostrate man, when suddenly a most extraordinary thing happened. Both their heads were brought together with fearful violence. One fell completely senseless, but the other staggered forward and groped for his rifle.

When Ernie told this part of the story he kept dabbing his forehead with his handkerchief.

'I never seen such a man as Martin, I don't think,' he said. 'Lord! he had a fist like a leg of mutton. He laid 'em out neatly on the grass, took off their coats and most of their other clothes, and flung 'em over the barbed wire, and then swarmed over like a cat. I had more difficulty, but he got me across too, somehow. Then we carted the clothes away to the next line.

'We got up into a wood that night, and Martin draws out his compass and he says: "We've got a hundred and seven miles to do in night shifts, cully. And if we make a slip we're shot as safe as a knife." It sounded the maddest scheme in the world, but somehow I felt that Martin would get through it. The only thing that saved me was that – that I didn't have to think. I simply left everything to him. If I'd started thinking I should have gone mad. I had it fixed in my mind, "Either he does it or he doesn't do it. I can't help it." I reelly don't remember much

about that journey. It was all a dream like. We did all our
travellin' at night by compass, and hid by day. Neither of us
had a word of German. But Gawd's truth! that man Martin
was a marvel! He turned our trousers inside out, and made 'em
look like ordinary labourers' trousers. He disappeared the first
night and came back with some other old clothes. We lived
mostly on raw potatoes we dug out of the ground with our
hands, but not always. I believe Martin could have stole an egg
from under a hen without her noticing it. He was the coolest
card there ever was. Of course there was a lot of trouble one
way and another. It wasn't always easy to find wooded country
or protection of any sort. We often ran into people and they
stared at us, and we shifted our course. But I think we were
only addressed three or four times by men, and then Martin's
methods were the simplest in the world. He just looked sort of
blank for a moment, and then knocked them clean out and
bolted. Of course they were after us all the time, and it was this
constant tacking and shifting ground that took so long. Fancy!
he had never a map, you know, nothing but the compass. We
didn't know what sort of country we were coming to, nothing.
We just crept through the night like cats. I believe Martin could
see in the dark . . . He killed a dog one night with his hands . . .
It was necessary.'

It was impossible to discover from Ernie how long this amazing
journey lasted – the best part of two months, I believe. He was
himself a little uncertain with regard to many incidents, whether
they were true or whether they were hallucinations. He suffered
greatly from his wound and had periods of feverishness. But
one morning, he said, Martin began 'prancing'. He seemed to
develop some curious sense that they were near the Dutch
frontier. And then, according to Ernie, 'a cat wasn't in it with
Martin'.

He was very mysterious about the actual crossing. I gather
that there had been some 'clumsy' work with sentries. It was at
that time that Ernie got a bullet through his arm. When he got
to Holland he was very ill. It was not that the wound was a
serious one, but, as he explained:

'Me blood was in a bad state. I was nearly down and out.'

He was very kindly treated by some Dutch Sisters in a convent hospital. But he was delirious for a long time, and when he became more normal they wanted to communicate with his people in England, but this didn't appeal to the dramatic sense of Ernie.

'I thought I'd spring a surprise packet on you,' he said, grinning.

We asked about Martin, but Ernie said he never saw him again. He went away while Ernie was delirious, and they said he had gone to Rotterdam to take ship somewhere. He thought Holland was a dull place.

During the relation of this narrative my attention was divided between watching the face of Ernie and the face of Ernie's mother.

I am quite convinced that she did not listen to the story at all. She never took her eyes from his face, and although her tongue was following the flow of his remarks, her mind was occupied with the vision of Ernie when he was a little boy, and when he ordered five tons of coal to be sent to the girls' school.

When he had finished, she said:

'Did you meet either of them young Stellings?'

And Ernie laughed rather uproariously and said no, he didn't have the pleasure of renewing their acquaintance.

On his way home, it appeared, he had reported himself at Headquarters, and his discharge was inevitable.

'So now you'll be able to finish the rabbit-hutch,' said Lily's husband, and we all laughed again, with the exception of Mrs Ward.

I found her later standing alone in the garden. It was a warm spring night. There was no moon, but the sky appeared restless with its burden of trembling stars. She had an old shawl drawn round her shoulders, and she stood there very silently with her arms crossed.

'Well, this is splendid news, Mrs Ward,' I said.

She started a little, and coughed, and pulled the shawl closer round her.

She said, 'Yes, sir,' very faintly.

I don't think she was very conscious of me. She still appeared immersed in the contemplation of her inner visions. Her eyes settled upon the empty house next door, and I thought I detected the trail of a tear glistening on her cheeks. I lighted my pipe. We could hear Ernie, and Lily, and Lily's husband still laughing and talking inside.

'She used to make a very good puddin',' Mrs Ward said suddenly, at random. 'Dried fruit inside, and that. My Ernie liked it very much . . .'

Somewhere away in the distance – probably outside the Unicorn – someone was playing a cornet. A train crashed by and disappeared, leaving a trail of foul smoke which obscured the sky. The smoke cleared slowly away. I struck another match to light my pipe.

It was quite true. On either side of her cheek a tear had trickled. She was trembling a little, worn out by the emotions of the evening.

There was a moment of silence, unusual for Dalston.

'It's all very . . . perplexin' and that,' she said quietly.

And then I knew for certain that in that great hour of her happiness her mind was assailed by strange and tremulous doubts. She was thinking of 'them others' a little wistfully. She was doubting whether one could rejoice – when the thing became clear and actual to one – without sending out one's thoughts into the dark garden to 'them others' who were suffering too. And she had come out into this little meagre yard at Dalston, and had gazed through the mist and smoke upwards to the stars, because she wanted peace intensely, and so she sought it within herself, because she knew that real peace is a thing which concerns the heart alone.

And so I left her standing there, and I went my way, for I knew that she was wiser than I.

# JOHN GALSWORTHY
# TOLD BY THE
# SCHOOLMASTER

We all remember still, I suppose, the singular beauty of the summer when the war broke out. I was then schoolmaster in a village on the Thames. Nearly fifty, with a game shoulder and extremely deficient sight, there was no question of my fitness for military service, and this, as with many other sensitive people, induced in me, I suppose, a mood abnormally receptive. The perfect weather, that glowing countryside, with corn harvest just beginning and the apples already ripening, the quiet nights trembling with moonlight and shadow and, in it all, this great horror launched and growing, the weazening of Europe deliberately undertaken, the death-warrant of millions of young men signed – Such summer loveliness walking hand in hand with murder thus magnified beyond conception was too piercingly ironical!

One of those evenings, towards the end of August, when the news of Mons was coming through, I left my house at the end of the village street and walked up towards the downs. I have never known anything more entrancing than the beauty of that night. All was still and coloured like the bloom of dark grapes; so warm, so tremulous. A rush of stars was yielding to the moon fast riding up, and from the corn-stooks of that early harvest the shadows were stealing out. We had no daylight-saving then, and it was perhaps half past nine when I passed two of my former scholars, a boy and a girl, standing silently at the edge of an old gravel pit opposite a beech clump. They looked up and gave me good evening. Passing on over the crest, I could see the unhedged fields to either hand; the corn stooked and the corn standing, just gilded under the moon; the swelling downs of a blue-grey; and the beech clump I had passed dark-cut against the brightening sky. The moon itself was almost golden, as if it would be warm to the touch, and from it came a rain of glamour over sky and fields, woods, downs, farmhouses and the river down below. All seemed in a conspiracy of unreality to one obsessed, like me, by visions of the stark and trampling carnage going on out there. Refuging from that grim comparison, I remember thinking that Jim Beckett and Betty Roofe were absurdly young to be sweethearting, if indeed they were, for they hadn't altogether looked like it. They could hardly be sixteen yet, for they had only left school last year. Betty Roofe had been head of the girls; an interesting child, alert, self-contained, with a well-shaped, dark-eyed little face and a head set on very straight. She was the daughter of the village laundress, and I used to think too good for washing clothes, but she was already at it and, as things went in that village, would probably go on doing it till she married. Jim Beckett was working on Carver's farm down there below me and the gravel pit was about half-way between their homes. A good boy, Jim, freckled, reddish in the hair and rather too small in the head; with blue eyes that looked at you very straight, and a short nose; a well-grown boy, very big for his age, and impulsive in spite of the careful stodginess of all young rustics; a curious vein of the sensitive in him, but a great deal of obstinacy, too – altogether an interesting blend!

I was still standing there when up he came on his way to Carver's and I look back to that next moment with as much regret as to any in my life.

He held out his hand.

'Good-bye, sir, in case I don't see you again.'

'Why, where are you off to, Jim?'

'Joinin' up.'

'Joining up? But, my dear boy, you're two years under age, at least.'

He grinned. 'I'm sixteen this month, but I bet I can make out to be eighteen. They ain't particular, I'm told.'

I looked him up and down. It was true, he could pass for eighteen well enough, with military needs what they were. And possessed, as everyone was just then, by patriotism and anxiety at the news, all I said was:

'I don't think you ought, Jim; but I admire your spirit.'

He stood there silent, sheepish at my words. Then:

'Well, good-bye, sir. I'm goin' to —ford to-morrow.'

I gave his hand a good hard squeeze. He grinned again, and without looking back, ran off down the hill towards Carver's farm, leaving me alone once more with the unearthly glamour of that night. God! what a crime was war! From this hushed moonlit peace boys were hurrying off to that business of man-made death as if there were not Nature's deaths galore to fight against. And we – we could only admire them for it! Well! I have never ceased to curse the sentiment which stopped me from informing the recruiting authorities of that boy's real age.

Crossing back over the crest of the hill towards home I came on the child Betty, at the edge of the gravel pit where I had left her.

'Well, Betty, was Jim telling you?'

'Yes, sir; he's going to join up.'

'What did you say to him?'

'I said he was a fool, but he's so headstrong, Jim!' Her voice was even enough, but she was quivering all over.

'It's very plucky of him, Betty.'

'M'm! Jim just gets things into his head. I don't see that he has any call to go and – and leave me.'

I couldn't help a smile. She saw it, and said sullenly:

'Yes, I'm young, and so's Jim; but he's my boy, for all that!'

And then, ashamed or startled at such expansiveness, she tossed her head, swerved into the beech clump like a shying foal, and ran off among the trees. I stood a few minutes, listening to the owls, then went home and read myself into forgetfulness on Scott's first Polar book.[1]

So Jim went and we knew him no more for a whole year. And Betty continued with her mother washing for the village.

In September, 1915, just after term had begun again, I was standing one afternoon in the village schoolroom pinning up on the wall a pictorial piece of imperial information for the benefit of my scholars, and thinking, as usual, of the war, and its lingering deadlock.[2] The sunlight slanted through on to my dusty forms and desks, and under the pollard lime-trees on the far side of the street I could see a soldier standing with a girl. Suddenly he crossed over to the school, and there in the doorway was young Jim Beckett in his absurd short-tailed khaki jacket, square and tanned to the colour of his freckles, looking, indeed, quite a man.

'How d'you do, sir?'

'And you, Jim?'

'Oh, I'm fine! I thought I'd like to see you. Just got our marching orders. Off to France tomorrow; been havin' my leave.'

I felt the catch at my throat that we all felt when youngsters whom we knew were going out for the first time.

'Was that Betty with you out there?'

'Yes – fact is, I've got something to tell you, sir. She and I were spliced last week at —mouth. We been stayin' there since, and I brought her home to-day, as I got to go to-night.'

I was staring hard, and he went on hurriedly:

'She just went off there and I joined her for my leave. We didn't want any fuss, you see, because of our bein' too young.'

'Young!'

The blankness of my tone took the grin off his face.

'Well, I was seventeen a week ago and she'll be seventeen next month.'

'Married? Honest Injun, Jim?'

He went to the door and whistled. In came Betty, dressed in dark blue, very neat and self-contained; only the flush on her round young face marked any disturbance.

'Show him your lines, Betty, and your ring.'

The girl held out the official slip and from it I read that a registrar had married them at —mouth, under right names and wrong ages.

Then she slipped a glove off and held up her left hand – there was the magic hoop! Well! the folly was committed; no use in crabbing it!

'Very good of you to tell me, Jim,' I said at last. 'Am I the first to know?'

'Yes, sir. You see, I've got to go at once, and like as not her mother won't want it to get about till she's a bit older. I thought I'd like to tell *you*, in case they said it wasn't all straight and proper.'

'Nothing I say will alter the fact that you've falsified your ages.'

Jim grinned again.

'That's all right,' he said. 'I got it from a lawyer's clerk in my platoon. It's a marriage all the same.'

'Yes; I believe that's so.'

'Well, sir, there she is till I come back.' Suddenly his face changed; he looked for all the world as if he were going to cry; and they stood gazing at each other exactly as if they were alone.

The lodger at the carpenter's, three doors down the street, was performing her usual afternoon solo on the piano, '*Connais-tu le pays?*' from *Mignon*.³ And whenever I hear it now, seldom enough in days contemptuous of harmony, it brings Jim and Betty back through a broad sunbeam full of dancing motes of dust; it epitomizes for me all the *Drang* –⁴ as the Germans call it – of those horrible years, when marriage, birth, death and every human activity were speeded up to their limit, and we did from year's end to year's end all that an enlightened humanity should not be doing, and left undone most of what it should have done.

'What time is it, sir?' Jim asked me suddenly.

'Five o'clock.'

'Lord! I must run for it. My kit's at the station. Could I leave her here, sir?'

I nodded and walked into the little room beyond. When I came back she was sitting where she used to sit in school, bowed over her arms spread out on the inky desk. Her dark bobbed hair was all I could see, and the quivering jerky movement of her young shoulders. Jim had gone. Well! That was the normal state of Europe, then! I went back into the little room to give her time, but when I returned once more she, too, had gone.

The second winter passed, more muddy, more bloody even than the first, and less shot through with hopes of an ending. Betty showed me three or four of Jim's letters, simple screeds with a phrase here and there of awkward and half-smothered feeling, and signed always 'Your loving hubby, Jim'. Her marriage was accepted in the village. Child-marriage was quite common then. In April it began to be obvious that their union was to be 'blessed', as they call it.

One day early in May I was passing Mrs Roofe's when I saw that lady in her patch of garden, and stopped to ask after Betty.

'Nearin' her time. I've written to Jim Beckett. Happen he'll get leave.'

'I think that was a mistake, Mrs Roofe. I would have waited till it was over.'

'Maybe you're right, sir; but Betty's that fidgety about him not knowin'. She's dreadful young, you know, t' 'ave a child. I didn't 'ave my first till I was twenty-one.'

'Everything goes fast these days, Mrs Roofe.'

'Not my washin'. I can't get the help, with Betty like this. It's a sad business this about the baby comin'. If he does get killed I suppose she'll get a pension, sir?'

Pension? Married in the wrong age, with the boy still under service age, if they came to look into it. I really didn't know.

'Oh, surely, Mrs Roofe! But we won't think about his being killed. Jim's a fine boy.'

Mrs Roofe's worn face darkened.

'He was a fool to join up before his time; plenty of chance after, seemingly; and then to marry my girl like this! Well, young folk *are* fools!'

I was sitting over my Pensions work one evening, a month later, for it had now fallen to me to keep things listed in the village, when someone knocked at my door, and who should be standing there but Jim Beckett!

'Why! Jim! Got leave?'

'Ah! I had to come and see her. I haven't been there yet; didn' dare. How is she, sir?'

Pale and dusty, as if from a hard journey, his uniform all muddy and unbrushed, and his reddish hair standing up any-how – he looked wretched, poor boy!

'She's all right, Jim. But it must be very near, from what her mother says.'

'I haven't had any sleep for nights, thinking of her – such a kid, she is!'

'Does she know you're coming?'

'No, I haven't said nothing.'

'Better be careful. I wouldn't risk a shock. Have you any-where to sleep?'

'No, sir.'

'Well, you can stay here if you like. They won't have room for you there.' He seemed to back away from me.

'Thank ye, sir. I wouldn' like to put you out.'

'Not a bit, Jim; delighted to have you and hear your adventures.'

He shook his head. 'I don't want to talk of them,' he said darkly. 'Don't you think I could see 'er to-night, sir? I've come a long way for it, my God! I have!'

'Well, try! But see her mother first.'

'Yes, sir,' and he touched his forehead. His face, so young a face, already had that look in the eyes of men who stare death down.

He went away and I didn't see him again that night. They had managed, apparently, to screw him into their tiny cottage. He was only just in time, for two days later Betty had a boy-child. He came to me the same evening, after dark, very excited.

'She's a wonder,' he said; 'but if I'd known I'd never ha' done it, sir, I never would. You can't tell what you're doing till it's too late, it seems.'

Strange saying from that young father, till afterwards it was made too clear!

Betty recovered quickly and was out within three weeks.

Jim seemed to have long leave, for he was still about, but I had little talk with him, for, though always friendly, he seemed shy of me, and as to talking of the war – not a word! One evening I passed him and Betty leaning on a gate, close to the river – a warm evening of early July, when the Somme battle was at its height. Out there hell incarnate; and here intense peace, the quietly flowing river, the willows, and unstirring aspens, the light slowly dying, and those two young things, with their arms round each other and their heads close together – her bobbed dark hair and Jim's reddish mop, getting quite long! I took good care not to disturb them. His last night, perhaps, before he went back into the furnace!

It was no business of mine to have my doubts, but I had been having them long before that very dreadful night when, just as I was going to bed, something rattled on my window, and going down I found Betty outside, distracted.

'Oh, sir, come quick! They've 'rested Jim.'

As we went over she told me:

'Oh, sir, I was afraid there was some mistake about his leave – it was so long; I thought he'd get into trouble over it, so I asked Bill Pateman' – (the village constable) – 'and now they've come and 'rested him for deserting. Oh! What have I done? What have I done?'

Outside the Roofes' cottage Jim was standing between a corporal's guard, and Betty flung herself into his arms. Inside I could hear Mrs Roofe expostulating with the corporal, and the baby crying. In the sleeping quiet of the village street, smelling of hay just harvested, it was atrocious.

I spoke to Jim. He answered quietly, in her arms:

'I asked for leave, but they wouldn't give it. I had to come. I couldn't stick it, knowing how it was with her.'

'Where was your regiment?'

'In the line.'

'Good God!'

Just then the corporal came out. I took him apart.

'I was his schoolmaster, Corporal,' I said. 'The poor chap joined up when he was just sixteen – he's still under age, you see; and now he's got this child-wife and a newborn baby!'

The corporal nodded; his face was twitching, a lined, decent face with a moustache.

'I know, sir,' he muttered. 'I know. Cruel work, but I've got to take him. He'll have to go back to France.'

'What does it mean?'

He lifted his arms from his sides and let them drop, and that gesture was somehow the most expressive and dreadful I ever saw.

'Deserting in face of the enemy,' he whispered hoarsely. 'Bad business! Can you get that girl away, sir?'

But Jim himself undid the grip of her arms and held her from him. Bending, he kissed her hair and face, then, with a groan, he literally pushed her into my arms and marched straight off between the guard.

And I was left in the dark, sweet-scented street with that distracted child struggling in my grasp.

'Oh, my God! My God! My God!' Over and over and over. And what could one say or do?

All the rest of that night, after Mrs Roofe had got Betty back into the cottage, I sat up writing in duplicate the facts about Jim Beckett. I sent one copy to his regimental headquarters, the other to the chaplain of his regiment in France. I sent fresh copies two days later with duplicates of his birth certificates to make quite sure. It was all I could do. Then came a fortnight of waiting for news. Betty was still distracted. The thought that, through her anxiety, she herself had delivered him into their hands nearly sent her off her head. Probably her baby alone kept her from insanity, or suicide. And all that time the battle of the Somme raged and hundreds of thousands of women in England and France and Germany were in daily terror for their menfolk. Yet none, I think, could have had quite the feeling of that child. Her mother, poor woman, would come over to me at the schoolhouse and ask if I had heard anything.

'Better for the poor girl to know the worst,' she said, 'if it is the worst. The anxiety's killin' 'er.'

But I had no news and could not get any at Headquarters. The thing was being dealt with in France. Never was the scale and pitch of the world's horror more brought home to me. This deadly little tragedy was as nothing – just a fragment of straw whirling round in that terrible wind.

And then one day I did get news – a letter from the chaplain – and seeing what it was I stuck it in my pocket and sneaked down to the river – literally afraid to open it till I was alone.

Crouched up there, with my back to a haystack, I took it out with trembling fingers.

DEAR SIR,
The boy Jim Beckett was shot to-day at dawn. I am distressed at having to tell you and the poor child his wife. War is a cruel thing indeed.

I had known it. Poor Jim! Poor Betty! Poor, poor Betty! I read on:

I did all I could; the facts you sent were put before the Court Martial and the point of his age considered. But all leave had been stopped; his request had been definitely refused; the regiment was actually in the line, with fighting going on – and the situation extremely critical in that sector. Private considerations count for nothing in such circumstances – the rule is adamant. Perhaps it has to be – I cannot say. But I have been greatly distressed by the whole thing, and the Court itself was much moved. The poor boy seemed dazed; he wouldn't talk; didn't seem to take in anything; indeed, they tell me that all he said after the verdict, certainly all I heard him say, was: 'My poor wife! My poor wife!' over and over again. He stood up well at the end.

He stood up well at the end! I can see him yet, poor impulsive Jim. Desertion, but not cowardice, by the Lord! No one who looked into those straight, blue eyes could believe that. But they bandaged them, I suppose. Well! a bullet in a billet more or less; what was it in that wholesale slaughter? As a raindrop on a willow tree drips into the river and away to sea – so that boy, like a million others, dripped to dust. A little ironical though, that his own side should shoot him, who went to fight for them two years before he need, to shoot him who wouldn't be legal food for powder for another month! A little ironical, perhaps, that he had left this son – legacy to such an implacable world! But there's no moral to a true tale like this – unless it be that the rhythm of life and death cares not a jot for any of us!

# D. H. LAWRENCE
# TICKETS, PLEASE

There is in the Midlands a single-line tramway system which boldly leaves the county town and plunges off into the black, industrial countryside, up hill and down dale, through the long ugly villages of workmen's houses, over canals and railways, past churches perched high and nobly over the smoke and shadows, through stark, grimy cold little market-places, tilting away in a rush past cinemas and shops down to the hollow where the collieries are, then up again, past a little rural church, under the ash trees, on in a rush to the terminus, the last little ugly place of industry, the cold little town that shivers on the edge of the wild, gloomy country beyond. There the green and creamy-coloured tram-car seems to pause and purr with curious satisfaction. But in a few minutes – the clock on the turret of the Co-operative Wholesale Society's Shops gives the time – away it starts once more on the adventure. Again there are the reckless swoops downhill, bouncing the loops: again the chilly wait in the hill-top market-place: again the breathless slithering round the precipitous drop under the church: again the patient halts at the loops, waiting for the outcoming car: so on and on, for two long hours, till at last the city looms beyond the fat gasworks, the narrow factories draw near, we are in the sordid streets of the great town, once more we sidle to a standstill at our terminus, abashed by the great crimson and cream-coloured city cars, but still perky, jaunty, somewhat dare-devil, green as a jaunty sprig of parsley out of a black colliery garden.

To ride on these cars is always an adventure. Since we are in war-time, the drivers are men unfit for active service: cripples and hunchbacks. So they have the spirit of the devil in them. The ride becomes a steeple-chase. Hurray! we have leaped in a clear jump over the canal bridges – now for the four-lane corner. With a shriek and a trail of sparks we are clear again. To be sure, a tram often leaps the rails – but what matter! It sits in a ditch till other trams come to haul it out. It is quite common for a car, packed with one solid mass of living people, to come to a dead halt in the midst of unbroken blackness, the heart of nowhere on a dark night, and for the driver and the girl con-ductor to call, 'All get off – car's on fire!' Instead, however, of rushing out in a panic, the passengers stolidly reply: 'Get on – get on! We're not coming out. We're stopping where we are. Push on, George.' So till flames actually appear.

The reason for this reluctance to dismount is that the nights are howlingly cold, black, and windswept, and a car is a haven of refuge. From village to village the miners travel, for a change of cinema, of girl, of pub. The trams are desperately packed. Who is going to risk himself in the black gulf outside, to wait perhaps an hour for another tram, then to see the forlorn notice 'Depôt Only,' because there is something wrong! Or to greet a unit of three bright cars all so tight with people that they sail past with a howl of derision. Trams that pass in the night.

This, the most dangerous tram-service in England, as the authorities themselves declare, with pride, is entirely conducted by girls, and driven by rash young men, a little crippled, or by delicate young men, who creep forward in terror. The girls are fearless young hussies. In their ugly blue uniform, skirts up to their knees, shapeless old peaked caps on their heads, they have all the *sang-froid* of an old non-commissioned officer. With a tram packed with howling colliers, roaring hymns downstairs and a sort of antiphony of obscenities upstairs, the lasses are perfectly at their ease. They pounce on the youths who try to evade their ticket-machine. They push off the men at the end of their distance. They are not going to be done in the eye – not they. They fear nobody – and everybody fears them.

'Hello, Annie!'

'Hello, Ted!'

'Oh, mind my corn, Miss Stone. It's my belief you've got a heart of stone, for you've trod on it again.'

'You should keep it in your pocket,' replies Miss Stone, and she goes sturdily upstairs in her high boots.

'Tickets, please.'

She is peremptory, suspicious, and ready to hit first. She can hold her own against ten thousand. The step of that tram-car is her Thermopylae.[1]

Therefore, there is a certain wild romance aboard these cars – and in the sturdy bosom of Annie herself. The time for soft romance is in the morning, between ten o'clock and one, when things are rather slack: that is, except market-day and Saturday. Thus Annie has time to look about her. Then she often hops off her car and into a shop where she has spied something, while the driver chats in the main road. There is very good feeling between the girls and the drivers. Are they not companions in peril, shipments aboard this careering vessel of a tram-car, for ever rocking on the waves of a stormy land?

Then, also, during the easy hours, the inspectors are most in evidence. For some reason, everybody employed in this tram-service is young: there are no grey heads. It would not do. Therefore the inspectors are of the right age, and one, the chief, is also good-looking. See him stand on a wet, gloomy morning, in his long oil-skin, his peaked cap well down over his eyes, waiting to board a car. His face is ruddy, his small brown moustache is weathered, he has a faint impudent smile. Fairly tall and agile, even in his waterproof, he springs aboard a car and greets Annie.

'Hello, Annie! Keeping the wet out?'

'Trying to.'

There are only two people in the car. Inspecting is soon over. Then for a long and impudent chat on the foot-board, a good, easy, twelve-mile chat.

The inspector's name is John Thomas Raynor – always called John Thomas, except sometimes, in malice, Coddy.[2] His face sets in fury when he is addressed, from a distance, with this abbreviation. There is considerable scandal about John Thomas in half a dozen villages. He flirts with the girl conductors in the morning, and walks out with them in the dark night, when they leave their tram-car at the depôt. Of course, the girls quit the service frequently. Then he flirts and walks out with the newcomer: always providing she is sufficiently attractive, and that she will consent to walk. It is remarkable, however, that most of the girls are quite comely, they are all young, and this roving life aboard the car gives them a sailor's dash and recklessness. What matter how they behave when the ship is in port? Tomorrow they will be aboard again.

Annie, however, was something of a Tartar, and her sharp tongue had kept John Thomas at arm's length for many months. Perhaps, therefore, she liked him all the more: for he always came up smiling, with impudence. She watched him vanquish one girl, then another. She could tell by the movement of his mouth and eyes, when he flirted with her in the morning, that he had been walking out with this lass, or the other, the night before. A fine cock-of-the-walk he was. She could sum him up pretty well.

In this subtle antagonism they knew each other like old friends, they were as shrewd with one another almost as man and wife. But Annie had always kept him sufficiently at arm's length. Besides, she had a boy of her own.

The Statutes fair,[3] however, came in November, at Bestwood. It happened that Annie had the Monday night off. It was a drizzling ugly night, yet she dressed herself up and went to the fair-ground. She was alone, but she expected soon to find a pal of some sort.

The roundabouts were veering round and grinding out their music, the side shows were making as much commotion as possible. In the cocoanut shies there were no cocoanuts, but artificial war-time substitutes, which the lads declared were fastened into the irons. There was a sad decline in brilliance and luxury. None the less, the ground was muddy as ever, there was the same crush, the press of faces lighted up by the flares and the electric lights, the same smell of naphtha and a few fried potatoes, and of electricity.

Who should be the first to greet Miss Annie on the show-ground but John Thomas. He had a black overcoat buttoned up to his chin, and a tweed cap pulled down over his brows, his face between was ruddy and smiling and handy as ever. She knew so well the way his mouth moved.

She was very glad to have a 'boy'. To be at the Statutes without a fellow was no fun. Instantly, like the gallant he was, he took her on the Dragons, grim-toothed, round-about switchbacks. It was not nearly so exciting as a tram-car actually. But, then, to be seated in a shaking, green dragon, uplifted above the sea of bubble faces, careering in a rickety fashion in the lower heavens, whilst John Thomas leaned over her, his cigarette in his mouth, was after all the right style. She was a plump, quick, alive little creature. So she was quite excited and happy.

John Thomas made her stay on for the next round. And therefore she could hardly for shame repulse him when he put his arm round her and drew her a little nearer to him, in a very warm and cuddly manner. Besides, he was fairly discreet, he kept his movement as hidden as possible. She looked down, and saw that his red, clean hand was out of sight of the crowd. And they knew each other so well. So they warmed up to the fair.

After the dragons they went on the horses. John Thomas paid each time, so she could but be complaisant. He, of course, sat astride on the outer horse – named Black Bess – and she sat sideways, towards him, on the inner horse – named Wildfire. But of course John Thomas was not going to sit discreetly on Black Bess, holding the brass bar. Round they spun and heaved, in the light. And round he swung on his wooden steed, flinging one leg across her mount, and perilously tipping up and down, across the space, half lying back, laughing at her. He was perfectly happy; she was afraid her hat was on one side, but she was excited.

He threw quoits on a table, and won for her two large, pale-blue hat-pins. And then, hearing the noise of the cinemas, announcing another performance, they climbed the boards and went in.

Of course, during these performances pitch darkness falls from time to time, when the machine goes wrong. Then there is a wild whooping, and a loud smacking of simulated kisses. In these moments John Thomas drew Annie towards him. After all, he had a wonderfully warm, cosy way of holding a girl with his arm, he seemed to make such a nice fit. And, after all, it was pleasant to be so held: so very comforting and cosy and nice. He leaned over her and she felt his breath on her hair; she knew he wanted to kiss her on the lips. And, after all, he was so warm and she fitted in to him so softly. After all, she wanted him to touch her lips.

But the light sprang up; she also started electrically, and put her hat straight. He left his arm lying nonchalantly behind her. Well, it was fun, it was exciting to be at the Statutes with John Thomas.

When the cinema was over they went for a walk across the dark, damp fields. He had all the arts of love-making. He was especially good at holding a girl, when he sat with her on a stile in the black, drizzling darkness. He seemed to be holding her in space, against his own warmth and gratification. And his kisses were soft and slow and searching.

So Annie walked out with John Thomas, though she kept her own boy dangling in the distance. Some of the tram-girls chose to be huffy. But there, you must take things as you find them, in this life.

There was no mistake about it, Annie liked John Thomas a good deal. She felt so rich and warm in herself whenever he was near. And John Thomas really liked Annie, more than usual. The soft, melting way in which she could flow into a fellow, as if she melted into his very bones, was something rare and good. He fully appreciated this.

But with a developing acquaintance there began a developing intimacy. Annie wanted to consider him a person, a man; she wanted to take an intelligent interest in him, and to have an intelligent response. She did not want a mere nocturnal presence, which was what he was so far. And she prided herself that he could not leave her.

Here she made a mistake. John Thomas intended to remain a nocturnal presence; he had no idea of becoming an all-round individual to her. When she started to take an intelligent interest

in him and his life and his character, he sheered off. He hated
intelligent interest. And he knew that the only way to stop it
was to avoid it. The possessive female was aroused in Annie.
So he left her.

It is no use saying she was not surprised. She was at first
startled, thrown out of her count. For she had been so *very* sure
of holding him. For a while she was staggered, and everything
became uncertain to her. Then she wept with fury, indignation,
desolation, and misery. Then she had a spasm of despair. And
then, when he came, still impudently, on to her car, still
familiar, but letting her see by the movement of his head that
he had gone away to somebody else for the time being, and
was enjoying pastures new, then she determined to have her
own back.

She had a very shrewd idea what girls John Thomas had
taken out. She went to Nora Purdy. Nora was a tall, rather
pale, but well-built girl, with beautiful yellow hair. She was
rather secretive.

'Hey!' said Annie, accosting her; then softly, 'Who's John
Thomas on with now?'

'I don't know,' said Nora.

'Why tha does,' said Annie, ironically lapsing into dialect.
'Tha knows as well as I do.'

'Well, I do, then,' said Nora. 'It isn't me, so don't bother.'

'It's Cissy Meakin, isn't it?'

'It is, for all I know.'

'Hasn't he got a face on him!' said Annie. 'I don't half like
his cheek. I could knock him off the foot-board when he comes
round at me.'

'He'll get dropped-on one of these days,' said Nora.

'Aye, he will, when somebody makes up their mind to drop
it on him. I should like to see him taken down a peg or two,
shouldn't you?'

'I shouldn't mind,' said Nora.

'You've got quite as much cause to as I have,' said Annie.
'But we'll drop on him one of these days, my girl. What? Don't
you want to?'

'I don't mind,' said Nora.

But as a matter of fact, Nora was much more vindictive than Annie.

One by one Annie went the round of the old flames. It so happened that Cissy Meakin left the tramway service in quite a short time. Her mother made her leave. Then John Thomas was on the *qui-vive*.[4] He cast his eyes over his old flock. And his eyes lighted on Annie. He thought she would be safe now. Besides, he liked her.

She arranged to walk home with him on Sunday night. It so happened that her car would be in the depôt at half past nine: the last car would come in at 10.15. So John Thomas was to wait for her there.

At the depôt the girls had a little waiting-room of their own. It was quite rough, but cosy, with a fire and an oven and a mirror, and table and wooden chairs. The half-dozen girls who knew John Thomas only too well had arranged to take service this Sunday afternoon. So, as the cars began to come in, early, the girls dropped into the waiting-room. And instead of hurrying off home, they sat around the fire and had a cup of tea. Outside was the darkness and lawlessness of war-time.

John Thomas came on the car after Annie, at about a quarter to ten. He poked his head easily into the girls' waiting-room.

'Prayer-meeting?' he asked.

'Aye,' said Laura Sharp. 'Ladies only.'

'That's me!' said John Thomas. It was one of his favourite exclamations.

'Shut the door, boy,' said Muriel Baggaley.

'On which side of me?' said John Thomas.

'Which tha likes,' said Polly Birkin.

He had come in and closed the door behind him. The girls moved in their circle, to make a place for him near the fire. He took off his great-coat and pushed back his hat.

'Who handles the teapot?' he said.

Nora Purdy silently poured him out a cup of tea.

'Want a bit o' my bread and drippin'?' said Muriel Baggaley to him.

'Aye, give us a bit.'

And he began to eat his piece of bread.

'There's no place like home, girls,' he said.

They all looked at him as he uttered this piece of impudence. He seemed to be sunning himself in the presence of so many damsels.

'Especially if you're not afraid to go home in the dark,' said Laura Sharp.

'Me! By myself I am.'

They sat till they heard the last tram come in. In a few minutes Emma Houselay entered.

'Come on, my old duck!' cried Polly Birkin.

'It *is* perishing,' said Emma, holding her fingers to the fire.

'"But – I'm afraid to, go home in, the dark,"'[5] sang Laura Sharp, the tune having got into her mind.

'Who're you going with to-night, John Thomas?' asked Muriel Baggaley, coolly.

'To-night?' said John Thomas. 'Oh, I'm going home by myself to-night – all on my lonely-O.'

'That's me!' said Nora Purdy, using his own ejaculation.

The girls laughed shrilly.

'Me as well, Nora,' said John Thomas.

'Don't know what you mean,' said Laura.

'Yes, I'm toddling,' said he, rising and reaching for his overcoat.

'Nay,' said Polly. 'We're all here waiting for you.'

'We've got to be up in good time in the morning,' he said, in the benevolent official manner.

They all laughed.

'Nay,' said Muriel. 'Don't leave us all lonely, John Thomas. Take one!'

'I'll take the lot, if you like,' he responded gallantly.

'That you won't, either,' said Muriel. 'Two's company; seven's too much of a good thing.'

'Nay – take one,' said Laura. 'Fair and square, all above board, and say which.'

'Aye,' cried Annie, speaking for the first time. 'Pick, John Thomas; let's hear thee.'

'Nay,' he said. 'I'm going home quiet to-night. Feeling good, for once.'

'Whereabouts?' said Annie. 'Take a good 'un, then. But tha's got to take one of us!'

'Nay, how can I take one?' he said, laughing uneasily. 'I don't want to make enemies.'

'You'd only make *one*,' said Annie.

'The chosen *one*,' added Laura.

'Oh, my! Who said girls!' exclaimed John Thomas, again turning, as if to escape. 'Well – good-night.'

'Nay, you've got to make your pick,' said Muriel. 'Turn your face to the wall, and say which one touches you. Go on – we shall only just touch your back – one of us. Go on – turn your face to the wall, and don't look, and say which one touches you.'

He was uneasy, mistrusting them. Yet he had not the courage to break away. They pushed him to a wall and stood him there with his face to it. Behind his back they all grimaced, tittering. He looked so comical. He looked around uneasily.

'Go on!' he cried.

'You're looking – you're looking!' they shouted.

He turned his head away. And suddenly, with a movement like a swift cat, Annie went forward and fetched him a box on the side of the head that sent his cap flying and himself staggering. He started round.

But at Annie's signal they all flew at him, slapping him, pinching him, pulling his hair, though more in fun than in spite or anger. He, however, saw red. His blue eyes flamed with strange fear as well as fury, and he butted through the girls to the door. It was locked. He wrenched at it. Roused, alert, the girls stood round and looked at him. He faced them, at bay. At that moment they were rather horrifying to him, as they stood in their short uniforms. He was distinctly afraid.

'Come on, John Thomas! Come on! Choose!' said Annie.

'What are you after? Open the door,' he said.

'We shan't – not till you've chosen!' said Muriel.

'Chosen what?' he said.

'Chosen the one you're going to marry,' she replied.

He hesitated a moment.

'Open the blasted door,' he said, 'and get back to your senses.' He spoke with official authority.

'You've got to choose!' cried the girls.

'Come on!' cried Annie, looking him in the eye. 'Come on! Come on!'

He went forward, rather vaguely. She had taken off her belt, and swinging it, she fetched him a sharp blow over the head with the buckle end. He sprang and seized her. But immediately the other girls rushed upon him, pulling and tearing and beating him. Their blood was now thoroughly up. He was their sport now. They were going to have their own back, out of him. Strange, wild creatures, they hung on him and rushed at him to bear him down. His tunic was torn right up the back, Nora had hold at the back of his collar, and was actually strangling him. Luckily the button burst. He struggled in a wild frenzy of fury and terror, almost mad terror. His tunic was simply torn off his back, his shirt-sleeves were torn away, his arms were naked. The girls rushed at him, clenched their hands on him and pulled at him: or they rushed at him and pushed him, butted him with all their might: or they struck him wild blows. He ducked and cringed and struck sideways. They became more intense.

At last he was down. They rushed on him, kneeling on him. He had neither breath nor strength to move. His face was bleeding with a long scratch, his brow was bruised.

Annie knelt on him, the other girls knelt and hung on to him. Their faces were flushed, their hair wild, their eyes were all glittering strangely. He lay at last quite still, with face averted, as an animal lies when it is defeated and at the mercy of the captor. Sometimes his eye glanced back at the wild faces of the girls. His breast rose heavily, his wrists were torn.

'Now, then, my fellow!' gasped Annie at length. 'Now then – now –'

At the sound of her terrifying, cold triumph, he suddenly started to struggle as an animal might, but the girls threw themselves upon him with unnatural strength and power, forcing him down.

'Yes – now, then!' gasped Annie at length.

And there was a dead silence, in which the thud of heart-beating was to be heard. It was a suspense of pure silence in every soul.

'Now you know where you are,' said Annie.

The sight of his white, bare arm maddened the girls. He lay in a kind of trance of fear and antagonism. They felt themselves filled with supernatural strength.

Suddenly Polly started to laugh – to giggle wildly – helplessly – and Emma and Muriel joined in. But Annie and Nora and Laura remained the same, tense, watchful, with gleaming eyes. He winced away from these eyes.

'Yes,' said Annie, in a curious low tone, secret and deadly. 'Yes! You've got it now! You know what you've done, don't you? You know what you've done.'

He made no sound nor sign, but lay with bright, averted eyes, and averted, bleeding face.

'You ought to be *killed*, that's what you ought,' said Annie, tensely. 'You ought to be *killed*.' And there was a terrifying lust in her voice.

Polly was ceasing to laugh, and giving long-drawn Oh-h-hs and sighs as she came to herself.

'He's got to choose,' she said vaguely.

'Oh, yes, he has,' said Laura, with vindictive decision.

'Do you hear – do you hear?' said Annie. And with a sharp movement, that made him wince, she turned his face to her.

'Do you hear?' she repeated, shaking him.

But he was quite dumb. She fetched him a sharp slap on the face. He started, and his eyes widened. Then his face darkened with defiance, after all.

'Do you hear?' she repeated.

He only looked at her with hostile eyes.

'Speak!' she said, putting her face devilishly near his.

'What?' he said, almost overcome.

'You've got to *choose*!' she cried, as if it were some terrible menace, and as if it hurt her that she could not exact more.

'What?' he said, in fear.

'Choose your girl, Coddy. You've got to choose her now. And you'll get your neck broken if you play any more of your tricks, my boy. You're settled now.'

There was a pause. Again he averted his face. He was cunning in his overthrow. He did not give in to them really – no, not if they tore him to bits.

'All right, then,' he said, 'I choose Annie.' His voice was strange and full of malice. Annie let go of him as if he had been a hot coal.

'He's chosen Annie!' said the girls in chorus.

'Me!' cried Annie. She was still kneeling, but away from him. He was still lying prostrate, with averted face. The girls grouped uneasily around.

'Me!' repeated Annie, with a terrible bitter accent.

Then she got up, drawing away from him with strange disgust and bitterness.

'I wouldn't touch him,' she said.

But her face quivered with a kind of agony, she seemed as if she would fall. The other girls turned aside. He remained lying on the floor, with his torn clothes and bleeding, averted face.

'Oh, if he's chosen –' said Polly.

'I don't want him – he can choose again,' said Annie, with the same rather bitter hopelessness.

'Get up,' said Polly, lifting his shoulder. 'Get up.'

He rose slowly, a strange, ragged, dazed creature. The girls eyed him from a distance, curiously, furtively, dangerously.

'Who wants him?' cried Laura, roughly.

'Nobody,' they answered, with contempt. Yet each one of them waited for him to look at her, hoped he would look at her. All except Annie, and something was broken in her.

He, however, kept his face closed and averted from them all. There was a silence of the end. He picked up the torn pieces of his tunic, without knowing what to do with them. The girls stood about uneasily, flushed, panting, tidying their hair and their dress unconsciously, and watching him. He looked at none of them. He espied his cap in a corner, and went and picked it up. He put it on his head, and one of the girls burst into a shrill, hysteric laugh at the sight he presented. He, however, took no heed, but went straight to where his overcoat hung on a peg. The girls moved away from contact with him as if he had been an electric wire. He put on his coat and buttoned it down. Then he rolled his tunic-rags into a bundle, and stood before the locked door, dumbly.

'Open the door, somebody,' said Laura.

'Annie's got the key,' said one.

Annie silently offered the key to the girls. Nora unlocked the door.

'Tit for tat, old man,' she said. 'Show yourself a man, and don't bear a grudge.'

But without a word or sign he had opened the door and gone, his face closed, his head dropped.

'That'll learn him,' said Laura.

'Coddy!' said Nora.

'Shut up, for God's sake!' cried Annie fiercely, as if in torture.

'Well, I'm about ready to go, Polly. Look sharp!' said Muriel.

The girls were all anxious to be off. They were tidying themselves hurriedly, with mute, stupefied faces.

# RADCLYFFE HALL
# MISS OGILVY
# FINDS HERSELF

Miss Ogilvy stood on the quay at Calais and surveyed the disbanding of her Unit, the Unit that together with the coming of war had completely altered the complexion of her life, at all events for three years.

Miss Ogilvy's thin, pale lips were set sternly and her forehead was puckered in an effort of attention, in an effort to memorize every small detail of every old war-weary battered motor on whose side still appeared the merciful emblem that had set Miss Ogilvy free.

Miss Ogilvy's mind was jerking a little, trying to regain its accustomed balance, trying to readjust itself quickly to this sudden and paralysing change. Her tall, awkward body with its queer look of strength, its broad, flat bosom and thick legs and ankles, as though in response to her jerking mind, moved uneasily, rocking backwards and forwards. She had this trick of rocking on her feet in moments of controlled agitation. As usual, her hands were thrust deep into her pockets, they seldom seemed to come out of her pockets unless it were to light a cigarette, and as though she were still standing firm under fire while the wounded were placed in her ambulances, she suddenly straddled her legs very slightly and lifted her head and listened. She was standing firm under fire at that moment, the fire of a desperate regret.

Some girls came towards her, young, tired-looking creatures whose eyes were too bright from long strain and excitement. They had all been members of that glorious Unit, and they still wore the queer little forage-caps and the short, clumsy tunics of the French Militaire. They still slouched in walking and smoked Caporals[1] in emulation of the Poilus. Like their founder and leader these girls were all English, but like her they had chosen to serve England's ally, fearlessly thrusting right up to the trenches in search of the wounded and dying. They had seen some fine things in the course of three years, not the least fine of which was the cold, hard-faced woman who commanding, domineering, even hectoring at times, had yet been possessed of so dauntless a courage and of so insistent a vitality that it vitalized the whole Unit.

'It's rotten!' Miss Ogilvy heard someone saying. 'It's rotten, this breaking up of our Unit!' And the high, rather childish voice of the speaker sounded perilously near to tears.

Miss Ogilvy looked at the girl almost gently, and it seemed, for a moment, as though some deep feeling were about to find expression in words. But Miss Ogilvy's feelings had been held in abeyance so long that they seldom dared become vocal, so she merely said, 'Oh?' on a rising inflection – her method of checking emotion.

They were swinging the ambulance cars in mid-air, those of them that were destined to go back to England, swinging them up like sacks of potatoes, then lowering them with much clanging of chains to the deck of the waiting steamer. The porters were shoving and shouting and quarrelling, pausing now and again to make meaningless gestures; while a pompous official was becoming quite angry as he pointed at Miss Ogilvy's own special car – it annoyed him, it was bulky and difficult to move.

'*Bon Dieu! Mais dépêchez-vous donc!*'[2] he bawled, as though he were bullying the motor.

Then Miss Ogilvy's heart gave a sudden, thick thud to see this undignified, pitiful ending; and she turned and patted the gallant old car as though she were patting a well-beloved horse, as though she would say: 'Yes, I know how it feels – never mind, we'll go down together.'

Miss Ogilvy sat in the railway carriage on her way from Dover to London. The soft English landscape sped smoothly past: small homesteads, small churches, small pastures, small lanes with small hedges; all small like England itself, all small like

Miss Ogilvy's future. And sitting there still arrayed in her tunic, with her forage-cap resting on her knees, she was conscious of a sense of complete frustration; thinking less of those glorious years at the Front and of all that had gone to the making of her, than of all that had gone to the marring of her from the days of her earliest childhood.

She saw herself as a queer little girl, aggressive and awkward because of her shyness; a queer little girl who loathed sisters and dolls, preferring the stable-boys as companions, preferring to play with footballs and tops, and occasional catapults. She saw herself climbing the tallest beech trees, arrayed in old breeches illicitly come by. She remembered insisting with tears and some temper that her real name was William and not Wilhelmina. All these childish pretences and illusions she remembered, and the bitterness that came after. For Miss Ogilvy had found as her life went on that in this world it is better to be one with the herd, that the world has no wish to understand those who cannot conform to its stereotyped pattern. True enough in her youth she had gloried in her strength, lifting weights, swinging clubs and developing muscles, but presently this had grown irksome to her; it had seemed to lead nowhere, she being a woman, and then as her mother had often protested: muscles looked so appalling in evening dress – a young girl ought not to have muscles.

Miss Ogilvy's relation to the opposite sex was unusual and at that time added much to her worries, for no less than three men had wished to propose, to the genuine amazement of the world and her mother. Miss Ogilvy's instinct made her like and trust men for whom she had a pronounced fellow-feeling; she would always have chosen them as her friends and companions in preference to girls or women; she would dearly have loved to share in their sports, their business, their ideals and their wide-flung interests. But men had not wanted her, except the three who had found in her strangeness a definite attraction, and those would-be suitors she had actually feared, regarding them with aversion. Towards young girls and women she was shy and respectful, apologetic and sometimes admiring. But their fads and their foibles, none of which she could share, while amusing her very often in secret, set her outside the sphere of their intimate lives, so that in the end she must blaze a lone trail through the difficulties of her nature.

'I can't understand you,' her mother had said, 'you're a very odd creature – now when I was your age . . .'

And her daughter had nodded, feeling sympathetic. There were two younger girls who also gave trouble, though in their case the trouble was fighting for husbands who were scarce enough even in those days. It was finally decided, at Miss Ogilvy's request, to allow her to leave the field clear for her sisters. She would remain in the country with her father when the others went up for the Season.

Followed long, uneventful years spent in sport, while Sarah and Fanny toiled, sweated and gambled in the matrimonial market. Neither ever succeeded in netting a husband, and when the Squire died leaving very little money, Miss Ogilvy found to her great surprise that they looked upon her as a brother. They had so often jibed at her in the past, that at first she could scarcely believe her senses, but before very long it became all too real: she it was who must straighten out endless muddles, who must make the dreary arrangements for the move, who must find a cheap but genteel house in London and, once there, who must cope with the family accounts which she only, it seemed, could balance.

It would be: 'You might see to that, Wilhelmina; you write, you've got such a good head for business.' Or: 'I wish you'd go down and explain to that man that we really can't pay his account till next quarter.' Or: 'This money for the grocer is five shillings short. Do run over my sum, Wilhelmina.'

Her mother, grown feeble, discovered in this daughter a staff upon which she could lean with safety. Miss Ogilvy genuinely loved her mother, and was therefore quite prepared to be leaned on; but when Sarah and Fanny began to lean too with the full weight of endless neurotic symptoms incubated in resentful virginity, Miss Ogilvy found herself staggering a little. For Sarah and Fanny were grown hard to bear, with their mania for telling their symptoms to doctors, with their unstable nerves and their acrid tongues and the secret dislike they now felt for their mother. Indeed, when old Mrs Ogilvy died, she was unmourned except by her eldest daughter who actually felt a void in her life – the unforeseen void that the ailing and weak will not infrequently leave behind them.

At about this time an aunt also died, bequeathing her fortune to her niece Wilhelmina who, however, was too weary to gird up her loins and set forth in search of exciting adventure – all she did was to move her protesting sisters to a little estate she had purchased in Surrey. This experiment was only a partial success, for Miss Ogilvy failed to make friends of her neighbours; thus at fifty-five she had grown rather dour, as is often the way with shy, lonely people.

When the war came she had just begun settling down – people do settle down in their fifty-sixth year – she was feeling quite glad that her hair was grey, that the garden took up so much of her time, that, in fact, the beat of her blood was slowing. But all this was changed when war was declared; on that day Miss Ogilvy's pulses throbbed wildly.

'My God! If only I were a man!' she burst out, as she glared at Sarah and Fanny, 'if only I had been born a man!' Something in her was feeling deeply defrauded.

Sarah and Fanny were soon knitting socks and mittens and mufflers and Jaeger trench-helmets.[3] Other ladies were busily working at depots, making swabs at the Squire's, or splints at the Parson's; but Miss Ogilvy scowled and did none of these things – she was not at all like other ladies.

For nearly twelve months she worried officials with a view to getting a job out in France – not in their way but in hers, and that was the trouble. She wished to go up to the front-line trenches, she wished to be actually under fire, she informed the harassed officials.

To all her inquiries she received the same answer: 'We regret that we cannot accept your offer.' But once thoroughly roused she was hard to subdue, for her shyness had left her as though by magic.

Sarah and Fanny shrugged angular shoulders: 'There's plenty of work here at home,' they remarked, 'though of course it's not quite so melodramatic!'

'Oh . . . ?' queried their sister, on a rising note of impatience – and she promptly cut off her hair: 'That'll jar them!' she thought with satisfaction.

Then she went up to London, formed her admirable Unit and finally got it accepted by the French, despite renewed opposition.

In London she had found herself quite at her ease, for many another of her kind was in London doing excellent work for the nation. It was really surprising how many cropped heads had suddenly appeared as it were out of space; how many Miss Ogilvys, losing their shyness, had come forward asserting their right to serve, asserting their claim to attention.

There followed those turbulent years at the Front, full of courage and hardship and high endeavour; and during those years Miss Ogilvy forgot the bad joke that Nature seemed to have played her. She was given the rank of a French lieutenant and she lived in a kind of blissful illusion; appalling reality lay on all sides and yet she managed to live in illusion. She was competent, fearless, devoted and untiring. What then? Could any man hope to do better? She was nearly fifty-eight, yet she walked with a stride, and at times she even swaggered a little.

Poor Miss Ogilvy sitting so glumly in the train with her manly trench-boots and her forage-cap! Poor all the Miss Ogilvys back from the war with their tunics, their trench-boots, and their childish illusions! Wars come and wars go but the world does not change: it will always forget an indebtedness which it thinks it expedient not to remember.

When Miss Ogilvy returned to her home in Surrey it was only to find that her sisters were ailing from the usual imaginary causes, and this to a woman who had seen the real thing was intolerable, so that she looked with distaste at Sarah and then at Fanny. Fanny was certainly not prepossessing, she was suffering from a spurious attack of hay fever.

'Stop sneezing!' commanded Miss Ogilvy, in the voice that had so much impressed the Unit. But as Fanny was not in the least impressed, she naturally went on sneezing.

Miss Ogilvy's desk was piled mountain-high with endless

tiresome letters and papers: circulars, bills, months-old correspondence, the gardener's accounts, an agent's report on some
fields that required land-draining. She seated herself before this
collection; then she sighed, it all seemed so absurdly trivial.

'Will you let your hair grow again?' Fanny inquired . . . she
and Sarah had followed her into the study. 'I'm certain the
Vicar would be glad if you did.'

'Oh?' murmured Miss Ogilvy, rather too blandly.

'Wilhelmina!'

'Yes?'

'You will do it, won't you?'

'Do what?'

'Let your hair grow; we all wish you would.'

'Why should I?'

'Oh, well, it will look less odd, especially now that the war
is over – in a small place like this people notice such things.'

'I entirely agree with Fanny,' announced Sarah.

Sarah had become very self-assertive, no doubt through
having mismanaged the estate during the years of her sister's
absence. They had quite a heated dispute one morning over the
south herbaceous border.

'Whose garden is this?' Miss Ogilvy asked sharply. 'I insist
on auricula-eyed sweet-williams! I even took the trouble to
write from France, but it seems that my letter has been ignored.'

'Don't shout,' rebuked Sarah, 'you're not in France now!'

Miss Ogilvy could gladly have boxed her ears: 'I only wish
to God I were,' she muttered.

Another dispute followed close on its heels, and this time it
happened to be over the dinner. Sarah and Fanny were living
on weeds – at least that was the way Miss Ogilvy put it.

'We've become vegetarians,' Sarah said grandly.

'You've become two damn tiresome cranks!' snapped their
sister.

Now it never had been Miss Ogilvy's way to indulge in acid
recriminations, but somehow, these days, she forgot to say:
'Oh?' quite so often as expediency demanded. It may have been
Fanny's perpetual sneezing that had got on her nerves; or it
may have been Sarah, or the gardener, or the Vicar, or even the

canary; though it really did not matter very much what it was just so long as she found a convenient peg upon which to hang her growing irritation.

'This won't do at all,' Miss Ogilvy thought sternly, 'life's not worth so much fuss, I must pull myself together.' But it seemed this was easier said than done; not a day passed without her losing her temper and that over some trifle: 'No, this won't do at all – it just mustn't be,' she thought sternly.

Everyone pitied Sarah and Fanny: 'Such a dreadful, violent old thing,' said the neighbours.

But Sarah and Fanny had their revenge: 'Poor darling, it's shell-shock, you know,' they murmured.

Thus Miss Ogilvy's prowess was whittled away until she herself was beginning to doubt it. Had she ever been that courageous person who had faced death in France with such perfect composure? Had she ever stood tranquilly under fire, without turning a hair, while she issued her orders? Had she ever been treated with marked respect? She herself was beginning to doubt it.

Sometimes she would see an old member of the Unit, a girl who, more faithful to her than the others, would take the trouble to run down to Surrey. These visits, however, were seldom enlivening.

'Oh, well . . . here we are . . .' Miss Ogilvy would mutter.

But one day the girl smiled and shook her blonde head: 'I'm not – I'm going to be married.'

Strange thoughts had come to Miss Ogilvy, unbidden, thoughts that had stayed for many an hour after the girl's departure. Alone in her study she had suddenly shivered, feeling a sense of complete desolation. With cold hands she had lighted a cigarette.

'I must be ill or something,' she had mused, as she stared at her trembling fingers.

After this she would sometimes cry out in her sleep, living over in dreams God knows what emotions; returning, maybe, to the battlefields of France. Her hair turned snow-white; it was not unbecoming yet she fretted about it.

'I'm growing very old,' she would sigh as she brushed her thick mop before the glass; and then she would peer at her wrinkles.

For now that it had happened she hated being old; it no longer appeared such an easy solution of those difficulties that had always beset her. And this she resented most bitterly, so that she became the prey of self-pity, and of other undesirable states in which the body will torment the mind, and the mind, in its turn, the body. Then Miss Ogilvy straightened her ageing back, in spite of the fact that of late it had ached with muscular rheumatism, and she faced herself squarely and came to a resolve.

'I'm off!' she announced abruptly one day; and that evening she packed her kit-bag.

Near the south coast of Devon there exists a small island that is still very little known to the world, but which, nevertheless, can boast an hotel; the only building upon it. Miss Ogilvy had chosen this place quite at random, it was marked on her map by scarcely more than a dot, but somehow she had liked the look of that dot and had set forth alone to explore it.

She found herself standing on the mainland one morning looking at a vague blur of green through the mist, a vague blur of green that rose out of the Channel like a tidal wave suddenly suspended. Miss Ogilvy was filled with a sense of adventure; she had not felt like this since the ending of the war.

'I was right to come here, very right indeed. I'm going to shake off all my troubles,' she decided.

A fisherman's boat was parting the mist, and before it was properly beached, in she bundled.

'I hope they're expecting me?' she said gaily.

'They du be expecting you,' the man answered.

The sea, which is generally rough off that coast, was indulging itself in an oily ground-swell; the broad, glossy swells struck the side of the boat, then broke and sprayed over Miss Ogilvy's ankles.

The fisherman grinned: 'Feeling all right?' he queried. 'It du be tiresome most times about these parts.' But the mist had suddenly drifted away and Miss Ogilvy was staring wide-eyed at the island.

She saw a long shoal of jagged black rocks, and between them the curve of a small sloping beach, and above that the lift of the island itself, and above that again, blue heaven. Near the beach stood the little two-storeyed hotel which was thatched, and built entirely of timber; for the rest she could make out no signs of life apart from a host of white seagulls.

Then Miss Ogilvy said a curious thing. She said: 'On the south-west side of that place there was once a cave – a very large cave. I remember that it was some way from the sea.'

'There du be a cave still,' the fisherman told her, 'but it's just above highwater level.'

'A-ah,' murmured Miss Ogilvy thoughtfully, as though to herself; then she looked embarrassed.

The little hotel proved both comfortable and clean, the hostess both pleasant and comely. Miss Ogilvy started unpacking her bag, changed her mind and went for a stroll round the island. The island was covered with turf and thistles and traversed by narrow green paths thick with daisies. It had four rock-bound coves of which the south-western was by far the most difficult of access. For just here the island descended abruptly as though it were hurtling down to the water; and just here the shale was most treacherous and the tide-swept rocks most aggressively pointed. Here it was that the seagulls, grown fearless of man by reason of his absurd limitations, built their nests on the ledges and reared countless young who multiplied, in their turn, every season. Yes, and here it was that Miss Ogilvy, greatly marvelling, stood and stared across at a cave; much too near the crumbling edge for her safety, but by now completely indifferent to caution.

'I remember . . . I remember . . .' she kept repeating. Then: 'That's all very well, but what do I remember?'

She was conscious of somehow remembering all wrong, of her memory being distorted and coloured – perhaps by the endless things she had seen since her eyes had last rested upon that cave. This worried her sorely, far more than the fact that she should be remembering the cave at all, she who had never set foot on the island before that actual morning. Indeed, except for the sense of wrongness when she struggled to piece her

memories together, she was steeped in a very profound content-
ment which surged over her spirit, wave upon wave.

'It's extremely odd,' pondered Miss Ogilvy. Then she laughed,
so pleased did she feel with its oddness.

That night after supper she talked to her hostess who was only
too glad, it seemed, to be questioned. She owned the whole
island and was proud of the fact, as she very well might be,
decided her boarder. Some curious things had been found on
the island, according to comely Mrs Nanceskivel: bronze
arrow-heads, pieces of ancient stone celts; and once they had
dug up a man's skull and thigh-bone – this had happened while
they were sinking a well. Would Miss Ogilvy care to have a
look at the bones? They were kept in a cupboard in the scullery.

Miss Ogilvy nodded.

'Then I'll fetch him this moment,' said Mrs Nanceskivel,
briskly.

In less than two minutes she was back with the box that
contained those poor remnants of a man, and Miss Ogilvy,
who had risen from her chair, was gazing down at those remnants. As she did so her mouth was sternly compressed, but her
face and her neck flushed darkly.

Mrs Nanceskivel was pointing to the skull: 'Look, Miss, he
was killed,' she remarked rather proudly, 'and they tell me
that the axe that killed him was bronze. He's thousands and
thousands of years old, they tell me. Our local doctor knows a
lot about such things and he wants me to send these bones to
an expert; they ought to belong to the Nation, he says. But I
know what would happen, they'd come digging up my island,
and I won't have people digging up my island, I've got enough
worry with the rabbits as it is.' But Miss Ogilvy could no longer
hear the words for the pounding of the blood in her temples.

She was filled with a sudden, inexplicable fury against the
innocent Mrs Nanceskivel: 'You ... *you* ...' she began, then
checked herself, fearful of what she might say to the woman.

For her sense of outrage was overwhelming as she stared at
those bones that were kept in the scullery; moreover, she knew
how such men had been buried, which made the outrage seem

all the more shameful. They had buried such men in deep, well-dug pits surmounted by four stout stones at their corners – four stout stones there had been and a covering stone. And all this Miss Ogilvy knew as by instinct, having no concrete knowledge on which to draw. But she knew it right down in the depths of her soul, and she hated Mrs Nanceskivel.

And now she was swept by another emotion that was even more strange and more devastating: such a grief as she had not conceived could exist; a terrible unassuageable grief, without hope, without respite, without palliation, so that with something akin to despair she touched the long gash in the skull. Then her eyes, that had never wept since her childhood, filled slowly with large, hot, difficult tears. She must blink very hard, then close her eyelids, turn away from the lamp and say rather loudly:

'Thanks, Mrs Nanceskivel. It's past eleven – I think I'll be going upstairs.'

Miss Ogilvy closed the door of her bedroom, after which she stood quite still to consider: 'Is it shell-shock?' she muttered incredulously. 'I wonder, can it be shell-shock?'

She began to pace slowly about the room, smoking a Caporal. As usual her hands were deep in her pockets; she could feel small, familiar things in those pockets and she gripped them, glad of their presence. Then all of a sudden she was terribly tired, so tired that she flung herself down on the bed, unable to stand any longer.

She thought that she lay there struggling to reason, that her eyes were closed in the painful effort, and that as she closed them she continued to puff the inevitable cigarette. At least that was what she thought at one moment – the next, she was out in a sunset evening, and a large red sun was sinking slowly to the rim of a distant sea.

Miss Ogilvy knew that she was herself, that is to say she was conscious of her being, and yet she was not Miss Ogilvy at all, nor had she a memory of her. All that she now saw was very familiar, all that she now did was what she should do, and all that she now was seemed perfectly natural. Indeed, she did not think of these things; there seemed no reason for thinking about them.

She was walking with bare feet on turf that felt springy and was greatly enjoying the sensation; she had always enjoyed it, ever since as an infant she had learned to crawl on this turf. On either hand stretched rolling green uplands, while at her back she knew that there were forests; but in front, far away, lay the gleam of the sea towards which the big sun was sinking. The air was cool and intensely still, with never so much as a ripple or birdsong. It was wonderfully pure – one might almost say young – but Miss Ogilvy thought of it merely as air. Having always breathed it she took it for granted, as she took the soft turf and the uplands.

She pictured herself as immensely tall; she was feeling immensely tall at that moment. As a matter of fact she was five feet eight which, however, was quite a considerable height when compared to that of her fellow-tribesmen. She was wearing a single garment of pelts, which came to her knees and left her arms sleeveless. Her arms and her legs, which were closely tattooed with blue zig-zag lines, were extremely hairy. From a leathern thong twisted about her waist there hung a clumsily made stone weapon, a celt, which in spite of its clumsiness was strongly hafted and useful for killing.

Miss Ogilvy wanted to shout aloud from a glorious sense of physical well-being, but instead she picked up a heavy, round stone which she hurled with great force at some distant rocks.

'Good! Strong!' she exclaimed. 'See how far it goes!'

'Yes, strong. There is no one so strong as you. You are surely the strongest man in our tribe,' replied her little companion.

Miss Ogilvy glanced at this little companion and rejoiced that they two were alone together. The girl at her side had a smooth brownish skin, oblique black eyes and short, sturdy limbs. Miss Ogilvy marvelled because of her beauty. She also was wearing a single garment of pelts, new pelts, she had made it that morning. She had stitched at it diligently for hours with short lengths of gut and her best bone needle. A strand of black hair hung over her bosom, and this she was constantly stroking and fondling; then she lifted the strand and examined her hair.

'Pretty,' she remarked with childish complacence.

'Pretty,' echoed the young man at her side.

'For you,' she told him, 'all of me is for you and none other. For you this body has ripened.'

He shook back his own coarse hair from his eyes; he had sad brown eyes like those of a monkey. For the rest he was lean and steel-strong of loin, broad of chest, and with features not too uncomely. His prominent cheekbones were set rather high, his nose was blunt, his jaw somewhat bestial; but his mouth, though full-lipped, contradicted his jaw, being very gentle and sweet in expression. And now he smiled, showing big, square, white teeth.

'You . . . woman,' he murmured contentedly, and the sound seemed to come from the depths of his being.

His speech was slow and lacking in words when it came to expressing a vital emotion, so one word must suffice and this he now spoke, and the word that he spoke had a number of meanings. It meant: 'Little spring of exceedingly pure water'. It meant: 'Hut of peace for a man after battle'. It meant: 'Ripe red berry sweet to the taste'. It meant: 'Happy small home of future generations'. All these things he must try to express by a word, and because of their loving she understood him.

They paused, and lifting her up he kissed her. Then he rubbed his large shaggy head on her shoulder; and when he released her she knelt at his feet.

'My master; blood of my body,' she whispered. For with her it was different, love had taught her love's speech, so that she might turn her heart into sounds that her primitive tongue could utter.

After she had pressed her lips to his hands, and her cheek to his hairy and powerful forearm, she stood up and they gazed at the setting sun, but with bowed heads, gazing under their lids, because this was very sacred.

A couple of mating bears padded towards them from a thicket, and the female rose to her haunches. But the man drew his celt and menaced the beast, so that she dropped down noiselessly and fled, and her mate also fled, for here was the power that few dared to withstand by day or by night, on the uplands or in the forests. And now from across to the left where a river would presently lose itself in the marshes, came a rhythmical thudding, as a herd of red deer with wide nostrils and starting eyes thundered past, disturbed in their drinking by the bears.

After this the evening returned to its silence, and the spell of its silence descended on the lovers, so that each felt very much alone, yet withal more closely united to the other. But the man became restless under that spell, and he suddenly laughed; then grasping the woman he tossed her above his head and caught her. This he did many times for his own amusement and because he knew that his strength gave her joy. In this manner they played together for a while, he with his strength and she with her weakness. And they cried out, and made many guttural sounds which were meaningless save only to themselves. And the tunic of pelts slipped down from her breasts, and her two little breasts were pear-shaped.

Presently, he grew tired of their playing, and he pointed towards a cluster of huts and earthworks that lay to the eastward. The smoke from these huts rose in thick straight lines, bending neither to right nor left in its rising, and the thought of sweet burning rushes and brushwood touched his consciousness, making him feel sentimental.

'Smoke,' he said.

And she answered: 'Blue smoke.'

He nodded: 'Yes, blue smoke – home.'

Then she said: 'I have ground much corn since the full moon. My stones are too smooth. You make me new stones.'

'All you have need of, I make,' he told her.

She stole closer to him, taking his hand: 'My father is still a black cloud full of thunder. He thinks that you wish to be head of our tribe in his place, because he is now very old. He must not hear of these meetings of ours, if he did I think he would beat me!'

So he asked her: 'Are you unhappy, small berry?'

But at this she smiled: 'What is being unhappy? I do not know what that means any more.'

'I do not either,' he answered.

Then as though some invisible force had drawn him, his body swung round and he stared at the forests where they lay and darkened, fold upon fold; and his eyes dilated with wonder and terror, and he moved his head quickly from side to side as a wild thing will do that is held between bars and whose mind is pitifully bewildered.

'Water!' he cried hoarsely, 'great water – look, look! Over there. This land is surrounded by water!'

'What water?' she questioned.

He answered: 'The sea.' And he covered his face with his hands.

'Not so,' she consoled, 'big forests, good hunting. Big forests in which you hunt boar and aurochs. No sea over there but only the trees.'

He took his trembling hands from his face: 'You are right . . . only trees,' he said dully.

But now his face had grown heavy and brooding and he started to speak of a thing that oppressed him: 'The Round-headed-ones, they are devils,' he growled, while his bushy black brows met over his eyes, and when this happened it changed his expression, which became a little sub-human.

'No matter,' she protested, for she saw that he forgot her and she wished him to think and talk only of love. 'No matter. My father laughs at your fears. Are we not friends with the Roundheaded-ones? We are friends, so why should we fear them?'

'Our forts, very old, very weak,' he went on, 'and the Round-headed-ones have terrible weapons. Their weapons are not made of good stone like ours, but of some dark, devilish sub-stance.'

'What of that?' she said lightly. 'They would fight on our side, so why need we trouble about their weapons?'

But he looked away, not appearing to hear her. 'We must barter all, all for their celts and arrows and spears, and then we must learn their secret. They lust after our women, they lust after our lands. We must barter all, all for their sly brown celts.'

'Me . . . bartered?' she queried, very sure of his answer other-wise she had not dared to say this.

'The Roundheaded-ones may destroy my tribe and yet I will not part with you,' he told her. Then he spoke very gravely: 'But I think they desire to slay us, and me they will try to slay first because they well know how much I mistrust them – they have seen my eyes fixed many times on their camps.'

She cried: 'I will bite out the throats of these people if they so much as scratch your skin!'

And at this his mood changed and he roared with amusement: 'You . . . woman!' he roared. 'Little foolish white teeth. Your teeth were made for nibbling wild cherries, not for tearing the throats of the Roundheaded-ones!'

'Thoughts of war always make me afraid,' she whimpered, still wishing him to talk about love.

He turned his sorrowful eyes upon her, the eyes that were sad even when he was merry, and although his mind was often obtuse, yet he clearly perceived how it was with her then. And his blood caught fire from the flame in her blood, so that he strained her against his body.

'You . . . mine . . .' he stammered.

'Love,' she said, trembling, 'this is love.'

And he answered: 'Love.'

Then their faces grew melancholy for a moment, because dimly, very dimly in their dawning souls, they were conscious of a longing for something more vast than this earthly passion could compass.

Presently, he lifted her like a child and carried her quickly southward and westward till they came to a place where a gentle descent led down to a marshy valley. Far away, at the line where the marshes ended, they discerned the misty line of the sea; but the sea and the marshes were become as one substance, merging, blending, folding together; and since they were lovers they also would be one, even as the sea and the marshes.

And now they had reached the mouth of a cave that was set in the quiet hillside. There was bright green verdure beside the cave, and a number of small, pink, thick-stemmed flowers that when they were crushed smelt of spices. And within the cave there was bracken newly gathered and heaped together for a bed; while beyond, from some rocks, came a low liquid sound

as a spring dripped out through a crevice. Abruptly, he set the
girl on her feet, and she knew that the days of her innocence
were over. And she thought of the anxious virgin soil that was
rent and sown to bring forth fruit in season, and she gave a
quick little gasp of fear:

'No . . . no . . .' she gasped. For, divining his need, she was
weak with the longing to be possessed, yet the terror of love
lay heavy upon her. 'No . . . no . . .' she gasped.

But he caught her wrist and she felt the great strength of his
rough, gnarled fingers, the great strength of the urge that leaped
in his loins, and again she must give that quick gasp of fear, the
while she clung close to him lest he should spare her.

The twilight was engulfed and possessed by darkness, which
in turn was transfigured by the moonrise, which in turn was
fulfilled and consumed by dawn. A mighty eagle soared up from
his eyrie, cleaving the air with his masterful wings, and beneath
him from the rushes that harboured their nests, rose other great
birds, crying loudly. Then the heavy-horned elks appeared on
the uplands, bending their burdened heads to the sod; while
beyond in the forests the fierce wild aurochs stamped as they
bellowed their love songs.

But within the dim cave the lord of these creatures had put
by his weapon and his instinct for slaying. And he lay there
defenceless with tenderness, thinking no longer of death but of
life as he murmured the word that had so many meanings. That
meant: 'Little spring of exceedingly pure water'. That meant:
'Hut of peace for a man after battle'. That meant: 'Ripe red
berry sweet to the taste'. That meant: 'Happy small home of
future generations'.

They found Miss Ogilvy the next morning; the fisherman saw
her and climbed to the ledge. She was sitting at the mouth of
the cave. She was dead, with her hands thrust deep into her
pockets.

# HUGH WALPOLE
# NOBODY

The only one of them all who perceived anything like the truth was young Claribel.

Claribel (how she hated the absurd name!) had a splendid opportunity for observing everything in life, simply because she was so universally neglected. The Matchams and the Dorsets and the Duddons (all the relations, in fact) simply considered her of no importance at all.

She did not mind this: she took it entirely for granted, as she did her plainness, her slowness of speech, her shyness in company, her tendency to heat spots, her bad figure, and all the other things with which an undoubtedly all-wise God had seen fit to endow her. It was only that having all these things, Claribel was additionally an unfortunate name; but then, most of them called her Carrie, and the boys 'Fetch and Carry' often enough.

She was taken with the others to parties and teas, in order, as she very well knew, that critical friends and neighbours should not say that 'the Dorsets always neglected that plain child of theirs, poor thing'.

She sat in a corner and was neglected, but that she did not mind in the least. She liked it. It gave her, all the more, the opportunity of watching people, the game that she liked best in all the world. She played it without any sense at all that she had unusual powers. It was much later than this that she was to realize her gifts.

It was this sitting in a corner in the Hortons flat that enabled her to perceive what it was that had happened to her Cousin Tom. Of course, she knew from the public standpoint well enough what had happened to him – simply that he had been wounded three times, once in Gallipoli and twice in France; that he had received the DSO and been made a Major. But it was something other than that that she meant. She knew that all the brothers and the sisters, the cousins, the uncles and the aunts proclaimed gleefully that there was nothing the matter with him at all. 'It's quite wonderful,' they all said, 'to see the way that dear Tom has come back from the war just as he went into it. His same jolly generous self. Everyone's friend. Not at all conceited. How wonderful that is, when he's done so well and has all that money!'

That was, Claribel knew, the thing that everyone said. Tom had always been her own favourite. He had not considered her the least little bit more than he had considered everyone else. He always was kind. But he gave her a smile and a nod and a pat, and she was grateful.

Then he had always seemed to her a miraculous creature; his whole history in the war had only increased that adoration. She loved to look at him, and certainly he must, in anyone's eyes, have been handsome, with his light, shining hair, his fine, open brow, his slim, straight body, his breeding and distinction and nobility.

To all of this was suddenly added wealth – his uncle, the head of the biggest biscuit factory in England, dying and leaving him everything. His mother and he had already been sufficiently provided for at his father's death; but he was now, through Uncle Bob's love for him, an immensely rich man. This had fallen to him in the last year of the war, when he was recovering from his third wound. After the Armistice, freed from the hospital, he had taken a delightful flat in Hortons (his mother preferred the country, and was cosy with dogs, a parrot, a butler, and bees in Wiltshire), and it was here that he gave his delightful parties. It was here that Claribel, watching from her corner, made her great discovery about him.

Her discovery quite simply was that he did not exist; that he was dead, that 'there was nobody there'.

She did not know what it was that caused her just to be aware of her ghostly surprise. She had in the beginning been taken in as they all had been. He had seemed on his first return from the hospital to be the same old Tom whom they had always known. For some weeks he had used a crutch, and his cheeks were pale, his eyes were sunk like bright jewels into dark pouches of shadow.

He had said very little about his experiences in France; that was natural, none of the men who had returned from there wished to speak of it. He had thrown himself with apparent eagerness into the dancing, the theatres, the house-parties, the shooting, the flirting – all the hectic, eager life that seemed to be pushed by everyone's hands into the dark, ominous silence that the announcement of the Armistice had created.

Then how they all had crowded about him! Claribel, seated in her dark little corner, had summoned them one by one – Mrs Freddie Matcham with her high, bright colour and wonderful hair, her two daughters, Claribel's cousins, Lucy and Amy, so pretty and so stupid, the voluminous Dorsets, with all their Beaminster connections, Hattie Dorset, Dollie Pym-Dorset, Rose and Emily; then the men – young Harwood Dorset, who was no good at anything, but danced so well, Henry Matcham, capable and intelligent would he only work, Pelham Duddon, ambitious and grasping; then her own family, her elder sisters, Morgraunt (what a name!), who married Rex Beaminster, and they hadn't a penny, and Lucile, unmarried, pretty and silly, and Dora, serious and plain and a miser – Oh! Claribel knew them all! She wondered, as she sat there, how she *could* know them all as she did, and, after that, how they could be so unaware that she *did* know them! She did not feel herself preternaturally sharp – only that they were unobservant or simply, perhaps, that they had better things to observe.

The thing, of course, that they were all just then observing was Tom and his money. The two things were synonymous, and if they couldn't have the money without Tom, they must have him with it. Not that they minded having Tom – he was exactly what they felt a man should be – beautiful to look at, easy and happy and casual, a splendid sportsman, completely free of all that tiresome 'analysis' stuff that some of the would-be clever ones thought so essential.

They liked Tom and approved of him, and oh! how they wanted his money! There was not one of them not in need of it! Claribel could see all their dazzling, shining eyes fixed upon those great piles of gold, their beautiful fingers crooked out towards it. Claribel did not herself want money. What she wanted, more than she allowed herself to think, was companionship and friendship and affection . . . And that she was inclined to think she was fated never to obtain.

The day when she first noticed the thing that was the matter with Tom, was one wet, stormy afternoon in March; they were all gathered together in Tom's lovely sitting-room in Hortons.

Tom, without being exactly clever about beautiful things, had a fine sense of the way that he wished to be served, and the result of this was that his flat was neat and ordered, everything always in perfect array. His man, Sheraton, was an ideal man; he had been Tom's servant before the war, and now, released from his duties, was back again; there was no reason why he should ever now depart from them, he having, as he once told Claribel, a contemptuous opinion of women. Under Sheraton's care, that long, low-ceilinged room, lined with bookcases (Tom loved fine bindings), with its gleaming, polished floor, some old family portraits and rich curtains of a gleaming dark purple – to Claribel this place was heaven. It would not, of course, have been so heavenly had Tom not been so perfect a figure moving against the old gold frames, the curtains, the leaping fire, looking so exactly, Claribel thought, 'the younger image of old Theophilus Duddon, stiff and grand up there on the wall in his white stock and velvet coat, Tom's great-grandfather'.

On this particular day Claribel's sister, Morgraunt Beaminster, and Lucile, Mrs Matcham, Hattie Dorset, and some men were present. Tom was sitting over the rim of a big leather chair near the fire, his head tossed back laughing at one of Lucile's silly jokes. Mrs Matcham was at the table, 'pouring out', and Sheraton, rather stout but otherwise a fine example of the Admirable Crichton, handed around the food. They were laughing, as they always did, at nothing at all, Lucile's shrill, barking laugh above the rest. From the babel Claribel caught phrases like 'Dear old Tom!' 'But he didn't – he hadn't got the

intelligence.' 'Tom, you're a pet . . .' 'Oh, but of *course* not.
What stuff! Why, Harriet herself . . . !' Through it all Sheraton
moved with his head back, his indulgent indifference, his
supremely brushed hair. It was just then Claribel caught the
flash from Mrs Matcham's beautiful eyes. Everyone had their
tea; there was nothing left for her to do. She sat there, her
lovely hands crossed on the table in front of her, her eyes lost,
apparently, in dim abstraction. Claribel saw that they were not
lost at all, but were bent, obliquely, with a concentrated and
almost passionate interest, upon Tom. Mrs Matcham wanted
something, and she was determined this afternoon to ask for it.
What was it? Money? Her debts were notorious. Jewels? She
was insatiable there . . . Freddie Matcham couldn't give her
things. Old Lord Ferris wanted to, but wasn't allowed to . . .
Claribel knew all this, young though she was. There remained,
then, as always, Tom.

Thrilled by this discovery of Mrs Matcham's eyes, Claribel
pursued her discoveries further, and the next thing that she saw
was that Lucile also was intent upon some prize. Her silly,
bright little eyes were tightened for some very definite purpose.
They fastened upon Tom like little scissors. Claribel knew that
Lucile had developed recently a passion for bridge and, being
stupid . . . Yes, Lucile wanted money. Claribel allowed herself
a little shudder of disgust. She was only seventeen, and wore
spectacles, and was plain, but at that moment she felt herself to
be infinitely superior to the whole lot of them. She had her own
private comfortable arrogances.

It was then, while she was despising them, that she made her
discovery about Tom. She looked across at him wondering
whether he had noticed any of the things that had struck her.
She at the same time sighed, seeing that she had made, as she
always did, a nasty sloppy mess in her saucer, and knowing
that Morgraunt (the watchdog of the family) would be certain
to notice and scold her for it.

She looked across at Tom and discovered suddenly that he
wasn't there. The shell of him was there, the dark clothes, the
black tie with the pearl pin, the white shirt, the faintly coloured
clear-cut mask with the shining hair, the white throat, the heavy

eyelashes – the shell, the mask, nothing else. She could never remember afterwards exactly what it was that made her certain that nobody was there. Lucile was talking to him, eagerly, repeating, as she always did, her words over and over again. He was, apparently, looking up at her, a smile on his lips. Morgraunt, so smart with the teasing blue feather in her hat, was looking across at them intent upon what Lucile was saying. He was apparently looking at Lucile, and yet his eyes were dead, sightless, like the eyes of a statue. In his hand he apparently held a cigarette, and yet his hand was of marble, no life ran through the veins. Claribel even fancied, so deeply excited had she become, that you could see the glitter of the fire through his dark body as he sat carefully balanced on the edge of the chair.

There was Nobody there, and then, as she began to reflect, there never had been anybody since the Armistice. Tom had never returned from France; only a framework with clothes hung upon it, a doll, an automaton, did Tom's work and fulfilled his place. Tom's soul had remained in France. He did not really hear what Lucile was saying. He did not care what any of them were doing, and that, of course, accounted for the wonderful way that, during these past weeks, he had acquiesced in every one of their proposals. They had many of them commented on Tom's extraordinary good nature now that he had returned. 'You really could do anything with him that you pleased,' Claribel had heard Morgraunt triumphantly exclaim. Well, so you can with a corpse! . . .

As she stared at him and realized the dramatic import of her discovery, she was suddenly filled with pity. Poor Tom! How terrible that time in France must have been to have killed him like that, and nobody had known. They had thought that he had taken it so easily, he had laughed and jested with the others, had always returned to France gaily . . . How terrified he must have been – before he died!

As she watched him, he got up from the chair and stood before the fire, his legs spread out. The others had gathered in a corner of the room, busied around Hattie, who was trying some new Jazz tunes on the piano. Mrs Matcham got up from her table and went over to Tom and began eagerly to talk to

him. Her hands were clasped behind her beautiful back, and
Claribel could see how the fingers twisted and untwisted again
and again over the urgency of her request.

Claribel saw Tom's face. The mask was the lovelier now
because she knew that there was no life behind it. She saw the
lips smile, the eyes shine, the head bend. It was to her as though
someone were turning an electric button behind there in the
middle of his back . . .

He nodded. Mrs Matcham laughed. 'Oh, you darling!'
Claribel heard her cry. 'If you only knew what you've done
for me!'

The party was over. They all began to go.

Claribel was right. There was Nobody there.

When everybody had gone that evening and the body of Tom
was alone, it surveyed the beautiful room.

Tom's body (which may for the moment be conveniently but
falsely called Tom) looked about and felt a wave of miserable,
impotent uselessness.

Tom summoned Sheraton.

'Clear all these things away,' he said.

'Yes, sir.'

'I'm going out.'

'Yes, sir.'

'Dinner jacket to-night, sir?'

'No, I'm not dressing.' He went to the door, then turned
round. 'Sheraton!'

'Yes, sir!'

'What's the matter with me?'

'I beg your pardon, sir!'

'What's the matter with me? You know what I mean as well
as I do. Ever since I came back . . . I can't take an interest in
anything – not in anything nor in anybody. To-day, for instance,
I didn't hear a word that they were saying, not one of them,
and they made enough noise, too! I don't care for anything, I
don't want anything, I don't like anything, I don't hate anything. It's as though I were asleep – and yet I'm not asleep
either. What's the matter with me, Sheraton?'

Sheraton's eyes, that had been so insistently veiled by decent society, as expressionless as a pair of marbles, were suddenly human; Sheraton's voice, which had been something like the shadow of a real voice, was suddenly full of feeling.

'Why, sir, of course I've noticed . . . being with you before the war and all, and being fond of you, if you'll forgive my saying so, so that I always hoped that I'd come back to you. Why, if you ask me, sir, it's just the bloody war – that's all it is. I've felt something of the same kind myself. I'm getting over it a bit. It'll pass, sir. The war leaves you kind o' dead. People don't seem real any more. If you could get fond of some young lady, Mr Duddon, I'm sure . . .'

'Thanks, Sheraton. I daresay you're right.' He went out.

It was a horrible night. The March wind was tearing down Duke Street,[1] hurling itself at the windows, plucking with its fingers at the doors, screaming and laughing down the chimneys. The decorous decencies of that staid bachelor St James's world seemed to be nothing to its mood of wilful bad temper. Through the clamour of banging doors and creaking windows the bells of St James's Church could be heard striking seven o'clock.

The rain was intermittent, and fell in sudden little gusts, like the subsiding agonies of a weeping child. Every once and again a thin wet wisp of a moon showed dimly grey through heavy piles of driving cloud. Tom found Bond Street almost deserted of foot passengers.

Buttoning his high blue collar up about his neck, he set himself to face the storm. The drive of the rain against his cheeks gave him some sort of dim satisfaction after the close warm comfort of his flat.

Somewhere, far, far away in him, a voice was questioning him as to why he had given Mrs Matcham that money. The voice reminded him of what indeed he very well knew, that it was exactly like throwing water down a well, that it would do Millie Matcham no good, that it was wasted money . . . Well, he didn't care. The voice was too far away, and altogether had too little concern with him to disturb him very deeply. Nothing disturbed him, damn it – nothing, nothing, nothing!

When he was almost upon Grosvenor Street, a sudden gust of wind drove at him so furiously that, almost without knowing what he was doing, instinctively he stepped back to take shelter beneath a wooden boarding. Here a street-lamp gave a pale yellow colour to the dark shadows, and from its cover the street shot like a gleaming track of steel into the clustered lights of Oxford Street.

Tom was aware that two people had taken shelter in the same refuge. He peered at their dim figures. He saw at once that they were old – an old man and an old woman.

He did not know what it was that persuaded him to stare at them as though they could be of any importance to him. Nothing could be of any importance to him, and he was attracted, perhaps, rather by a kind of snivelling, sniffling noise that one of them made. The old lady – she had a terrible cold. She sneezed violently, and the old man uttered a scornful 'chut-chut' like an angry, battered bird. Then he peered up at Tom and said in a complaining, whining voice:

'What a night!'

'Yes, it is,' said Tom. 'You'd better get home.'

His eyes growing accustomed to the gloom, he saw the pair distinctly. The old man was wearing a high hat, battered and set rakishly on the side of his head. The collar of a threadbare overcoat was turned up high over his skinny neck. He wore shabby black gloves. The old lady, sheltering behind the old man, was less easily discerned. She was a humped and disconcerted shadow, with a feather in her hat and a sharp nose.

'You'd better be getting home,' Tom repeated, wondering to himself that he stayed.

The old man peered up at him.

'You're out for no good, I reckon,' he mumbled. 'Waiting like this on a night like this.' There was a note in his voice of scornful patronage.

'I'm not out for anything particular,' said Tom. 'Simply taking a walk.' The old lady sneezed again. 'You'd really better be going home. Your wife's got a terrible cold.'

'She's not my wife,' said the old man. 'She's my sister, if you want to know.'

'I don't want to know especially,' said Tom. 'Well, good-night: I see the rain's dropped.'

He stepped out into Bond Street, and then (on looking back he could never define precisely the impulse that drove him) he hurried back to them.

'You'd better let me get you a cab or something,' he said. 'You really ought to go home.'

The old man snarled at him. 'You let us alone,' he said. 'We haven't done you any harm.'

The impulse persisted.

'I'm going to get you a cab,' he said. 'Whether you like it or no.'

'None of your bloody philanthropy,' said the old man. 'I know you. M'rier and me's all right.'

It was Maria then who took the next step in the affair. Tom, although he was afterwards to have a very considerable knowledge of that old lady, could never definitely determine as to whether the step that she took was honest or no. What she did was to collapse into the sodden pavement in a black and grimy heap. The feather stood out from the collapse with a jaunty, ironical gesture.

''Ere, M'rier,' said the old man, very much as though he were addressing a recalcitrant horse, 'you get hup.'

No sound came from the heap. Tom bent down. He touched her soiled velvet coat, lifted an arm, felt the weight sink beneath him. 'Well,' he said, almost defiantly, to the old man, 'what are you going to do now?'

'She's always doing it,' he answered, 'and at the most aggravating moments.' Then with something that looked suspiciously like a kick, he repeated: 'You get hup, M'rier.'

'Look here, you can't do that,' Tom cried. 'What an old devil you are! We've got to get her out of this.'

A voice addressed them from the street: 'Anything the matter?' it said.

Tom turned and found that the driver of a taxi had pulled up his machine and was peering into the shadow.

'Yes. There's been an accident,' Tom said. 'This lady's fainted. We'd better get her home.'

'Where's she going to?' said the driver suspiciously.

'What business is that of yours?' cried the old man furiously. 'You just leave us alone.'

'No, you couldn't do that,' Tom answered. 'There'll be a policeman here in a moment, and he'll have you home whether you want it or not. You never can lift her yourself, and you can't leave her there. You'd better help me get her into the cab!'

The old man began to gargle strangely in his throat.

'Policeman!' he seemed to say. 'If I 'ad my way –'

'Well, for once you haven't,' said Tom shortly. 'Here, driver, help me lift her in.'

'Where's she going?' he repeated.

'If you don't help me at once I'll see that a policeman *is* here. I've got your number. You'll hear from me in the morning.'

The man got off his box, cursing. He hesitated a moment, then came across. Together he and Tom lifted the inert mass, pushed it through the door of the cab and settled it in the seat.

'Makin' my cab dirty and all,' growled the driver.

'Well,' said Tom to the old man, 'are you going to see your sister home? If not, I shall take her to the nearest hospital.'

For a moment the old man remained perched up against the wall, his top hat flaunting defiance to the whole world. Suddenly, as though he had been pushed, he came across to the driver.

'Eleven D Porker's Buildings, Victoria,'[2] he said.

'B?' asked the driver.

'D, you damned fool,' the old man almost shouted.

'Thought you said B,' remarked the driver very amiably.

The old man got in. He was on one side of the motionless Maria, Tom on the other.

That was a remarkable and even romantic ride. The roads were slippery, and the driver, it appeared, a little drunk. The cab rocked like a drunken boat, and the watery moon, now triumphant over the clouds, the gleaming pavement, the houses, gaunt in the uncertain moonlight, and thin as though they had been cut from black paper, seemed to be inebriated too. Maria shared in the general irresponsibility, lurching from side to side, and revealing, now that her hat was on Tom's lap, an ancient peeked face with as many lines on it as an Indian's, and grey, untidy hair. She seemed a lifeless thing enough, and yet Tom had a strange notion that one eye was open, and not only watching, but winking as well.

It would have been the natural thing to have opened her dress and given her air, to have poured whisky or brandy down her throat, to have tickled her with feathers! Tom did none of these things: afterwards he imagined that his inaction was due to the fact that he knew all the time that she had not really fainted.

Not a word was exchanged during the journey. They drove down Victoria Street, turned off on the right of Westminster Cathedral, and drew up in a narrow, dirty street.

A high block had 'Porker's Buildings' printed in large, ugly letters on the fanlight near the door.

'You'd better help me lift her in,' Tom said to the driver. 'The old man's not good for anything.'

The driver grunted, but helped Maria into the street. The fresh night air seemed to refresh her. She sighed and then sneezed.

'Maybe she can walk herself,' said the driver.

The door opened of itself, and Tom was in a dark, dingy hall with a faint gas-jet like a ghostly eye to guide him. The old man started up the stairs.

'Can you walk a bit?' Tom asked the old lady.

She nodded. Tom paid the driver and the door closed behind him. It was a hard fight to conquer the stairs, and Maria clung like a heavy bag round her deliverer's neck, but on the third floor the old man unlocked a door, walked in before them and lighted a candle. He then sat himself down with his back to them, pulled a grimy piece of newspaper out of his pocket, and was apparently at once absorbed in reading.

The room was a wretched enough place. One of the windows was stuffed with brown paper; a ragged strip of carpet covered only a section of the cracked and dirty boards. There was a grimy bed; the fireplace was filled with rubbish.

Tom helped Maria on to the bed and looked about him. Then in a sudden fit of irritation he went up to the old man and shook him by the shoulder.

'Look here,' he said. 'This won't do. You've got to do

something for her. She may die in the night, or anything. I'll fetch a doctor, if that's what you want, or get something from the chemist's –'

'Oh! go to hell!' said the old man without turning.

An impulse of rage seized Tom, and he caught the old man by the collar, swung him out of the chair, shook him until he was breathless and coughing, then said:

'Now be civil.'

The old man collapsed on the bed near his sister, struggled for breath, then screamed:

'You damned aristocrat! I'll have you up before the courts for this; invading a man's peaceable 'ome –'

Then Maria unexpectedly interfered. She sat up, smoothing her hair with her old trembling fingers. 'I'm sure,' she said, in a mincing, apologetic voice, 'that we ought to be grateful to the gentleman, Andrew. If it 'adn't been for him, I'm sure I don't know where we'd 'ave been. It's your wicked temper you're always losing. I've told you of it again and again – I'm much better now, thank you, sir, and I'm sure I'm properly grateful.'

Tom looked around him, then back at the two old people.

'What a filthy place,' he said. 'Haven't you got anybody to look after you?'

'Me daughter run away with a musical gentleman,' said Maria. 'My 'usband died of DT's[3] three years back. Andrew and meself's alone now. We get the Old Age Pension, and manage very nicely, thank you.'

'Well, I'm coming back to-morrow,' said Tom fiercely, turning on the old man. 'Do you hear that?'

'If yer do,' said Andrew, 'I'll 'ave the perlice after you.'

'Oh, no, 'e won't,' said Maria. 'That's only 'is little way. I'm sure we'll be pleased to see you.'

Tom put some money on the bed and left.

Out in the street he paused. What was the matter with him? He stood in the street looking up at the Westminster Cathedral tower and the thin sheeting of sky now clear – a pale, boundless sea in which two or three little stars were remotely sailing. What was the matter with him?

He felt a strange stirring and trembling about him. He had

some of the pain and hurt that a man feels when he is first revived from some drowning adventure. But it was a pain and hurt of the soul, not of the body. His heart beat expectantly, as though around the corner of the lonely street a wonderful stranger might suddenly be expected to appear. He even strained his eyes against the shadows, piercing them and finding only more shadows behind them.

He even felt tired and exhausted, as though he had but now passed through a great emotional experience.

And all these sensations were clear and precious to him. He treasured them, standing there, breathing deeply, as though he were in new air of some high altitude. The boom of Big Ben came suddenly across the silence like a summoning voice across waste, deserted country, and he went home . . .

When he awoke next morning he was aware that something had happened to him, and he did not know what it was. He lay there definitely beating back an impulse to spring out of bed, hurry through his bath, dress, and have breakfast, and then – what? He had not felt such an impulse since his return from France, and it could not be that he felt it now simply because he had, last night, met two dirty, bedraggled old people and helped them home.

He laughed. Sheraton, hanging his shirt on the back of a chair, turned.

'Well, you're feeling better this morning, sir,' he said.

'Yes, I am,' said Tom, 'and I'm damned if I know why.' Nevertheless, although he did not know why, before the morning was out he found himself once more behind Victoria Street and climbing the stairs of Porker's Buildings. He had strange experiences that morning. To many they would have been disappointing. The old man was silent: not a word would he say. His attitude was one of haughty, autocratic superiority. Maria disgusted Tom. She was polite, cringing even, and as poisonous as a snake. She stated her wants quite modestly: had it not been for her age you would have thought her a typical image of the down-trodden, subjected poor. Her eyes glittered.

'Well, you *are* a nasty old creature.' Tom turned from her and shook Andrew by the shoulder.

'Well?' said Andrew.

'There's nothing now I can do?' asked Tom.

'Except get out,' said Andrew.

Another old woman came in – then a young man. A fine specimen this last – a local prize-fighter, it appeared – chest like a wall, thick, stumpy thighs, face of a beetroot colour, nose twisted, ears like saucers. The old woman, Maria's friend, was voluble. She explained a great deal to Tom. She was used, it seemed, to speaking in public. They could afford, she explained, to be indifferent to the 'Quality' now, because a time was very shortly coming when they would have everything, and the Quality nothing. It had happened far away in Russia, and it was about to happen here. A good thing too . . . At last the poor people could appear as they really were, hold their heads up. Only a month or two . . .

'You're a Bolshevist,' said Tom.

Long words did not distress the old lady. 'A fine time's coming,' she said.

Maria did not refuse the food and the finery and the money. 'You think,' said Tom, as a final word to her old lady friend, 'that I'm doing this because I'm charitable, because I love you, or some nonsense of that kind. Not at all. I'm doing it because I'm interested, and I haven't been interested in anything for months.'

He arranged with the pugilist to be present at his next encounter, somewhere in Blackfriars,[4] next Monday night.

'It's against the Bermondsey Chick,' Battling Bill explained huskily. 'I've got one on him. Your money's safe enough . . .'

Tom gave Maria a parting smile.

'I don't like you,' he said, 'and I can see that you positively hate me, but we're getting along very nicely . . .'

It is at this point that Claribel again takes up the narrative. It was, of course, not many days before, in Tom's own world, 'What's happened to Tom?' was on everyone's lips.

Claribel was interested as anyone, and she had, of course, her own theories. These theories changed from day to day, but the fact, potent to the world and beyond argument, was that

Tom was 'Nobody' no longer. Life had come back to him; he was eagerly, passionately 'out' upon some secret quest.

It amused Claribel to watch her friends and relations as they set forth, determined to lay bare Tom's mystery. Mrs Matcham, who had her own very definite reasons for not allowing Tom to escape, declared that of course it was a 'woman'. But this did not elucidate the puzzle. Had it been some married woman, Tom would not have been so perfectly 'open' about his disappearances. He never denied for a moment that he disappeared; he rather liked them to know that he did. It was plainly nothing of which he was ashamed. He had been seen at no restaurants with anyone – no chorus-girl, no girl at all, in fact. Dollie Pym-Dorset, who was a little sharper than the others, simply because she was more determinedly predatory, declared that Tom was learning a trade.

'He will turn up suddenly one day,' she said, 'as a chauffeur, or an engineer, or a bootblack. He's trying to find something to fill up his day.'

'He's found it,' Lucile cried with her shrill laugh. 'Whatever it is, it keeps him going. He's never in; Sheraton declares he doesn't know where he goes. It's disgusting . . .'

Old Lord Ferris, who took an indulgent interest in all the Duddon developments because of his paternal regard for Mrs Matcham, declared that it was one of these new religions. 'They're simply all over the place; a feller catches 'em as he would the measles. Why, I know a chap . . .'

But no. Tom didn't look as though he had found a new religion. He had made no new resolutions, dropped no profanities, lost in no way his sense of humour. No, it didn't look like a religion.

Claribel's convictions about it were not very positive. She was simply so glad that he had become 'Somebody' again, and she had perhaps a malicious pleasure in the disappointment of 'the set'. It amused her to see the golden purse slipping out of their eager fingers, and they so determined to stay it.

The pursuit continued for weeks. Everyone was drawn into it. Even old Lord John Beaminster, who was beset with debts and gout, stirred up his sister Adela to see whether she couldn't 'discover' something . . .

It was Henry Matcham who finally achieved the revelation. He came bursting in upon them all. The secret was out. Tom had turned 'pi – '[5] He was working down in the East End[6] to save souls.

The news was greeted with incredulity. 'Tom soul-saving? Impossible! Tom the cynic, the irreligious, the despiser of dogma, the arbitrator of indifference – Incredible.'

But Matcham knew. There could be no doubt. A man he knew in Brooks's had a brother a parson in an East-End Settlement.[7] The parson knew Tom well, said he was always down there, in the men's clubs and about the streets.

They looked at one another in dismay. Claribel laughed to see them. What was to be done? Tom must be saved, of course; but how? No plan could be evoked. 'Well, the first thing we must do,' said Mrs Matcham, 'is to get a plain statement from himself about it.'

They sent Claribel as their ambassador, realizing, apparently suddenly, that 'she had some sense', and that Tom liked her.

She told him, with a twinkle in her eye, what they wanted.

'They're all very much upset by what you're doing, Tom. They don't want to lose you, you see. They're fond of you. And they don't think it *can* be good for you being all the time with Bolsheviks and dirty foreigners. You'll only be taken in by them, they think, and robbed; and that they can't bear. Especially they think that now after the war everyone ought to stand together, shoulder to shoulder, you know, class by class. That's the way Henry Matcham puts it.

'Of course, they admire you very much, what you're doing – they think it very noble. But all this slumming seems to them ... what did Dollie call it? ... Oh, yes, *vieux jeu*[8] ... the sort of thing young men did in the nineties, centuries ago. Oxford House,[9] and all that. It seems rather stupid to them to go back to it now, especially when the war's shown the danger of Bolshevism.'

Tom laughed. 'Why, Carrie,' he said, 'how well you know them!'

She laughed too. 'Anyway,' she said, 'I know you better than they do.'

Tom agreed that it would be a very good thing for them all
to meet.

'They've got what's happened just a trifle wrong,' he said.
'It's only fair to clear things up.'

They all appeared on the appointed day – Mrs Matcham, as
president, in a lovely rose-coloured tulle for which she was
just a little too old, Hattie, Dollie, Harwood Dorset, Henry
Matcham, Pelham Duddon, Morgraunt and Lucile, Dora, and
of course Claribel. The event had the appearance of one of the
dear old parties.

The flat was just as beautiful, the tea as sumptuous, Sheraton
as perfect. They hung around the same chairs, the same table,
in all their finery and beauty and expense. They were as sure of
conquest as they had ever been.

Tom sat on the red leather top of the fire-guard and faced them.

Mrs Matcham led the attack.

'Now, dear old Tom,' she said, in that cooing and persuasive
voice of hers, so well known and so well liked; 'you know that
we all love you.'

'Yes, I know you do,' said Tom, grinning.

'We do. All of us. You've just been a hero, and we're all
proud to death of you. It's only our pride and our love for you
that allows us to interfere. We don't *want* to interfere, but we
do want to know what's happening. Henry has heard that
you're working down in the East End, doing splendidly, and
it's just like your dear old noble self, but is it wise? Are you
taking advice? Won't those people down there do you in, so to
speak? I know that this is a time, of course, when we've all got
to study social conditions. No thinking man or woman can
possibly look round and *not* see that there is a great deal . . . a
whole lot . . . well, anyway, you know what I mean, Tom. But
is it right, without consulting any of us, to go down to all those
queer people? They can't like you really, you know. It's only
for what they can get out of you, and all that. After all, your
*own* people *are your own people*, aren't they, Tom dear?'

'I don't know.' Tom looked up at her smiling. 'But I don't
think that's exactly the point. They may be or they may not . . .
Look here. You've got one or two wrong ideas about this.

I want you to have the truth, and then we won't have to bother one another any more. You talk about my working and being noble, and so on. That's the most awful Tommy-rot. I'll tell you exactly what happened. I came back from France. At least, no, I didn't come back; but my body came back, if you know what I mean. I stayed over there. At least, I suppose that is what happened. I didn't know myself what it was. I just know that I didn't exist. You all used to come to tea here and be awfully nice and so on, but I didn't hear a word any of you said. I hope that doesn't sound rude, but I'm trying to tell exactly what occurred. I didn't know what was the matter with me – I wasn't anybody at all. I was Nobody. I didn't exist; and I asked Sheraton, and he didn't know either. And then, one night –'

Tom paused. The dramatic moment had come. He knew the kind of thing that they were expecting, and when he thought of the reality he laughed.

'One night – well, you won't believe me, I suppose, if I tell you I was very unhappy – no, unhappy is too strong – I was just nothing at all. You'd all been here to tea, and I went out for a walk down Bond Street to clear my head. It was raining and I found two old things taking shelter under a wooden standing. The old lady fainted while I was talking to them, and I saw them home – and – well, that's all!'

'That's all!' cried Millie Matcham. 'Do you mean, Tom, that you fell in love with the old woman?'

Her laugh was shrill and anxious.

He laughed back. 'Fell in love! That's just like you, Millie. You think that love must be in it every time. There isn't any love in this – and there isn't any devotion, or religion, or high-mindedness, or trying to improve them, or any of the things you imagine. On the contrary, *they* hate *me*, and I don't think that I'm very fond of *them* – except that I suppose one has a sort of affection for anybody who's brought one back to life again – when one didn't want to die!'

Henry Matcham broke in: 'Tom, look here – upon my word, I don't believe that one of us has the least idea *what* you're talking about.'

Tom looked around at them all and, in spite of himself, he was surprised at the change in their faces. The surprise was a shock. They were no longer regarding him with a gaze of tender, almost proprietary interest. The eyes that stared at his were almost hostile, at any rate suspicious, alarmed. Alarmed about what? Possibly his sanity – possibly the misgiving that in a moment he was going to do or say something that would shock them all.

He realized as he looked at them that he had come, quite unexpectedly, upon the crisis of his life. They could understand it, were he philanthropic, religious, sentimental. They were prepared for those things; they had read novels, they knew that such moods did occur. What they were not prepared for, what they most certainly would not stand, was exactly the explanation that he was about to give them. That would insult them, assault the very temple of their most sacred assurances. As he looked he knew that if he now spoke the truth he would for ever cut himself off from them. They would regard his case as hopeless. It would be in the future 'Poor Tom'.

He hated that – and for what was he giving them up? For the world that distrusted him, disbelieved in him, and would kill him if it could . . .

The Rubicon[10] was before him. He looked at its swirling waters, then, without any further hesitation, he crossed it. He was never to return again . . .

'I'm sorry to disappoint you all,' he said. 'There's no senti mental motive behind my action – no desire to make any people better, nothing fine at all. It simply is, as I've said already, that those two people brought me back to life again. I don't know what, except that I was suddenly interested in them. I didn't like them, and they *hated* me. Now I've become interested in their friends and relations. I don't want to *improve* them. They wouldn't let me if I did. I came back from France nobody at all. What happened there had simply killed all my interest in life. And – I'm awfully sorry to say it – but none of you brought my interest back. I think the centre of interests changed. It's as though there were some animal under the floor, and the part of the room that he's under is the part that you look at, because he's restless and it quivers. Well, he's shifted his position, that's all. You aren't on the interesting part of the floor any longer. I do hate to be rude and personal – but you have driven me to it. All of you are getting back to exactly what you were before the war: there's almost no change at all! And you're none of you interesting. I'm just as bad – but I want to go where the interesting human beings are, and there are more in the dirty streets than the clean ones. In books like *Marcella*,[11] years ago people went out of their own class because they wanted to do "good". I don't want to do good to anyone, but I do want to keep alive now that I've come back to life again. And – that's all there is to it,' he ended lamely.

He had done as he had expected. He had offended them all mortally. He was arrogant, proud, supercilious, and a little mad. And they saw, finally, that they had lost him. No more money for any of them.

'Well,' said Henry Matcham at last, 'if you want to know, Tom, I think that's about the rottenest explanation I've ever heard. Of course, you're covering something up. But I'm sure we don't want to penetrate your secret if you don't like us to.'

'There *isn't* any secret.' Tom was beginning to be angry. 'I tell you for the hundredth time I'm not going to start soup kitchens, or found mission rooms, or anything like that, but I don't want any more of these silly tea-parties or perpetual revues, or – or –'

'Or any of us,' Dollie, her cheeks flushed with angry colour, broke in. 'All Tom's been trying to explain to us is that he thinks we're a dull lot, and the Bolsheviks in the slums are more lively –'

'No,' Tom broke in; 'Dollie, that isn't fair. I don't want to pick and choose according to class any more. I don't want to be anything ever again with a name to it – like a Patriot, or a Democrat, or a Bolshevik, or an Anti-Bolshevik, or a Capitalist. I'm going by Individuals wherever they are. I – Oh, forgive me,' he broke off, 'I'm preaching; I didn't mean to. It's a thing I hate. But it's so strange – you none of you know how strange it is – being dead, so that you felt nothing, and minded nothing, and thought nothing, and then suddenly waking –'

But they had had enough. Tommy was trying to teach them. Teach *them*! And *Tommy*! . . .

They 'must be going' – sadly, angrily, indignantly they melted away. Tom was very sorry: there was nothing to be done.

Only Claribel, taking his hand for a moment, whispered:

'It's all right. They'll all come back later. They'll be wanting things.'

They were gone – all of them. He was alone in his room. He drew back the curtains and looked down over the grey misty stream of Duke Street scattered with the marigolds of the evening lights.

He threw open a window, and the roar of London came up to him like the rattle-rattle-rattle of a weaver's shuttle.

He laughed. He was happier than he had ever been before. The whole world seemed to be at his feet, and he no longer wished to judge it, to improve it, to dictate to it, to dogmatize it, to expect great things of it, to be disappointed in it . . .

He would never do any of those things again.

He addressed it:

'I did passionately wish you to be improved,' he said, 'but I didn't love you. Now I know you will never be improved, but I love you dearly – all of you, not a bit of you. Life simply isn't long enough for all I'm going to see!'

# 4

# IN RETROSPECT

# HAROLD BRIGHOUSE
# ONCE A HERO

Standing in a sheltered doorway a tramp, with a slouch hat crammed low over a notably unwashed face, watched the outside of the new works canteen of the Sir William Rumbold Ltd, Engineering Company. Perhaps because they were workers while he was a tramp, he had an air of compassionate cynicism as the audience assembled and thronged into the building, which, as prodigally advertised throughout Calderside, was to be opened that night by Sir William in person.

There being no one to observe him, the tramp could be frank with his cynicism; but inside the building, in the platform ante-room, Mr Edward Fosdike, who was Sir William's locally resident secretary, had to discipline his private feelings to a suave concurrence in his employer's florid enthusiasm. Fosdike served Sir William well, but no man is a hero to his (male) secretary.

'I hope you will find the arrangements satisfactory,' Fosdike was saying, tugging nervously at his maltreated moustache. 'You speak at seven and declare the canteen open. Then there's a meal.' He hesitated. 'Perhaps I should have warned you to dine before you came.'

Sir William was aware of being a very gallant gentleman. 'Not at all,' he said heroically, 'not at all. I have not spared my purse over this War Memorial. Why should I spare my feelings? Well, now, you've seen about the Press?'

'Oh, yes. The reporters are coming. There'll be flash-light photographs. Everything quite as usual when you make a public appearance, sir.'

Sir William wondered if this resident secretary of his were

quite adequate. Busy in London, he had left all arrangements in his local factotum's hands, and he was doubting whether those hands had grasped the situation competently. 'Only as usual?' he said sharply. 'This War Memorial has cost me ten thousand pounds.'

'The amount,' Fosdike hastened to assure him, 'has been circulated, with appropriate tribute to your generosity.'

'Generosity,' criticized Rumbold. 'I hope you didn't use that word.'

Mr Fosdike referred to his notebook. 'We said,' he read, ' "The cost, though amounting to ten thousand pounds, is entirely beside the point. Sir William felt that no expense was excessive that would result in a fitting and permanent expression of our gratitude to the glorious dead." '

'Thank you, Fosdike. That is exactly my feeling,' said the gratified Sir William, paying Fosdike the unspoken compliment of thinking him less of a fool than he looked. 'It is,' he went on, 'from no egotistic motive that I wish the Press to be strongly represented to-night. I believe that in deciding that Calderside's War Memorial should take the form of a Works Canteen, I am setting an example of enlightenment which other employers would do well to follow. I have erected a monument, not in stone, but in goodwill, a club-house for both sexes to serve as a centre of social activities for the firm's employees, wherein the great spirit of the noble work carried out at the Front by the YMCA will be recaptured and adapted to peace conditions in our local organization in the Martlow Works Canteen. What are you taking notes for?'

'I thought –' began Fosdike.

'Oh, well, perhaps you are right. Reporters have been known to miss one's point, and a little first aid, eh? By the way, I sent you some notes from town of what I intended to say in my speech. I just sent them ahead in case there was any local point I'd got wrong.'

He put it as a question, but actually it was an assertion and a challenge. It asserted that by no possible chance could there be anything injudicious in the proposed speech, and it challenged Fosdike to deny that assertion if he dared.

And Fosdike had to dare; he had to accuse himself of assuming too easily that Rumbold's memory of local Calderside detail was as fresh as the memory of the man on the spot.

'I did want to suggest a modification, sir,' he hazarded timidly.

'Really?' – quite below zero – 'Really? I felt very contented with the speech.'

'Yes, sir, it's masterly. But on the spot here –'

'Oh, agreed. Quite right, Fosdike. I am speaking tonight to the world – no; let me guard against exaggeration. The world includes the Polynesians and Esquimaux – I am speaking to the English-speaking races of the world, but first and foremost to Calderside. My own people. Yes? You have a little something to suggest? Some happy local allusion?'

'It's about Martlow,' said Fosdike shortly.

Sir William took him up. 'Ah, now you're talking,' he approved. 'Yes, indeed, anything you can add to my notes about Martlow will be most welcome. I have noted much, but too much is not enough for such an illustrious example of conspicuous gallantry, so noble a life, so great a deed, and so self-sacrificing an end. Any details you can add about Timothy Martlow will indeed –'

Fosdike coughed. 'Excuse me, sir, that's just the point. If you talk like that about Martlow down here, they'll laugh at you.'

'Laugh?' gasped Rumbold, his sense of propriety outraged. 'My dear Fosdike, what's come to you? I celebrate a hero. Our hero. Why, I'm calling the Canteen after Martlow when I might have given it my own name. That speaks volumes.' It did.

But Fosdike knew too well what would be the attitude of a Calderside audience if he allowed his chief to sing in top-notes an unreserved eulogy of Tim Martlow. Calderside knew Tim, the civilian, if it had also heard of Tim, the soldier. 'Don't you remember Martlow, sir? Before the war, I mean.'

'No. Ought I to?'

'Not on the bench?'

'Martlow? Yes, now I think of the name in connection with the old days, there was a drunken fellow. To be sure, an awful blackguard, continually before the bench. Dear me! Well, well, but a man is not responsible for his undesirable relations, I hope.'

'No, sir. But that was Martlow. The same man. You really can't speak to Calderside of his as an ennobling life and a great example. The war changed him, but – well, in peace, Tim was absolutely the local bad man, and they all know it. I thought you did, or –'

Sir William turned a face expressive of awe-struck wonder. 'Fosdike,' he said with deep sincerity, 'this is the most amazing thing I've heard of the war. I never connected Martlow the hero with – well, well, *de mortuis*.' He quoted:

> ' "Nothing in his life
> Became him like the leaving it; he died
> As one that had been studied in his death
> To throw away the dearest thing he owed
> As 'twere a careless trifle." [1]

'Appropriate, I think? I shall use that.'

It was, at least, a magnificent recovery from an unexpected blow, administered by the very man whose duty it was to guard Sir William against just that sort of blow. If Fosdike was not the local watchdog, he was nothing; and here was an occasion when the dog had omitted to bark until the last minute of the eleventh hour.

'Very apt quotation, sir, though there have never been any exact details of Martlow's death.'

Sir William meditated. 'Do you recall the name of the saint who was a regular rip before he got religion?' he asked.

'I think that applies to most of them,' said Fosdike.

'Yes, but the one in particular. Francis. That's it.' He filled his chest. 'Timothy Martlow,' he pronounced impressively, 'is the St Francis of the Great War, and this Canteen is his shrine. Now, I think I will go into the hall. It is early, but I shall chat with the people. Oh, one last thought. When you mentioned Martlow, I thought you were going to tell me of some undesirable connections. There are none?'

'There is his mother. A widow. You remember the Board voted her an addition to her pension.'

'Oh, yes. And she?'

'Oh, most grateful. She will be with you on the platform. I have seen myself that she is – fittingly attired.'

'I think I can congratulate you, Fosdike,' said Sir William magnanimously. 'You've managed very well. I look forward to a pleasant evening, a widely reported speech, and –'

Then Dolly Wainwright came into the ante-room.

'If you please, sir,' she said, 'what's going to be done about me?'

Two gentlemen who had all but reached the smug bathos of a mutual admiration society turned astonished eyes at the intruder.

She wore a tam,[2] and a check blanket coat, which she un buttoned as they watched her. Beneath it, suitable to the occasion, was a white dress, and Sir William, looking at it, felt a glow of tenderness for this artless child who had blundered into the privacy of the ante-room. Something daintily virginal in Dolly's face appealed to him; he caught himself thinking that her frock was more than a miracle in bleached cotton – it was moonshine shot with alabaster; and the improbability of that combination had hardly struck him when Fosdike's voice forced itself harshly on his ears.

'How did you get in here?'

Sir William moved to defend the girl from the anger of his secretary, but when she said, with a certain challenge, 'Through the door,' he doubted if she were so defenceless as she seemed.

'But there's a doorkeeper at the bottom,' said Fosdike. 'I gave him my orders.'

'I gave him my smile,' said Dolly. 'I won.'

'Upon my word –' Fosdike began.

'Well, well,' interrupted Sir William, 'what can I do for you?'

The reply was indirect, but caused Sir William still further to readjust his estimate of her.

'I've got friends in the meeting to-night,' she concluded. 'They'll speak up for me, too, if I'm not righted. So I'm telling you.'

'Don't threaten me, my girl,' said Sir William without

severity. 'I am always ready to pay attention to any legitimate grievance, but –'

'Legitimate?' she interrupted. 'Well, mine's not legitimate. So there!'

'I beg your pardon?' She puzzled Sir William. 'Come now,' he went on in his most patriarchal manner, 'don't assume I'm not going to listen to you. I am. To-night there is no thought in my mind except the welfare of Calderside.'

'Oh, well,' she said apologetically, 'I'm sorry if I riled you, but it's a bit awkward to speak it out to a man. Only' (the unconscious cruelty of youth – or was it conscious?) 'you're both old, so perhaps I can get through. It's about Tim Martlow.'

'Ah,' said Sir William encouragingly, 'our glorious hero.'

'Yes,' said Dolly. 'I'm the mother of his child.'

We are all balloons dancing our lives amongst pins. Therefore, be compassionate towards Sir William. He collapsed speechlessly on a hard chair.

Fosdike reacted more alertly. 'This is the first I've heard of Martlow's being married,' he said aggressively.

Dolly looked up at him indignantly. 'You ain't heard it now, have you?' she protested. 'I said it wasn't legitimate. I don't say we'd not have got married if there'd been time, but you can't do everything on short leave.'

There seemed an obvious retort. Rumbold and Fosdike looked at each other, and neither made the retort. Instead, Fosdike asked: 'Are you employed in the works here?'

'I was here, on munitions,' she said, 'and then on doles.'

'And now you're on the make,' he sneered.

'Oh, I dunno,' she said. 'All this fuss about Tim Martlow. I ought to have my bit out of it.'

'Deplorable,' grieved Sir William. 'The crass materialism of it all. This is so sad. How old are you?'

'Twenty,' said Dolly. 'Twenty, with a child to keep, and his father's name up in gold lettering in that hall there. I say somebody ought to do something.'

'I suppose now, Miss –' Fosdike baulked.

'Wainwright, Dolly Wainwright, though it ought to be Martlow.'

'I suppose you loved Tim very dearly?'

'I liked him well enough. He was good-looking in his khaki.'

'Liked him? I'm sure it was more than that.'

'Oh, I dunno. Why?' asked the girl, who said she was the mother of Martlow's child.

'I am sure,' said Fosdike gravely, 'you would never do any-thing to bring a stain upon his memory.'

Dolly proposed a bargain. 'If I'm rightly done by,' she said, 'I'll do right by him.'

'Anything that marred the harmony of to-night's ceremony, Miss Wainwright, would be unthinkable,' said Sir William, coming to his lieutenant's support.

'Right,' said Dolly cheerfully. 'If you'll take steps according, I'm sure I've no desire to make a scene.'

'A scene,' gasped Sir William.

'Though,' she pointed out, 'it's a lot to ask of anyone, you know. Giving up the certain chance of getting my photograph in the papers. I make a good picture, too. Some do and some don't, but I take well and when you know you've got the looks to carry off a scene, it's asking something of me to give up the idea.'

'But you said you'd no desire to make a scene.'

'Poor girls have often got to do what they don't wish to. I wouldn't make a scene in the usual way. Hysterics and all that. Hysterics means cold water in your face and your dress messed up and no sympathy. But with scenes, the greater the occasion the greater the reward, and there's no denying this is an occasion, is there? You're making a big to-do about Tim Mart-low and the reward would be according. I don't know if you've noticed that if a girl makes a scene and she's got the looks for it, she gets offers of marriage, like they do in the police-court when they've been wronged and the magistrate passes all the men's letters on to the court missionary and the girl and the missionary go through them and choose the likeliest fellow out of the bunch?'

'But my dear young lady –' Fosdike began.

She silenced him. 'Oh, it's all right. I don't know that I want to get married.'

'Then you ought to,' said Sir William virtuously.

'There's better things in life than getting married,' Dolly said. 'I've weighed up marriage, and I don't see what there is in it for a girl nowadays.'

'In your case, I should have thought there was everything.'

Dolly sniffed. 'There isn't liberty,' she said. 'And we won the fight for liberty, didn't we? No; if I made that scene it 'ud be to get my photograph in the papers where the film people could see it. I've the right face for the pictures, and my romantic history will do the rest.'

'Good heavens, girl,' cried the scandalized Sir William, 'have you no reverence at all? The pictures! You'd turn all my disinterested efforts to ridicule. You'd – oh, but there! You're not going to make a scene?'

'That's a matter of arrangement, of course,' said the cool lady. 'I'm only showing you what a big chance I shall miss if I oblige you. Suppose I pipe up my tale of woe just when you're on the platform with the Union Jack behind you and the reporters in front of you, and that tablet in there that says Tim is the greatest glory of Calderside –'

Sir William nearly screamed. 'Be quiet, girl. Fosdike,' he snarled, turning viciously on his secretary, 'what the deuce do you mean by pretending to keep an eye on local affairs when you miss a thing like this?'

' 'Tisn't his fault,' said Dolly. 'I've been saving this up for you.'

'Oh,' he groaned, 'and I'd felt so happy about to-night.' He took out a fountain pen. 'Well, I suppose there's no help for it. Fosdike, what's the amount of the pension we allow Martlow's mother?'

'Double it, add a pound a week, and what's the answer. Mr Fosdike?' asked Dolly quickly.

Sir William gasped ludicrously.

'I mean to say,' said Dolly, conferring on his gasp the honour of an explanation, 'she's old and didn't go on munitions, and didn't get used to wangling income tax on her wages, and never had no ambitions to go on the pictures, neither. What's compensation to her isn't compensation to me. I've got a higher standard.'

'The less you say about your standards, the better, my girl,' retorted Sir William. 'Do you know that this is blackmail?'

'No, it isn't. Not when I ain't asked you for nothing. And if I pass the remark how that three pounds a week is my idea of a minimum wage, it isn't blackmail to state the fact.'

Sir William paused in the act of tearing a page out of Fosdike's note-book. 'Three pounds a week!'

'Well,' said Dolly reasonably, 'I didn't depreciate the currency. Three pounds a week is little enough these times for the girl who fell from grace through the chief glory of Calderside.'

'But suppose you marry,' suggested Mr Fosdike.

'Then I marry well,' she said, 'having means of my own. And I ought to, seeing I'm kind of widow to the chief glory of –'

Sir William looked up sharply from the table. 'If you use that phrase again,' he said, 'I'll tear this paper up.'

'Widow to Tim Martlow,' she amended it, defiantly. He handed her the document he had drawn up. It was an undertaking in brief, unambiguous terms to pay her three pounds a week for life. As she read it, exulting, the door was kicked open.

The tramp, whose name was Timothy Martlow, came in and turning, spoke through the doorway to the janitor below. 'Call out,' he said, 'and I'll come back and knock you down again.' Then he locked the door.

Fosdike went courageously towards him. 'What do you mean by this intrusion? Who are you?'

The tramp assured himself that his hat was well pulled down over his face. He put his hands in his pockets and looked quizzically at the advancing Mr Fosdike. 'So far,' he said, 'I'm the man that locked the door.'

Fosdike started for the second door, which led directly to the platform. The tramp reached it first, and locked it, shouldering Fosdike from him. 'Now,' he said.

Sir William was searching the wall. 'Are there no bells?' he asked desperately.

'No.'

'No?' jeered the tramp. 'No bell. No telephone. No nothing. You're scotched without your rifle this time.'

Fosdike consulted Sir William. 'I might shout for the police,' he suggested.

'It's risky,' commented the tramp. 'They sometimes come when they're called.'

'Then –' began the secretary.

'It's your risk,' emphasized the tramp. 'And I don't advise it. I've gone to a lot of trouble this last week to keep out of sight of the Calderside police. They'd identify me easy, and Sir William wouldn't like that.'

'I wouldn't like?' said Rumbold. 'I? Who are you?'

'Wounded and missing, believed dead,' quoted the tramp. 'Only there's been a lot of beliefs upset in this war, and I'm one of them.'

'One of what?'

'I'm telling you. One of the strayed sheep that got mislaid and come home at the awkwardest times.' He snatched his hat off. 'Have a good look at that face, your worship.'

'Timothy Martlow,' cried Sir William.

Fosdike staggered to a chair while Dolly, who had shown nothing but amusement at the tramp, now gave a quick cry and shrank back against the wall, exhibiting every symptom of the liveliest terror. Of the trio, Sir William, for whom surely this inopportune return had the most serious implications, alone stood his ground, and Martlow grimly appreciated his pluck.

'It's very near made a stretcher-case of him,' he said, indicating the prostrated Fosdike. 'You're cooler. Walking wounded.'

'I . . . really . . .'

'Shake hands, old cock,' said Martlow, 'I know you've got it writ up in there' – he jerked his head towards the hall – 'that I'm the chief glory of Calderside, but damme if you're not the second best yourself, and I'll condescend to shake your hand if it's only to show you I'm not a ghost.'

Sir William decided that it was politic to humour this visitor. He shook hands. 'Then, if you know,' he said, 'if you know what this building is, it isn't accident that brings you here to-night.'

'The sort of accident you set with a time-fuse,' said Martlow grimly. 'I told you I'd been dodging the police for a week lest any of my old pals should recognize me. I was waiting to get you to-night, and sitting tight and listening. The things I heard! Nearly made me take my hat off to myself. But not quite. Not quite. I kept my hat on and I kept my hair on. It's a mistake to act premature on information received. If I'd sprung this too soon, the wrong thing might have happened to me.'

'What wrong thing, Martlow?' asked Sir William with some indignation. If the fellow meant anything, it was that he would have been spirited away by Sir William.

'Oh, anything,' replied Martlow. 'Anything would be wrong that made me miss this pleasure. You and me conversing affable here. Not a bit like it was in the old days before I rose to being the chief glory of Calderside. Conversation was one-sided then, and all on your side instead of mine. "Here again, Martlow," you'd say, and then they'd gabble the evidence, and you'd say, "Fourteen days," or "Twenty-one days," if you'd got up peevish and that's all there was to our friendly intercourse. This time, I make no doubt you'll be asking me to stay at the Towers to-night. And,' he went on blandly, enjoying every wince that twisted Sir William's face in spite of his efforts to appear unmoved, 'I don't know that I'll refuse. It's a levelling thing, war. I've read that war makes us all conscious we're members of one brotherhood, and I know it's true now. Consequently the chief glory of the place ain't got no right to be too high and mighty to accept your humble invitation. The best guest-room for Sergeant Martlow, you'll say See there's a hot water-bottle in his bed, you'll say, and in case he's thirsty in the night, you'll tell them to put the whisky by his side.'

After all, a man does not rise to become Sir William Rumbold by being flabby. Sir William struck the table heavily. Somehow he had to put a period to this mocking harangue. 'Martlow,' he said, 'how many people know you're here?'

Tim gave a good imitation of Sir William's gesture. He, too, could strike a table. 'Rumbold,' he retorted, 'what's the value of a secret when it's not a secret? You three in this room know, and not another soul in Calderside.'

'Not even your mother?' queried Rumbold.

'No. I been a bad son to her in the past. I'm a good one now

I'm dead. She's got a bit o' pension, and I'll not disturb that. I'll stay dead – to her,' he added forcibly, dashing the hope which leaped in Rumbold.

'Why have you come here? Here – to-night?'

The easy mockery renewed itself in Martlow's voice. 'People's ideas of fun vary,' he stated. 'The fly's idea ain't the same as the spider's. This 'ere is my idea – shaking your hand and sitting cosy with the bloke that's sent me down more times than I can think. And the fun 'ull grow furious when you and I walk arm in arm on to that platform, and you tell them all I'm resurrected.'

'Like this?' the proper Mr Fosdike interjected.

'Eh?' said Tim. 'Like what?'

'You can't go on to the platform in those clothes, Martlow. Have you looked in a mirror lately? Do you know what you look like? This is a respectable occasion, man.'

'Yes,' said Tim drily. 'It's an occasion for showing respect to me. I'll do as I am, not having had time to go to the tailor's for my dress suit yet.'

'Martlow,' said Sir William briskly, 'time's short. I'm due on that platform.'

'Right, I'm with you.' Tim moved towards the platform door.

Sir William, with a serene air of triumph, played his trump card. He took out his cheque-book. 'No,' he said. 'You're not coming. Instead –'

He shrank back hastily as a huge fist was projected vehemently towards his face. But the fist swerved and opened. The cheque-book, not Sir William's person, was its objective. 'Instead be damned,' said Tim Martlow, pitching the cheque-book to the floor. 'To hell with your money. Thought I was after money, did you?'

Sir William met his eye. 'Yes, I did,' he said hardily.

'That's the sort of mean idea you would have, Sir William Rumbold. They say scum rises. You grew a handle to your name during the war, but you ain't grown manners to go with it. War changes them that's changeable. T'others are too set to change.'

Sir William felt a strange glow of appreciation for this man who, with so easy an opportunity to grow rich, refused money. 'It's changed you,' he said with ungrudging admiration that had no tincture of diplomacy in it.

'Has it?' mused Tim. 'From what?'

'Well –' Sir William was embarrassed. 'From what you were.'

'What was I?' demanded Tim. 'Go on, spit it out. What sort of character would you have given me then?'

'I'd have called you,' said Sir William boldly, 'a disreputable drunken loafer who never did an honest day's work in his life.' Which had the merit of truth, and, he thought, the demerit of rashness.

To his surprise he found that Tim was looking at him with undisguised admiration. 'Lummy,' he said, 'you've got guts. Yes, that's right. "Disreputable drunken loafer". And if I came back now?' he asked.

'You were magnificent in the war, Martlow.'

'First thing I did when I got civvies on was to get blind and skinned. Drink and civvies go together in my mind.'

'You'll get over that,' said Sir William encouragingly; but he was puzzled by the curiously wistful note which had replaced Tim's hectoring.

'There's a chance,' admitted Tim. 'A bare chance. Not a chance I'd gamble on. Not when I've a bigger chance than that. You wouldn't say, weighing me up now, that I've got a reformed look, would you?'

Sir William couldn't. 'But you'll pull yourself together. You'll remember –'

'I'll remember the taste of beer,' said Tim with fierce conviction. 'No, I never had a chance before, but I've got one now, and, by heaven, I'm taking it.' Sir William's apprehension grew acute; if money was not the question, what outrageous demand was about to be made of him? Tim went on, 'I'm nothing but a dirty, drunken tramp to-day. Yes, drunk when I can get it and craving when I can't. That's Tim Martlow when he's living. Tim Martlow dead's a different thing. He's a man with his name wrote up in letters of gold in a dry canteen. Dry! By God, that's funny! He's somebody, honoured in Calderside for ever and ever, amen. And we won't spoil a good thing by taking chances on my reformation. I'm dead. I'll stay dead.' He paused in enjoying the effect he made.

Sir William stooped to pick his cheque-book from the floor. 'Don't do that,' said Tim sharply. 'It isn't out of your mind yet that money's what I came for. Fun's one thing that brought me. Just for the treat of showing you myself and watching your quick-change faces while I did it. And I've had my fun.' His voice grew menacing. 'The other thing I came for isn't fun. It's this.' Dolly screamed as he took her arm and jerked her to her feet from the corner where she had sought obscurity. He shook her urgently. 'You've been telling tales about me. I've heard of it. You hear all the news when you lie quiet yourself and let other people do the talking. You came in here to-night to spin a yarn. I watched you in. Well, is it true?'

'No,' said Dolly, gasping for breath.

'I mean –' he insisted, 'what you said about you and me. That isn't true?'

She repeated her denial. 'No,' he said, releasing her, 'it 'ud have a job to be seeing this is the first time I've had the pleasure of meeting you. That'll do.' He opened the platform door politely. 'I hope I haven't made you late on the platform, sir,' he said.

Both Sir William and the secretary stared fascinated at Dolly, the enterprising young person who had so successfully bluffed them. 'I repeat, don't let me make you late,' said Tim from the now wide open door.

Rumbold checked Fosdike who was, apparently, bent on doing Dolly a personal violence. 'That can wait,' he said. 'What can't wait is this.' He held out his hand to Martlow. 'In all sincerity, I beg the honour.'

Tim shook his hand, and Rumbold turned to the door. Fosdike ran after him with the notes of his speech. 'Your speech, sir.'

Sir William turned on him angrily. 'Man,' he said, 'haven't you heard? That muck won't do now. I have to try to do Martlow justice.' He went out to the platform, Fosdike after him.

Tim Martlow sat at the table and took a bottle from his pocket. He drew the cork with his teeth, then felt a light touch on his arm. 'I was forgetting you,' he said, replacing the bottle.

'I ain't likely to forget you,' said Dolly ruefully.

He gripped her hard. 'But you are going to forget me, my girl,' he said. 'Tim Martlow's dead, and his letters of gold ain't going to be blotted by the likes of you. You that's been putting it about Calderside I'm the father of your child, and I ain't never seen you in my life till to-night.'

'Yes, but you're getting this all wrong,' she blubbered. 'I didn't have a baby. I was going to borrow one if they'd claimed to see it.'

'What? No baby? And you put it across old Rumbold?' Laughter and sheer admiration of her audacity were mingled in his voice. With a baby it was a good bluff; without one, the girl's ingenuity seemed to him to touch genius.

'He gave me that paper,' she said, pride subduing tears as she handed him her splendid trophy.

'Three pounds a week for life,' he read, with profound reverence. 'If you ain't a blinkin' marvel.' He complimented her, giving her the paper back. Then he realized that, through him, her gains were lost.

'Gawd, I done wrong. I got no right to mess up a thing like that. I didn't know. See, I'll tell him I made you lie. I'll own the baby's mine.'

'But there ain't no baby,' she persisted.

'There's plenty of babies looking for a mother with three pounds a week,' he said.

She tore the paper up. 'Then they'll not find me,' she said. 'Three pounds a week's gone. And your letters of gold, Mr Martlow, remain.'

The practised voice of Sir William Rumbold, speaking on the platform, filled the ante-room, not with the rhetorician's counterfeit of sincerity, but, unmistakably, with sincerity itself. 'I had prepared a speech,' he was saying. 'A prepared speech is useless in face of the emotion I feel at the life of Timothy Martlow. I say advisedly to you that when I think of Martlow, I know myself for a worm. He was despised and rejected. What had England done for him that he should give his life for her? We wronged him. We made an outcast of him. I personally wronged him from the magistrate's bench, and he pays us back like this, rising from an undeserved obscurity to a height where he rests secure for ever, a reproach to us, and a great example of the man who won. And against what odds he played it out to a supreme end, and –'

'You're right,' said Tim Martlow, motioning the girl to close the door. He wasn't used to hearing panegyrics on himself, nor was he aware that, mechanically, he had raised the bottle to his lips.

Dolly meant to close the door discreetly; instead, she threw it from her and jumped at the bottle. Tim was conscious of a double crash, putting an emphatic stop to the sound of Sir William's eulogy – the crash of the door and the bottle which Dolly snatched from him and pitched against the wall.

'Letters of gold,' she panted, 'and you shan't tarnish them. I'll see to that.'

He gaped for a moment at the liquor flowing from the bottle, then raised his eyes to hers. 'You?' he said.

'I haven't got a baby to look after,' said Dolly. 'But – I've you. Where were you thinking of going now?'

His eyes went to the door behind which Sir William was, presumably, still praising him, and his head jerked resolutely. 'Playing it out,' he said. 'I've got to vanish good and sure after that. I'll play it out, by God. I was a hero once, I'll be a hero still.' His foot crunched broken glass as he moved. 'I'm going to America, my girl. It's dry.'

Perhaps she distrusted the absolute dryness of America, and perhaps that had nothing to do with Dolly. She examined her hand minutely. 'Going to the Isle of Man on a rough day, I wasn't a bit ill,' she said casually. 'I'm a good sailor.'

'You put it across Sir William,' he said. 'You're a blinkin' marvel.'

'No,' she said, 'but a thing that's worth doing is worth doing well. I'm not a marvel, but I might be the metal polish in those gold letters of yours if you think it worth while.'

His trampish squalor seemed to him suddenly appalling. 'There, don't do that,' he protested – her arm had found its way into his. 'My sleeve's dirty.'

'Idiot!' said Dolly Wainwright, drawing him to the door.

# KATHERINE MANSFIELD
# THE FLY

'Y'are very snug in here,' piped old Mr Woodifield, and he peered out of the great, green-leather armchair by his friend the boss's desk as a baby peers out of its pram. His talk was over; it was time for him to be off. But he did not want to go. Since he had retired, since his . . . stroke, the wife and the girls kept him boxed up in the house every day of the week except Tuesday. On Tuesday he was dressed and brushed and allowed to cut back to the City for the day. Though what he did there the wife and girls couldn't imagine. Made a nuisance of himself to his friends, they supposed . . . Well, perhaps so. All the same, we cling to our last pleasures as the tree clings to its last leaves. So there sat old Woodifield, smoking a cigar and staring almost greedily at the boss, who rolled in his office chair, stout, rosy, five years older than he, and still going strong, still at the helm. It did one good to see him.

Wistfully, admiringly, the old voice added, 'It's snug in here, upon my word!'

'Yes, it's comfortable enough,' agreed the boss, and he flipped the *Financial Times* with a paper-knife. As a matter of fact he was proud of his room; he liked to have it admired, especially by old Woodifield. It gave him a feeling of deep, solid satisfaction to be planted there in the midst of it in full view of that frail old figure in the muffler.

'I've had it done up lately,' he explained, as he had explained for the past – how many? – weeks. 'New carpet,' and he pointed to the bright red carpet with a pattern of large white rings. 'New furniture,' and he nodded towards the massive bookcase and the table with legs like twisted treacle. 'Electric heating!'

He waved almost exultantly towards the five transparent, pearly sausages glowing so softly in the tilted copper pan.

But he did not draw old Woodifield's attention to the photograph over the table of a grave-looking boy in uniform standing in one of those spectral photographers' parks with photographers' storm-clouds behind him. It was not new. It had been there for over six years.

'There was something I wanted to tell you,' said old Woodifield, and his eyes grew dim remembering. 'Now what was it? I had it in my mind when I started out this morning.' His hands began to tremble, and patches of red showed above his beard.

Poor old chap, he's on his last pins, thought the boss. And, feeling kindly, he winked at the old man, and said jokingly, 'I tell you what. I've got a little drop of something here that'll do you good before you go out into the cold again. It's beautiful stuff. It wouldn't hurt a child.' He took a key off his watch-chain, unlocked a cupboard below his desk, and drew forth a dark, squat bottle. 'That's the medicine,' said he. 'And the man from whom I got it told me on the strict QT it came from the cellars at Windsor Castle.'

Old Woodifield's mouth fell open at the sight. He couldn't have looked more surprised if the boss had produced a rabbit.

'It's whisky, ain't it?' he piped feebly.

The boss turned the bottle and lovingly showed him the label. Whisky it was.

'D'you know,' said he, peering up at the boss wonderingly, 'they won't let me touch it at home.' And he looked as though he was going to cry.

'Ah, that's where we know a bit more than the ladies,' cried the boss, swooping across for two tumblers that stood on the table with the water-bottle, and pouring a generous finger into each. 'Drink it down. It'll do you good. And don't put any water with it. It's sacrilege to tamper with stuff like this. Ah!' He tossed off his, pulled out his handkerchief, hastily wiped his moustaches, and cocked an eye at old Woodifield, who was rolling his in his chaps.

The old man swallowed, was silent a moment, and then said faintly, 'It's nutty!'

But it warmed him; it crept into his chill old brain – he remembered.

'That was it,' he said, heaving himself out of his chair. 'I thought you'd like to know. The girls were in Belgium last week having a look at poor Reggie's grave, and they happened to come across your boy's. They're quite near each other, it seems.'

Old Woodifield paused, but the boss made no reply. Only a quiver in his eyelids showed that he heard.

'The girls were delighted with the way the place is kept,' piped the old voice. 'Beautifully looked after. Couldn't be better if they were at home. You've not been across, have yer?'

'No, no!' For various reasons the boss had not been across.

'There's miles of it,' quavered old Woodifield, 'and it's all as neat as a garden. Flowers growing on all the graves. Nice broad paths.' It was plain from his voice how much he liked a nice broad path.

The pause came again. Then the old man brightened wonderfully.

'D'you know what the hotel made the girls pay for a pot of jam?' he piped. 'Ten francs! Robbery, I call it. It was a little pot, so Gertrude says, no bigger than a half-crown. And she hadn't taken more than a spoonful when they charged her ten francs. Gertrude brought the pot away with her to teach 'em a lesson. Quite right, too; it's trading on our feelings. They think because we're over there having a look round we're ready to pay anything. That's what it is.' And he turned towards the door.

'Quite right, quite right!' cried the boss, though what was quite right he hadn't the least idea. He came round by his desk, followed the shuffling footsteps to the door, and saw the old fellow out. Woodifield was gone.

For a long moment the boss stayed, staring at nothing, while the grey-haired office messenger, watching him, dodged in and out of his cubby-hole like a dog that expects to be taken for a run. Then: 'I'll see nobody for half an hour, Macey,' said the boss. 'Understand? Nobody at all.'

'Very good, sir.'

The door shut, the firm heavy steps recrossed the bright

carpet, the fat body plumped down in the spring chair, and leaning forward, the boss covered his face with his hands. He wanted, he intended, he had arranged to weep . . .

It had been a terrible shock to him when old Woodifield sprang that remark upon him about the boy's grave. It was exactly as though the earth had opened and he had seen the boy lying there with Woodfield's girls staring down at him. For it was strange. Although over six years had passed away, the boss never thought of the boy except as lying unchanged, unblemished in his uniform, asleep for ever. 'My son!' groaned the boss. But no tears came yet. In the past, in the first months and even years after the boy's death, he had only to say those words to be overcome by such grief that nothing short of a violent fit of weeping could relieve him. Time, he had declared then, he had told everybody, could make no difference. Other men perhaps might recover, might live their loss down, but not he. How was it possible? His boy was an only son. Ever since his birth the boss had worked at building up this business for him; it had no other meaning if it was not for the boy. Life itself had come to have no other meaning. How on earth could he have slaved, denied himself, kept going all those years without the promise for ever before him of the boy's stepping into his shoes and carrying on where he left off?

And that promise had been so near being fulfilled. The boy had been in the office learning the ropes for a year before the war. Every morning they had started off together; they had come back by the same train. And what congratulations he had received as the boy's father! No wonder; he had taken to it marvellously. As to his popularity with the staff, every man jack of them down to old Macey couldn't make enough of the boy. And he wasn't in the least spoilt. No, he was just his bright natural self, with the right word for everybody, with that boyish look and his habit of saying, 'Simply splendid!'

But that was all over and done with as though it never had been. The day had come when Macey had handed him the telegram that brought the whole place crashing about his head. 'Deeply regret to inform you . . .' And he had left the office a broken man, with his life in ruins.

Six years ago, six years . . . How quickly time passed! It might
have happened yesterday. The boss took his hands from his
face; he was puzzled. Something seemed to be wrong with him.
He wasn't feeling as he wanted to feel. He decided to get up and
have a look at the boy's photograph. But it wasn't a favourite
photograph of his; the expression was unnatural. It was cold,
even stern-looking. The boy had never looked like that.

At that moment the boss noticed that a fly had fallen into his
broad inkpot, and was trying feebly but desperately to clamber
out again. Help! help! said those struggling legs. But the sides
of the inkpot were wet and slippery; it fell back again and began
to swim. The boss took up a pen, picked the fly out of the ink,
and shook it on to a piece of blotting-paper. For a fraction of
a second it lay still on the dark patch that oozed round it. Then
the front legs waved, took hold, and, pulling its small, sodden
body up, it began the immense task of cleaning the ink from its
wings. Over and under, over and under, went a leg along a
wing as the stone goes over and under the scythe. Then there
was a pause, while the fly, seeming to stand on the tips of its
toes, tried to expand first one wing and then the other. It
succeeded at last, and, sitting down, it began, like a minute cat,
to clean its face. Now one could imagine that the little front
legs rubbed against each other lightly, joyfully. The horrible
danger was over; it had escaped; it was ready for life again.

But just then the boss had an idea. He plunged his pen back
into the ink, leaned his thick wrist on the blotting-paper, and
as the fly tried its wings down came a great heavy blot. What
would it make of that? What indeed! The little beggar seemed
absolutely cowed, stunned, and afraid to move because of what
would happen next. But then, as if painfully, it dragged itself
forward. The front legs waved, caught hold, and, more slowly
this time, the task began from the beginning.

He's a plucky little devil, thought the boss, and he felt a real
admiration for the fly's courage. That was the way to tackle
things; that was the right spirit. Never say die; it was only a
question of . . . But the fly had again finished its laborious task,
and the boss had just time to refill his pen, to shake fair and
square on the new-cleaned body yet another dark drop. What

about it this time? A painful moment of suspense followed. But behold, the front legs were again waving; the boss felt a rush of relief. He leaned over the fly and said to it tenderly, 'You artful little b . . .' And he actually had the brilliant notion of breathing on it to help the drying process. All the same, there was something timid and weak about its efforts now, and the boss decided that this time should be the last, as he dipped the pen deep into the inkpot.

It was. The last blot fell on the soaked blotting-paper, and the draggled fly lay in it and did not stir. The back legs were stuck to the body; the front legs were not to be seen.

'Come on,' said the boss. 'Look sharp!' And he stirred it with his pen – in vain. Nothing happened or was likely to happen. The fly was dead.

The boss lifted the corpse on the end of the paper-knife and flung it into the waste-paper basket. But such a grinding feeling of wretchedness seized him that he felt positively frightened. He started forward and pressed the bell for Macey.

'Bring me some fresh blotting-paper,' he said sternly, 'and look sharp about it.' And while the old dog padded away he fell to wondering what it was he had been thinking about before. What was it? It was . . . He took out his handkerchief and passed it inside his collar. For the life of him he could not remember.

# WINIFRED HOLTBY
# THE CASUALTY LIST

Mrs Lancing came into her drawing-room and added another silk poppy to the bunch growing annually in the cloisonné vase. Another Armistice Day's duty done; another Two Minutes' Silence observed at the Memorial Service in the Parish Church which the dear Rector always held. He had lost one of his own boys in 1917. It was very sad.

It was all very sad. The war had been terrible, terrible. Going to see *Journey's End*[1] with Margaret last month had brought it all back to her. She had been thinking about that play all through the service; about poor young Stanhope, drinking like that, and the funny servant; but most of all about that queer, tense, terrifying yet exciting call, 'Stretcher-bearer! Stretcher-bearer!' in the last act. It had a curious effect upon her, as though it almost, but not quite, released the secret of a hidden fear.

Well, she was tired now. Those new patent-leather shoes were not really comfortable. It had been a relief to get into slippers again. Thank goodness there was still half an hour before lunch-time in which she could rest and look at *The Times*. Arthur had left it on the sofa as usual. He had not looked very well that morning; but then, who could look well every morning? When you were eighty-two. Why, she hadn't felt any too well herself, and she was nearly nine years younger. She sat down in the big arm-chair and stretched out her feet towards the dancing fire.

Of course, it wasn't as if she had had boys herself. With Arthur too old really, even to be a special constable, and the girls doing a little light secretarial and orderly work at the local hospital, she had never been able to feel that she was really in the war. She had done her bit, rolled bandages, and knitted socks, and served on the Refugees Committee, and rationed her own household so sternly that two of her best maids left; but that had not been quite the same thing. And she had always hated to feel out of anything – of the best set in the town, or the Hospital Ball, or the craze for roller-skating – or even the war. She had read the Casualty List every morning carefully, and written sympathetic, admiring notes to those other women whose husbands and sons were among the wounded or the fallen; but she could not sometimes help wishing that her own situation was a little more heroic. Those Wonderful Mothers Who Gave Their Sons held an immense moral advantage over the ordinary women who only coped with a sugar shortage and the servant problem, and the regulations about darkening windows. When Nellie Goodson's only son was killed, she had felt almost envious, of the boy for his Glorious End, of the mother for her honourable grief. Her sin had always been to covet honour.

During the ten years following the war, she had nearly forgotten this strange feeling of envy, just as she had forgotten the taste of lentil cutlets and the fuss about meat cards. There had been so much to think about, Margaret's wedding to her smart young Deryck, and Celia's wedding to Dr Studdley. Funny she could never think of him as Eric – always as Dr Studdley – and the grand-children, and the new bathroom, and Arthur's operation, and putting in Central Heating and her own neuritis. Life had been very full and complicated and busy, for Arthur's business had not done so badly during the war, and though of course he had retired, he still drew dividends.

It was a pity that she had never been able to persuade him to settle anything on the girls. That night she stayed with Margaret to go to *Journey's End* she remembered the girl, already in her becoming blue theatre frock, setting the grapefruit glasses on the polished table – for she was always up to date although she kept only a day-woman – and sighing, 'If only we had a little capital.' If Deryck had had a little capital, perhaps they would have felt that they could afford a baby. These modern ways were all wrong, thought Mrs Lancing. And yet, when she

remembered Celia and her four, and another coming, and the
untidiness of the Studdleys' little house, with one meal always
on top of the next, she could not reproach Margaret. It seemed
a pity, perhaps, that young people needed the money, while old
people always had it.

Of course she had paid for the theatre seats and taxis and
everything. She had not really wanted to see *Journey's End*, but
everyone had been talking about it, and she felt so silly when
she said she had only listened in on Arthur's wireless. She really
liked a nice, amusing play, something you could laugh over,
with a little love story and pretty frocks. Still, Margaret had
seemed quite glad to take her, and it had been a change from
hurrying back after visiting poor Nancy.

Once a month since Nancy's second stroke, Mrs Lancing had
gone up to town to see her sister. She was astonished at the
difference that Nancy's illness made to her. The sisters had
never been deeply devoted to each other, and for many years
their relationship had been one of mutual tolerance and irritation. Yet ever since Mrs Lancing had seen Nancy lying in bed,
between the chintz curtains covered with hollyhocks, her poor
mouth twisted and her speech all thick and blurred, she had
been afraid. The weeks passed, and a sudden ringing of the
telephone had only meant that the butcher could not send the
kidneys in time for dinner, or that the Burketts wanted a fourth
for bridge; but still Mrs Lancing was afraid. They said that the
third stroke was always fatal, and Mrs Lancing did not want
her sister to die. For when she had gone there would be no one
left to share those memories of her childhood which grew
more vivid with each passing year. There was no one else who
remembered the hollow at the roots of the weeping ash-tree,
that had made a beautiful kitchen range whenever they had
played at Keeping House. No one else remembered poor Miss
Wardle, the governess, who had lost the third finger of her left
hand and spoke with a lisp. And no one else remembered that
exciting night when the wheel came off the brougham driving
home from the Hilaries, and they had to walk in their party
slippers through the snow.

Even Rita Washburn, naughty little Rita who came over from

the Rectory to do lessons with them, was dead now. Only two months ago Mrs Lancing had covered the blue front of her black dress with a scarf, before she set off to Golders Green Cemetery for Rita's funeral.

Perhaps it would be as well to ask Madame Challette to make her next dress with two detachable fronts, one black, and one coloured. For in these days one never knew. Every time Mrs Lancing picked up *The Times* she looked down the Deaths' Column with apprehension. She never knew who might go next. Why, there were hardly any of the old Bromley people left. That was the worst of being the baby of a set. Everyone else seemed to grow old so soon. Mrs Lancing did not feel old at all, only sometimes she got a little tired, and always nowadays she was conscious of that lurking fear.

She picked up *The Times* and held it between her and the fire. Well, there was one comfort, she would never see Nancy's death there, as she had seen their father's, because she was on holiday in Scotland with Arthur and they had not known where to find her. She had made arrangements with Nancy's household now to telephone to her at once if anything happened, because she knew so well how, in the confusion of death, important things were neglected.

She knew so well. She had become quite expert recently in the technicalities of sudden illness, death and funerals. There had been her mother, her elder brother Henry, cousin Jane, and her great friend, Millie Waynwright. Millie's children had both been abroad when it happened, and she had had to arrange everything. Somehow it was just like Millie to give everyone as much trouble as possible. Dear, wayward, lovely, petulant Millie, a spoiled pretty woman to the end, her white hair waved and shingled, her neck tied up with pale mauve tulle, and fresh flowers brought by her husband every day. But she had never really got over Roddie's death. He had been killed accidentally by a bomb exploding in England, and somehow that was really worse than if it had happened in France.

Mrs Lancing picked up *The Times* and looked at the Deaths' Column in the front page. 'Adair, Bayley, Blaynes, Brintock, Carless.' Frederick Carless – now, would that be Daisy's hus-

band? Seventy-five – why, not so much older than she was. Mrs
Lancing had begun to count her friends' ages eagerly, finding
comfort in her own comparative youth. 'Davies, Dean, Dikes.'
It was a heavy list to-day. There must have been an offensive.

How absurd. She was thinking of it as though it were a
casualty list; but this was peace-time. The war had been over
for more than ten years. It was Armistice Day, the day on which
the nation thought proudly of its glorious dead.

> They shall not grow old, as we that are left grow old,
> Age shall not weary them nor the years condemn;
> At the going down of the sun and in the morning,
> We will remember them.[2]

We who are left grow old, thought Mrs Lancing. The years
condemn us. We fall in a war with Time which knows no
armistice. This column in *The Times* is the Casualty List.

She looked up at the scarlet silk poppies in the vase. In
Flanders fields the poppies grow,[3] because the young men died,
so the Rector had said only an hour ago, in order that the world
might be a better place for those who stayed behind. But the
old who died because the years condemned them, was there no
honour in their going? Of course, they had to pass on some
time, and leave the world to the young. Mrs Lancing thought
of Margaret, and her sigh, 'If only we had a little capital!'
breathed without malice and without intention. She did not
mean to hint anything to her mother, but of course she knew
that when her parents went, there would be £12,000 each for
her and Celia. The old must pass on. The young must inherit.

The shadow of death darkened the world when one was over
seventy; yet save for one fear it was not unfriendly; it was not
dishonourable. It was just part of life. Only she had not liked
the look of Arthur's face that morning and she did wish that
his heart was stronger.

The sudden opening of the drawing-room door roused her. She
sat up, and saw the scared, white face of the young parlourmaid.

'Oh, please, 'm, will you come? The master's had a fainting
attack or something in the smoking-room.'

Arthur's heart. Of course. It had to come.

As though with her bodily ears, Mrs Lancing heard ringing through the house the queer, exciting, alarming, sinister cry of 'Stretcher-bearer! Stretcher-bearer!'

She knew that this was the fear she had not dared to face, that this was the hour she had awaited with unspoken terror. Yet now that it had come, she was unshaken.

She rose quietly from her chair, placed *The Times* again upon the sofa, said to Ethel, 'Very well. I will come at once. Please telephone to Dr Burleigh.' And with a steady step walked to the door.

She was not out of it this time. This was her war, and she had learned how to behave.

# ROBERT GRAVES
# CHRISTMAS TRUCE

Young Stan comes around yesterday about tea-time – you know my grandson Stan? He's a Polytechnic student, just turned twenty, as smart as his dad was at the same age. Stan's all out to be a commercial artist and do them big coloured posters for the hoardings. Doesn't answer to 'Stan', though – says it's 'common'; says he's either 'Stanley' or he's nothing.

Stan's got a bagful of big, noble ideas; all schemed out carefully, with what he calls 'captions' attached.

Well, I can't say nothing against big, noble ideas. I was a red-hot Labour-man myself for a time, forty years ago now, when the Kayser's war ended and the war-profiteers began treading us ex-heroes into the mud. But that's all over long ago – in fact, Labour's got a damn sight too respectable for my taste! Worse than Tories, most of their leaders is now – especially them that used to be the loudest in rendering 'We'll Keep the Red Flag Flying Still'.[1] They're all Churchwardens now, or country gents, if they're not in the House of Lords.

Anyhow, yesterday Stan came around, about a big Ban-the-Bomb march all the way across England to Trafalgar Square. And couldn't I persuade a few of my old comrades to form a special squad with a banner marked 'First World War Veterans Protest Against the Bomb'? He wanted us to head the parade, ribbons, crutches, wheel-chairs and all.

I put my foot down pretty hard. 'No, Mr Stanley,' I said politely, 'I regret as I can't accept your kind invitation.'

'But why?' says he. 'You don't want another war, Grand-father, do you? You don't want mankind to be annihilated? This time it won't be just a few unlucky chaps killed, like Uncle

Arthur in the First War, and Dad in the Second . . . It will be all mankind.'

'Listen, young 'un,' I said. 'I don't trust nobody who talks about mankind – not parsons, not politicians, nor anyone else. There ain't no such thing as "mankind", not practically speaking there ain't.'

'Practically speaking, Grandfather,' says young Stan, 'there *is*. Mankind means all the different nations lumped together – us, the Russians, the Americans, the Germans, the French, and all the rest of them. If the bomb goes off, everyone's finished.'

'It's not going off,' I says.

'But it's gone off twice already – at Hiroshima and Nagasaki,' he argues, 'so why not again? The damage will be definitely final when it *does* go off.'

I wouldn't let Stan have the last word. 'In the crazy, old-fashioned war in which I lost my foot,' I said, a bit sternly, 'the Fritzes used poison gas. They thought it would help 'em to break through at Wipers. But somehow the line held, and soon our factories were churning out the same stinking stuff for us to use on them. All right, and now what about Hitler's war?'

'What about it?' Stan asks.

'Well,' I says, 'everyone in England was issued an expensive mask in a smart-looking case against poison-gas bombs dropped from the air – me, your dad, your ma, and yourself as a tiny tot. But how many poison-gas bombs were dropped on London, or on Berlin? Not a damned one! Both sides were scared stiff. Poison-gas had got too deadly. No mask in the market could keep the new sorts out. So there's not going to be no atom bombs dropped neither, I tell you, Stanley my lad; not this side of the Hereafter! Everyone's scared stiff again.'

'Then why do both sides manufacture quantities of atom bombs and pile them up?' he asks.

'Search me,' I said, 'unless it's a clever way of keeping up full employment by making believe there's a war on. What with bombs and fall-out shelters, and radar equipment, and unsink-able aircraft-carriers, and satellites, and shooting rockets at the moon, and keeping up big armies – takes two thousand quid nowadays to maintain a soldier in the field, I read the other day

– what with all that play-acting, there's full employment assured for everyone, and businessmen are rubbing their hands.'

'Your argument has a bad flaw, Grandfather. The Russians don't need to worry about full employment.'

'No,' said I, 'perhaps they don't. But their politicians and commissars have to keep up the notion of a wicked Capitalist plot to wipe out the poor workers. And they have to show that they're well ahead in the Arms Race. Forget it, lad, forget it! Mankind, which is a term used by maiden ladies and bun-punchers, ain't going to be annihilated by no atom bomb.'

Stan changed his tactics. 'Nevertheless, Grandfather,' he says, 'we British want to show the Russians that we're not engaged in any such Capitalist plot. All men are brothers, and I for one have nothing against my opposite number in Moscow, Ivan Whoever-he-may-be . . . This protest march is the only logical way I can show him my dislike of organized propaganda.'

'But Ivan Orfalitch[2] ain't here to watch you march; nor the Russian telly ain't going to show him no picture of it. If Ivan thinks you're a bleeding Capitalist, then he'll go on thinking you're a bleeding Capitalist; and he won't be so far out, neither, in my opinion. No, Stan, you can't fight organized propaganda with amachoor propaganda.'[3]

'Oh, can it, Grandfather!' says Stan. 'You're a professional pessimist. And you didn't hate the Germans even when you were fighting them – in spite of the newspapers. What about that Christmas Truce?'

Well, I'd mentioned it to him one day, I own; but it seems he'd drawn the wrong conclusions and didn't want to be put straight. However, I'm a lucky bloke – always being saved by what other blokes call 'coincidences', but which I don't; because they always happen when I need 'em most. In the trenches we used to call that 'being in God's pocket'. So, of course, we hear a knock at the door and a shout, and in steps my old mucking-in chum Dodger Green, formerly 301691, Pte Edward Green of the 1st Batt., North Wessex Regiment – come to town by bus for a Saturday-night booze with me, every bit of twenty miles.

'You're here in the exact nick, Dodger,' says I, 'as once before.' He'd nappooed[4] a Fritz officer one day when I was

lying with one foot missing outside Delville Wood,[5] and the
Fritz was kindly putting us wounded out of our misery with an
automatic pistol.

'What's new, Fiddler?' he asks.

'Tell this lad about the *two* Christmas truces,' I said. 'He's
trying to enlist us for a march to Moscow, or somewhere.'

'Well,' says Dodger, 'I don't see no connexion, not yet. And
marching to Moscow ain't no worse nor marching to Berlin,
same as you and me did – and never got more nor a few hundred
yards forward in the three years we were at it. But, all right, I'll
give him the facts, since you particularly ask me.'

Stan listened quietly while Dodger told his tale. I'd heard it
often enough before, but Dodger's yarns improve with the
telling. You see, I missed most of that first Christmas Truce, as
I'll explain later. But I came in for the second; and saw a part
of it what Dodger didn't. And the moral I wanted to impress
on young Stan depended on there being *two* truces, not one:
them two were a lot different from one another.

I brings a quart bottle of wallop from the kitchen, along with
a couple of glasses – not three, because young Stan don't drink
anything so 'common' as beer – and Dodger held forth. Got
a golden tongue, has Dodger – I've seen him hold an audience
spellbound at The Three Feathers from opening-time to stop-
tap, and his glass filled every ten minutes, free.

'Well,' he says, 'the first truce was in 1914, about four months
after the Kayser's war began. They say that the old Pope suggested it, and that the Kayser agreed, but that Joffre,[6] the French
C-in-C wouldn't allow it. However, the Bavarians were sweating on a short spell of peace and goodwill, being Catholics, and
sent word around that the Pope was going to get his way.
Consequently, though we didn't have the Bavarians in front of
us, there at Boy Greneer,[7] not a shot was fired on our sector
all Christmas Eve. In those days we hadn't been issued with
Mills bombs,[8] or trench-mortars, or Very pistols, or steel helmets, or sandbags, or any of them later luxuries; and only two
machine-guns to a battalion. The trenches were shallow and
knee-deep in water, so that most of the time we had to crouch
on the fire step. God knows how we kept alive and smiling

... It wasn't no picnic, was it, Fiddler? – and the ground half-frozen, too!

'Christmas Eve, at seven thirty p.m., the enemy trenches suddenly lit up with a row of coloured Chinese lanterns, and a bonfire started in the village behind. We stood to arms, prepared for whatever happened. Ten minutes later the Fritzes began singing a Christmas carol called "Stilly Nucked".[9] Our boys answered with "Good King Wenceslas", which they'd learned the first verse of as Waits, collecting coppers from door to door. Unfortunately no one knew more than two verses, because Waits always either get a curse or a copper before they reach the third verse.

'Then a Fritz with a megaphone shouts, "Merry Christmas, Wessex!"

'Captain Pomeroy was commanding us. Colonel Baggie had gone sick, second-in-command still on leave, and most of the other officers were young second-lieutenants straight from Sandhurst – we'd taken such a knock, end of October. The Captain was a real gentleman: father, grandfather, and great-grandfather all served in the Wessex. He shouts back: "Who are you?" And they say that they're Saxons, same as us, from a town called Hully in West Saxony.[10]

' "Will your commanding officer meet me in no man's land to arrange a Christmas truce?" the Captain shouts again. "We'll respect a white flag," he says.

'That was arranged, so Captain Pomeroy and the Fritz officer, whose name was Lieutenant Coburg, climbed out from their trenches and met half-way. They didn't shake hands, but they saluted, and each gave the other word of honour that his troops wouldn't fire a shot for another twenty-four hours. Lieutenant Coburg explained that his Colonel and all the senior officers were back taking it easy at Regimental HQ. It seems they liked to keep their boots clean, and their hands warm: not like our officers.

'Captain Pomeroy came back pleased as Punch, and said: "The truce starts at dawn, Wessex; but meanwhile we stay in trenches. And if any man of you dares break the truce tomorrow," he says, "I'll shoot him myself, because I've given that German officer my word. All the same, watch out, and don't let go of your bundooks."[11]

'That suited us; we'd be glad to get up from them damned fire steps and stretch our legs. So that night we serenaded the Fritzes with all manner of songs, such as "I want to go Home!"[12] and "The Top of the Dixie Lid",[13] and the one about "Old Von Kluck, He Had a Lot of Men";[14] and they serenaded us with "*Deutschland Über Alles*",[15] and songs to the concertina.

'We scraped the mud off our puttees and shined our brasses, to look a bit more regimental next morning. Captain Pomeroy, meanwhile, goes out again with a flashlight and arranges a Christmas football match – kick-off at ten thirty – to be followed at two o'clock by a burial service for all the corpses what hadn't been taken in because of lying too close to the other side's trenches.

' "Over the top with the best of luck!" shouts the Captain at eight a.m., the same as if he was leading an attack. And over we went, a bit shy of course, and stood there waiting for the Fritzes. They advanced to meet us, shouting, and five minutes later, there we were . . .

'Christmas was a peculiar sort of day, if ever I spent one. Hobnobbing with the Hun, so to speak: swapping fags and rum and buttons and badges for brandy, cigars and souvenirs. Lieutenant Coburg and several of the Fritzes talked English, but none of our blokes could sling a word of their bat.

'No man's land had seemed ten miles across when we were crawling out on a night patrol; but now we found it no wider than the width of two football pitches. We provided the football, and set up stretchers as goalposts; and the Reverend Jolly, our Padre,[16] acted as ref. They beat us three–two, but the Padre had showed a bit too much Christian charity – their outside-left shot the deciding goal, but he was miles offside and admitted it soon as the whistle went. And we spectators were spread nearly two deep along the touch-lines with loaded rifles slung on our shoulders.

'We had Christmas dinner in our own trenches, and a German bugler obliged with the mess call – same tune as ours. Captain Pomeroy was invited across, but didn't think it proper to accept. Then one of our sentries, a farmer's son, sees a hare loping down the line between us. He gives a view halloo, and everyone rushes to the parapet and clambers out and runs forward to cut it off. So do the Fritzes. There ain't no such thing as harriers in Germany; they always use shot-guns on hares. But they weren't allowed to shoot this one, not with the truce; so they turned harriers same as us.

'Young Totty Fahy and a Saxon corporal both made a grab for the hare as it doubled back in their direction. Totty catches it by the forelegs and the Corporal catches it by the hindlegs, and they fall on top of it simultaneous.

'Captain Pomeroy looked a bit worried for fear of a shindy about who caught that hare; but you'd have laughed your head off to see young Totty and the Fritz both politely trying to force the carcase on each other! So the Lieutenant and the Captain gets together, and the Captain says: "Let them toss a coin for it." But the Lieutenant says: "I regret that our men will not perhaps understand. With us, we draw straws." So they picked some withered stems of grass, and Totty drew the long one. He was in our section, and we cooked the hare with spuds that night in a big iron pot borrowed from Duck Farm; but Totty gave the Fritz a couple of bully-beef tins, and the skin. Best stoo I ever ate!

'We called 'em "Fritzes" at that time. Afterwards they were "Jerries", on account of their tin hats. Them helmets with spikes called *Pickelhaubes* was still the issue in 1914, but only for parade use. In the trenches caps were worn; like ours, but grey, and no stiffening in the top. Our blokes wanted *pickelhaubes* badly to take their fiancées when they went home on leave; but Lieutenant Coburg says, sorry, all *pickelhaubes* was in store behind the lines. They had to be content with belt-buckles.

'General French[17] commanded the BEF at the time – decent old stick. Said afterwards that if he'd been consulted about the truce, he'd have agreed for chivalrous reasons. He must have reckoned that whichever side beat, us or the Germans, a Christmas truce would help considerably in signing a decent peace at the finish. But the Kayser's High Command were mostly Prussians, and Lieutenant Coburg told us that the Prussians were against the truce, which didn't agree with their "frightful-ness" notions; and though other battalions were fraternizing with the Fritzes up and down the line that day – but we didn't know it – the Prussians weren't having any. Nor were some English regiments: such as the East Lancs on our right flank and the Sherwood Foresters on the left – when the Fritzes came out with white flags, they fired over their heads and waved 'em back. But they didn't interfere with our party. It was worse in the French line: them Frogs machine-gunned all the "Merry Christmas" parties . . . Of course, the French go in for New Year celebrations more than Christmas.

'One surprise was the two barrels of beer that the Fritzes rolled over to us from the brewery just behind their lines. I don't fancy French beer; but at least this wasn't watered like what they sold us English troops in the *estaminets*. We broached them out in the open, and the Fritzes broached another two of their own.

'When it came to the toasts, the Captain said he wanted to keep politics out of it. So he offered them "Wives and Sweet-hearts!" which the Lieutenant accepted. Then the Lieutenant proposed "The King!"[18] which the Captain accepted. There was a King of Saxony too, you see, in them days, besides a King of England; and no names were mentioned. The third toast was "A Speedy Peace!" and each side could take it to mean victory for themselves.

'After dinner came the burial service – the Fritzes buried their corpses on their side of the line; we buried ours on ours. But we dug the pits so close together that one service did for both. The Saxons had no Padre with them; but they were Protestants, so the Reverend Jolly read the service, and a German divinity student translated for them. Captain Pomeroy sent for the drummers and put us through that parade in proper regimental fashion: slow march, arms reversed, muffled drums, a Union Jack and all.

'An hour before dark, a funny-faced Fritz called Putzi came up with a trestle table. He talked English like a Yank. Said he'd been in Ringling's Circus over in the United States. Called us "youse guys", and put on a hell of a good gaff with conjuring tricks and juggling – had his face made up like a proper clown. Never heard such applause as we gave Herr Putzi!

'Then, of course, our bastard of a Brigadier, full of turkey and plum pudding and mince pies, decides to come and visit the trenches to wish us Merry Christmas! Captain Pomeroy got the warning from Fiddler here, who was away down on light duty at Battalion HQ. Fiddler arrived in the nick, running split-arse across the open, and gasping out: "Captain, sir, the Brigadier's here; but none of us hasn't let on about the truce."

'Captain Pomeroy recalled us at once. "*Imshi*,[19] Wessex!" he shouted. Five minutes later the Brigadier came sloshing up the communication trench, keeping his head well down. The Captain tried to let Lieutenant Coburg know what was happening; but the Lieutenant had gone back to fetch him some warm gloves as a souvenir. The Captain couldn't speak German; what's more, the Fritzes were so busy watching Putzi that they wouldn't listen. So Captain Pomeroy shouts to me: "Private Green, run along the line and order the platoon commanders from me to fire three rounds rapid over the enemies' heads." Which I did; and by the time the Brigadier turns up, there wasn't a Fritz in sight.

'The Brigadier, whom we called "Old Horseflesh", shows a lot of Christmas jollity. "I was very glad," he says, "to hear that Wessex fusillade, Pomeroy. Rumours have come in of fraternization elsewhere along the line. Bad show! Disgraceful! Can't interrupt a war for freedom just because of Christmas! Have you anything to report?"

'Captain Pomeroy kept a straight face. He says: "Our sentries report that the enemy have put up a trestle table in no man's land, sir. A bit of a puzzle, sir. Seems to have a bowl of goldfish on it." He kicked the Padre, and the Padre kept his mouth shut.

'Old Horseflesh removes his brass hat, takes his binoculars, and cautiously peeps over the parapet. "They *are* goldfish, by Gad!" he shouts. "I wonder what new devilish trick the Hun will invent next. Send out a patrol tonight to investigate." "Very good, sir," says the Captain.

'Then Old Horseflesh spots something else: it's Lieutenant Coburg strolling across the open between his reserve and front lines; and he's carrying the warm gloves. "What impudence! Look at that swaggering German officer! Quick, here's your rifle, my lad! Shoot him down point-blank!" It seems Lieutenant Coburg must have thought that the fusillade came from the Foresters on our flank; but now he suddenly stopped short and looked at no man's land, and wondered where everyone was gone.

'Old Horseflesh shoves the rifle into my hand. "Take a steady aim," he says. "Squeeze the trigger, don't pull!" I aimed well above the Lieutenant's head and fired three rounds rapid. He staggered and dived head-first into a handy shell-hole.

'"Congratulations," said Old Horseflesh, belching brandy in my face. "You can cut another notch in your rifle butt. But what effrontery! Thought himself safe on Christmas Day, I suppose! Ha, ha!" He hadn't brought Captain Pomeroy no gift of whisky or cigars, nor nothing else; stingy bastard, he was. At any rate, the Fritzes caught on, and their machine-guns began traversing tock-tock-tock, about three feet above our trenches. That sent the Brigadier hurrying home in such a hurry that he caught his foot in a loop of telephone wire and went face forward into the mud. It was his first and last visit to the front line.

'Half an hour later we put up an ALL CLEAR board. This time us and the Fritzes became a good deal chummier than before. But Lieutenant Coburg suggests it would be wise to keep quiet about the lark. The General Staff might get wind of it and kick up a row, he says. Captain Pomeroy agrees. Then the Lieutenant warns us that the Prussian Guards are due to relieve his Saxons the day after Boxing Day. "I suggest that we continue the truce until then, but with no more fraternization," he says. Captain Pomeroy agrees again. He accepts the warm gloves and in return gives the Lieutenant a Shetland wool scarf. Then he asks whether, as a great favour, the Wessex might be permitted to capture the bowl of goldfish, for the Brigadier's sake. Herr Putzi wasn't too pleased, but Captain Pomeroy paid him for it with a gold sovereign and Putzi says: "Please, for Chrissake, don't forget to change their water!"

'God knows what the Intelligence made of them goldfish

when they were sent back to Corps HQ, which was a French luxury *shadow* . . . I expect someone decided the goldfish have some sort of use in trenches, like the canaries we take down the coal pits.

'Then Captain Pomeroy says to the Lieutenant: "From what I can see, Coburg, there'll be a stalemate on this front for a year or more. You can't crack our line, even with massed machine-guns; and we can't crack yours. Mark my words: our Wessex and your West Saxons will still be rotting here next Christmas – what's left of them."

'The Lieutenant didn't agree, but he didn't argue. He answered: "In that case, Pomeroy, I hope we both survive to meet again on that festive occasion; and that our troops show the same gentlemanly spirit as today."

'"I'll be very glad to do so," says the Captain, "if I'm not scuppered meanwhile." They shook hands on that, and the truce continued all Boxing Day. But nobody went out into no man's land, except at night to strengthen the wire where it had got trampled by the festivities. And of course we couldn't prevent our gunners from shooting; and neither could the Saxons prevent theirs. When the Prussian Guards moved in, the war started again; fifty casualties we had in three days, including young Totty who lost an arm.

'In the meantime a funny thing had happened: the sparrows got wind of the truce and came flying into our trenches for biscuit crumbs. I counted more than fifty in a flock on Boxing Day.

'The only people who objected strongly to the truce, apart from the Brigadier and a few more like him, was the French girls. Wouldn't have nothing more to do with us for a time when we got back to billets. Said we were *no bon* and *boko camarade*[20] with the *Allemans*.'

Stan had been listening to this tale with eyes like stars. 'Exactly,' he said. 'There wasn't any feeling of hate between the individuals composing the opposite armies. The hate was all whipped up by the newspapers. Last year, you remember, I attended the Nürnberg Youth Rally.[21] Two other fellows whose fathers had been killed in the last war, like mine, shared the same tent with four German war-orphans. They weren't at all bad fellows.'

'Well, lad,' I said, taking up the yarn where Dodger left off, 'I didn't see much of that first Christmas Truce owing to a spent bullet what went into my shoulder and lodged under the skin: the Medico cut it out and kept me off duty until the wound healed. I couldn't wear a pack for a month, so, as Dodger told you, I got Light Duty down at Battalion HQ, and missed the fun. But the second Christmas Truce, now that was another matter. By then I was Platoon Sergeant to about twenty men signed on for the Duration of the War – some of them good, some of 'em His Majesty's bad bargains.

'We'd learned a lot about trench life that year; such as how to drain trenches and build dugouts. We had barbed wire entanglements in front of us, five yards thick, and periscopes, and listening-posts out at sap-heads;[22] also trench-mortars and rifle-grenades, and bombs, and steel-plates with loop-holes for sniping through.

'Now I'll tell you what happened, and Dodger here will tell you the same. Battalion orders went round to Company HQ every night in trenches, and the CO was now Lieutenant-Colonel Pomeroy – DSO with bar. He'd won brevet rank[23] for the job he did rallying the battalion when the big German mine[24] blew C Company to bits and the Fritzes followed up with bombs and bayonets. However, when he sent round Orders two days before Christmas 1915, Colonel Pomeroy (accidentally on purpose) didn't tell the Adjutant to include the "Official Warning to All Troops" from General Sir Douglas Haig.[25] Haig was our new Commander-in-Chief. You hear about him on Poppy Day – the poppies he sowed himself, most of 'em! He'd used his influence with King George, to get General French booted out and himself shoved into the job. His "Warning" was to the effect that any man attempting to fraternize with His Majesty's enemies on the poor excuse of Christmas would be court-martialled and shot. But Colonel Pomeroy never broke his word, not even if he swung for it; and here he was alongside the La Bassée Canal,[26] and opposite us were none other than the same West Saxons from Hully!

'The Colonel knew who they were because we'd coshed and caught a prisoner in a patrol scrap two nights before, and after the Medico plastered his head, the bloke was brought to Battalion HQ under escort (which was me and another man). The Colonel questioned him through an interpreter about the geography of the German trenches: where they kept that damned minny-werfer,[27] how and when the ration parties came up, and so on. But this Fritz wouldn't give away a thing; said he'd lost his memory when he'd got coshed. So at last the Colonel remarked in English: "Very well, that's all. By the way, is Lieutenant Coburg still alive?"

'"Oh, yeah," says the Fritz, surprised into talking English. "He's back again after a coupla wounds. He's a Major now, commanding our outfit."

'Then a sudden thought struck him. "For Chrissake," he says, "ain't you the Wessex officer who played Santa Claus last year and fixed that truce?"

'"I am," says the Colonel, "and you're Putzi Cohen the Conjurer, from whom I once bought a bowl of goldfish! It's a small war!"

'That's why, you see, the Colonel hadn't issued Haig's warning. About eighty or so of us old hands were still left, mostly snobs,[28] hobbajers,[29] drummers, transport men, or wounded blokes rejoined. The news went the rounds, and they all rushed Putzi and shook his hand and asked couldn't he put on another conjuring gaff for them? He says: "Ask Colonel Santa Claus! He's still feeding my goldfish."

'I was Putzi's escort, before I happened to have coshed him and brought him in; but I never recognized him without his greasepaint – not until he started talking his funny Yank English.

'The Colonel sends for Putzi again, and says: "I don't think you're quite well enough to travel. I'm keeping you here as a hospital case until after Christmas."

'Putzi lived like a prize pig the next two days, and put on a show every evening – card tricks mostly, because he hadn't his accessories. Then came Christmas Eve, and a sergeant of the Holy Boys who lay on our right flank again, remarked to me it was a pity that "Stern-Endeavour" Haig[30] had washed out our Christmas fun. "First I've heard about," says I, "and what's more, chum, I don't want to hear about it, see? Not officially, I don't."

'I'd hardly shut my mouth before them Saxons put out Chinese lanterns again and started singing "Stilly Nucked". They hadn't fired a shot, neither, all day.

'Soon word comes down the trench: "Colonel's orders: no firing as from now, without officer's permission."

'After stand-to next morning, soon as it was light, Colonel Pomeroy he climbed out of the trench with a white handker-chief in his hand, picked his way through our wire entangle-ments and stopped half-way across no man's land. "Merry Christmas, Saxons!" he shouted. But Major Coburg had already advanced towards him. They saluted each other and shook hands. The cheers that went up! "Keep in your trenches, Wessex!" the Colonel shouted over his shoulder. And the Major gave the same orders to his lot.

'After jabbering a bit they agreed that any bloke who'd attended the 1914 party would be allowed out of trenches, but not the rest – they could trust only us regular soldiers. Regulars, you see, know the rules of war and don't worry their heads about politics nor propaganda; them Duration blokes sickened us sometimes with their patriotism and their lofty skiting, and their hatred of "the Teuton foe" as one of 'em called the Fritzes.

'Twice more Saxons than Wessex came trooping out. We'd strict orders to discuss no military matters – not that any of our blokes had been studying German since the last party. Football was off, because of the overlapping shell holes and the barbed wire, but we got along again with signs and a bit of café French, and swapped fags and booze and buttons. But the Colonel wouldn't have us give away no badges. Can't say we were so chummy as before. Too many of ours and theirs had gone west that year and, besides, the trenches weren't flooded like the first time.

'We put on three boxing bouts: middle, welter and light; won the welter and light with KOs, lost the middle on points. Colonel Pomeroy took Putzi up on parole, and Putzi gave an

even prettier show than before, because Major Coburg had sent
back for his greasepaints and accessories. He used a parrakeet
this time instead of goldfish.

'After dinner we found we hadn't much more to tell the
Fritzes or swap with them, and the officers decided to pack up
before we all got into trouble. The Holy Boys had promised
not to shoot, and the left flank was screened by the Canal bank.
As them two was busy discussing how long the no-shooting
truce should last, all of a sudden the Christmas spirit flared up
again. We and the Fritzes found ourselves grabbing hands and
forming a ring around the pair of them – Wessex and West
Saxons all mixed anyhow and dancing from right to left to the
tune of "Here We Go Round the Mulberry Bush", in and out
of shell holes. Then our RSM pointed to Major Coburg, and
some of our blokes hoisted him on their shoulders and we all
sang "For He's a Jolly Good Fellow". And the Fritzes hoisted
our Colonel up on their shoulders too, and sang "*Hock Solla
Leeben*",[31] or something . . . Our Provost-sergeant took a photo
of that; pity he got his before it was developed.

'Now here's something I heard from Lightning Collins, an
old soldier in my platoon. He'd come close enough to overhear
the Colonel and the Major's conversation during the middle-
weight fight when they thought nobody was listening. The
Colonel says: "I prophesied last year, Major, that we'd still be
here this Christmas, what was left of us. And now I tell you
again that we'll still be here *next* Christmas, *and* the Christmas
after. If we're not scuppered; and that's a ten to one chance.
What's more, next Christmas there won't be any more fun and
games and fraternization. I'm doubtful whether I'll get away
with this present act of insubordination; but I'm a man of my
word, as you are, and we've both kept our engagement."

' "Oh, yes, Colonel," says the Major. "I too will be lucky if
I am not court-martialled. Our orders were as severe as yours."
So they laughed like crows together.

'Putzi was the most envied man in France that day: going
back under safe escort to a prison camp in Blighty. And the
Colonel told the Major: "I congratulate you on that soldier. He
wouldn't give away a thing!"

'At four o'clock sharp we broke it off; but the two officers waited a bit longer to see that everyone got back. But no, young Stan, that's not the end of the story! I had a bloke in my platoon called Gipsy Smith, a dark-faced, dirty soldier, and a killer. He'd been watching the fun from the nearest sap-head, and no sooner had the Major turned his back than Gipsy aimed at his head and tumbled him over.

'The first I knew of it was a yell of rage from everyone all round me. I see Colonel Pomeroy run up to the Major, shouting for stretcher-bearers. Them Fritzes must have thought the job was premeditated, because when our stretcher-bearers popped out of the trench, they let 'em have it and hit one bloke in the leg. His pal popped back again.

'That left the Colonel alone in no man's land. He strolled calmly towards the German trenches, his hands in his pockets – being too proud to raise them over his head. A couple of Fritzes fired at him, but both missed. He stopped at their wire and shouted: "West Saxons, my men had strict orders not to fire. Some coward has disobeyed. Please help me carry the Major's body back to your trenches! Then you can shoot me, if you like; because I pledged my word that there'd be no fighting."

'The Fritzes understood, and sent stretcher-bearers out. They took the Major's body back through a crooked lane in their wire, and Colonel Pomeroy followed them. A German officer bandaged the Colonel's eyes as soon as he got into the trench, and we waited without firing a shot to see what would happen next. That was about four o'clock, and nothing did happen until second watch. Then we see a flashlight signalling, and presently the Colonel comes back, quite his usual self.

'He tells us that, much to his relief, Gipsy's shot hadn't killed the Major but only furrowed his scalp and knocked him senseless. He'd come to after six hours, and when he saw the Colonel waiting there, he'd ordered his immediate release. They'd shaken hands again, and said: "Until after the war!", and the Major gives the Colonel his flashlight.

'Now the yarn's nearly over, Stan, but not quite. News of the truce got round, and General Haig ordered first an Inquiry and then a Court Martial on Colonel Pomeroy. He wasn't shot, of course; but he got a severe reprimand and lost five years' seniority. Not that it mattered, because he got shot between the eyes in the 1916 Delville Wood show where I lost my foot.

'As for Gipsy Smith, he said he'd been obeying Haig's strict orders not to fraternize, and also he'd felt bound to avenge a brother killed at Loos.[32] "Blood for blood," he said, "is our gipsy motto." So we couldn't do nothing but show what we thought by treating him like the dirt he was. And he didn't last long. I sent Gipsy back with the ration party on Boxing Night. We were still keeping up our armed truce with the Saxons, but again their gunners weren't a party to it, and outside the Quartermaster's hut Gipsy got his backside removed by a piece of howitzer shell. Died on the hospital train, he did.

'Oh, I was forgetting to tell you that no sparrows came for biscuit crumbs that Christmas. The birds had all cleared off months before.

'Every year that war got worse and worse. Before it ended, nearly three years later, we'd have ten thousand officers and men pass through that one battalion, which was never at more than the strength of five hundred rifles. I'd had three wounds by 1916; some fellows got up to six before it finished. Only Dodger here came through without a scratch. That's how he got his name, dodging the bullet that had his name and number on it. The Armistice found us at Mons, where we started. There was talk of "Hanging the Kayser"; but they left him to chop wood in Holland[33] instead. The rest of the Fritzes had their noses properly rubbed in the dirt by the Peace Treaty.[34] But we let them rearm in time for a second war, Hitler's war, which is how your dad got killed. And after Hitler's war there'd have been a third war, just about now, which would have caught you, Stanley my lad, if it weren't for that blessed bomb you're asking me to march against.

'Now, listen, lad: if two real old-fashioned gentlemen like Colonel Pomeroy and Major Coburg – never heard of him again, but I doubt if he survived, having the guts he had – if two real men like them two couldn't hope for a third Christmas Truce in the days when "mankind", as you call 'em, was still a little bit civilized, tell me, what can you hope for now?

'Only fear can keep the peace,' I said. 'The United Nations are a laugh, and you know it. So thank your lucky stars that the Russians have H-bombs and that the Yanks have H-bombs, stacks of 'em, enough to blow your "mankind" up a thousand times over; and that everyone's equally respectful of everyone else, though not on regular visiting terms.'

I stopped, out of breath, and Dodger takes Stan by the hand. 'You know what's right for *you*, lad?' he says. 'So don't listen to your granddad. Don't be talked out of your beliefs! He's one of the Old and Bold, but maybe he's no wiser nor you and I.'

# MURIEL SPARK
# THE FIRST YEAR
# OF MY LIFE

I was born on the first day of the second month of the last year of the First World War, a Friday. Testimony abounds that during the first year of my life I never smiled. I was known as the baby whom nothing and no one could make smile. Everyone who knew me then has told me so. They tried very hard, singing and bouncing me up and down, jumping around, pulling faces. Many times I was told this later by my family and their friends; but, anyway, I knew it at the time.

You will shortly be hearing of that new school of psychology, or maybe you have heard of it already, which, after long and far-adventuring research and experiment, has established that all of the young of the human species are born omniscient. Babies, in their waking hours, know everything that is going on everywhere in the world; they can tune in to any conversation they choose, switch on to any scene. We have all experienced this power. It is only after the first year that it was brainwashed out of us; for it is demanded of us by our immediate environment that we grow to be of use to it in a practical way. Gradually, our know-all brain-cells are blacked out, although traces remain in some individuals in the form of ESP,[1] and in the adults of some primitive tribes.

It is not a new theory. Poets and philosophers, as usual, have been there first. But scientific proof is now ready and to hand. Perhaps the final touches are being put to the new manifesto in some cell at Harvard University. Any day now it will be given to the world, and the world will be convinced.

Let me therefore get my word in first, because I feel pretty sure, now, about the authenticity of my remembrance of things past. My autobiography, as I very well perceived at the time, started in the very worst year that the world had ever seen so far. Apart from being born bedridden and toothless, unable to raise myself on the pillow or utter anything but farmyard squawks or police-siren wails, my bladder and my bowels totally out of control, I was further depressed by the curious behaviour of the two-legged mammals around me. There were those black-dressed people, females of the species to which I appeared to belong, saying they had lost their sons. I slept a great deal. Let them go and find their sons. It was like the special pin for my nappies which my mother or some other hoverer dedicated to my care was always losing. These careless women in black lost their husbands and their brothers. Then they came to visit my mother and clucked and crowed over my cradle. I was not amused.

'Babies never really smile till they're three months old,' said my mother. 'They're not *supposed* to smile till they're three months old.'

My brother, aged six, marched up and down with a toy rifle over his shoulder:

> The Grand old Duke of York
> He had ten thousand men;
> He marched them up to the top of the hill
> And he marched them down again.
>
> And when they were up, they were up.
> And when they down, they were down.
> And when they were neither down nor up
> They were neither up nor down.[2]

'Just listen to him!'
'Look at him with his rifle!'
I was about ten days old when Russia stopped fighting. I tuned in to the Czar, a prisoner, with the rest of his family, since evidently the country had put him off his throne and there had been a revolution not long before I was born. Everyone was talking about it. I tuned in to the Czar. 'Nothing would

ever induce me to sign the treaty of Brest-Litovsk,'[3] he said to his wife. Anyway, nobody had asked him to.

At this point I was sleeping twenty hours a day to get my strength up. And from what I discerned in the other four hours of the day I knew I was going to need it. The Western Front on my frequency was sheer blood, mud, dismembered bodies, blistering crashes, hectic flashes of light in the night skies, explosions, total terror. Since it was plain I had been born into a bad moment in the history of the world, the future bothered me, unable as I was to raise my head from the pillow and as yet only twenty inches long. 'I truly wish I were a fox or a bird,'[4] D. H. Lawrence was writing to somebody. Dreary old creeping Jesus. I fell asleep.

Red sheets of flame shot across the sky. It was 21 March, the fiftieth day of my life, and the German Spring Offensive had started before my morning feed. Infinite slaughter. I scowled at the scene, and made an effort to kick out. But the attempt was feeble. Furious, and impatient for some strength, I wailed for my feed. After which I stopped wailing but continued to scowl.

> *The Grand old Duke of York*
> *He had ten thousand men . . .*

They rocked the cradle. I never heard a sillier song. Over in Berlin and Vienna the people were starving, freezing, striking, rioting and yelling in the streets. In London everyone was bustling to work and muttering that it was time the whole damn business was over.

The big people around me bared their teeth; that meant a smile, it meant they were pleased or amused. They spoke of ration cards for meat and sugar and butter.

'Where will it all end?'

I went to sleep. I woke and tuned in to Bernard Shaw who was telling someone to shut up.[5] I switched over to Joseph Conrad who, strangely enough, was saying precisely the same thing. I still didn't think it worth a smile, although it was expected of me any day now. I got on to Turkey. Women

draped in black huddled and chattered in their harems; yak-yak-
yak. This was boring, so I came back to home base.

In and out came and went the women in British black. My
mother's brother, dressed in his uniform, came coughing. He
had been poison-gassed in the trenches. '*Tout le monde à la
bataille!*'[6] declaimed Marshal Foch, the old swine. He was now
Commander-in-Chief of the Allied Forces. My uncle coughed
from deep within his lungs, never to recover but destined to
return to the Front. His brass buttons gleamed in the firelight.
I weighed twelve pounds by now; I stretched and kicked for
exercise, seeing that I had a lifetime before me, coping with this
crowd. I took six feeds a day and kept most of them down by
the time the *Vindictive* was sunk in Ostend harbour,[7] on which
day I kicked with special vigour in my bath.

In France the conscripted soldiers leapfrogged over the dead
on the advance and littered the fields with limbs and hands, or
drowned in the mud. The strongest men on all fronts were dead
before I was born. Now the sentries used bodies for barricades
and the fighting men were unhealthy from the start. I checked
my toes and my fingers, knowing I was going to need them.
*The Playboy of the Western World*[8] was playing at the Court
Theatre in London, but occasionally I beamed over to the
House of Commons, which made me drop off gently to sleep.
Generally, I preferred the Western Front where one got the true
state of affairs. It was essential to know the worst, blood and
explosions and all, for one had to be prepared, as the Boy
Scouts said. Virginia Woolf yawned and reached for her diary.
Really, I preferred the Western Front.

In the fifth month of my life I could raise my head from my
pillow and hold it up. I could grasp the objects that were held
out to me. Some of these things rattled and squawked. I gnawed
on them to get my teeth started. 'She hasn't smiled yet?' said
the dreary old aunties. My mother, on the defensive, said I was
probably one of those late smilers. On my wavelength Pablo
Picasso was getting married[9] and early in that month of July
the Silver Wedding of King George V and Queen Mary[10] was
celebrated in joyous pomp at St Paul's Cathedral. They drove
through the streets of London with their children. Twenty-five

years of domestic happiness. A lot of fuss and ceremonial handing over of swords went on at the Guildhall where the King
and Queen received a cheque for £53,000 to dispose of for
charity as they thought fit. *Tout le monde à la bataille!* Income
tax in England had reached six shillings in the pound. Everyone was talking about the Silver Wedding, yak-yak-yak, and
ten days later the Czar and his family, now in Siberia, were
invited to descend to a little room in the basement.[11] Crack,
crack, went the guns; screams and blood all over the place, and
that was the end of the Romanoffs. I flexed my muscles. 'A fine
healthy baby,' said the doctor; which gave me much satisfaction.

   *Tout le monde à la bataille!* That included my gassed uncle.
My health had improved to the point where I was able to crawl
in my playpen. Bertrand Russell was still cheerily in prison for
writing something seditious about pacifism.[12] Tuning in as usual
to the Front Lines it looked as if the Germans were winning all
the battles yet losing the war. And so it was. The upper-income
people were upset about the income tax at six shillings to the
pound. But all women over thirty got the vote. 'It seems a long
time to wait,' said one of my drab old aunts, aged twenty-two.
The speeches in the House of Commons always sent me to sleep
which was why I missed, at the actual time, a certain oration
by Mr Asquith[13] following the Armistice on 11 November. Mr
Asquith was a greatly esteemed former prime minister later to
be an earl, and had been ousted by Mr Lloyd George. I clearly
heard Asquith, in private, refer to Lloyd George as 'that damned
Welsh goat'.[14]

   The Armistice was signed and I was awake for that. I pulled
myself on to my feet with the aid of the bars of my cot. My
teeth were coming through very nicely in my opinion, and well
worth all the trouble I was put to in bringing them forth. I
weighed twenty pounds. On all the world's fighting fronts the
men killed in action or dead of wounds numbered 8,538,315
and the warriors wounded and maimed were 21,219,452. With
these figures in mind I sat up in my high chair and banged my
spoon on the table. One of my mother's black-draped friends
recited:

*I have a rendezvous with Death*
*At some disputed barricade,*
*When spring comes back with rustling shade*
*And apple blossoms fill the air –*
*I have a rendezvous with Death.*[15]

Most of the poets, they said, had been killed. The poetry made them dab their eyes with clean white handkerchiefs.

Next February on my first birthday, there was a birthday-cake with one candle. Lots of children and their elders. The war had been over two months and twenty-one days. 'Why doesn't she smile?' My brother was to blow out the candle. The elders were talking about the war and the political situation. Lloyd George and Asquith. Asquith and Lloyd George. I remembered recently having switched on to Mr Asquith at a private party where he had been drinking a lot. He was playing cards and when he came to cut the cards he tried to cut a large box of matches by mistake. On another occasion I had seen him putting his arm around a lady's shoulder in a Daimler motor car,[16] and generally behaving towards her in a very friendly fashion. Strangely enough she said, 'If you don't stop this nonsense immediately I'll order the chauffeur to stop and I'll get out.' Mr Asquith replied, 'And pray, what reason will you give?' Well anyway it was my feeding time.

The guests arrived for my birthday. It was so sad, said one of the black widows, so sad about Wilfred Owen who was killed so late in the war, and she quoted from a poem of his:

*What passing bells for these who die as cattle?*
*Only the monstrous anger of the guns.*[17]

The children were squealing and toddling around. One was sick and another wet the floor and stood with his legs apart gaping at the puddle. All was mopped up. I banged my spoon on the table of my high chair.

*But I've a rendezvous with Death*
*At midnight in some flaming town;*

> When spring trips north again this year,
> And I to my pledged word am true,
> I shall not fail that rendezvous.

More parents and children arrived. One stout man who was warming his behind at the fire, said, 'I always think those words of Asquith's after the Armistice were so apt . . .'

They brought the cake close to my high chair for me to see, with the candle shining and flickering above the pink icing. 'A pity she never smiles.'

'She'll smile in time,' my mother said, obviously upset.

'What Asquith told the House of Commons just after the war,' said that stout gentleman with his backside to the fire, 'so apt, what Asquith said. He said that the war has cleansed and purged the world, by God! I recall his actual words: "All things have become new. In this great cleansing and purging it has been the privilege of our country to play her part . . ."' [18]

That did it. I broke into a decided smile and everyone noticed it, convinced that it was provoked by the fact that my brother had blown out the candle on the cake. 'She smiled!' my mother exclaimed. And everyone was clucking away about how I was smiling. For good measure I crowed like a demented raven. 'My baby's smiling!' said my mother.

'It was the candle on her cake,' they said.

The cake be damned. Since that time I have grown to smile quite naturally, like any other healthy and house-trained person, but when I really mean a smile, deeply felt from the core, then to all intents and purposes it comes in response to the words uttered in the House of Commons after the First World War by the distinguished, the immaculately dressed and the late Mr Asquith.

# ROBERT GROSSMITH
# COMPANY

Ever since the old woman, his niece, left the house and joined their vaporous host, he had spent the day idly wandering from room to room in the grip of ancient memories. Here was the room he was born in, here the attic he played in as a lad, the log cabin, crow's nest, castle turret of his solitary, always solitary fantasies; here the bathroom where he passed a guilty adolescence poring over chiaroscuro nudes in fear and circumspection; here the room he died in, not yet a man, lungs full of mustard gas, already turning vaporous. They were all dead now of course, his mother, father, sisters, grandparents, even the old woman, his niece, all together again, though hardly a family. The blood-ties that had seemed to bind them while alive had loosened with the prospect of a common eternity, blood after all proving no thicker than air. No, it was the memories that held him, the memories he subsisted on, like a diet of ersatz foodstuffs, knowing he would never taste real nourishment again.

It was therefore with something resembling a sense of physical pleasure that, sitting one day at the foot of the stairs gazing glumly at the worn patterns on the carpet, his attention was alerted by the bright metallic tinkling of a key in the lock. He looked up, doubting the evidence of his phantom senses. With an ill-fitting shudder the door burst open to admit a wedge of dusted sunlight and three haloed figures, almost transparent in the light.

The corpulent sales-pitching estate agent – for such he took him to be – led the prospective buyers into the hall, a handsome smiling couple in their thirties. Ignoring the agent's patter, they surveyed the gloomy baroque interior with a sceptical eye, taking in at a single glance the high dust-dark ceiling, the peeling paintwork, antique banister, heavy oak-panelled doors. Of course it needed some work doing on it, the old woman had let it get into quite a state as you could see, but nothing a good sweep and a few coats of paint wouldn't fix.

He stood up and joined the group in the kitchen, nodding his agreement. As for the structural condition of the building, it was really first-rate – well, the surveyor's report would confirm that – and it couldn't be better situated as far as local services were concerned. He followed the trio from room to room, admiring with them the view of the fens from the upstairs windows, echoing the estate agent's paean to the housebuilders of yore, endorsing his exaggerated claims about the costs of heating and upkeep. It was surprising, they'd find the fuel bills were actually quite low, the walls retained the heat, you see, and –

Well, they'd think about it. It was a bit bigger than they'd had in mind, they only had one child, a little girl (a little girl!), but on the other hand they had to admit they did like it, it had a sort of friendly lived-in feel, didn't it, Clive?

Time passed, the surveyor did his surveying, other viewers came to view, and somewhat to his surprise the couple returned, complete with rubber plants, budgie, colour TV, modern aluminium-frame furniture and their little girl, Angela, four. He took to her instantly, as she took to the house. The bright green, improbably large eyes, the head of dark ringlets that tumbled as she ran, the dimpled cheeks, the freckles, the busy legs pounding the stairs – 'It's like a castle, Mummy!' – there was something in her so saturated with vibrancy, vitality, that one could almost have persuaded oneself that decay was an illusion. Who would dare predict that one day this hair would be white, these gums toothless, this delicate blooming skin as blotched and tough as old shoe leather? As his fondness for her grew and he began to appreciate the depths of emotional attachment of which he was still unexpectedly capable, it struck him that what he was experiencing was a kind of love; a chaste, fraternal or paternal love, as befitted his condition.

At first he was content to remain in the role of onlooker. Settling below the ceiling in the corner of the room where she played, he would gratefully observe her solitary games, eavesdrop shamelessly on her conversations with her dolls, beguiled by her guileless charms. When bedtime came he would follow her upstairs, installing himself on top of her wardrobe or like a dog at the foot of her bed, watching over her through the night. It was as if, through her, he was able to live again, to recover a vicarious existence of his own. He waited impatiently for her return each day from school, cursed the sunshine that took her out to play in the garden, dreaded the inevitable summer holidays and impromptu weekends away that deprived him of her company, leaving him alone in the vast desert empire of his solitude, murdering time till her return. He was happiest when she was sick and forced to keep to her bed; nothing too serious, a chill would do, or a mild lingering tummy upset. Sometimes, when especially lonely and bold, he would sidle in beside her, nestling his formless form against her sleeping curves, enfolding her with his fleshless arms. He managed not to waste time dwelling on the future – her future of course, he had none, or rather too much of it – on what would happen when she grew up and – well, he managed not to think of such things.

The idea took shape slowly. After all, he didn't want to frighten her. Besides, he knew how the others scorned such diversions. Accept the facts, they said or seemed to imply (they seldom spoke), the world of the living is lost to you for ever, you have no place there, let it go. Most of the others had made the transition successfully. The earthly world had faded for them, dimmed, dissolved, grown remote and insubstantial, as spectral in their eyes as their world was to the living.

But the idea would not go away, it pursued him, niggled at him, refused to let him rest. If only he could become her friend, her secret friend, no one else need know. They both needed a friend. What possible harm could there be in that?

He chose to materialize one afternoon when her mother was out shopping and her father busy mowing the lawn. Dressed in his old army uniform with his decorations prominently displayed, he looked, he thought, rather handsome, distinguished, even a little dapper. No burglar or child-molester would affect such an elaborate disguise.

'Hello,' he said, standing in the open doorway of the living-room – an apt location for his first appearance, he thought.

She looked up from the floor where she lay mutely mouthing the captions of a brightly coloured comic; studied him with interest and suspicion.

'Who are you?'

'I used to live here.' He took a step into the room, closing the door behind him. 'Just popped in to see what the old place looks like. What's your name? Mine's William. You can call me Billy.'

'How did you get in? My mummy and daddy told me not to speak to strange men.'

'I'm not a strange man. I told you, I used to live here. Do you want to play a game?'

'What sort of game?'

'I don't know, you choose. How about hide-and-seek?'

'My name's Angela,' she said. 'I'm five.'

'Hello, Angela.'

'You look funny. Are you a soldier?'

'Sort of, yes.'

'Mr Green was a soldier. I know because he told me.'

'Who's Mr Green?'

'The man in the sweet shop.' Then, her suspicions aroused again, 'If you used to live here you'd know that.'

'I've been away a long time,' he said. 'In the army. Just got back. Mr Green didn't work in the sweet shop when I lived here. There wasn't a sweet shop.'

They continued to talk. As he felt himself gaining her confidence he advanced slowly into the room, rediscovering the forgotten art of ambulation. With excessive caution he skirted those areas where the sunlight streaming through the french windows threatened to penetrate his disguise, expose him for the shadow he was. He rested against a mahogany table supporting an empty fruit bowl and a red ceramic vase. The polished surface of the table, he noted with the usual regret, disdained to return his reflection.

'Do you have many friends, Angela?'

'Hilary's my friend. Her daddy's a policeman.'

'Can I be your friend, Angela?'

He could only assume she was about to answer in the affirmative because at that moment the door he had closed behind
him was flung briskly open – 'I'm back, Popsie!' – and the head
of Angela's mother thrust itself into the room. He evaporated
instantly but with such precipitateness that the vase on the table
against which he had been leaning was sent rocking on its
base and crashing to the floor, fracturing into a dozen pieces.
Angela's mother turned to the noise with a start. She closed the
door and threw it open again, repeating the experiment without
success: the fruit bowl refused to budge. Puzzled, she knelt
down and began gathering the shards of pottery from the floor.

'It was the man.'

'What man?'

'The man who was here. The soldier. He made himself invisible when you came in.'

'Come and help me unpack the shopping, there's a good girl.'

The next time he visited her he was more careful. Angela was
in her bedroom feeding and dressing her dolls, her father in the
garage tinkering with his car, her mother in the kitchen with
her arms in a sinkful of grey suds – a conventional tripartition
of roles he was pleased to see had survived the disastrous
changes of modern life.

'Hello, it's me, Billy,' he said, stepping out from behind the
wardrobe with a nervous smile meant to deprive his sudden
entrance of menace.

She looked up from where she stood by a miniature crib in
which a naked pink doll contentedly sucked air from the tiny
plastic bottle nuzzled in its face. A slight furrowing of the brow
and narrowing of the eyes betokened the tentative shaping of a
question.

'Are you a magician? I saw a magician on the telly once who
could do that. He could make himself invisible. Pouf,' she went,
mimicking with ten tremulous fingers two rising balls of smoke.

'That's right, I'm a magician. I can do lots of tricks.'

'Will you teach me them? I like tricks.'

'Well, I don't know, they're secrets really. I'm not supposed to tell anyone.'

'If you were my friend you'd tell me. Friends aren't supposed to have secrets.'

'Well, we'll see, we'll see. Perhaps when you're a bit older.'

'Grown-ups always say that,' she complained. 'My mummy and daddy don't think you're real. I told them about you but they don't believe me. They think I made you up.'

'You believe I'm real, don't you?' – the note of anxiety in his voice betraying him.

'Of course. I can see you, can't I? And I can touch you if I want.' She took a step towards him.

'No, don't do that!' Backing away towards the wardrobe.

'Why not?'

'Because, because I'm all dirty, my clothes are dirty. You don't want to get your nice clean frock all dirty, do you?'

'Why do you wear those funny army clothes? You don't look like a proper soldier.'

She was asking too many questions, it was time to leave.

'Look, shall I do my trick again? Do you want to see me disappear?'

She shrugged her shoulders. 'If you want.'

'All right, but this time you count to three, all right? Then say the magic word: Alacazam. Got it? Alacazam. Any time you want me to appear, just say the magic word.'

She counted with ponderous deliberation. 'Alka seltz!'

Running into the space he had vacated, she palpated the air with her fingers as if searching for a hidden crevice, then skipped back with a giggle to her dollies.

Those were the happiest days of his death. He floated freely about the house, borne up by a sense of belonging once more to the land of the living, or if not quite belonging then at least being accepted as a sort of naturalized alien, or, more appropriately perhaps, a soldier on furlough, a prisoner on parole.

His euphoria made him reckless. Sliding under the covers that night when he had assured himself she was asleep, he took it into his head to materialize. Using words like 'materialize', or for that matter 'head', in connection with what was at best an ethereal act is liable to be misleading. To materialize, in this context, simply meant that, had she opened her eyes, she would have seen him there beside her, or imagined she did. Unfortunately, this was precisely what happened. He evaporated before the shrill piping scream had time to leave her lungs, scrambling to the top of the wardrobe, curling into a ball, imploring her soundlessly, invisibly, to curb her cries, be quiet, he hadn't meant any harm, he'd just wanted some company, that was all.

'It was the man, the man,' she gave out between huge gulping sobs, burying her face in her mother's shoulder.

'Ssh ssh, it was just a dream, darling, just a dream, Mummy's here now, it's all right, all right.'

'He was in my bed, the man.'

It irked him that she had reacted in this way. He'd been friendly, after all, he'd been nice to her, what was she afraid of? If only he could talk to her, explain, apologize, he'd never do it again, honestly, not if she didn't want him to, cross his heart and hope to – well, never mind. But to appear before her now, he knew, would only make things worse, increase her fear, alienate her further. Especially as the so-called 'dream' in which he'd entered her bed was succeeded by a series of real (that is to say illusory) nightmares in which he apparently repeated and elaborated on the act. Night after night she would awake in a tangle of sweat-soaked sheets, screaming she'd seen him again. He came to despise this shadowy reflection of his already shadowy self, this impostor, this double, this malevolent twin, spreading a trail of terror and laying it at his door.

There was nothing for it, he had to speak to her again. He waited till she'd been tucked in and read to and was lying awake in the yellow glow of her bedside lamp, now left on all through the night, humming quietly to herself. She halted mid-phrase and looked up at him, lips parted in preparation for the automatic scream.

'Don't cry, Angela, please. I don't want to hurt you, just be your friend.'

'I don't like you,' she said uncertainly. 'You've been scaring me. You're not a nice man. I'm going to call my daddy.'

'Don't, Angela, please. Look, I promise I won't visit you again if you don't want me to. Just say so and I'll go away, I promise.'

'Go away!' she said. 'I don't want to see you ever again.'

He was beginning to lose patience with her. 'Come on now, don't be silly. Look, I told you I'm your friend, didn't I? You can't send me away, I'm your friend, for God's sake!'

'Mummy! Daddy! Mummee-ee!'

In a fit of pique he swept a phosphorescent arm across the desktop cluttered with dolls and dolls' clothing, dolls' hairbrushes, dolls' toys, dolls' dolls, sent them clattering to the floor. 'Play with these, don't you? Bloody dolls! Just bits of plastic, dead bloody plastic! What about me, what about me?' The momentum of his anger and frustration, suddenly finding a release after a deathtime of denial, proved impossible to contain. He charged through the room in a swirling vortical haze, upsetting the furniture, ripping the posters from the walls, lifting up a mirror and shattering it against the desk, stamping hysterically on the dolls that littered the floor at his feet, crushing their hollow unfeeling skulls, tearing them limb from limb, flinging the mutilated remains at the walls and windows, howling. He evaporated in a heap as the door flew open behind him.

Everything was going wrong, why was everything going wrong? He hadn't meant to fly off the handle like that, it just happened, ghosts had emotions too, he wasn't perfect. And now he had spoiled everything, everything.

He took once more to roaming the house without aim, borne down by the weight of his solitude and grief. When even movement proved beyond him, he would retire to a dusty corner of the attic or huddle in a foetal ball in the grate of an unlit fireplace, roasting in the cold ashes of self-pity and self-hate. How could he now enjoy watching over her through the night when aware that she might awake at any moment, denouncing him for dream crimes he had had no part in? How could he even enter her room when afraid that the icy draught he bore in his train might alert her to his presence, set into irresistible motion the whole familiar histrionic routine?

Slouched one evening before the television set, watching a

daft late-night horror movie with Angela's parents, he heard them talking about him.

'Poltergeist! So the place is haunted, is that it? Bloody ridiculous! What's he want us to do, get in a priest to exorcize it?'

'Please, darling, try and stay calm, I'm just telling you what he said, that's all. Apparently it's got nothing to do with ghosts, it's quite a common phenomenon, especially among young girls. Some sort of release of psychic energy or something. They can break things, start fires, you know, cause a lot of damage.'

'But Christ, Shirl, you saw that room. That wasn't just breaking things. She must have done that physically, with her hands. But why, why?'

'I know, I know, I'm just telling you what he said, that's all.'

How endearing the living were with their obstinate refusal to countenance any but the most grossly physical of explanations in their commerce with the spirit, how they feared the intangible, the unknown. Sometimes it seemed to him that for all the arid lunar emptiness of his own existence, the real tragedy was theirs. He at least knew how things stood, he had had time – so much time! – to adjust, while they still had to live through the monstrous metamorphosis of death, still had to suffer the pain of that fatal wrench. How differently they would treat their bodies, how they would glory and exult in the flesh, how plunder its pleasures, if they knew the hollow ache of facing eternity without it. How they will miss that heavenly machine when it gasps up its infernal ghost.

Things had come to a head, they couldn't go on as they were. It was clear their relationship was fractured beyond repair. It was equally clear that he couldn't continue indefinitely in his present condition, slinking and skulking round the house, wilting under the burden of an oppressive guilt. He must appear before her one final time, explain what had happened, quietly, without rancour, obtain her forgiveness, then vanish for ever in the penetralia of the house till nature made them equal again.

He selected for his day of valediction one sultry Sunday afternoon when both parents were in the garden sunbathing; prostrate, beach-clad, toning up their cancerous tans. It was too hot for Angela, who lay on her bed by an open window, listlessly turning the pages of a well-thumbed comic, sipping a glass of orange squash through two thin coloured straws.

The main thing was not to frighten her. He materialized inside the wardrobe – less alarming, he thought, than suddenly appearing unannounced in the middle of the room – and pushed the door gently open with a sly forewarning creak. So innocent and incorruptible she looked, lying there in her red (what was it called?) jumpsuit on the bed. As cherubic as her name. He coughed to signal his presence and assumed a simpering, as he thought disarming, smile.

Instantly she was up on the bed and backing away from him. Her lips parted, breaking not in a cry but in a thin gasp and bubble of saliva like one of the speech-bubbles in the comic she'd been reading.

'It's all right, Angela, it's all right, I've come to say goodbye, don't be frightened, please.'

She had retreated dangerously close to the open window. In a single movement she turned on her heels, thrust her torso over the sill and split the air with a spirit-curdling scream. 'Mummee-ee!'

Her body was extended so far across the sill he was afraid the slightest movement would topple her, send her tumbling, plummeting to the patio below. He rushed towards her to prevent her fall, grab her ankles, hold her down, but even as his ghostly fingers grazed the fabric of her trouser-leg he knew he was too late, she had gone, overbalanced, was already somersaulting through the air like one of her own dolls, swooping to embrace the geometric grid of flagstones flying up to meet her. He could only look on with her parents in mute helpless horror as the implacable laws of gravity were fatally confirmed.

He didn't wait to see if she was dead. Dead or alive, what was the difference? Either way he had to leave. If alive, she would never want to see him again. If dead, he would be haunted by the ghost of her memory, by the permanent presence of her absence from the family where she belonged. The thought of all those unlived years, those untasted experiences, would pursue him like a life sentence, a death sentence, through eternity. Besides, how should he explain himself to her newly arrived spirit, how convince her of his thoughtless good intentions, how justify what he had done? No, the crime was clear, parole would be revoked, and escape was the only option. Shimmering through the open window and passing silently over the huddled scene of grief being played out below, he drifted sluggishly towards the whispering fens, then slowly up, up, up, like a child's gas-filled balloon, on his way to heaven knows where.

# JULIAN BARNES

# EVERMORE

All the time she carried them with her, in a bag knotted at the neck. She had bayoneted the polythene with a fork, so that condensation would not gather and begin to rot the frail card. She knew what happened when you covered seedlings in a flower-pot: damp came from nowhere to make its sudden climate. This had to be avoided. There had been so much wet back then, so much rain, churned mud and drowned horses. She did not mind it for herself. She minded it for them still, for all of them, back then.

There were three postcards, the last he had sent. The earlier ones had been divided up, lost perhaps, but she had the last of them, his final evidence. On the day itself, she would unknot the bag and trace her eyes over the jerky pencilled address, the formal signature (initials and surname only), the obedient crossings-out. For many years she had ached at what the cards did not say; but nowadays she found something in their official impassivity which seemed proper, even if not consoling.

Of course she did not need actually to look at them, any more than she needed the photograph to recall his dark eyes, sticky-out ears, and the jaunty smile which agreed that the fun would be all over by Christmas. At any moment she could bring the three pieces of buff field-service card[1] exactly to mind. The dates: Dec 24, Jan 11, Jan 17, written in his own hand, and confirmed by the postmark which added the years: 16, 17, 17. 'NOTHING is to be written on this side except the date and signature of the sender. Sentences not required may be erased. If anything else is added the postcard will be destroyed.' And then the brutal choices.

```
I am quite well
I have been admitted into hospital
  ⎰ sick    ⎱  and am going on well
  ⎱ wounded ⎰  and hope to be discharged soon
I am being sent down to the base
                      ⎧ letter dated............
I have received your ⎨ telegram................
                      ⎩ parcel..................
Letter follows at first opportunity
I have received no letter from you
  ⎰ Lately
  ⎱ For a long time
```

He was quite well on each occasion. He had never been admitted into hospital. He was not being sent down to the base. He had received a letter of a certain date. A letter would follow at the first opportunity. He had not received no letter. All done with thick pencilled crossing-out and a single date. Then, beside the instruction <u>Signature only</u>, the last signal from her brother. S. Moss. A large looping S with a circling full stop after it. Then Moss, written without lifting from the card what she always imagined as a stub of pencil-end studiously licked.

On the other side, their mother's name – Mrs Moss, with a grand M and a short stabbing line beneath the *rs* – then the address. Another warning down the edge, this time in smaller letters. 'The address only to be written on this side. If anything else is added, the postcard will be destroyed.' But across the top of her second card, Sammy had written something, and it had not been destroyed. A neat line of ink without the rough loopiness of his pencilled signature: '<u>50 yds</u> from the Germans. Posted from Trench.' In fifty years, one for each underlined yard, she had not come up with the answer. Why had he written it, why in ink, why had they allowed it? Sam was a cautious and responsible boy, especially towards their mother, and he would not have risked a worrying silence. But he had undeniably written these words. And in ink, too. Was it code for something else? A premonition of death? Except that Sam was not the sort to have premonitions. Perhaps it was simply excitement, a desire to impress. Look how close we are. 50 yds from the Germans. Posted from Trench.

She was glad he was at Cabaret Rouge, with his own headstone. Found and identified. Given known and honoured burial. She had a horror of Thiepval,[2] one which failed to diminish in spite of her dutiful yearly visits. Thiepval's lost souls. You had to make the right preparation for them, for their lostness. So she always began elsewhere, at Caterpillar Valley, Thistle Dump, Quarry, Blighty Valley, Ulster Tower,[3] Herbécourt.

> No Morning Dawns
> No Night Returns
> But What We Think Of Thee

That was at Herbécourt, a walled enclosure in the middle of fields, room for a couple of hundred, most of them Australian, but this was a British lad, the one who owned this inscription. Was it a vice to have become such a connoisseur of grief? Yet it was true, she had her favourite cemeteries. Like Blighty Valley and Thistle Dump, both half-hidden from the road in a fold of valley; or Quarry, a graveyard looking as if it had been abandoned by its village; or Devonshire, that tiny, private patch for the Devonshires who died on the first day of the Somme, who fought to hold that ridge and held it still. You followed signposts in British racing green, then walked across fields guarded by wooden martyred Christs to these sanctuaries of orderliness, where everything was accounted for. Headstones were lined up like dominoes on edge; beneath them, their owners were present and correct, listed, tended. Creamy altars proclaimed that THEIR NAME LIVETH FOR EVERMORE.[4] And so it did, on the graves, in the books, in hearts, in memories.

Each year she wondered if this would be her last visit. Her life no longer offered up to her the confident plausibility of two decades more, one decade, five years. Instead, it was now renewed on an annual basis, like her driving licence. Every April Dr Holling had to certify her fit for another twelve months behind the wheel. Perhaps she and the Morris would go kaput on the same day.

Before, it had been the boat train, the express to Amiens, a local stopper, a bus or two. Since she had acquired the Morris, she had in theory become freer; and yet her routine remained almost immutable. She would drive to Dover and take a night ferry, riding the Channel in the blackout alongside burly lorry-drivers. It saved money, and meant she was always in France for daybreak. No Morning Dawns . . . He must have seen each daybreak and wondered if that was the date they would put on his stone . . . Then she would follow the N43 to St-Omer, to Aire and Lillers, where she usually took a croissant and *thé à l'anglaise*. From Lillers the N43 continued to Béthune, but she flinched from it: south of Béthune was the D937 to Arras, and there, on a straight stretch where the road did a reminding elbow, was Brigadier Sir Frank Higginson's domed portico.[5] You should not drive past it, even if you intended to return. She had done that once, early in her ownership of the Morris, skirted Cabaret Rouge in second gear, and it had seemed the grossest discourtesy to Sammy and those who lay beside him: no, it's not your turn yet, just you wait and we'll be along. No, that was what the other motorists did.

So instead she would cut south from Lillers and come into Arras with the D341. From there, in that thinned triangle whose southern points were Albert and Péronne, she would begin her solemn and necessary tour of the woods and fields in which, so many decades before, the British Army had counter-attacked to relieve the pressure on the French at Verdun. That had been the start of it, anyway. No doubt scholars were by now having second thoughts, but that was what they were for; she herself no longer had arguments to deploy or positions to hold. She valued only what she had experienced at the time: an outline of strategy, the conviction of gallantry, and the facts of mourning.

At first, back then, the commonality of grief had helped: wives, mothers, comrades, an array of brass hats, and a bugler amid gassy morning mist which the feeble November sun had failed to burn away. Later, remembering Sam had changed: it became work, continuity; instead of anguish and glory, there was fierce unreasonableness, both about his death and her com-memoration of it. During this period, she was hungry for the solitude and the voluptuous selfishness of grief: her Sam, her loss, her mourning, and nobody else's similar. She admitted as much: there was no shame to it. But now, after half a century, her feelings had simply become part of her. Her grief was a calliper, necessary and supporting; she could not imagine walking without it.

When she had finished with Herbécourt and Devonshire, Thistle Dump and Caterpillar Valley, she would come, always with trepidation, to the great red-brick memorial at Thiepval. An arch of triumph, yes, but of what kind, she wondered: the triumph over death, or the triumph *of* death? 'Here are recorded names of officers and men of the British armies who fell on the Somme battlefields July 1915 – February 1918 but to whom the fortune of war denied the known and honoured burial given to their comrades in death.' Thiepval Ridge, Pozières Wood, Albert, Morval, Ginchy, Guillemont, Ancre, Ancre Heights, High Wood, Delville Wood, Bapaume, Bazentin Ridge, Miraumont, Transloy Ridges, Flers-Courcelette. Battle after battle, each accorded its stone laurel wreath, its section of wall: name after name after name, the Missing of the Somme, the official graffiti of death. This monument by Sir Edwin Lutyens[6] revolted her, it always had. She could not bear the thought of these lost men, exploded into unrecognizable pieces, engulfed in the mud-fields, one moment fully there with pack and gaiters, baccy and rations, with their memories and their hopes, their past and their future crammed into them, and the next moment only a shred of khaki or a sliver of shin-bone to prove they had ever existed. Or worse: some of these names had first been given known and honoured burial, their allotment of ground with their name above it, only for some new battle with its heedless artillery to tear up the temporary graveyard and bring a second, final extermination. Yet each of those scraps of uniform and flesh – whether newly killed or richly decomposed – had been brought back here and reorganized, conscripted into the eternal regiment of the missing, kitted out and made to dress by the right. Something about the way they had vanished and the way they were now reclaimed was more than she could bear: as if an army which had thrown them away so lightly now chose to

own them again so gravely. She was not sure whether this was
the case. She claimed no understanding of military matters. All
she claimed was an understanding of grief.

Her wariness of Thiepval always made her read it with a
sceptical, a proof-reader's eye. She noticed, for instance, that
the French translation of the English inscription listed – as the
English one did not – the exact number of the Missing. 73,367.
That was another reason she did not care to be here, standing
in the middle of the arch looking down over the puny Anglo-
French cemetery (French crosses to the left, British stones to
the right) while the wind drew tears from an averting eye.
73,367: beyond a certain point, the numbers became uncount-
able and diminishing in effect. The more dead, the less pro-
portionate the pain. 73,367: even she, with all her expertise in
grief, could not imagine that.

Perhaps the British realized that the number of the Missing
might continue to grow through the years, that no fixed total
could be true; perhaps it was not shame, but a kind of sensible
poetry which made them decline to specify a figure. And they
were right: the numbers had indeed changed. The arch was
inaugurated in 1932 by the Prince of Wales, and all the names
of all the Missing had been carved upon its surfaces, but still,
here and there, out of their proper place, hauled back tardily
from oblivion, were a few soldiers enlisted only under the
heading of Addenda. She knew all their names by now:
Dodds T., Northumberland Fusiliers; Malcolm H. W., The
Cameronians; Lennox F. J., Royal Irish Rifles; Lovell F. H. B.,
Royal Warwickshire Regiment; Orr R., Royal Inniskillins;
Forbes R., Cameron Highlanders; Roberts J., Middlesex Regi-
ment; Moxham A., Wiltshire Regiment; Humphries F. J.,
Middlesex Regiment; Hughes H. W., Worcestershire Regiment;
Bateman W. T., Northamptonshire Regiment; Tarling E., The
Cameronians; Richards W., Royal Field Artillery; Rollins S.,
East Lancashire Regiment; Byrne L., Royal Irish Rifles;
Gale E. O., East Yorkshire Regiment; Walters J., Royal
Fusiliers; Argar D., Royal Field Artillery. No Morning Dawns,
No Night Returns . . .

She felt closest to Rollins S., since he was an East Lancashire;

she would always smile at the initials inflicted upon Private
Lovell; but it was Malcolm H. W. who used to intrigue her
most. Malcolm H. W., or, to give him his full inscription:
'Malcolm H. W. The Cameronians (Sco. Rif.) served as
Wilson H.' An addendum and a corrigendum all in one. When
she had first discovered him, it had pleased her to imagine his
story. Was he under age? Did he falsify his name to escape
home, to run away from some girl? Was he wanted for a crime,
like those fellows who joined the French Foreign Legion? She
did not really want an answer, but she liked to dream a little
about this man who had first been deprived of his identity and
then of his life. These accumulations of loss seemed to exalt
him; for a while, faceless and iconic, he had threatened to rival
Sammy and Denis as an emblem of the war. In later years she
turned against such fancifulness. There was no mystery really.
Private H. W. Malcolm becomes H. Wilson. No doubt he was
in truth H. Wilson Malcolm, and when he volunteered they
wrote the wrong name in the wrong column; then they were
unable to change it. That would make sense: man is only a
clerical error corrected by death.

She had never cared for the main inscription over the central
arch:

AUX ARMEES
FRANCAISE ET
BRITANNIQUE
L'EMPIRE
BRITANNIQUE
RECON
NAISSANT

Each line was centred, which was correct, but there was
altogether too much white space beneath the inscription. She
would have inserted 'less #' on the galley-proof. And each
year she disliked more and more the line-break in the word
*reconnaissant*. There were different schools of thought about
this – she had argued with her superiors over the years – but
she insisted that breaking a word in the middle of a doubled

consonant was a nonsense. You broke a word where the word itself was perforated. Look what this military, architectural or sculptural nincompoop had produced: a fracture which left a separate word, *naissant*, by mistake. *Naissant* had nothing to do with *reconnaissant*, nothing at all; worse, it introduced the notion of birth on to this monument to death. She had written to the War Graves Commission about it, many years ago, and had been assured that the proper procedures had been followed. They told *her* that!

Nor was she content with EVERMORE. Their name liveth for evermore: here at Thiepval, also at Cabaret Rouge, Caterpillar Valley, Combles Communal Cemetery Extension, and all the larger memorials. It was of course the correct form, or at least the more regular form; but something in her preferred to see it as two words. EVER MORE: it seemed more weighty like this, with an equal bell-toll on each half. In any case, she had a quarrel with the Dictionary about *evermore*. 'Always, at all times, constantly, continually'. Yes, it could mean this in the ubiquitous inscription. But she preferred sense 1: 'For all future time'. Their name liveth for all future time. No morning dawns, no night returns, but what we think of thee. This is what the inscription meant. But the Dictionary had marked sense 1 as '*Obs*. exc. *arch*.' Obsolete except archaic. No, oh certainly not, no. And not with a last quotation as recent as 1854. She would have spoken to Mr Rothwell about this, or at least pencilled a looping note on the galley-proof; but this entry was not being revised, and the letter E had passed over her desk without an opportunity to make the adjustment.

EVERMORE. She wondered if there was such a thing as collective memory, something more than the sum of individual memories. If so, was it merely coterminous, yet in some way richer; or did it last longer? She wondered if those too young to have original knowledge could be given memory, could have it grafted on. She thought of this especially at Thiepval. Though she hated the place, when she saw young families trailing across the grass towards the red-brick *arc-de-triomphe* it also roused in her a wary hopefulness. Christian cathedrals could inspire religious faith by their vast assertiveness; why then should not

Lutyens's memorial provoke some response equally beyond the rational? That reluctant child, whining about the strange food its mother produced from plastic boxes, might receive memory here. Such an edifice assured the newest eye of the pre-existence of the profoundest emotions. Grief and awe lived here; they could be breathed, absorbed. And if so, then this child might in turn bring its child, and so on, from generation to generation, EVERMORE. Not just to count the Missing, but to understand what those from whom they had gone missing knew, and to feel her loss afresh.

Perhaps this was one reason she had married Denis. Of course she should never have done so. And in a way she never had, for there had been no carnal connection: she unwilling, he incapable. It had lasted two years and his uncomprehending eyes when she delivered him back were impossible to forget. All she could say in her defence was that it was the only time she had behaved with such pure selfishness: she had married him for her own reasons, and discarded him for her own reasons. Some might say that the rest of her life had been selfish too, devoted as it was entirely to her own commemorations; but this was a selfishness that hurt nobody else.

Poor Denis. He was still handsome when he came back, though his hair grew white on one side and he dribbled. When the fits came on she knelt on his chest and held his tongue down with a stub of pencil. Every night he roamed restlessly through his sleep, muttered and roared, fell silent for a while, and then with parade-ground precision would shout *Hip! hip! hip!* When she woke him, he could never remember what had been happening. He had guilt and pain, but no specific memory of what he felt guilty about. She knew: Denis had been hit by shrapnel and taken back down the line to hospital without a farewell to his best pal Jewy Moss, leaving Sammy to be killed during the next day's Hun bombardment. After two years of this marriage, two years of watching Denis vigorously brush his patch of white hair to make it go away, she had returned him to his sisters. From now on, she told them, they should look after Denis and she would look after Sam. The sisters had gazed at her in silent astonishment. Behind them, in the hall, Denis, his chin wet and his brown eyes uncomprehending, stood with an awkward patience which implied that this latest event was nothing special in itself, merely one of a number of things he failed to grasp, and that there would surely be much more to come, all down the rest of his life, which would also escape him.

She had taken the job on the Dictionary a month later. She worked alone in a damp basement, at a desk across which curled long sheets of galley-proof. Condensation beaded the window. She was armed with a brass table-lamp and a pencil which she sharpened until it was too short to fit in the hand. Her script was large and loose, somewhat like Sammy's; she deleted and inserted, just as he had done on his field-service postcards. Nothing to be written on this side of the galley-proof. If anything else is added to the galley-proof it will be destroyed. No, she did not have to worry; she made her marks with impunity. She spotted colons which were italic instead of roman, brackets which were square instead of round, inconsistent abbreviations, misleading cross-references. Occasionally she made suggestions. She might observe, in looping pencil, that such-and-such a word was in her opinion vulgar rather than colloquial, or that the sense illustrated was figurative rather than transferred. She passed on her galley-proofs to Mr Rothwell, the joint deputy editor, but never enquired whether her annotations were finally acted upon. Mr Rothwell, a bearded, taciturn and pacific man, valued her meticulous eye, her sure grasp of the Dictionary's conventions, and her willingness to take work home if a fascicle was shortly going to press. He remarked to himself and to others that she had a strangely disputatious attitude over words labelled as obsolete. Often she would propose *?Obs.* rather than *Obs.* as the correct marking. Perhaps this had something to do with age, Mr Rothwell thought; younger folk were perhaps more willing to accept that a word had had its day.

In fact, Mr Rothwell was only five years younger than she; but Miss Moss – as she had become once more after her disposal of Denis – had aged quickly, almost as a matter of will. The years passed and she grew stout, her hair flew a little more wildly away from her clips, and her spectacle lenses became thicker. Her stockings had a dense, antique look to them, and she never took her raincoat to the dry-cleaner. Younger lexicographers entering her office, where a number of back files were stored, wondered if the faint smell of rabbit-hutch came from the walls, the old dictionary slips, Miss Moss's raincoat, or Miss Moss herself. None of this mattered to Mr Rothwell, who saw only the precision of her work. Though entitled by the Press to an annual holiday of fifteen working days, she never took more than a single week.

At first this holiday coincided with the eleventh hour of the eleventh day of the eleventh month;[7] Mr Rothwell had the delicacy not to ask for details. In later years, however, she would take her week in other months, late spring or early autumn. When her parents died and she inherited a small amount of money, she surprised Mr Rothwell by arriving for work one day in a small grey Morris with red leather seats. It sported a yellow metal AA badge on the front and a metal GB plate on the back. At the age of fifty-three she had passed her driving-test first time, and manoeuvred her car with a precision bordering on *élan*.

She always slept in the car. It saved money; but mainly it helped her be alone with herself and Sam. The villages in that thinned triangle south of Arras became accustomed to the sight of an ageing British car the colour of gun-metal drawn up beside the war memorial; inside, an elderly lady wrapped in a travelling rug would be asleep in the passenger seat. She never locked the car at night, for it seemed impertinent, even disrespectful on her part to feel any fear. She slept while the villages slept, and would wake as a drenched cow on its way to milking softly shouldered a wing of the parked Morris. Every so often she would be invited in by a villager, but she preferred not to accept hospitality. Her behaviour was not regarded as peculiar, and cafés in the region knew to serve her *thé à l'anglaise* without her having to ask.

After she had finished with Thiepval, with Thistle Dump and Caterpillar Valley, she would drive up through Arras and take the D937 towards Béthune. Ahead lay Vimy, Cabaret Rouge, ND de Lorette. But there was always one other visit to be paid first: to Maison Blanche.[8] Such peaceful names they mostly had. But here at Maison Blanche were 40,000 German dead, 40,000 Huns laid out beneath their thin black crosses, a sight as orderly as you would expect from the Huns, though not as splendid as the British graves. She lingered there, reading a few names at random, idly wondering, when she found a date just a little later than 21st January 1917, if this could be the Hun that had killed her Sammy. Was this the man who squeezed the trigger, fed the machine-gun, blocked his ears as the howitzer[9] roared? And see how short a time he had lasted afterwards: two days, a week, a month or so in the mud before being lined up in known and honoured burial, facing out once more towards her Sammy, though separated now not by barbed wire and 50 yds but by a few kilometres of asphalt.

She felt no rancour towards these Huns; time had washed from her any anger at the man, the regiment, the Hun army, the nation that had taken Sam's life. Her resentment was against those who had come later, and whom she refused to dignify with the amicable name of Hun. She hated Hitler's war for diminishing the memory of the Great War, for allotting it a number, the mere first among two. And she hated the way in which the Great War was held responsible for its successor, as if Sam, Denis and all the East Lancashires who fell were partly the cause of that business. Sam had done what he could – he had served and died – and was punished all too quickly with becoming subservient in memory. Time did not behave rationally. Fifty years back to the Somme; a hundred beyond that to Waterloo; four hundred more to Agincourt, or Azincourt as the French preferred. Yet these distances had now been squeezed closer to one another. She blamed it on 1939–1945.

She knew to keep away from those parts of France where the second war happened, or at least where it was remembered. In the early years of the Morris, she had sometimes made the mistake of imagining herself on holiday, of being a tourist. She might thoughtlessly stop in a lay-by, or be taking a stroll down a back lane in some tranquil, heat-burdened part of the country, when a neat tablet inserted in a dry wall would assault her. It would commemorate Monsieur Un Tel,[10] *lâchement assassiné par les Allemands*, or *tué*, or *fusillé*, and then an insulting modern date: 1943, 1944, 1945. They blocked the view, these deaths and these dates; they demanded attention by their recency. She refused, she refused.

When she stumbled like this upon the second war, she would hurry to the nearest village for consolation. She always knew where to look: next to the church, the *mairie*, the railway station; at a fork in the road; on a dusty square with cruelly pollarded limes and a few rusting café tables. There she would find her damp-stained memorial with its heroic *poilu*, grieving widow, triumphant Marianne,[11] rowdy cockerel.[12] Not that the story she read on the plinth needed any sculptural illustration. 67 against 9, 83 against 12, 40 against 5, 27 against 2: here was the eternal corroboration she sought, the historical corrigendum. She would touch the names cut into stone, their gilding washed away on the weather-side. Numbers whose familiar proportion declared the terrible primacy of the Great War. Her eye would check down the bigger list, snagging at a name repeated twice, thrice, four, five, six times: one male generation of an entire family taken away to known and honoured burial. In the bossy statistics of death she would find the comfort she needed.

She would spend the last night at Aix-Noulette (101 to 7); at Souchez (48 to 6), where she remembered Plouvier, Maxime, Sergent, killed on 17th December 1916, the last of his village to die before her Sam; at Carency (19 to 1); at Ablain-Saint-Nazaire (66 to 9), eight of whose male Lherbiers had died, four on the *champ d'honneur*, three as *victimes civiles*, one a *civil fusillé par l'ennemi*. Then, the next morning, cocked with grief, she would set off for Cabaret Rouge while dew was still on the grass. There was consolation in solitude and damp knees. She no longer talked to Sam; everything had been said decades ago. The heart had been expressed, the apologies made, the secrets given. She no longer wept, either; that too had stopped. But the hours she spent with him at Cabaret Rouge were the most vital of her life. They always had been.

The D937 did its reminding elbow at Cabaret Rouge, making sure you slowed out of respect, drawing your attention to

Brigadier Sir Frank Higginson's handsome domed portico, which served as both entrance gate and memorial arch. From the portico, the burial ground dropped away at first, then sloped up again towards the standing cross on which hung not Christ but a metal sword. Symmetrical, amphitheatrical, Cabaret Rouge held 6,676 British soldiers, sailors, marines and airmen; 732 Canadians; 121 Australians; 42 South Africans; 7 New Zealanders; 2 members of the Royal Guernsey Light Infantry; 1 Indian; 1 member of an unknown unit; and 4 Germans.

It also contained, or more exactly had once had scattered over it, the ashes of Brigadier Sir Frank Higginson, Secretary to the Imperial War Graves Commission,[13] who had died in 1958 at the age of sixty-eight. That showed true loyalty and remembrance. His widow, Lady Violet Lindsley Higginson, had died four years later, and her ashes had been scattered here too. Fortunate Lady Higginson. Why should the wife of a brigadier who, whatever he had done in the Great War, had not died, be allowed such enviable and meritorious burial, and yet the sister of one of those soldiers whom the fortune of war had led to known and honoured burial be denied such comfort? The Commission had twice denied her request, saying that a military cemetery did not receive civilian ashes. The third time she had written they had been less polite, referring her brusquely to their earlier correspondence.

There had been incidents down the years. They had stopped her coming for the eleventh hour of the eleventh day of the eleventh month by refusing her permission to sleep the night beside his grave. They said they did not have camping facilities; they affected to sympathize, but what if everybody else wanted to do the same? She replied that it was quite plain that no one else wanted to do the same but that if they did then such a desire should be respected. However, after some years she ceased to miss the official ceremony: it seemed to her full of people who remembered improperly, impurely.

There had been problems with the planting. The grass at the cemetery was French grass, and it seemed to her of the coarser type, inappropriate for British soldiers to lie beneath. Her campaign over this with the Commission led nowhere. So one spring she took out a small spade and a square yard of English turf kept damp in a plastic bag. After dark she dug out the offending French grass and relaid the softer English turf, patting it into place, then stamping it in. She was pleased with her work, and the next year, as she approached the grave, saw no indication of her mending. But when she knelt, she realized that her work had been undone: the French grass was back again. The same had happened when she had surreptitiously planted her bulbs. Sam liked tulips, yellow ones especially, and one autumn she had pushed half a dozen bulbs into the earth. But the following spring, when she returned, there were only dusty geraniums in front of his stone.

There had also been the desecration. Not so very long ago. Arriving shortly after dawn, she found something on the grass which at first she put down to a dog. But when she saw the same in front of 1685 Private W. A. Andrade 4th Bn. London Regt. R. Fus. 15th March 1915, and in front of 675 Private Leon Emanuel Levy The Cameronians (Sco. Rif.) 16th August 1916 aged 21 And the Soul Returneth to God Who Gave It – Mother, she judged it most unlikely that a dog, or three dogs, had managed to find the only three Jewish graves in the cemetery. She gave the caretaker the rough edge of her tongue. He admitted that such desecration had occurred before, also that paint had been sprayed, but he always tried to arrive before anyone else and remove the signs. She told him that he might be honest but he was clearly idle. She blamed the second war. She tried not to think about it again.

For her, now, the view back to 1917 was uncluttered: the decades were mown grass, and at their end was a row of white headstones, domino-thin. 1358 Private Samuel M. Moss East Lancashire Regt. 21st January 1917, and in the middle the Star of David. Some graves in Cabaret Rouge were anonymous, with no identifying words or symbols; some had inscriptions, regimental badges, Irish harps, springboks, maple leaves, New Zealand ferns. Most had Christian crosses; only three displayed the Star of David. Private Andrade, Private Levy and Private Moss. A British soldier buried beneath the Star of David: she kept her eyes on that. Sam had written from training camp that the fellows chaffed him, but he had always been Jewy Moss at school, and they were good fellows, most of them, as good inside the barracks as outside, anyway. They made the same remarks he'd heard before, but Jewy Moss was a British soldier, good enough to fight and die with his comrades, which is what he had done, and what he was remembered for. She pushed away the second war, which muddled things. He was a British soldier, East Lancashire Regiment, buried at Cabaret Rouge beneath the Star of David.

She wondered when they would plough them up, Herbécourt, Devonshire, Quarry, Blighty Valley, Ulster Tower, Thistle Dump and Caterpillar Valley; Maison Blanche and Cabaret Rouge. They said they never would. This land, she read everywhere, was 'the free gift of the French people for the perpetual resting place of those of the allied armies who fell . . .' and so on. EVERMORE, they said, and she wanted to hear: for all future time. The War Graves Commission, her successive members of parliament, the Foreign Office, the commanding officer of Sammy's regiment, all told her the same. She didn't believe them. Soon – in fifty years or so – everyone who had served in the War would be dead; and at some point after that, everyone who had known anyone who had served would also be dead. What if memory-grafting did not work, or the memories themselves were deemed shameful? First, she guessed, those little stone tablets in the back lanes would be chiselled out, since the French and the Germans had officially stopped hating one another years ago, and it would not do for German tourists to be accused of the cowardly assassinations perpetrated by their ancestors. Then the war memorials would come down, with their important statistics. A few might be held to have architectural interest; but some new, cheerful generation would find them morbid, and dream up better things to enliven the villages. And after that it would be time to plough up the cemeteries, to put them back to good agricultural use: they had lain fallow for too long. Priests and politicians would make it all right, and the farmers would get their land back, fertilized with blood and bone. Thiepval might become a listed building, but would they keep Brigadier Sir Frank Higginson's domed portico? That elbow in the D937 would be declared a traffic hazard; all it needed was a drunken casualty for the road to be made straight again after all these years. Then the great forgetting could begin, the fading into the landscape. The war would be levelled to a couple of museums, a set of demonstration trenches, and a few names, shorthand for pointless sacrifice.

Might there be one last fiery glow of remembering? In her own case, it would not be long before her annual renewals ceased, before the clerical error of her life was corrected; yet even as she pronounced herself an antique, her memories seemed to sharpen. If this happened to the individual, could it not also happen on a national scale? Might there not be, at some point in the first decades of the twenty-first century, one final moment, lit by evening sun, before the whole thing was handed over to the archivists? Might there not be a great looking-back down the mown grass of the decades, might not a gap in the trees discover the curving ranks of slender headstones, white tablets holding up to the eye their bright names and terrifying dates, their harps and springboks, maple leaves and ferns, their Christian crosses and their Stars of David? Then, in the space of a wet blink, the gap in the trees would close and the mown grass disappear, a violent indigo cloud would cover the sun, and history, gross history, daily history, would forget. Is this how it would be?

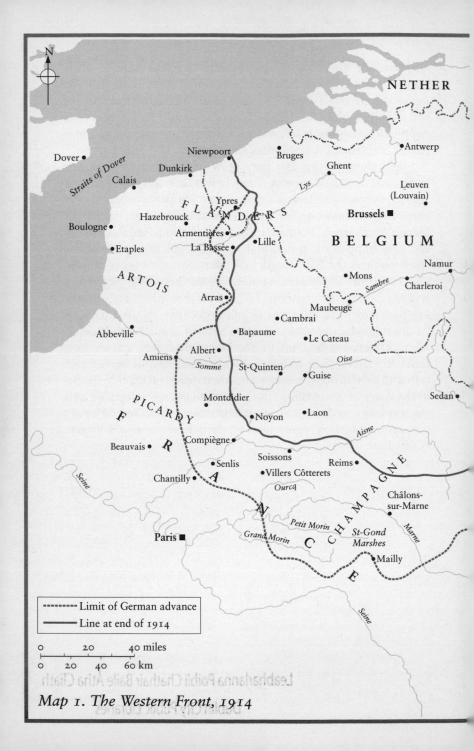

Map 1. *The Western Front, 1914*

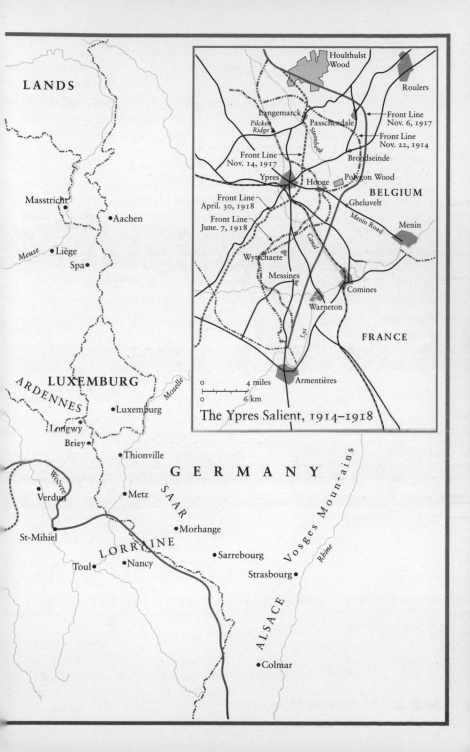

LANDS

Masstricht

Meuse  •Liège

•Aachen

Spa •

## The Ypres Salient, 1914–1918

Houlthulst
Wood

Roulers

Langemarck
*Pilcken
Ridge*

Passchendaele

Front Line
Nov. 6, 1917

Front Line
Nov. 22, 1914

Front Line
Nov. 14, 1917

*Steenbeek*

Broodseinde

Ypres

Hooge

Polygon Wood

BELGIUM

Front Line
April. 30, 1918

Gheluvelt

*Menin Road*

Menin

Front Line
June. 7, 1918

Canal

Wytschaete

Messines

Comines

Warneton

*Lys*

FRANCE

0 ___ 4 miles
0 ___ 6 km

Armentières

ARDENNES

LUXEMBURG

*Moselle*

•Luxemburg

•Longwy

Briey •

•Thionville

GERMANY

Vosges Mountains

*Wavre*

Verdun •

•Metz

SAAR

St-Mihiel •

•Morhange

LORRAINE

Toul •   •Nancy

•Sarrebourg

Strasbourg

*Rhine*

ALSACE

•Colmar

N

NETHER

Dover
Straits of Dover
Calais
Dunkirk
Bruges
Ghent
Antwerp

British Flanders Offensive, 1917

Second Battle of
Ypres, April 1917

Ypres
Paschendale
FLANDERS
Brussels
Hazebrouck
ARTOIS
Boulogne
Aubers Ridge Lille
Etaples
(May)
British
attacks, 1917
(March)
Neuve Chapelle
BELGIUM
(Sept.–Oct)
Festubert
Loos
Mons
French
attacks, 1917
(May–June)
Souchez
(Sept.–Oct)
Vimy
Arras
Bullcourt
Cambrai
Abbeville
Thiepval
Bapaume
Battle of the Somme,
July–Nov. 1916
German Winter
Withdrawal, 1917
Amiens
Somme
Oise
Sedan

PICARDY
Montdidier
Noyon
F
R
Chamin des Dames
Malmaison
Aisne
Compiègne
Jan, 1915
Soissons
Reims
A
French Spring
Offensive, 1917
CHAMPAGNE
Chantilly
N
Seine
Marne
French attacks in
Champagne
Feb.–March 1915,
Sept.–Nov. 1915
Petit Morin
C CHAMPAGNE
Grand Morin
Paris
E

Seine

① Fort Vaux
② Fort Douaumont

0        20        40 miles
0    20    40    60 km

*Map 2. The Western Front, 1915–1917*

LANDS

RUHR

•Düsseldorf

Cologne•

•Aachen

GERMANY

*Meuse* •Liège

•Koblenz

•Frankfurt

•Mainz

Bad Kreuznach•

ARDENNES

LUXEMBURG

*Moselle*

•Luxemburg

Longwy•

Battle of Verdun
Feb.–Aug. 1917

•Briey

•Thionville

①

*Woëvre*

②

Verdun

•Metz

SAAR

St-Mihiel

LORRAINE

French attack
April 1915

Toul•

•Nancy

Strasbourg•

*Rhine*

Vosges Mountains

ALSACE

•Colmar

N

Dover
Straits of Dover
Calais
Boulogne •
Etaples •

NETHER

• Antwerp

Dunkirk •
Bruges •
Ghent •

Lys

Cassel •
Ypres • Paschendale
Hazebrouck •
Lille •
FLANDERS

■ Brussels

BELGIUM

ARTOIS

Drocourt •

Mons •

Abbeville •
Arras •

Somme
Doullens •
Quéant • Cambrai •
Flesquiéres •
Bapaume •
Busigny •
Albert •
Amiens •
Hamel •
St-Quinten •
Oise
Villers-Bretonneux •
Montdidier •
La Fère •
Méziers •
Sedan •
PICARDY
Noyon •
F
Chamin des Dames
Malmaison •
Aisne
Compiègne •
Beauvais •
Soissons •
CHAMPAGNE
R
Senlis •
Reims •
Villets •
A
Chantilly •
Côtterets
N
Châlons-sur-Marne •
C
Petit Morin
E
Grand Morin
Marne
Paris ■

Seine

Seine

Somme Offensive ('Michael'), 21 March–5 April
Lys Offensive ('Georgette'), 9–29 April
Aisne Offensive ('Blucher–Yorck'), 27 May–4 June
Matz Offensive ('Gneisenau'), 9–12 June
Champagne–Marne Offensive ('Friedenssturm'), 15–17 July

0       20       40 miles
0    20    40    60 km

*Map 3. The Western Front, 1918*

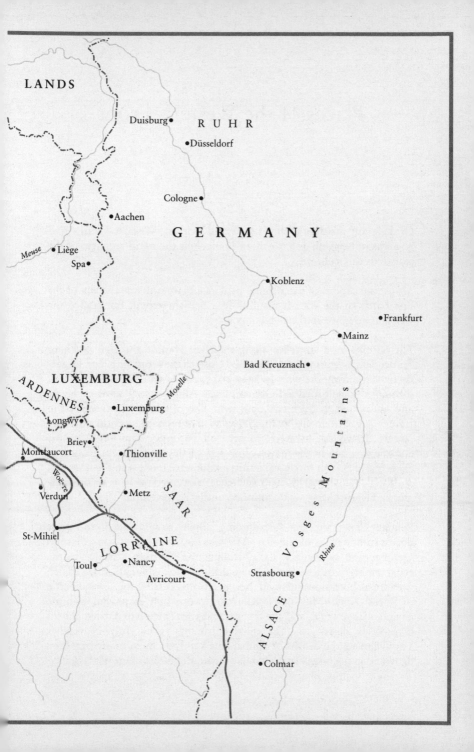

LANDS

Duisburg•

R U H R

•Düsseldorf

Cologne•

•Aachen

G E R M A N Y

*Meuse* •Liège

Spa•

•Koblenz

•Frankfurt

•Mainz

Bad Kreuznach•

LUXEMBURG

*Moselle*

ARDENNES

•Luxembourg

Longwy•

Briey•

Montfaucort

•Thionville

*Woëvre*

•Verdun

SAAR

•Metz

V o s g e s   M o u n t a i n s

St-Mihiel•

LORRAINE

Toul•

•Nancy

Avricourt•

Strasbourg•

*Rhine*

A L S A C E

•Colmar

# Places of the Western Front

Of the many theatres of the First World War, the Western Front – that is, areas in Belgium and northern France – is the main scenario of the stories in this volume.

*Mons*, the capital of the Belgian province Hainaut, was the site of the first battle of the war. It resulted in a British retreat, but stalled the German advance to the Belgian coast.

The Somme area stretches along the river Somme through northern France and Belgium. *Arras*, situated close to the front line, was largely destroyed during the war. In May 1915, Allied troops failed to break through the well-fortified German lines. Allied casualties were heavy and amounted to over 130,000 men. The offensive was renewed in June 1915, but to no avail. *Béthune* saw repeated action and was largely destroyed, as were Albert and Péronne. The battle of the Somme was one of the major offensives of the war, a co-operation of French and British forces on a thirty-kilometre front. On the first day, 1 July 1916, almost 60,000 casualties occurred on the British side alone. The offensive was continued until 18 November 1916.

Belgian *Ypres* and the surrounding salient saw some of the most devastating battles of the war. The first battle of Ypres took place in October and November 1914, stalling the German advance to the coast at high Allied cost and resulting in the stagnation of trench warfare as both sides fortified their positions. During the second battle of Ypres (April–May 1915), German troops first employed chlorine gas on a large scale, and the city of Ypres was evacuated, then almost completely destroyed. The third battle of Ypres (July–November 1917) caused the deaths of almost half a million men, many of whom drowned in the boggy marshlands surrounding the village of *Passchen-*

*daele*. Menin Gate Memorial, opened in Ypres in July 1927, commemorates all missing British and Commonwealth soldiers of the salient. The Belgian village of *Zillebecke*, or Zillebeke, near Ypres, is the site of seventeen war cemeteries.

*Verdun* was a French fortress of high symbolic value since it had long withstood the Prussians in the war of 1870–71 and was therefore well-known to most French citizens. The German army attacked Verdun in February 1916 and succeeded in engaging the French troops in a long drawn-out siege designed to weaken the French army in other parts of the frontline.

# Glossary

**Blighty:** Britain; coined originally by British expatriates in India, but taken up by homesick soldiers during the First World War. A 'Blighty wound' required a trip home for treatment and convalescence.

**Boche:** French derogatory term for Germans, used by the British during the war.

**Bully:** 'bully-beef', or corned beef, formed an important part of the British soldiers' rations.

**Estaminet:** French tavern or public-house, frequented by locals as well as British soldiers during the war.

**Fritz:** German male Christian name; used as nickname for all Germans.

**Hun:** derogatory term for Germans during the war.

**Jerry:** a German or German soldier.

**Poilu:** nickname for French soldiers of the First World War. It derives from the adjective *poilu*, translating literally as 'hairy' and referring to the unshaven faces of the soldiers, who had to spend long periods in the trenches.

**Subaltern:** in the British army, a junior commissioned officer below the rank of captain.

**Very lights:** flare fired by a pistol at night, either for temporary illumination, or for signalling.

**Wipers:** soldiers' slang for Ypres.

# Military Abbreviations

**Admiralty Court KC**: King's Counsel in Britain's Admiralty Court, responsible for all cases pertaining to maritime law.

**ASC**: Army Signal Command.

**BEF**: British Expeditionary Force – the professional army sent to France and Belgium in 1914. The term applied primarily to British soldiers stationed on the Western Front until November 1914; they were later supplemented by the volunteers of 'Kitchener's Army', who had been recruited and trained from August 1914 onwards. The BEF landed at Boulogne on 14 August 1914, and engaged in action at Mons and Ypres during the first months of the war.

**Batt. HQ**: Battalion Headquarters.

**CB**: confinement to barracks, a military punishment.

**C-in-C**: Commander-in-Chief.

**CO**: Commanding Officer.

**CSM**: Company Sergeant Major.

**Corps HQ**: Corps Headquarters.

**DCM**: Distinguished Conduct Medal; a military decoration for non commissioned officers established in 1854.

**DSO**: Distinguished Service Order; a military decoration for officers created in 1886. The DSO was awarded nearly nine thousand times during the First World War.

**GHQ**: General Headquarters.

**NCO**: Non-commissioned Officer. In the British army of the First World War, NCOs were members of the so-called enlisted personnel. They took over administrative or supervisory tasks delegated to them by a commissioned officer.

**OC**: Officer Commanding – that is, the Company Commander.

**OTC**: Officer Training Corps.

**QM**: Quartermaster.

**RSM**: Regimental Sergeant Major; a warrant officer obliged to maintain discipline and ensure high standards of performance in his regiment or battalion.

**VC**: Victoria Cross; a military decoration awarded to members of the Commonwealth armed services. It was created in 1856 by Queen Victoria to acknowledge conspicuous acts of bravery.

# Notes

## Arthur Machen: The Bowmen

First appeared in the *Evening News* on 29 September 1914. It sparked the legend about the 'Angels of Mons', who were subsequently claimed in other sources to have appeared during the British retreat from the town. Machen was at first willing to exploit the story's popularity commercially and republished 'The Bowmen' in a short collection of war tales under the title *The Angels of Mons: The Bowmen and Other Legends of the War* (1915), but he was bewildered when the 'incident' in his story was taken as fact by many, particularly the Church. He tried to expose it as fiction in his introduction to the volume.

1. *the retreat of the eighty thousand*: the British retreat at Mons in 1914.
2. *Sedan*: a decisive victory over the French during the Franco-Prussian war, on 1 September 1870, by the German army under General Helmuth von Moltke (1800–91). French forces were vastly outnumbered.
3. *'Good bye, good-bye to Tipperary'*: In the autumn of 1914, 'It's a Long Way to Tipperary' (1912) was a popular song among English soldiers and civilians.
4. *What price Sidney Street?*: Sidney Street, in Stepney, east London, was the scene of a showdown between the Metropolitan Police and a group of Eastern European anarchists in January 1911. Cornered after a failed robbery and the shooting of several policemen, two anarchists set fire to the building in which they were hiding and died during their attempt to escape. 'The Siege of Sidney Street' or 'the Battle of Stepney' was widely reported and even depicted on postcards.
5. *World without end. Amen*: final words of the 'Song of Mary' (Luke 1:46–55), sung as the Magnificat during Anglican evensong.

6.  *Harow*: an Anglo-Norman battle cry.
7.  *the contemptible English*: reference to a remark attributed to the
    Kaiser – but probably invented by the War Office – to the effect
    that the English were 'a contemptible little army'. The name
    'Old Contemptibles' was subsequently adopted as a term for the
    soldiers of the BEF.

## 'Sapper' (Herman Cyril McNeile): Private Meyrick – Company Idiot

Like most of McNeile's war stories, 'Private Meyrick – Company
Idiot' was first published in the *Daily Mail* during the war, and later
appeared in his collection *Men, Women and Guns* (1916).

1.  *Expeditionary Force*: the BEF.
2.  *a contemptible little army*: see 'The Bowmen', note 7.
3.  *Kipling*: Rudyard Kipling (1865–1936, see Biographies, p. 395).
4.  *Pay Corporal*: a non-commissioned officer who, in addition to his
    usual duties, was in charge of a regiment's payroll and connected
    administration.
5.  *Musketry returns*: the records of the most recent shooting
    practice.
6.  *A Company*: military unit, typically 190 to 200 soldiers; see also
    'Victory', note 1.
7.  *Savez*: 'Understand?'
8.  *through the charge that won the day*: the Charge of the Light
    Brigade – the British cavalry against Russian forces during the
    Crimean war in 1854, commemorated in 'The Charge of the
    Light Brigade' (1855) by Alfred, Lord Tennyson (1809–1892).
    The small British force attacked on a misinterpreted order and
    suffered heavy casualties.
9.  *If your officer's dead and the sergeants look white*: from Rudyard
    Kipling's (1865–1936) 'The Young British Soldier', published in
    Kipling's *Barrack-Room Ballads* (1892), which, by 1915, was in
    its forty-second edition.

## C. E. Montague: A Trade Report Only

First appeared in Montague's collection of war stories *Fiery Particles*
(1923). On 28 April 1923, *Time* magazine judged the volume as 'not
so important' as Montague's war recollections in *Disenchantment*
(1922), but praised the author's 'humour, irony, [and] sympathy'.

1.  *Proserpine's garden*: Proserpine, the Roman goddess of the underworld, was the daughter of Demeter, the goddess of fertility. Dividing her time between her husband, Hades, and her mother, Proserpine spends four months of the year in the underworld and the remaining eight above ground with her mother. Her return to the upper world was believed to herald spring.
2.  *Mais assez gentil*: 'but pleasant enough'.
3.  *Le bon Dieu Boche*: 'the good German God'.
4.  *ne faut pas les embêter*: 'you don't need to annoy them'.
5.  *Paisiblement*: 'peacefully'.
6.  *dixie-lid*: the lid of a cooling pot.
7.  *Pas d'inquiétude*: 'no trouble'.

## Richard Aldington: Victory

First appeared in the author's *Roads to Glory* (1930), and was published a year after his war novel *Death of a Hero* (1929).

1.  *C Company*: military unit, typically 190 to 200 soldiers. The British army identifies its rifle companies by letter (usually, but not always, A, B and C).
2.  *the Dormouse in Alice*: a character in *Alice's Adventures in Wonderland* (1865), by Lewis Carroll (1832–98).
3.  *bally*: euphemism meaning 'bloody'.
4.  *zero hour*: the co-ordinated moment of attack when the soldiers had to go over the top.
5.  *Siegfried Line*: a defensive line of trenches and five forts, established in 1916–17 by the German army as a section of the Hindenburg Line in northern France, and named after characters from the medieval German epic *Nibelungenlied*.
6.  *Rosinante*: Don Quixote's horse.
7.  *maffick*: from 'mafeking', to describe riotous celebrating, such as took place after the relief of Mafeking on 17 May 1900.

## Anne Perry: Heroes

In 2000 'Heroes' won an Edgar Award, the Mystery Writers of America award for the best short story. It was first published in an anthology of mystery stories, *Murder and Obsession* (2000), edited by Otto Penzler.

1.  *God's an Englishman*: popular nineteenth-century maxim of obscure origin, further popularized by R. F. Delderfield's *God Is An Englishman* (1970).

## Mary Borden: Blind

First appeared in its author's *The Forbidden Zone* (1929), a collection of sketches and stories based on her experiences as a nurse on the Western Front.

1.  *Casse-croûte*: a snack.
2.  *Briquet*: cigarette-lighter.

## Katherine Mansfield: An Indiscreet Journey

Published posthumously in *Something Childish and other Stories* (1924). Katherine Mansfield based the story on her affair with a 'little corporal', the French officer and writer Francis Carco (1886–1958).

1.  *ma mignonne*: 'sweetheart'.
2.  *mignonette*: a plant with fragrant green-grey flowers.
3.  *ma France adorée*: 'my beloved France'.
4.  *kepi*: uniform cap worn by French soldiers.
5.  *vous êtes tout à fait aimable*: 'You're very kind'.
6.  *toute de suite*: 'Now; immediately'.
7.  *juste en face de la gare*: 'directly opposite the railway station'.
8.  *Venez vite, vite*: 'Come quickly!'
9.  *un espèce de sea-gull couché sur votre chapeau*: 'a kind of sea-gull perched on your hat'.
10. *Non, je ne peux pas manger ça*: 'No, I can't eat that'.
11. *Matin*: *Le Matin* (1883–1944) was a French newspaper, with a print run of 670,000 in 1914.
12. *Montez vite, vite!*: 'Get in quickly!'.
13. *Ah, je m'en f . . .*: polite abbreviation for '*Je m'en fou*', meaning 'I couldn't care less!'
14. *Prends ça, mon vieux*: 'Take this, old friend'.
15. *Dodo, mon homme, fais vit' dodo*: a lullaby – *faire dodo* is French baby-talk, meaning 'to fall asleep'.
16. *Premier Rencontre*: 'First Meeting'.
17. *Triomphe D'Amour*: 'The Triumph of Love'.
18. *Il pleure de colère*: 'He's crying with rage'.
19. *Picon*: an alcoholic drink.

20. *Mais vous savez c'est un peu dégoûtant, ça*: 'This is rather disgusting, you know.'
21. *N'est-ce pas, Mademoiselle?*: 'Isn't that so, Miss?'
22. *bifteks*: beefsteaks.
23. *souvenir tendre*: 'a fond memory'.
24. *épatant*: 'jolly good; terrific'.

## Joseph Conrad: The Tale

First published in the *Strand Magazine* in October 1917. The text reprinted here has been taken from *The Complete Short Fiction of Joseph Conrad*, vol. 2 (1992).

## A. W. Wells: 'Chanson Triste'

First published in *The English Review* in November 1924, and subsequently included in *The Best Short Stories of 1925*, edited by Edward J. O'Brien.

1. *'Chanson Triste'*: a short piece for the piano by Peter Tchaikovsky (1840–1893), Opus 40 No. 2.
2. *a common Bulgar soldier*: Bulgaria had fought Romania in the Second Balkans War of 1913, and while Serbia, Greece, Romania and Montenegro joined the Allies, Bulgaria fought alongside Germany in the First World War. Britain and France declared war on Bulgaria in October 1914.
3. *Dorrain*: a town on the border between Macedonia and Bulgaria.
4. *Rupert Brooke*: English poet (1887–1915), made famous by his *War Sonnets* (1915) and 'The Soldier' in particular. He died of blood poisoning on a hospital ship in the Mediterranean. Brooke became a tragic symbol of Edwardian youth destroyed by the war.
5. *and I shall find some girl, perhaps*: the final lines of Brooke's 'The Chilterns' (1916).
6. *Omar Khayyám*: twelfth-century Persian poet. He became famous in Victorian England when his *Rubáiyát* was translated by Edward FitzGerald (1809–1883).
7. *Johnny*: soldiers' slang for enemy soldier.

## Arthur Conan Doyle: His Last Bow

First published in the September 1917 issue of *Strand Magazine*, sub-titled 'The War Service of Sherlock Holmes'. It also appeared in *Collier's* on 22 September 1917 and in a collection of Sherlock Holmes stories, entitled *His Last Bow: Some Reminiscences of Sherlock Holmes* (1917).

1.  *the Kaiser*: William II (1859–1941), the last German emperor and a grandson of Queen Victoria.
2.  *our good Chancellor*: Theobald von Bethmann Hollweg (1856–1921), in office since 14 July 1909. Even before the outbreak of war, Bethmann Hollweg doubted that Germany would win. He opposed unrestricted submarine warfare and was dismissed on 13 July 1917 under pressure from generals Hindenburg and Ludendorff.
3.  *four-in-hand*: carriage drawn by four horses.
4.  *window-breaking furies*: the suffragettes of the Women's Social and Political Union, led by Emmeline and Christabel Pankhurst. The WSPU was founded in 1903, and from 1905 embraced acts of violence such as window-breaking or even arson to draw attention to their claim for women's suffrage.
5.  *Rosyth*: naval base and dockyard on the south coast of Fife, built between 1909 and 1916.
6.  *Carlton House Terrace*: location of the German embassy in 1914.
7.  *Duke of York's steps*: the steps below the York Column, in London's Waterloo Place, Westminster.
8.  *semaphore*: optical telegraph or sign transmission with two flags or paddles, fixed to a series of relay-station towers to cover longer distances.
9.  *lamp-code*: a means of transmitting information with signal lamps. The flashes can convey even complex information, and were used in the British Royal Navy well into the twentieth century during periods of radio silence.
10. *Marconi*: Guglielmo Marchese Marconi (1874–1937) developed the wireless radio-telegraph system, which he had patented in Britain in 1897.
11. *Portland*: a prison and naval base on the Devonshire coast, sur-rounded by artificial breakwaters.
12. *Franz Joseph*: Franz Joseph I (1830–1916), Emperor of Austria, King of Hungary and Bohemia since 1848.

13.  *Schoenbrunn Palace*: residence of the Austrian royal family in Vienna.
14.  *Behold the fruit of pensive nights and laborious days*: from William Shakespeare's *Coriolanus* (Act V scene 6).
15.  *the constabulary at Skibbereen*: the Royal Irish Constabulary, one of Ireland's two police forces in the early twentieth century.

## W. Somerset Maugham: Giulia Lazzari

Included in Maugham's *Ashenden, Or, The British Agent* (1928), a cycle of short stories based loosely on Maugham's own experiences as an agent during the war.

1.  *cochon*: 'swine'.
2.  *Allons, levez-vous*: 'Come on, get up'.

## John Buchan: The Loathly Opposite

First appeared in Buchan's *The Runagates Club* (1928), a collection of stories told by the members of the eponymous and fictitious London dinner club.

1.  *Generalstabsoffizier*: General Staff Officer in the German army.
2.  *Falkenhayn*: Erich von Falkenhayn (1861–1922), infantry general and chief of the German General Staff from 1914 to 1916. He was responsible for planning the German Western Offensive of 1915, and advocated total submarine warfare.
3.  *a place called Rosensee in the Sächischen Sweitz*: Rosensee, a lake in a mountainous region of Saxony (*Sächsische Schweiz*).
4.  *violet rays*: ultra-violet rays.
5.  *Junkers*: a German country squire.
6.  *capercailzie*: the wood-grouse, a large game bird found in mountainous regions.
7.  *Homburg*: Bad Homburg; a popular German spa.
8.  *Champagne*: in the autumn of 1915, the Allies resumed their offensive in Champagne.

## Rudyard Kipling: Mary Postgate

First appeared in the *Century*, September 1915, and subsequently published in Kipling's *A Diversity of Creatures* (1917).

1.  *cassowary*: a large flightless bird.

2.  *Contrexeville*: a spa in Lorraine. The name here refers to the mineral water bottled in the town.

3.  *Hentys, Marryats, Levers; Stevensons, Baroness Orczys, Garvices*: popular novelists, widely read by the young: George Alfred Henty (1832–1902), Captain Frederick Marryat (1792–1848), Charles James Lever (1806–1872), Robert Louis Stevenson (1850–1894), Baroness Emma Orczy (1865–1947) and Charles Garvice (1833–1920).

4.  *assegai*: spear used in South Africa, and the name of the tree whose timber is used in its manufacture.

5.  *Brooklands*: motor-racing track and aviation centre in Surrey, built in 1907.

6.  *'Laty!'*: 'Lady!'

7.  *Cassée. Toute cassée*: 'Broken, all broken'.

8.  *Che me rends. Le médicin! Toctor!*: 'I surrender. The doctor! Doctor!' The pilot speaks French and English with a German accent: 'che' = 'je', and 'toctor' = 'doctor'.

9.  *Ich haben der todt Kinder gesehn*: literally, 'I have seen the dead children', but Mary Postgate's German is faulty: *'Ich habe die toten Kinder gesehen'* is correct.

## Stacy Aumonier: Them Others

First published in the *Century* in August 1917, and subsequently appeared in Aumonier's *The Love-A-Duck and Other Stories* (1921), and *Great Short Stories of the War* (1930), ed. H. C. Minchin. In his study *Aspects of the Modern Short Story* (1924), A. C. Ward claimed that the protagonist of the story, Mrs Ward, was 'a shining symbol of all bereaved mothers – not of England only, but of all the warring nations, friends and enemies made one in grief'.

## John Galsworthy: Told By the Schoolmaster

First appeared in *Argosy* in May 1927, then in Galsworthy's *Forsytes, Pendyces and Others* (1933).

1.  *Scott's first Polar book*: Robert Falcon Scott (1868–1912), the most famous (and tragic) figure of the 'heroic' age of Antarctic exploration; he reached the South Pole behind his Norwegian rival, Roald Amundsen (1872–1928). Scott died with four companions while trying to return to base after reaching the Pole.

He had published his account of the first National Antarctic Expedition (1901–4) in *The Voyage of the Discovery* (1905).

2. *its lingering deadlock*: from mid-September 1914 onwards, the Allied and German armies were caught up in stalemate on the Western Front. With increasingly deep trench systems on both sides, the cratered and wired no man's land between them, the front hardly moved until the German spring offensive of March 1918.

3. *'Connais-tu le pays?' from* Mignon: the opera *Mignon* (1866), by Ambroise Thomas (1811–1896), is based on a character from Johann Wolfgang Goethe's novel *Wilhelm Meisters Lehrjahre* (1795–6). The aria referred to here is the French version of Goethe's poem from the novel, 'Know you the land where the lemon-trees bloom'.

4. *All the Drang – as the Germans call it*: *Drang* translates literally as 'urge'; the reference is to the German literary *Sturm und Drang* movement (i.e. 'Storm and Stress').

## D. H. Lawrence: Tickets, Please

First published in April 1919, in *Strand Magazine*. During the war women temporarily replaced men in the home economy and public-service sectors. The version of the text reproduced here appeared in Lawrence's collection *England, My England* (1922).

1. *Thermopylae*. a narrow mountain pass, site of a famous battle in 480 BC in which the ancient Greeks, led by the Spartans, successfully held back an army of Persian invaders in a desperate last stand.

2. *Coddy*: the nickname is ambiguous, since it implies that Thomas resembles a fish, but may also refer to the abbreviation 'cod' for 'codswallop' and reflect negatively on his conversation.

3. *The Statutes Fair*: a fun-fair.

4. *on the qui-vive*: on the look-out.

5. *I'm afraid to, go home in, the dark*: an allusion to the song 'I'm Afraid to Come Home in the Dark' (1908), by Egbert van Alstyne and Harry Williams. In it, a husband explains his nightly absences to his newlywed wife by claiming that he has had to stay at the club, not daring to venture out after dark.

## Radclyffe Hall: Miss Ogilvy Finds Herself

Written in 1926, and taken from the author's short-story collection of the same title, which first appeared in 1934. It is one of two stories addressing the First World War. The other, 'Fräulein Schwartz', relates the story of an elderly German spinster who experiences the war in London lodgings and is bullied into suicide by her hostile fellow lodgers.

1. *Caporals*: the American cigarette brand, Sweet Caporals.
2. *Bon Dieu! Mais dépêchez-vous donc!*: 'Good God! Hurry up!'
3. *Jaeger trench-helmets*: a close-fitting woollen cap of the balaclava type. Jaeger, the British knitwear company, offered a range of products for the forces during the First World War.

## Hugh Walpole: Nobody

First published in the author's *The Thirteen Travellers* (1921).

1. *Duke Street*: Tom is taking his walk in the prosperous neighbour-hoods of Mayfair, Soho and Marylebone in the London Borough of Westminster. Bond Street and Oxford Street were then promi-nent shopping streets. Mayfair and Marylebone were well-to-do residential and commercial areas, while Soho was one of London's less respectable areas, with many public-houses, res-taurants and brothels; it was frequented particularly by artists and intellectuals.
2. *Victoria*: the area around Victoria station in the Borough of Westminster; it consisted mainly of commercial buildings and social housing.
3. *DT*: delirium tremens, caused by alcohol abuse.
4. *Blackfriars*: an area south-west of the City of London, bordering the river Thames.
5. *pi—*: pious, but used in a derogatory fashion.
6. *the East End*: notorious for its sub-standard accommodation and the poverty of its inhabitants.
7. *East-End Settlement*: the charitable settlement movement en-abled future clergymen to experience the problems of the poor at first hand. Originating at Oxford University, the first settle-ment, a forerunner of community centres, opened in Bethnal Green in 1884, and in the following two years four more opened in London and one in New York.

8.   *vieux jeu*: 'old hat'.
9.   *Oxford House*: the Bethnal Green settlement.
10.  *Rubicon*: 'to cross the Rubicon' means 'to take a significant step, or momentous decision'.
11.  *Marcella*: a novel by Mary Ward – 'Mrs Humphrey Ward' (1851–1920) – published in 1894. Marcella, the novel's socialist heroine, falls in love with a conservative landowner.

## Harold Brighouse: Once A Hero

First appeared in *Pan* in July 1921, and exists in two versions: the short story, and a one act play, published by Gowans and Grey in 1922. The story appeared in *The Best British Short Stories of 1922* (1923), eds. Edward J. O'Brien and John Cournos.

1.   *Nothing in his life*: from William Shakespeare's *Macbeth* (Act I scene 4).
2.   *She wore a tam*: tam-o'-shanter, a Scottish cap.

## Katherine Mansfield: The Fly

First published during the author's lifetime in the *Nation*, March 1922, then in her collection, *The Dove's Nest* (1923).

## Winifred Holtby: The Casualty List

First published in the author's collection, *Truth Is Not Sober* (1934).

1.   *Journey's End*: a highly successful play by R. C. Sherriff (1896–1975), first performed in 1928. It is set in March 1918 and explores the relationships between a group of infantry officers, sharing a dugout on the front line prior to a major German offensive. In the most emotional scene of the play, the protagonist Stanhope watches helplessly as his friend Raleigh dies in his arms from a shrapnel injury. Sherriff had served as a captain in the British army during the war.
2.   *They shall not grow old . . .*: the best-known lines of Robert Laurence Binyon's (1869–1943) poem 'To the Fallen', first published in *The Times*, 21 September 1914; often referred to as the 'Ode of Remembrance'.
3.   *In Flanders fields the poppies grow*: from 'In Flanders Fields', a

war poem by the Canadian officer John Alexander McCrae (1872–1918). It became famous even during the war and remains one of its most frequently quoted poems.

## Robert Graves: Christmas Truce

First published in the *Saturday Evening Post* as 'Wave No Banners' on 15 December 1962; subsequently appeared in Graves's *Collected Short Stories* (1965).

1.  *We'll keep the Red Flag Flying Still*: correctly, 'We'll keep the red flag flying here'; from the anthem of the British Labour Party, 'The Red Flag', by Irish socialist James Connell (1852–1929).
2.  *Ivan Orfalitch*: not an authentic Russian name, but used in the sense of 'the next man in Russia' or 'my opposite number in Russia'.
3.  *amachoor propaganda*: amateur propaganda.
4.  *nappooed*: killed – 'nappoo' was a common term for 'gone', 'dead' or 'done for' among the soldiers; from the French expression *il n'y a plus*, 'there is nothing left'.
5.  *Delville Wood*: the battle of Delville Wood was a subsidiary attack of the Somme offensive, lasting from July to September 1916.
6.  *Joffre*: Joseph Joffre (1852–1931) was Commander-in-Chief of the French army from 1911 to 1916; he was replaced by General Robert Georges Nivelle (1856–1924) after heavy French losses at Verdun, and was given the ceremonial post Marshal of France.
7.  *Boy Greneer*: soldiers' term for the village of Bois Grenier, near Armentières.
8.  *Mills bombs*: a type of hand grenade adopted by the British army as its standard grenade in 1915.
9.  *Stilly Nucked*: 'Stille Nacht'.
10. *Hully in West Saxony*: the East German city of Halle, on the banks of the Saale river.
11. *bundooks*: a transliteration of the Hindi word for 'gun'.
12. *I want to go Home!*: opening line of a popular soldiers' song.
13. *Dixie Lid*: lid of an army cooking pot.
14. *Old Von Kluck, He Had a Lot of Men*: a popular First World War marching song, which began 'Oooh, we don't give a f***/ For old von Kluck/And all his German army'. General Alexander von Kluck (1846–1934) had been in charge of the failed 'march on Paris' in August 1914.

15. *'Deutschland Über Alles'*: opening line of the patriotic song 'Das Lied der Deutschen' (1841). August Heinrich Hoffmann von Fallersleben (1798–1874) composed the lyrics, which expressed love of country. It was adopted as the German national anthem after the First World War.

16. *Padre*: regimental chaplain.

17. *General French*: Sir John Denton Pinkstone French (1852–1925) was chief of the Imperial General Staff from 1912 to 1913; in 1913, he was made field marshal, and in August 1914 took command of the BEF. He was replaced in December 1915 by Field Marshal Sir Douglas Haig (see note 26), and appointed commander of the British Home Forces until the end of the war.

18. *The King!*: the toast is sufficiently neutral to be embraced by both sides: it might refer either to King George V (1865–1936) or Kaiser William II (1859–1941), who was also King of Prussia. Saxony, moreover, still had its own king, Friedrich August III (1865–1932).

19. *Imshi*: an Arabic phrase for 'take off' or 'get lost', here meant as an order to hide.

20. *boko camarade*: '*beaucoup camarade*', i.e. great friends.

21. *Nürnberg Youth Rally*: a peace camp between young people from all countries that had participated in the Second World War. It was held in 1956–7 in Nuremberg, a town particularly associated with Nazi atrocities; also, the Hitler Youth Movement had held rallies there.

22. *sap-heads*: shallow holes – usually shell craters – in no man's land used as comparatively sheltered listening posts to monitor activities in enemy trenches.

23. *brevet rank*: a rank one degree higher than one is paid for, held on a temporary basis.

24. *the big German mine*: during the war, the German and British armies employed tunnelling companies to plant mines. As early as December 1914, ten German mines exploded under the British lines near Festubert; Graves's own regiment, the Royal Welch Fusiliers, witnessed a major detonation in June 1916.

25. *General Sir Douglas Haig*: Field Marshal Sir Douglas Haig (1861–1928) was made Commander-in-Chief of the British army in December 1915. He had served in Sudan and the Boer War, and in 1909 had been appointed Chief of the General Staff for India after working in the War Office for two years. Haig was responsible for the British campaign of slow attrition after the battle of the Somme.

26. *La Bassée Canal*: La Bassée is a town on the Somme connected

to nearby Aire by an industrial canal. The area saw the last heavy battles of the early war in October 1914, prior to the establishment of the British lines.

27. *minny-werfer*: from the German word for trench mortar, 'Minenwerfer'.

28. *snobs*: junior officers. Well-connected public-school men were likely to enter the army with a commission, unlike their working-class contemporaries.

29. *bobbajers*: bombardiers, or Royal Artillery corporals.

30. *'Stern-Endeavour' Haig*: Field Marshal Sir Douglas Haig (1861–1928) was substituted for General French (see note 18) in the belief that he would instil the British war effort with new vigour.

31. *Hock Solla Leeben*: A German song used for birthdays and anniversary celebrations – correctly, 'Hoch soll er leben' (i.e. 'three cheers for him').

32. *a brother killed at Loos*: the battle of Loos, 25–28 September 1915, during the wider Artois–Loos offensive by the French and British in the autumn of 1915.

33. *chop wood in Holland*: the Kaiser fled to the Netherlands from Belgium on 10 November 1918. The Dutch government granted him asylum on the condition that he would abstain from future political activity, and Wilhelm II confirmed his resignation on 28 November. He spent the rest of his life at his house in Doorn, reportedly passing his time in chopping wood.

34. *Peace Treaty*: Treaty of Versailles, signed on 28 June 1919. It was strongly opposed in Germany and by many Allied politicians due to its particularly harsh reparation demands and the fact that Germany had to acknowledge sole responsibility for the war.

## Muriel Spark: The First Year of My Life

First published in the *New Yorker* in June 1975. The text used here has been taken from *The Penguin Book of British Comic Short Stories* (1990).

1. *ESP*: extra-sensory perception.

2. *The Grand Old Duke of York*: A popular nursery rhyme.

3. *treaty of Brest-Litowsk*: peace treaty between Russia, Germany and its allies, signed on 3 March 1918, in which Russia ceded a third of its population in the Baltic region, Finland and Poland, to the German Empire.

4. *'I truly wish I were a fox or a bird'*: from a letter D. H. Lawrence (1885–1930, see Biographies, p. 395) wrote to his former neighbour in Cornwall, the Scottish composer Cecil Gray (1895–1951) on 12 March 1918. Having been evicted from their Cornish cottage the previous spring, the Lawrences were about to take a new house, which inspired Lawrence with panic.

5. *Bernard Shaw who was telling somebody to shut up*: the Irish playwright, Nobel Prize winner and socialist George Bernard Shaw (1856–1950) strongly opposed the war and wrote numerous essays and articles against it. He was also an open critic of the Versailles peace treaty. His wartime writings were collected and published as *What I Really Wrote About the War* (1930).

6. *Tout le monde à la bataille!*: 'Everyone to arms!' A reference to General Foch's (1851–1929) Meuse-Argonne offensive, 26 September–11 November 1918. French, British and American forces were to attack along the entire Western Front, joining forces in a final effort at breaking the German lines.

7. *the time the* Vindictive *was sunk in Ostend harbour*: In a massive military action, British naval forces attacked the German bases at Ostend and Zeebrugge in April 1918, aiming to block the harbours. HMS *Vindictive*, laden with cement, was sunk to effect this blockade.

8. *The Playboy of the Western World*: a play by J. M. Synge, first performed in Dublin and subsequently in 1907 at the Court Theatre in London. It is set in a public-house during the early 1900s, where the main character, Christy Mahon, thrills a large audience with an account of how he allegedly killed his father.

9. *Picasso was getting married*: he married Russian ballerina Olga Khokhlova on 18 June 1918.

10. *the Silver Wedding of King George V and Queen Mary*: the celebrations took place on 6 July 1918.

11. *the Czar and his family*: the assassination of the Romanov family in the wake of the Russian revolution. On 17 July 1918, Nicholas II (1868–1918), his wife and five children were shot in the basement of Ipatiev House in Yekaterinburg to prevent their rescue by counter-revolutionary forces.

12. *Bertrand Russell*: an ardent pacifist, the philosopher Bertrand Russell (1872–1970) opposed British participation in the war, and worked for the No Conscription Fellowship from 1916 onwards. In January 1918 he published an article in the *Tribunal*, suggesting that American soldiers might be used as strike-breakers in England after East End dockworkers had refused to

load a ship bound for Russia, the *Jolly George*, with munitions
in early 1918. Russell's article was seen as criminal agitation,
and he was sentenced to six months' imprisonment.

13. *A certain oration by Mr Asquith*: Herbert Henry Asquith (1852–
1928), prime minister 1908–16. Blamed by many for the unsuc-
cessful conduct of the Somme offensive, Asquith had resigned in
December 1916 and was succeeded by David Lloyd George
(1863–1945). As Liberal opposition leader, however, he remained a public figure, and gave the speech referred to here in
Parliament, following Lloyd George's, on 18 November 1918.
Asquith's eldest son, Raymond, was killed during the battle of
the Somme in September 1916 (see note 18).

14. *that damned Welsh goat*: despite his public proclamations of
(professional) friendship, Asquith did not like Lloyd George,
whose takeover as prime minister ended Asquith's tenure in
1916. Lloyd George was commonly considered a more fitting
wartime leader; Asquith's hesitant policies had been much
criticized in the press.

15. *I have a rendezvous with death*: a poem by the American Alan
Seeger (1888–1916), who served in the French Foreign Legion
during the First World War.

16. *Putting his arm around a lady's shoulder in a Daimler motor
car*: Asquith was well known as a ladies' man and had a number
of intimate female correspondents, even though he was happily
married. He had a prominent affair with young socialite Venetia
Stanley (1887–1948), a friend of his daughter Violet, who
eventually married one of Asquith's *protégés*, the Liberal MP
Edwin Samuel Montagu.

17. *What passing bells for these who die as cattle?*: the opening lines
to 'Anthem for Doomed Youth' by Wilfred Owen (1893–1918).

18. *All things have become new*: From Asquith's speech, on
18 November 1918, to the House of Commons, in support of a
resolution to congratulate King George V on the conclusion of
the Armistice. Asquith's interpretation of the war stressed its
'purifying' effect on the British people and the righteousness of
the British cause, stating that the war 'is and will remain by itself
as a record of everything Humanity can dare or endure – of the
extremes of possible heroism and . . . of possible baseness, and
above and beyond all, the slow moving but in the end irresistible
power of a great ideal'. The full text can be found in *Speeches
by the Earl of Oxford and Asquith, KG* (1927).

## Robert Grossmith: Company

First appeared in the *Spectator*, 23/30 December 1989. It was subsequently included in two anthologies of short stories, *Best English Short Stories* 2 (1990) and *The Minerva Book of Short Stories 3* (1991).

## Julian Barnes: Evermore

First published in the *New Yorker*, 13 November 1995, and subsequently appeared in the author's *Cross Channel* (1996).

The cemeteries mentioned in this story – Cabaret Rouge, Caterpillar Valley, Thistle Dump, Quarry and Blighty Valley – are all British and Commonwealth war cemeteries on the Somme. Herbécourt has one for troops from the United Kingdom and Australia. Some accommodate a few German graves.

1. *field-service card*: field postcards, given out in the trenches to be sent as a faster substitute for letters and speed up the process of censoring. The soldiers could delete information that did not apply to them, but were not allowed to add any message of their own.

2. *Thiepval*: the Thiepval Memorial to the Missing of the Somme was opened in 1932. Thiepval is the largest British war memorial in the world, displaying the names of nearly 74,000 British and Commonwealth soldiers who fell on the Somme between July 1916 and March 1918 without a known place of burial.

3. *Ulster Tower*: commemorates the men of the 36th Ulster Division, who fought and died on the Western Front.

4. *THEIR NAME LIVETH FOR EVERMORE*: from the Book of Ecclesiastes, chosen for the Imperial War Graves Commission by Rudyard Kipling, who also composed the standard inscription for the headstones of the unknown, 'A soldier of the Great War . . . Known unto God'.

5. *Brigadier Sir Frank Higginson's domed portico*: shelter building at the entrance to Cabaret Rouge cemetery, designed by Higginson (1890–1958) in his function as secretary of the Imperial War Graves Commission.

6. *Sir Edwin Lutyens*: the distinguished architect (1869–1944), appointed to the Imperial War Graves Commission in 1917–18.

7. *the eleventh hour of the eleventh day of the eleventh month*: the exact time of the Armistice of 1918. Since 1945, the Armistice

has been commemorated on Remembrance Sunday, the second Sunday in November, when the fallen of all conflicts since 1914 are remembered. On 7 November 1919 King George V issued a proclamation calling for the observance of a two-minute silence in 'reverent remembrance of the glorious dead'; it still takes place on 11 November each year, and at the services of Remembrance across the United Kingdom.

8.  *Maison Blanche*: German war cemetery north of Arras.

9.  *howitzer*: a gun for high-angle firing of shells.

10. *Monsieur Un Tel*: 'Mr So-and-So'.

11. *triumphant Marianne*: idealized female figure, symbolizing Liberty, Reason, and the French Republic.

12. *cockerel*: the cockerel is a French national symbol, which derives from the Latin *gallus*: it translates both as 'inhabitant of Gaul' (i.e. France) and 'cockerel'.

13. *Imperial War Graves Commission*: from 1914, a branch of the Red Cross was charged with marking the graves of fallen soldiers. In 1915 the duty was transferred to the army's newly set up Graves Registration Commission, at which point it was decided that all British and Commonwealth dead soldiers were to be interred abroad where they had fallen. In 1917 the Imperial War Graves Commission was founded by Sir Fabian Arthur Goulstone Ware (1869–1949), and in 1960 it became the Commonwealth War Graves Commission. Ware had led the original Red Cross unit.

# Biographies

## Aldington, Richard (1892–1962)

Born in Portsmouth as Edward Godfree Aldington, he grew up in Dover. He studied at University College, London, but left without a degree to become a writer and journalist. In 1912 Aldington joined the Imagist movement, and edited the avant-garde literary periodical the *Egoist*. He was a close friend of Ezra Pound, T. S. Eliot and D. H. Lawrence. He went to France as a soldier in mid-1916 and remained in the army until the end of the war. Soon afterwards he published a collection of poems, *Images of War* (1919), and his novel *Death of a Hero* (1929) deals with what he perceived as the soldiers' archetypal experience of the war: profound disillusionment with and loss of faith in humanity.

## Aumonier, Stacy (1887–1928)

The descendant of an old Huguenot family, Aumonier was an artist before he turned to writing in 1913. John Galsworthy regarded him as 'one of the best short-story writers of all time'; and A. C. Ward claimed, in his *Aspects of the Modern Short Story* (1924), that Aumonier's war stories resembled 'an English epic of the Great War' (252). Aumonier captured the varied reactions to war of his fellow countrymen, and portrayed the destruction of what many thought of as an English pre-war idyll in 'The Match' (1916).

## Barnes, Julian (1946–)

Educated in London and at Oxford, Barnes has worked as a lexicographer, reviewer, editor and television critic. He is now a full-time writer and occasional translator, and lives in London. He has published crime fiction under the pseudonym Dan Kavanagh. For his 'serious' novels,

Barnes has won numerous awards, both in Britain and abroad, and his works have been shortlisted frequently for the Man Booker Prize. To date, he has published two volumes of short stories – *Cross Channel* (1996) and *The Lemon Table* (2004).

## Borden, Mary (1886–1968)

Born in Chicago, the daughter of a businessman. While travelling in Europe at the outbreak of the war, Borden decided to set up a hospital unit on the Western Front. She stayed in France for the duration, and was awarded the Croix de Guerre by the French government. She met her second husband, Edward Spears, while serving in France, and went to live with him in England. Of Borden's novels, *Sarah Gay* (1931) is also loosely based on her own war experiences. Her collection of sketches, poetry and short stories, *The Forbidden Zone* (1929), derives entirely from her war experiences.

## Brighouse, Harold (1882–1958)

Brighouse grew up in Manchester as the son of a businessman, and, after an apprenticeship in a company selling shipping equipment, went to work in the cotton trade. In 1902 he moved to London, where he embarked on his writing career. Brighouse was a prolific playwright, who also wrote eight novels, a number of short stories and worked as literary critic of the *Manchester Guardian*. Many of his plays feature Lancastrians, and the factory setting of *Once a Hero* may also owe much to his roots in a manufacturing town.

## Buchan, John (1875–1940)

Educated in Glasgow and at Oxford, Buchan was a barrister, journalist, publisher and politician. He wrote and published his first novels while still at university. During the war he was a correspondent for *The Times*, and, in 1917, was made director of information for the Secret Service. Buchan was created Baron Tweedsmuir, and in 1935 moved to Canada as its governor general. He wrote a large number of historical novels and many short stories, published in seven collections and in magazines such as the *Spectator* and *Blackwood's*. However, his literary fame rests primarily on his spy thrillers, most famously *The Thirty-Nine Steps* (1915).

# Conrad, Joseph (1857–1924)

Józef Teodor Konrad Korzeniowski was born in Ukraine, then part of
the Russian Empire. His parents were Polish nationalists and belonged
to the impoverished gentry, but Conrad was orphaned young and
moved to Marseille at sixteen to seek his fortune at sea. After several
years as an apprentice on sailing ships, he joined the British Merchant
Navy in 1879. Once he had passed the required exams, he became a
captain and a naturalized British subject. He embarked on a professional writing career in the 1890s, drawing on his travels and
experiences abroad. Of his many novels and short stories, 'The Tale'
is the only one to address the First World War.

# Doyle, Sir Arthur Conan (1859–1930)

The son of Irish immigrants, Doyle grew up in southern Scotland and
studied medicine in Edinburgh. He soon began to write, producing
historical novels, plays, poetry, treatises on military history and spiritualism, but he is best known for his Sherlock Holmes stories. An
ardent patriot, he had already been an apologist of the Boer War,
about which he wrote a propaganda pamphlet and a history. During
the First World War, he agreed to work for the War Propaganda
Bureau, alongside other popular writers like Rudyard Kipling, John
Galsworthy, H. G. Wells and Thomas Hardy. In the war he lost not
only his son, Kingsley, but a brother, two brothers-in-law and two
nephews.

# Galsworthy, John (1867–1933)

After Harrow, Galsworthy studied law at Oxford, but decided to
become a writer. As a novelist he remained one of the most widely
read British authors until the 1950s. His fiction won him many awards,
most notably the Nobel Prize for Literature in 1932, for *The Forsyte
Saga*. During the war, Galsworthy donated all his literary income to
the war effort and various relief funds; he also wrote for the War
Propaganda Bureau. However, his attitude towards the war, and particularly towards the vilification of the enemy in the press, was not
uncritical. His sister Lilian was married to the Bavarian painter Georg
Sauter, who was interned during the war, to Galsworthy's indignation.

## Graves, Robert von Ranke (1895–1985)

Graves was born in London. He enlisted at the beginning of the war, although he had an Oxford scholarship, and his first poems appeared while he was serving in the army. At the battle of the Somme he was wounded so severely that his family was informed of his death, but he recovered, albeit with lasting damage to his lungs. After the war, Graves took up his place at Oxford, and later lived in Cairo, Mallorca and Pennsylvania. From 1961 to 1966, he was professor of Poetry at Oxford University. He perceived himself primarily as a poet, although he produced several successful novels, such as the best-selling *I, Claudius* (1934), a memoir and works of non-fiction.

## Grossmith, Robert (1954–)

Born in Dagenham, Essex, Grossmith spent seven years in Sweden as a translator and teacher, then did a PhD at the University of Keele. His doctoral thesis, *Other States of Being: Nabokov's Two-world Metaphysic*, was published in 1987, followed by a novel, *The Empire of Lights* (1990).

## Hall, Radclyffe (1880–1943)

Marguerite Radclyffe Hall was born in Bournemouth. Her parents separated shortly after her birth, and after her mother remarried, she was brought up by governesses. Hall attended King's College in London and lived in Germany until a legacy enabled her to move to London at the age of twenty-one. There, she lived first with her older (married) lover Mabel Batten, then with Batten's young cousin, Una Troubridge. Early on Hall had realized her lesbianism and had many unhappy youthful love affairs. She and Troubridge remained together until Hall's death, from cancer, in 1943. Hall remains best-known for her overtly lesbian – and initially banned – novel, *The Well of Loneliness* (1928).

## Holtby, Winifred (1898–1935)

Born into a wealthy Yorkshire farming family, she went to school in Scarborough. There, she witnessed the shelling of the town by German destroyers in December 1914 and wrote about it for a local paper, and later in her novel, *The Crowded Street* (1924). She gained a place at Somerville College, Oxford, but took a year off in 1917–18 to join

the Women's Auxiliary Army Corps. After the war, Holtby formed a
lifelong friendship with Vera Brittain. Holtby's best-known literary
work is her novel *South Riding* (1936). An ardent socialist, feminist
and human-rights campaigner, she also wrote for various newspapers and magazines, including the *Manchester Guardian* and *Good
Housekeeping*.

## Kipling, Rudyard (1865–1936)

Kipling was born in Bombay, but educated in England. After his return
to India, he wrote for newspapers, in which many of his early poems
and stories were also published. After a wave of success with his short
stories about British colonial life he returned to England in 1889. In
his collection of verses *Barrack-Room Ballads* (1892), he coined the
archetype of the British soldier, Tommy Atkins. Kipling was a patriot,
and some of his texts – notoriously his poem 'The White Man's
Burden' (1899) – have been read as inherently racist. However, he was
also a critic of the Empire, and pointed out social problems at home.
He first witnessed warfare in South Africa during the Boer War. During
the First World War, he worked for the War Propaganda Bureau and
was later appointed to advise the Imperial War Graves Commission.
His son Jack was killed at the age of eighteen in 1915, and several of
his First World War stories betray a loathing of the enemy. In his
post-war story 'The Gardener' (1926), Kipling emphasizes remembrance and mourning rather than hatred.

## Lawrence, D. H. (1885–1930)

Born into a Midlands mining family, Lawrence was educated in Not
tingham and worked as a teacher before he became a full-time writer.
In 1914 he married Frieda von Richthofen Weekley – a distant cousin
of fighter pilot Manfred von Richthofen. In 1917, suspected of being
German spies, the Lawrences were forced to leave their home in
Cornwall. They were denied passports while the war lasted, but left
England in 1919. The novel *Kangaroo* (1923) reflects the Lawrences'
experiences during these years, but Lawrence also wrote a number of
short stories about the war, which were published in *England, My
England* (1922). The title story of this volume was first published in
the *English Review*, October 1915, and presents the war as the means
of self-destruction for a doomed and decadent English society.

## Machen, Arthur Llewellyn Jones (1863–1947)

Machen was born to a clergyman father in Monmouthshire, Wales.
Growing up in a lonely environment, immersed in Roman remains
and Welsh folklore, he developed a lifelong fascination with the mythi-
cal and supernatural, and became famous for his 'supernatural' fiction
and ghost stories, which had been popular in Britain since Victorian
times. At various times Machen earned a living as an actor and journalist, most notably for the *Evening News*.

## Mansfield, Katherine (1888–1923)

Katherine Mansfield is one of the best-known authors of the modernist
short story. Born in Wellington, New Zealand, she moved to London
to attend Queen's College, then took up writing. She had many affairs,
and eventually contracted gonorrhoea, which was left untreated and
may have led to her infection with tuberculosis, of which she died.
Her second husband, John Middleton Murry, edited her letters and
unpublished works after her death. During the First World War, her
brother was killed at the front, but 'The Fly' and 'An Indiscreet Journey' are her only two stories that address the war directly.

## Maugham, W. Somerset (1874–1965)

Born in Paris, he lived in France until the age of ten, when he was
orphaned and moved to the home of a clergyman uncle in Kent.
He attended King's School, Canterbury, and subsequently went to
Heidelberg University, then to London to study medicine. Maugham
qualified as a doctor in 1897, the same year in which his first novel,
*Liza of Lambeth*, was published. Maugham habitually drew on autobiographical experience for his writing. Too old to enlist for military
service, he served as an ambulance driver at the Western Front for
five months during the First World War. He also worked for British
Intelligence in Switzerland and Russia.

## Montague, C. E. (1867–1928)

Born to Irish Catholic parents, who had emigrated to England, Montague was educated in London and at Oxford. He was invited to work
for the *Manchester Guardian* on trial after his graduation, and wrote
in favour of Irish Home Rule, opposed the Boer War and, initially,
the First World War. Once war had been declared, though, he hoped

that full support of the British war effort would help to end the conflict quickly. Already over forty-one, he was allowed in the trenches for a brief spell in 1916, but went on to work for Military Intelligence, writing articles and censoring letters and news reports. Montague's later writings about the First World War, above all his book of essays *Disenchantment* (1922), attempt to expose the inhumanity of warfare and show his disillusionment with the war.

## Perry, Anne (1938–)

Born in London as Juliet Marion Hulme, she grew up mostly in New Zealand and now lives in Scotland. Perry was educated privately – her health was poor – and later worked in a variety of jobs before becoming a writer in 1972. As well as her two series of Victorian detective tales – one featuring Inspector Pitt, the other private-investigator Monk – Perry began in 2003 a new series set during the First World War. She has published several First World War novels, in which Cambridge professor and military chaplain Joseph Reavley solves mysterious criminal cases at the front and, aided by his agent brother and two sisters, fights the machinations of the mysterious 'Peacemaker' behind the lines.

## 'Sapper': McNeile, Herman Cyril (1888–1937)

Born to a Royal Navy captain, then educated at Cheltenham and Woolwich, McNeile joined the Corps of Royal Engineers in 1907. His pseudonym 'Sapper' is taken from the equivalent rank to 'private' with the Engineers. A prolific and popular short-story writer, McNeile turned out numerous stories about his war experiences, which were first published in the *Daily Mail* and collected in one volume in 1930. He remains best known for his *Bulldog Drummond* stories, written after the war, featuring a former British army captain turned private investigator. During the war, McNeile was awarded the Military Cross and rose to the rank of lieutenant colonel. While his later works have been characterized as racist and kitsch, his war stories are marked by his 'professional' viewpoint: although realistic, they do not condemn the war but stress the endurance and hardiness of British soldiers.

## Spark, Muriel (1918–2006)

Muriel Sarah Camberg, of Jewish-Scottish descent, was educated in Edinburgh. At nineteen, she went to Southern Rhodesia (today Zimbabwe) to marry teacher Sidney Oswald Spark. The marriage soon ended in divorce. In 1944 Spark went back to Britain, where she worked for MI6 until the end of the Second World War. Besides writing poetry and fiction, she was also a journalist and editor, and published critical works on writers such as Mary Shelley and John Masefield. During the early 1960s Spark moved to New York to work for the *New Yorker*, and in 1967 settled in Italy, where she remained until her death. She published more than twenty novels – most famously *The Prime of Miss Jean Brodie* (1961) – and numerous short stories, which appeared in a Penguin edition, *Collected Stories* (1994). The recipient of a great number of honorary degrees and awards, Spark was created Dame Commander of the British Empire in 1993.

## Walpole, Sir Hugh (1884–1941)

Born in New Zealand to an Anglican priest, Walpole was educated in Canterbury and Cambridge. After his studies, he remained in Britain, eventually settling in the Lake District. A successful and popular novelist, critic and playwright, he worked for the Red Cross in Russia during the war. His war experiences inspired two of his best-known novels, *The Dark Forest* (1916), which ran into several editions even in the first year after its publication, and *The Secret City* (1919). In the Second World War, Walpole again engaged in volunteer war work, during which he was killed in 1941.

## Wells, A. W. (1894–1977)

Wells, about whom little biographical information is obtainable, was the author of one collection of short stories, *All This Is Ended* (1936) and a travel book on South Africa, *South Africa: A Planned Tour of the Country To-day*, which was first published in 1939 and ran into several editions during the 1940s and 1950s. His only novel, *The Secret of a City*, was published in 1958.

# Acknowledgements

'The Bowmen' from *The Collected Arthur Machen* by Arthur Machen, copyright © 1988 by The Estate of Arthur Machen. Published by Gerald Duckworth. Reprinted by permission of A. M. Heath & Co. Ltd.

'Private Meyrick – Company Idiot' from *Men, Women and Guns* by 'Sapper' Herman Cyril McNeile. Published by Hodder & Stoughton.

'A Trade Report Only' from *Fiery Particles* by C. E. Montague. Published by Chatto & Windus.

'Victory' from *Roads to Glory* by Richard Aldington, copyright © 1930 by The Estate of Richard Aldington. Published by Chatto & Windus. Reprinted by permission of Rosica Colin Ltd.

'Heroes' by Anne Perry from *Murder and Obsession*, ed. Otto Penzler, copyright © 1999 by Anne Perry. Published by Orion. Reprinted by permission of the author.

'Blind' from *The Forbidden Zone* by Mary Borden, published by William Heinemann. Reprinted by permission of Duff Hart-Davis.

'An Indiscreet Journey' from *Something Childish and Other Stories* by Katherine Mansfield. Published by Constable. Reprinted by permission of Constable & Robinson Ltd.

'The Tale' from the *Complete Short Fiction of Joseph Conrad*, Vol. 2, by Joseph Conrad. Published by Pickering.

'Chanson Triste' by Arthur Walter Wells from *Best Short Stories of 1925*, ed. Edward J. O'Brien. Published by Jonathan Cape.

'His Last Bow' by Arthur Conan Doyle from *Strand Magazine*.

'Giulia Lazzari' from *Ashenden* by W. Somerset Maugham. Published by William Heinemann. Reprinted by permission of The Random House Group Ltd.

'The Loathly Opposite' from *The Runagates Club* by John Buchan, copyright © 1928 by The Estate of John Buchan. Published by Thomas Nelson. Reprinted by permission of A. P. Watt Ltd.

'Mary Postgate' from *A Diversity of Creatures* by Rudyard Kipling.
Published by Macmillan.

'Them Others' by Stacy Aumonier from *Great Short Stories of the
War*, ed. H. C. Minchin. Published by Eyre & Spottiswoode.

'Told by the Schoolmaster' from *Forsytes, Pendyces and Others* by
John Galsworthy. Published by William Heinemann.

'Tickets, Please' from *England, My England* by D. H. Lawrence.
Published by Thomas Seltzer.

'Miss Ogilvy Finds Herself' from *Miss Ogilvy Finds Herself* by Radclyffe Hall. Published by William Heinemann. Reprinted by permission of Jonathan Lovat Dickson/A. M. Heath & Co. Ltd.

'Nobody' from *The Thirteen Travellers* by Hugh Walpole.
Published by Hutchinson.

'Once a Hero' by Harold Brighouse from *Best British Short Stories of
1922*, eds. Edward J. O'Brien and John Cournos. Published by
Longmans Green.

'The Fly' from *The Dove's Nest* by Katherine Mansfield. Published by
Constable. Reprinted by permission of Constable & Robinson Ltd.

'The Casualty List' from *Truth Is Not Sober* by Winifred Holtby.
Published by Collins. Reprinted by permission of HarperCollins
Publishers Ltd.

'Christmas Truce' from *Collected Short Stories* by Robert Graves,
copyright © 1962 by The Estate of Robert Graves. Published by
Cassell. Reprinted by permission of Carcanet Press Ltd.

'The First Year of My Life' by Muriel Spark from *The Penguin Book
of British Comic Short Stories*, ed. Patricia Craig, copyright © 1975
by The Estate of Muriel Spark. Published by Viking. Reprinted by
permission of David Higham Associates Ltd.

'Company' by Robert Grossmith from *The Minerva Book of Short
Stories 3*, eds. Giles Gordon and David Hughes, copyright © 1989
by Robert Grossmith. Published by Mandarin. Reprinted by permission of the author.

'Evermore' from *Cross Channel* by Julian Barnes, copyright © 1996
by Julian Barnes. Published by Jonathan Cape (UK) and Alfred A.
Knopf (USA). Reprinted by permission of Jonathan Cape, an
imprint of The Random House Group Ltd, and by permission of
Alfred A. Knopf, a division of Random House, Inc.

Every effort has been made to trace copyright holders. The publishers
would be interested to hear from any copyright holders not here
acknowledged, and will be pleased to rectify any mistakes or omissions
in subsequent editions.

The editors wish to thank Adam Freudenheim and Mariateresa Boffo at Penguin for making this project possible and supporting us over the long months of preparing this book. Professor Franz-Josef Brüggemeier, Professor Wolfgang Hochbruck and Mr Taff Gillingham provided valuable hints for the annotations. We also thank Dr Stefanie Lethbridge, Christina Spittel, Johanna Kunze and Nikolaus Reusch for assisting with researching the notes and reading early stages of the manuscript.

# PENGUIN CLASSICS

**THE LOST ESTATE (LE GRAND MEAULNES)**
**HENRI ALAIN-FOURNIER**

*'Meaulnes was everywhere, everything was filled with memories of our adolescence, now ended'*

When Meaulnes first arrives at the local school in Sologne, everyone is captivated by his good looks, daring and charisma. But when he disappears for several days, and returns with tales of a strange party at a mysterious house and a beautiful girl hidden within it, Meaulnes has been changed forever. In his restless search for his Lost Estate and the happiness he found there, Meaulnes, observed by his loyal friend François, may risk losing everything he ever had. Poised between youthful admiration and adult resignation, Alain-Fournier's compelling narrator carries the reader through this evocative and often unbearably moving portrayal of desperate friendship and vanished adolescence.

Robin Buss's major new translation sensitively and accurately renders *Le Grand Meaulnes*'s poetically charged, expressive and deceptively simple style, while the introduction by *New Yorker* writer Adam Gopnik discusses the life of Alain-Fournier, who was killed in the First World War after writing this, his only novel.

'I find its depiction of a golden time and place just as poignant now' Nick Hornby

Translated by Robin Buss
With an introduction by Adam Gopnik

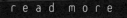

# PENGUIN CLASSICS

## THE WOMAN WHO RODE AWAY/ST. MAWR/THE PRINCESS
D. H. LAWRENCE

These three works, all written in 1924, explore the profound effects on protagonists who embark on psychological voyages of liberation. In *St. Mawr*, Lou Witt buys a beautiful, untamable bay stallion and discovers an intense emotional affinity with the horse that she cannot feel with her husband. This superb novella displays Lawrence's mastery of satirical comedy in a scathing depiction of London's fashionable high society. In 'The Woman Who Rode Away' a woman's religious quest in Mexico brings great danger – and astonishing self-discovery, while 'The Princess' portrays the intimacy between an aloof woman and her male guide as she ventures into the wilderness of New Mexico in search of new experiences.

In his introduction, James Lasdun discusses the theme of liberation and the ways in which it is conveyed in these works. Using the restored texts of the Cambridge edition, this volume includes a new chronology by Paul Poplawski.

'Lawrence urged men and women to live ... to glory in the exhilarating terror of this brief life' Frederic Raphael, *Sunday Times*

Edited by Brian Finney, Christa Jansohn and Dieter Mehl
with notes by Paul Poplawski and an introduction by James Lasdun

# PENGUIN CLASSICS

**THE THIRTY-NINE STEPS**
JOHN BUCHAN

'My guest was lying sprawled on his back. There was a long knife through his heart which skewered him to the floor'

Adventurer Richard Hannay has just returned from South Africa and is thoroughly bored with his London life – until a murder is committed in his flat, just days after the victim had warned him of an assassination plot that could bring Britain to the brink of war. An obvious suspect for the police and an easy target for the killers, Hannay goes on the run in his native Scotland, where he must use all his wits to stay one step ahead of the game – and warn the government before it is too late. One of the most popular adventure stories ever written, *The Thirty-Nine Steps* established John Buchan as the original thriller writer and inspired many other novelists and filmmakers including Alfred Hitchcock.

In his introduction to this new edition, John Keegan compares Buchan's life – his experiences in South Africa, his love of Scotland and his moral integrity – with his fictional hero. This edition also includes notes, a chronology and further reading.

Edited with an introduction by John Keegan

# PENGUIN CLASSICS

### THE HISTORY OF MARY PRINCE

*The History of Mary Prince* (1831) was the first narrative of a black woman to be published in Britain. It describes Prince's sufferings as a slave in Bermuda, Turks Island and Antigua, and her eventual arrival in London with her brutal owner Mr Wood in 1828. Prince escaped from him and sought assistance from the Anti-Slavery Society, where she dictated her remarkable story to Susanna Strickland (later Moodie). A moving and graphic document, *The History* drew attention to the continuation of slavery in the Caribbean, despite an 1807 Act of Parliament officially ending the slave trade. It inspired two libel actions and ran into three editions in the year of its publication. This powerful rallying cry for emancipation remains an extraordinary testament to Prince's ill-treatment, suffering and survival.

In her introduction, Sara Salih sets the work in its context as a significant early example of Black Atlantic literature. This edition also includes further reading, a chronology, the brief *Narrative of Louis Asa-Asa*, notes and appendices providing further contexts for Prince's *History*.

Edited with an introduction and notes by Sara Salih

# PENGUIN CLASSICS

**THE WONDERFUL ADVENTURES OF MRS SEACOLE IN MANY LANDS** MARY SEACOLE

*The Wonderful Adventures of Mrs Seacole in Many Lands* (1857) is the autobiography of a Jamaican woman whose fame rivalled Florence Nightingale's during the Crimean War. Seacole travelled widely before eventually arriving in London, where her offer to volunteer as a nurse in the war was met with racism and refusal. Undaunted, Seacole set out independently to the Crimea where she acted as doctor and 'mother' to wounded soldiers while running her business, the 'British Hotel'. A witness to key battles, she gives vivid accounts of how she coped with disease, bombardment and other hardships at the Crimean battlefront. Told with energy, warmth and humour, her remarkable life story is a key work of nineteenth-literature that provides significant insights into the history of race politics.

This new Penguin Classic is accompanied by an introduction by Sara Salih, placing *Wonderful Adventures* in its historical and political contexts, and discussing Seacole's attitudes to race, slavery and war. This edition also includes suggestions for further reading, a chronology, appendices, notes and a map.

Edited with an introduction and notes by Sara Salih

# PENGUIN CLASSICS

**THE STORM**
DANIEL DEFOE

'Horror and Confusion seiz'd upon all ... No Pen can describe it, no Tongue can express it, no Thought conceive it'

On the evening of 26 November 1703, a hurricane from the north Atlantic hammered into Britain: it remains the worst storm the nation has ever experienced. Eyewitnesses saw cows thrown into trees and windmills ablaze from the friction of their whirling sails – and some 8,000 people lost their lives. For Defoe, bankrupt and just released from prison for his 'seditious' writings, the storm struck during one of his bleakest moments. But it also furnished him with material for his first book, and in this powerful depiction of suffering and survival played out against a backdrop of natural devastation, we can trace the outlines of Defoe's later masterpieces, *A Journal of the Plague Year* and *Robinson Crusoe*.

This new Penguin Classics edition marks the 300th anniversary of the first publication of The Storm. It also includes two other pieces by Defoe inspired by that momentous night, an introduction, chronology, further reading, notes and maps.

'Astonishing ... a masterpiece of reportage' Sunday Telegraph

Edited with an introduction by Richard Hamblyn

# PENGUIN CLASSICS

## THE COLLECTED LETTERS OF MARY WOLLESTONECRAFT

Mary Wollstonecraft is one of the most distinctive letter writers of the eighteenth century: to read her letters today is to trace her thoughts on paper. In this unique single volume of her correspondence, we follow her from the girl of fourteen leaving home to become a lady's companion, to the woman of thirty-eight, facing death in childbirth. The letters reveal her desire to reconcile personal integrity and sexual longing; motherhood and intellectual life; reason and passion. Touching and engaging, they form a compelling autobiographical document of one of Britain's most radical thinkers and writers.

Janet Todd's introduction places the letters in their biographical context and discusses Wollstonecraft's relationships with her correspondents. This edition also includes notes and an index.

'A remarkable record of intimate conversation 200 years ago, allowing us to eavesdrop on the past' Lydall Gordon, *Independent on Sunday*

'An exemplary edition ... providing vividly detailed and accessible footnotes' Kate Chisholm, *Telegraph*

Edited with an introduction and notes by Janet Todd

# PENGUIN CLASSICS

---

**THE COSSACKS AND OTHER STORIES**
**LEO TOLSTOY**

*'You will see war ... in its authentic expression – as blood, suffering and death'*

In 1851, at the age of twenty-two, Tolstoy travelled to the Caucasus and joined the army there as a cadet. The four years that followed were among the most significant in his life, and deeply influenced the stories collected here. Begun in 1852 but unfinished for a decade, 'The Cossacks' describes the experiences of Olenin, a young cultured Russian who comes to despise civilization after spending time with the wild Cossack people. 'Sevastopol Sketches', based on Tolstoy's own experiences of the siege of Sevastopol in 1854–55, is a compelling description and consideration of the nature of war. In 'Hadji Murat', written towards the end of his life, Tolstoy returns to the Caucasus of his youth and portrays the life of a great leader, torn apart and destroyed by a conflict of loyalties: it is amongst the greatest of his shorter works.

The translations in this volume convey the beauty and power of the original pieces, while the introduction reflects on Tolstoy's own wartime experiences. This edition also includes notes and maps.

Translated with notes by David McDuff and Paul Foote
With an introduction by Paul Foote

---

# THE STORY OF PENGUIN CLASSICS

**Before 1946** ... 'Classics' are mainly the domain of academics and students; readable editions for everyone else are almost unheard of. This all changes when a little-known classicist, E. V. Rieu, presents Penguin founder Allen Lane with the translation of Homer's *Odyssey* that he has been working on in his spare time.

**1946** Penguin Classics debuts with *The Odyssey*, which promptly sells three million copies. Suddenly, classics are no longer for the privileged few.

**1950s** Rieu, now series editor, turns to professional writers for the best modern, readable translations, including Dorothy L. Sayers's *Inferno* and Robert Graves's unexpurgated *Twelve Caesars*.

**1960s** The Classics are given the distinctive black covers that have remained a constant throughout the life of the series. Rieu retires in 1964, hailing the Penguin Classics list as 'the greatest educative force of the twentieth century.'

**1970s** A new generation of translators swells the Penguin Classics ranks, introducing readers of English to classics of world literature from more than twenty languages. The list grows to encompass more history, philosophy, science, religion and politics.

**1980s** The Penguin American Library launches with titles such as *Uncle Tom's Cabin*, and joins forces with Penguin Classics to provide the most comprehensive library of world literature available from any paperback publisher.

**1990s** The launch of Penguin Audiobooks brings the classics to a listening audience for the first time, and in 1999 the worldwide launch of the Penguin Classics website extends their reach to the global online community.

**The 21st Century** Penguin Classics are completely redesigned for the first time in nearly twenty years. This world-famous series now consists of more than 1300 titles, making the widest range of the best books ever written available to millions – and constantly redefining what makes a 'classic'.

The Odyssey continues ...

*The best books ever written*

PENGUIN CLASSICS

SINCE 1946